College life 202;

Core Principles

J.B. Vample

Book Four

The College life series

COLLEGE LIFE 202-CORE PRINCIPLES

Printed in the United States of America

First Printing, 2017

ISBN-10: 0-9969817-7-2 (eBook edition)
ISBN-13: 978-0-9969817-7-4 (eBook edition)

ISBN-10: 0-9969817-6-4 (Paperback edition)
ISBN-13: 978-0-9969817-6-7 (Paperback edition)

For information contact; email: JBVample@yahoo.com

Website: www.jbvample.com

Book cover design by: Najla Qamber Designs

This is a work of fiction. Names, characters, places and incidents are either the product of the author's imagination or are used fictitiously, and any resemblance to actual persons, living or dead, business establishments, events or locales is entirely coincidental.

This book is dedicated to my amazing grandmother, Marlene.

Ganmum, when you told me how proud you were of me and that you're living your dream of being a writer *through* me…you have no idea how happy that made me. I am truly honored to be carrying this writing torch for the both of us. God willing, I will take this torch to the top. Thank you for all your love and support throughout my *entire* life. I love you to the moon and back.

Chapter 1

"So y'all really not gonna walk me back up to my room?" Malajia Simmons barked into her cell phone as she navigated the hallway of Paradise Terrace. Listening to the stern voice on the other end of the line, Malajia sucked her teeth. "Dad, you hype worrying about some snow flurries that probably won't even happen... Y'all are petty," she spat. "Can you at *least* put some money in my account? ... Huh? That's not enough... Hello? Dad? ... Seriously?" she hissed; the line had gone dead.

Malajia's displeasure at her father was short-lived. After weeks of being home on winter break, Malajia was finally back at her second home—Paradise Valley University—for the start of the second half of her sophomore year.

Shoving her phone into her coat pocket, she breathed a sigh of relief when she reached her room door. Twisting the knob and giving the door a push, she stepped inside, dropping her large overnight bag on the floor.

Hearing noise coming from her private bathroom, Malajia smiled. "Hey boo boo!" she bellowed.

Chasity Parker opened the bathroom door, shooting Malajia an unenthused glance. "Ugh," she scoffed, much to Malajia's amusement.

"Did you just get here?" Malajia asked, removing her red coat. "I didn't see you when I came up earlier."

Chasity placed something on her dresser, then pushed some of her long, jet black hair behind her ear. "You just answered your own question," she jeered.

Malajia made a face. "Whatever, smart ass." She unzipped one of her suitcases. "I swear, my parents are so ignorant," she griped.

"What did they do *now*?" Chasity wondered, tone even.

"They just dropped my shit off and rolled." Malajia pulled several pairs of high-heeled shoes from the bag. "Talkin' 'bout they gotta hit the road before the snow flurries starts... Nobody said shit about no damn flurries, with their lyin' asses."

Hanging some clothes in her closet, Chasity shook her head. "Can you spare me your bitch fest about your family for a day?" she requested.

"Nope," Malajia immediately put out, looking up at Chasity.

Chasity threw her head back in agitation, but decided against replying.

"And do you know that my dad had the *nerve* to think that two hundred dollars is enough to last me for two weeks?" Malajia continued to gripe.

"God, shut up!" Chasity snapped, unable to hold her tongue any longer.

Malajia was taken back. "Why are you hollering at me? I ain't do shit to you," she sneered.

"Like *always*, you run your fuckin' mouth like I feel like hearing that shit," Chasity spat out. "You *still* haven't learned to shut up?"

Malajia stared at Chasity, a blank expression on her brown face. "Why must we do this every time we see each other?" she mocked, tone calm. "You already know that I'm gonna irritate you, so just *deal* with it." She held her arms out. "Calm down, come over here and let me hug you, you sexy, light-skinned, female specimen you."

Chasity stared back, disgusted. "I'll let you hug me if I can slap your tracks loose afterwards," she hissed.

Malajia made a face, putting her arms down in the process. "You know what, *fuck* you," she barked, returning to her unpacking. "Uptight, angry ass. I think it's time for another bang session with Jason."

Chasity's eyes widened as she clenched her jaw in agitation. Malajia busted out laughing. Malajia had been successful in refraining from teasing Chasity about losing her virginity to Jason Adams during a one night encounter over Thanksgiving break. But she figured since Chasity's attitude was on ten, that her teasing was appropriate.

"Uh huh, stop being a bitch to me," Malajia teased.

Chasity silently made her way to the door. In passing, she kicked Malajia's bag from under her.

"You asshole!" Malajia wailed.

Chasity flipped her the middle finger as she left.

Chasity's journey took her to the dorm lobby. Hearing someone call her name as she headed for the door, she spun around to be greeted by a familiar, smiling face. "Hey Sid," she said.

Sidra Howard held her arms out and embraced her old roommate. "How was the rest of your break?" she asked, adjusting her purse on her shoulder. "I haven't heard much from you since we left New York."

Chasity looked away momentarily. Sidra was right, Chasity had been rather mute with Sidra and the rest of the girls since leaving the group ski trip in New York. That was a little over two weeks ago. "It was fine," Chasity put out finally.

"Good," Sidra smiled, her grey eyes flashing bright. "Well, I might as well tell *you* first, I got a car."

"Oh really?"

Sidra nodded enthusiastically. "Mama and Daddy surprised me the other day."

"So you drove here?"

"Of *course*," Sidra replied.

Chasity eyed her skeptically, to which Sidra frowned. "What's with the look?" Sidra chortled.

"I'm just trying to figure out how Miss I'm-scared-of-the-damn-highway drove from Delaware to Virginia without having a nervous breakdown."

Sidra rolled her eyes. During the girls' road trip to Florida for spring break freshman year, Sidra avoided the highway when it was her turn to drive and took the group on the back roads, costing them hours.

"I am not *afraid* of the highway, okay," Sidra ground out, flinging her long, straight ponytail over her shoulder. "I just don't *like* it very much."

Chasity slowly folded her arms, staring at her.

Sidra, feeling like Chasity's hazel-eyed gaze was a spotlight, shifted her eyes. "Josh drove," she admitted.

Chasity broke into laughter. "Uh huh."

"Shut up, Chaz," Sidra pouted, waving at her with a dismissive gesture. As the girls went to go their separate ways, Sidra spun back around. "Is Malajia back yet?"

"Yeah, she's up there looking stupid as usual," Chasity threw over her shoulder as she headed out.

Sidra shook her head and giggled, continuing on her way.

"Shit, it's cold," Chasity griped to herself, folding her arms to her chest. Going out without her coat, even if it *was* only to run to her car, wasn't the brightest of ideas. Her black turtleneck sweater didn't provide nearly enough heat.

She shivered as she unlocked her trunk, opening it the rest of the way to grab her last bag. It slipped from her fingers and fell to the ground. Chasity let out a loud groan as she bent down to retrieve it. Just as she grabbed for it, another hand picked it up.

Chasity's eyes immediately shot up and locked with the person. Fixing her eyes on Jason Adams, the glare gave way to a relaxed expression. Jason, crouched in front of her, smiled back.

"Jason," she said, almost breathlessly. Seeing his handsome, light-brown face, made her forget about the biting cold.

"Hey beautiful," he returned, slinging the bag on his shoulder as they both stood up right. Jason moved in for an embrace, and Chasity welcomed it. A few weeks ago, she never thought that the two of them would be back at a place where they could be in the same space, let alone embrace.

After Jason confessed his love for her and they crossed the friendship line and slept together, Chasity ran from her feelings and hurt Jason's in the process. Jason, not knowing how to handle it, abruptly ended their friendship. It wasn't until their chance meetup during their group ski trip in New York that they agreed to try to be friends again.

"You just getting back?" Chasity asked, breaking their embrace.

Jason had to compose himself. Feeling her in his arms again brought back memories of the night that they shared—and the hope of a future together. "No, I've been back for a few hours now."

Chasity pushed some hair out of her face, folding her arms over her chest. "Did you come back to a single room again?"

Jason laughed. "Yeah, I did."

Chasity shook her head. "Lucky you."

"That I am," he teased. He focused on Chasity's face, her slender body...which was shivering. "You need to get out of this cold," he urged, guiding her in the direction of her dorm with his hand.

"I know," Chasity agreed, shutting her trunk.

"You don't need to be out without a coat on, Chaz," he chided, adjusting the bag on his shoulder. "It's not good for your anemia."

Chasity rolled her eyes as they walked side by side towards the dorm entrance. "I know, I know," she grunted. She didn't need to be reminded about being anemic; she was diagnosed last semester after passing out while on a date with Jason. The iron pills she was forced to take every day were a big enough reminder.

"Sidra, if you're gonna continue to talk shit about my dance moves, you *and* your ponytail can skip right back out my damn room," Malajia hurled, dancing to the music blasting from the radio.

"I didn't even skip *in* here," Sidra threw back, her hands on her hips. "And I've had to endure you shaking your behind in my face for the past five minutes. I think I'm entitled to comment."

Malajia flagged the girl with her hand as she clicked the radio off with a remote.

"Chaz is gonna kill you for touching her radio," Sidra warned, sitting on Malajia's bed.

"Ain't nobody scared of that demon," Malajia dismissed. "Get your ass off my bed and drive me to Mega Mart."

Sidra looked at Malajia as if she had lost her mind. "I'm not driving you *any* damn place," she refused. "*Especially* when you're talking to me like you're crazy."

"Then get out my damn room," Malajia ordered.

Sidra opened her mouth to give Malajia a verbal lashing, but was interrupted by the door opening. "Jason!" Sidra shrieked, jumping up from the bed. She darted over to him, brushing past Malajia in the process.

"Damn Sid!" Malajia bellowed, sliding to the floor, then rolling in dramatic fashion, earning confused looks from her friends.

"Get your dumb ass off the floor," Chasity demanded, annoyed by Malajia's dramatics.

"I barely touched you!" Sidra exclaimed.

Jason shook his head in amusement at the silly look on Malajia's face as he and Sidra embraced.

Chasity caught herself shooting Sidra a glare as Jason hugged her. It was a platonic hug and not unusual; the girls and guys embraced all the time. But since coming to terms with her true feelings for Jason, she couldn't help but feel a tinge of irritation seeing him hug someone else. Even if it *was* harmless.

Malajia picked herself up from the floor. Dusting her clothes off, she walked over to Jason.

"You good Mel?" Jason chuckled.

Malajia sucked her teeth. "She hype as shit, like she ain't just see everybody not too long ago," she snapped at Sidra.

"*You're* the one who fell over like an idiot for *nothing*," Chasity hurled, leaning back against the wall.

Malajia shot Chasity a side-glance as she hugged Jason. She stared tauntingly at Chasity as she purposely held on tight. "You been working out Jase?" she asked.

Jason frowned in confusion, realizing that Malajia was running her hand up and down his right arm. "Uh… Yeah, a little," he put out, feeling a tad bit uncomfortable.

Chasity narrowed her eyes at Malajia. *I'm about to smack this bitch.*

"You smell good, whatchu' got on?" Malajia teased as Jason broke from their embrace.

"Knock it the fuck off," Chasity hissed through clenched teeth.

Malajia laughed and stuck her tongue out at Chasity. "Too easy."

"Okay ladies, I gotta go finish some stuff, I'll see you a little later," Jason announced, reaching for the doorknob.

Sidra waved to him. "Later Jase."

Jason smiled back, then refocused his attention on Chasity, who was still leaning against the wall near the door. "Can I call you later?" he asked, taking hold of her hand.

"Sure," Chasity replied.

"Cool." As Jason opened the door, Chasity had neglected to let go of his hand right away. Slightly embarrassed, she let go. Once he left and the door closed, she was met with knowing glances.

"Shut up," Chasity spat out.

"Uh huh," Sidra teased. "We saw those looks you were giving him."

"And *us* while we were hugging him," Malajia added, flopping down on her bed. "Jealous ass."

Chasity pointed at Malajia. "No, you were doing that flirting bullshit on *purpose*," she threw back.

"True," Malajia boasted. "But what about *Sidra*?"

Chasity looked at Sidra, whose mouth had fallen open in shock.

"She wasn't doing shit but giving her friend a hug," Malajia egged on. "It was one of those church hugs too. No crotch touching at *all*, and you looked like you wanted to rip her face in half."

"Chasity," Sidra cried out.

"Huh?" Chasity answered.

"Did you really want to rip my face in half?" she asked, holding her hand to her chest.

"I didn't realize that I was looking like that," Chasity admitted.

"*I* did," Malajia joked.

"Shut up," Chasity sniped, moving across the room.

Sidra giggled. "Okay Mel, stop teasing her."

"I'm not gonna stop *shit*," Malajia refused. "Something about Miss Parker has changed since I last saw her. She's getting all possessive over her big sexy hymen breaker."

"Will you stop it?" Chasity barked, as Sidra busted out laughing.

Sidra playfully smacked a laughing Malajia on her arm. "Malajia, you are so disrespectful."

Malajia put her hands up in surrender. "My bad Chaz, that was my last one, I promise," she laughed. "…for the day."

Chasity slowly folded her arms as she continued to stare Malajia down.

"Please let the heat be on in this room," Alexandra

Chisolm pleaded to herself as she walked the halls of Paradise Terrace, holding two large overnight bags. She was exhausted. After a long bus ride from New Jersey and making the long walk from the campus bus station to her dorm, Alex couldn't wait to get into her room.

Sticking her key in the door, she gave it a push and smiled once she stepped foot into her room. "Ah, home sweet home," she mused. Setting her bags on the floor near her bed, she glanced around. Her roommates' belongings were placed neatly by one of the closets; she clapped at the sight. "Yay, Sidra's back." Removing her coat, she made a move for the bathroom, but was distracted by commotion in the hallway.

Alex darted out. Witnessing the scene in front of her, Alex frowned. *Why am I not surprised it's those two?* she wondered. Chasity and Malajia had each other in a headlock, while Sidra, laughter in her voice, yelled at them to stop.

"What's going on out here?" Alex charged, heading over.

Sidra glanced over. "Alex, can you help me with these two, please?"

"What the hell happened?" Alex asked, watching Malajia and Chasity struggle with one another.

Sidra shook her head, rubbing the back of her neck. "Girl, we were on our way to the SDC, and Malajia started yelling at Chaz about *something*, finger all in her face. Then she accidentally poked her in the cheek," she huffed.

Alex folded her arms and shook her head.

"Chaz got mad and slapped Malajia on the arm. Malajia slapped her back, and then *this* happened," Sidra concluded, gesturing to the two of them.

"Malajia, why are you always messing with her?" Alex wondered, annoyed.

"Get off me, Malajia," Chasity fumed.

"No bitch, you get off *me* first," Malajia demanded, ignoring Alex's question.

Completely over the whole situation, Chasity maneuvered her way out of Malajia's headlock, then grabbed

Malajia's arm and twisted it behind her back. Malajia started screaming at the top of her lungs.

"God Malajia, you can wake the damn dead with your mouth," Sidra stated, exasperated.

"She's breaking my fuckin' arm!" Malajia screamed,

"You gonna keep your fuckin' fingers out my damn face?" Chasity taunted, holding her grip.

"Okay, okay," Malajia relented.

Chasity let go, then gave her a shove. Malajia immediately grabbed her sore arm. "You always gotta go overboard," she complained, giving it a rub. "And you messed up my damn hair. You better not have loosened a damn track." She ran a quick hand over her shoulder-length, burgundy extensions.

"I always tell you that you play too much," Alex commented.

Malajia rolled her eyes at Alex as she continued to rub her shoulder.

Alex shook her head at Malajia, then moved in to give Chasity a hug.

Chasity backed away with a frown. "You smell like some bullshit," she jeered. Malajia snickered, much to Alex's agitation.

Alex pointed at them. "You know what—" she paused as she caught a whiff of her sweater. "Eww, you're right," she groaned.

"How you come out the house smelling like that?" Malajia laughed. "Nasty ass."

"Shut up, Malajia," Alex threw back, pulling the sweater fabric away from her skin. "No, I was sitting next to this funky ass man for the *entire* bus ride from Jersey. I can't believe his stench ate all the way through my damn coat like that… I'm so disgusted."

"Alex, stop lying. You know you smelled like that before that man sat next to you," Malajia mocked.

Alex glared at her, then turned to head into her room. The girls followed.

"What were you doing in Jersey?" Sidra asked, taking a seat on her bed. "I thought you would've caught a ride from Chaz."

"I wouldn't have let her in my damn car, smelling like that," Chasity joked.

Alex, snatched the sweater over her head. "I told you! It was the damn man—never mind you jerk," she hissed, holding the shirt in her hands. "Anyway, one of my aunts came to Philly a few days ago to visit and wanted me to spend some time at her house in Jersey. So instead of going back to Philly, then having to take the bus to West Chester to meet Chasity, I just decided to ride the bus back from *there*."

Malajia stared at Alex as she sat next to Sidra on her bed. "Nobody needed to *hear* all that," she bit out.

If it wasn't for Alex's dark brown complexion, the redness in her face would have been noticeable. *She always has something smart to say.*

"And that *still* don't justify your big ass lying about sitting next to some funky ass man, when you *know* you left the house without washing this morning," Malajia goaded.

Fed up, Alex tossed her smelly, soiled sweater directly at Malajia's face; it landed right on its target.

"Oh God!" Malajia wailed, knocking it to the floor. "It burns!"

Sidra put her hand over her face, shaking her head at Malajia's antics.

Malajia stood from the bed and rubbed her face. "I think it burned my eyebrows off," she panicked, walking over to Chasity. "Chaz, are my brows still here?"

"Get out my damn face!" Chasity snapped, making Malajia flinch at the bass in her voice.

"Alex, did you hear from Emily yet?" Sidra asked, ignoring the commotion.

Alex ran her hands through her thick, wavy, dark brown, shoulder-length hair, then dug around in one of her bags. "Yeah, I talked to her briefly yesterday." She sighed, retrieving a bottle of body wash. "She won't be back until sometime tomorrow."

"Her mom wanted to breast feed her one more day, huh?" Malajia joked.

Alex rolled her eyes. "Don't start," she warned. "Cut the girl a break. She was able to get away from her mom long enough to come skiing with us over the break, remember? Give her some credit."

Malajia shrugged. "I'm not taking that away from her," she assured. "But without her Dad's help in concocting that lie about her staying with him that weekend, she would've never been able to go."

"Does it matter—"

"That her mom is still a smothering jackass? *Yes*, yes it does," Chasity cut in, interrupting Alex's question.

Alex looked to Sidra for support, but Sidra just turned away and ran her hand over her hair. *Thanks for the backup Sid.* "Look, Evil and Shit-starter," Alex snarled at Chasity and Malajia. "Can you refrain from making those smart-ass comments about her situation this semester?"

"No," Chasity said at the same time that Malajia said, "Why?"

Alex stomped her foot on the floor in frustration. "I'm *serious* now," she fussed. "Em has been feeling down enough... I swear there's something different about her these days."

"If her mother would let her breathe every now and then, she'd be fine," Sidra muttered, examining her manicured nails.

Chapter 2

Malajia barged through her door later that evening. "I got drinks for us!" she bellowed.

The dramatic entrance and loud voice startled Chasity, who was trying to watch TV. "Girl!" she snapped, annoyed at the interruption.

"Oh shut up," Malajia returned, unfazed. "Come on, let's drink."

"No," Chasity replied. "I'm not in the mood for a hangover."

Malajia rolled her eyes. "You won't get a hangover as long as you eat while drinking, duh," she mocked, holding the bottle up. "Now, come on, drink with me. I'm bored."

Chasity eyed the bottle of blue liquid in Malajia's hand and frowned. "So your idea of curing boredom is to get pissy drunk?" Chasity questioned smartly, reaching for her bottle of water on the nightstand.

Malajia thought for a moment. "Yes," she shrugged, placing the bottle to her lips.

"Do you even know what the hell that *is*?" Chasity asked when Malajia coughed after taking a long sip.

"No, but *whatever* it is, it's strong as shit," Malajia commented, patting her chest. "Shit, I'm about to start going back to Praz for drinks. The girl who made *this* one was hype as shit with the liquor."

"Yeah, I'm not drinking that bullshit," Chasity refused.

Malajia once again shrugged. "Suit yourself," she said. "Come in," she said as a knock sounded on the door. Not bothering to turn around when the guests entered the room, Malajia put the bottle back to her lips. But before the liquid could touch Malajia's tongue, Alex swooped in and snatched it from her.

"No you don't," Alex declared, holding the bottle out of Malajia's reach.

Malajia spun around and tried to grab it. "Give that back, you nappy-headed bitch!" she erupted.

Chasity, who was taking a sip of water, spat it out as she busted out laughing.

"Damn Malajia!" Sidra exclaimed at the harsh reaction.

Alex regarded Malajia with anger, holding the bottle out of her reach. "That whole comment was uncalled for," she raged.

"So was *you* rollin' up in here, snatching my damn drink," Malajia countered.

"I'm looking out for *your* careless behind," Alex threw back. "Calling me nappy and *especially* a bitch, was rude."

Malajia flagged Alex with her hand. "Don't nobody care about your feelings," she hissed.

"*Clearly*," Alex fumed, then turned her attention to Chasity, who was still laughing. "It wasn't that damn funny."

Chasity tried to stop laughing, but couldn't, much to Alex's agitation.

"My hair is *far* from nappy okay," Alex harped.

"We know sweetie," Sidra consoled. "You know you have to ignore her."

Alex appreciated Sidra's words, but she was still highly offended by *Malajia's*. "I'm tired of you making comments about my damn hair, Malajia," she continued, pointing at her. "Just because I don't straighten it, it doesn't—"

"All right, shut up already," Malajia snapped. "You

actin' all sensitive and shit."

"You don't know what to say out your damn mouth," Alex hurled.

"I say what I *want*," Malajia spat, pointing at her. "You shouldn't have taken my damn drink."

Alex put her free hand on her hip and held her fiery gaze on Malajia, who stared back with a challenging look.

"Okay fine, my bad," Malajia gave in after a few seconds of the non-verbal standoff. Alex rolled her eyes and Malajia sucked her teeth. "I take it back, fuck you *and* your mop," Malajia ground out.

"That's enough you two, chill," Sidra cut in, retrieving the bottle from Alex. She put the bottle to her nose and sniffed.

"Get your damn nose off my bottle," Malajia barked.

"Girl, this smells like straight rubbing alcohol," Sidra complained, ignoring Malajia's outburst. "Do you *want* to tear your insides up?"

"What are you two doing here?" Chasity asked, clicking the TV off.

"We're finished unpacking and we're bored. We wanted to see if you ladies wanted to do something," Alex answered, now calm.

"What *I* want to do, doesn't involve *you*," Chasity muttered.

Alex sucked her teeth. Between Malajia's mouth and Chasity's attitude, Alex felt like she could slap either one of them at any given time.

Malajia snickered, gesturing to Chasity. "She wanna rub one out real quick," she teased, much to girls' disgust.

"Come *on*," Sidra complained. "Always so damn inappropriate."

"Oh shut it up. You act like *you* don't do it," Malajia hurled back, earning a searing look from Sidra. "I saw those books in your drawer."

Embarrassed and angry, Sidra stomped her foot on the floor. "Stay out of my stuff!"

"I was looking for candy," Malajia explained, amused.

Alex looked over at Chasity. "Chaz, if that's what you were—"

"I was talking about finishing my damn *movie*," Chasity hissed. "Why do you even bother *listening* to Malajia's lying ass?"

"I'm still trying to figure that out," Sidra grunted, folding her arms.

Malajia found her friends' agitation amusing. She cracked up laughing.

Chasity looked over at Malajia, annoyed. "Alex, give that simple bitch her drink back so she can leave people the hell alone."

Malajia glanced at Alex, a grin on her face and hope in her eyes.

"No," Alex refused.

"Well, when all else fails. We order food," Alex joked, grabbing a slice of pizza from the box.

"Yeah well, you lucky there's no party in the clusters," Malajia sneered, dipping a french fry into some ketchup.

Alex shrugged. After debating with the girls on what to do, coming up with nothing that wouldn't involve them going out into the cold, they decided to order takeout and eat in the dorm's massive lounge. "*Whatever* the reason, it's good to be back here relaxing with you girls," she said. "I miss you guys when we're on break."

Sidra nodded in agreement. "*My* sentiments exactly." She reached for an eggroll. "What did you girls do once you got back from New York?"

"I ain't do shit," Malajia dryly answered. "But Chasity slept with Jason again."

Reaching for her turkey burger, Chasity let out a loud groan. "Make *one* more goddamn comment, Malajia," she warned, angry.

Sidra slapped her forehead with her palm in frustration.

Malajia never ceased to push peoples' buttons.

Alex regarded Chasity with shock. "Chaz, *tell* me you didn't do that," she said.

"No, I *didn't*," Chasity sneered. "But even if I *did*, that's *my* damn business."

"Uh, *not* when the *last* time it happened, it affected the whole damn group," Alex threw back.

Chasity rolled her eyes. Leave it to Alex to throw up the past. When Jason decided to end his and Chasity's friendship, both Chasity and Jason took their pain out on the group by withdrawing from it. It made their friends feel that not only were they caught in the middle, but that their group would never be the same.

"Are things not fine between Jason and I *now*?" Chasity challenged, trying to keep her temper in check.

Alex, ran her hand through her hair. "*Sure* they're fine, thank God," she admitted. "But for *how long*? I swear, this 'just friends' thing that you two are doing—when you *both* know that you belong together as a couple—is ridiculous."

Chasity just stared at Alex as she continued.

"You're both putting off the inevitable... No, scratch that, Jason's not because everybody and their mother knows that he loves you. It's *you*," Alex pointed to Chasity. "*You're* the one running from what you truly feel, and it's not fair to *him* or to you*rself*."

Chasity frowned as she processed everything Alex had to say. "Wow," she replied, voice deceptively calm. "Did you think that up earlier, during your time on that funky ass bus?"

Malajia nearly spat out her soda as she tried to hold in her laugh.

Alex's eyes became slits, resisting the urge to slap the smirk off Chasity's face.

Sidra shook her head, then gave Malajia's arm a tap for laughing. "Geez Alex, how long were you holding *that* in?" Sidra teased.

"A while," Alex grumbled, taking a bite out of her pizza. "She knows I'm right."

"Alex, don't get slapped tonight." Chasity spat.

"Your threats mean nothing," Alex returned.

Sidra snapped her head towards Malajia. "You see what you started?" she chided.

Malajia shrugged, relishing the tension. "The first day back would *not* be complete without a good old fashioned argument."

Sidra's response was halted once she saw two familiar faces walk through the door. "Hey guys," she smiled.

Malajia had the opposite reaction. "God, can we have *one* night?" she complained, smacking her hand on the arm of the couch.

Josh Hampton and David Summers walked over; Josh took a seat on the arm of the couch, David elected to sit on the floor. "Nice to see you *too* Malajia," Josh jeered, setting a bottle of soda on the coffee table.

"Who invited y'all?" Malajia hissed.

"*I* did, you jackass," Sidra barked, tired of Malajia's nonsense.

David pushed his silver glasses up on his nose. "We brought dessert," he smiled, setting a box of brownies on the table.

Malajia's mood instantly lifted. "Ooh, chocolate," she beamed, reaching for the box.

Sidra leaned forward and smacked Malajia's hand away. "No, you don't get any," she ground out. "You've been starting trouble all day."

Malajia folded her arms like a child and sat back in her seat.

Josh shook his head. He was amused by the byplay between his two childhood friends. "Have you ladies talked to Jason and Mark?" he asked. "Are they back?"

"Jason's back," Alex answered. "But I haven't seen Mark."

"*I* talked to him earlier," Sidra revealed, opening a packet of sauce for another egg roll. "He said that he's coming back tomorrow."

Malajia loudly clapped, tossing her arms in the air in excitement. "Thank God!" she bellowed. "*Fuck* them brownies. That news just made my night."

David successfully hid a laugh. It was no secret that Malajia had much disdain for Mark, a feeling that was mutual for Mark as well. "It'll be nice to have the room to myself, if only for one night," he mused.

"David, I feel sorry that you have to spend another semester being the roommate of that fool," Malajia jeered.

"Why *did* he decide to come back tomorrow anyway?" Alex asked, curious.

"Oh, he didn't *decide*, he has no *choice*," Sidra chortled. "As soon as he pulled out of the driveway, his car ran out of gas."

"Typical," Josh laughed. "He always runs that car dry."

"Well, he has to wait for his parents to get back in town tomorrow to take him to the gas station," Sidra added.

"His ass betta *walk*," Malajia scoffed.

"You know he's not crossing that four-lane highway to get to that gas station," David chuckled.

"I already cussed his behind out about being that irresponsible," Sidra said, reaching for a brownie.

"Why are we still talkin' 'bout him?" Malajia sneered. "Please, I just ate; I wanna keep my food down."

Before anybody could respond, they heard a familiar, loud voice. "Oh God no," David grumbled, putting his hand over his face.

"Damn it!" Malajia yelled, voice not masking her contempt. "Y'all done went and talked his loud ass up."

"Well, there goes *my* night," Chasity complained, closing her food container.

"Hey homies!" Mark Johnson hollered as he strolled into the lounge, sunglasses on his face. His friends were stunned to say the least.

"Mark...it's dark out, what's with the sunglasses?" Alex drew her question out slowly.

Mark removed the glasses from his handsome, dark

brown face. "They cool, though," he explained.

"How did you know where we were?" Malajia sneered and slapped her leg. "Oh I forgot, you probably sniffed us out, you're a *dog* after all."

Mark narrowed his eyes at her. "You wish I *would* sniff your lonely ass," he bit back; she flipped him off in retaliation. "Where the hell *else* would y'all asses be?" Mark mocked. "I dropped my shit off and saw that David was back. He ain't got nowhere else to go but *here* any-damn-way, so I walked over."

David rolled his eyes. *So much for my one night of insult-free peace.*

"It's good to see you man, but what are you doing here tonight?" Josh quipped. "Your parents came back early to take you for gas?"

Mark walked over and squeezed his tall, solid body on the couch in between Chasity and Sidra, who were none too happy about it.

"Your ass just touched my fuckin' leg," Chasity griped, slapping his leg.

He smiled at her. "You want me to touch something *else*?" he teased, then proceeded to repeatedly flick his tongue at her.

Chasity turned her lip up. "Ugh," she scoffed in disgust, moving to another seat.

Sidra, smacked him on the back of the head. "Stop being nasty," she chastised.

"Anyway," Mark began, rubbing the back of his head. "I didn't really run out of gas. I made that up." His confession was met with confused looks.

"Um...why?" Alex asked.

"I wanted to surprise you guys," Mark smiled. "What better way than to make you guys think that I was coming tomorrow, then actually show up *tonight*?" It was silence for a few moments as the group tried to process what he said.

"What kind of bullshit?" Chasity bit out.

"Man, that ain't no damn surprise," Malajia fussed, "The

damn surprise would've been if you didn't come back at *all*."

Mark's face fell as laughter erupted from the guys.

"Yo, why would you think that that was a good idea?" Josh laughed.

"That *was* pretty lame," Sidra added.

Alex shook her head. "Who *does* that?" she griped. "Who really sits there and concocts a stupid, pointless lie like that?"

Annoyed and embarrassed, Mark rose from his seat and stormed out of the lounge without saying a word.

"Wait, did he just throw a temper tantrum?" Malajia mocked.

David sighed. "Looks like," he confirmed.

"Fool," Malajia berated.

Chapter 3

I can't wait to get out of this car, Emily Harris thought, shifting in the passenger's seat of her mother's sedan.

"Traffic is a mess today, isn't it?" Ms. Harris commented at an attempt to start a conversation.

Emily just looked at her, forcing a smile. The ride from New Jersey to Virginia seemed twenty-hours long; it was only five. For Emily, winter break couldn't have come to an end soon enough. Between her mother's nagging and smothering, she felt like she was going to pull her mid-neck length sandy brown hair out, strand by strand.

"We're here," Ms. Harris announced after a few more moments of driving.

Emily stepped out of the parked car and commenced to retrieving her bags from the trunk.

Before Emily could grab all of her belongings, Ms. Harris was right there helping.

I can get it myself! she fumed. Emily rolled her eyes out of her mother's view as the two women headed up the steps of the campus apartment complex.

Opening the door to her single room, Emily let out a sigh. *I hate this room.* Emily felt that the room kept her isolated from her friends, who had the luxury of rooming with each other. It was a constant reminder of the lengths that her mother would go just to control her life; the woman had put her name on the list behind her back for a single room.

Emily tossed her bags near her bed and flopped down.

"No time for rest Emily, you need to unpack," Ms. Harris said. "Then we can go grab something to eat."

"Mommy, I'm not hungry and I'm really tired right now," Emily replied meekly.

"I don't see how you're tired, you were up in your room all night last night," Ms. Harris spat, folding her arms. "I assumed you were asleep."

Emily just looked up at her mother, not saying a word. If she spoke, she might let it slip that she was up in her room drinking the small bottles of liquor that she had taken from the hotel in New York.

"I didn't sleep that well," she finally put out, tone low.

Ms. Harris rolled her eyes and proceeded to unpack Emily's suitcase.

Emily just stared at the back of her mother's head, fuming. *Get out!* After the night that she had, if she didn't see her mother for the rest of the year, Emily would've been perfectly happy. After all, her mother was the cause of her almost having a nervous breakdown the night before.

"Mommy, I can do that," Emily offered, standing up from her bed.

"No, you said you're tired. You rest and *I'll* do it," Ms. Harris argued.

Emily sighed, reaching for one of her sweaters. "It's fine—"

"I *said*, I'll do it," Ms. Harris snapped. Emily flinched from the bass in her mother's voice. Irritated, Emily walked out of the room and closed the door behind her.

Chasity's eyes were focused on the laptop screen in front of her. "No, no, don't stall damn it," she barked, giving the screen a tap. She sucked her teeth when she heard a knock on the door "It's open."

"Hey Chaz," Jason said, walking in and shutting the door behind him.

Chasity felt her heart jump, but her face never changed expressions as she turned in her seat, facing him. "What's up?"

"I just came from getting my schedule, so I figured I'd stop by and see what you were up to," he answered.

Chasity felt like she was staring at him longer than normal. "Okay," she replied. *God I want you*, she thought, watching him walk over to her desk. She kept her eyes focused on the muscular tone of his tall body as he moved.

He leaned against her desk. "What are you doing?"

Chasity ran her hand through her hair as she tried not to focus on how close he was to her. "Adding some new software to my laptop," she replied. "It's a pain in my ass."

Jason chuckled. "I can imagine," he sympathized. "Which is why I haven't bought any new software for *mine* yet."

Chasity shook her head. "You have Programming 3 this semester, right?"

Jason nodded.

"Yeah well, you're gonna *need* new software," she advised.

"I'll be sure to get it," Jason chortled. He stared at her as she went back to hitting keys on her laptop. He tried to form more words to say, but couldn't. All he could think about was grabbing her, kissing her, and carrying her to her bed to relive their first night together. Jason shook his head to get the image out of his mind.

Stop man, she's not ready, he thought. Recalling their last conversation in New York, Jason was well aware that Chasity wasn't ready for them to be anything more than friends. Jason promised himself that he would fall back from pursing her and just focus on trying to regain the friendship that they shared prior to everything getting crazy between them.

Jason looked at his watch. "I should probably go and get

that software now," he said, standing up right.

Chasity took a deep breath as the smell of his cologne brushed by her. His taste was always good. "Um…the software that I have can be added to up to three devices," she said, looking at him. "I can add it to your laptop for you, if you want."

"I appreciate it, but you don't have to do that," he replied.

"I know I don't *have* to," Chasity returned.

"You know I can buy my *own*, right?" Jason threw back, fixing a stern gaze upon her.

"You know I didn't *ask* you that, right?" she frowned.

Jason laughed. *Yep, she's back to her old, smart-mouthed self. I missed that.* "Well, thank you, I appreciate it."

Chasity rolled her eyes. "Yeah, yeah, just bring your laptop over here so I can do it," she sneered, much to his amusement.

"Yes ma'am," he relented, heading for the door. "You want me to bring it right *now*? Or—"

"Just bring the freakin' laptop, Jason," she barked.

"Thanks, I owe you," he smiled.

"Yeah, yeah," she ground out as he walked out of the door. Once the door was shut, she dropped her hardened expression. "You're welcome," she mumbled to an empty room. Chasity closed her eyes and let out a whine as she placed her head on her desk. "Stupid," she hissed at herself.

Sidra wiped the sink counter of her adjoined bathroom with a sponge, tossing it into a nearby trash can. She washed her hands and gave herself a once-over in the wall-sized mirror, before adjusting the pins in her up-do. She rolled her eyes when she heard the doorknob turn at the other end of the bathroom.

Great, she thought.

"Hi Sidra," her next-door neighbor and cohabiter of the

bathroom put out as she stepped in.

Sidra forced a smile. She was hoping that her messy neighbors would have fallen off the face of the earth, or at least not returned to school that semester. "Hi Dee." Her tone was less than unenthused as she turned back to the mirror.

Dee resisted the urge to roll her eyes. *I swear, this girl and her snotty ass attitude.* "How was your break?" she asked, plunking a basket full of toiletry items on the sink.

Sidra gave the basket a quick side-eye. "It was fine." *Please stop talking to me.* After the confrontations with both Dee and her roommate last semester about their messy antics in their shared bathroom, Sidra wasn't in the mood to play nice.

"Good." Dee could feel the tension. Sidra moved her arm and Dee caught sight of the sparkly cuff bracelet on her wrist. "That's a pretty bracelet," she complimented, pointing.

Sidra glanced down at it, almost as if she had forgotten that it was there. "Thanks. Christmas gift," she replied.

"You seem to have a thing for bracelets," Dee chortled. Recalling every occasion that she saw Sidra, not only was she dressed as if she was working in a corporate office, but she was always wearing a unique bracelet.

Sidra smiled. "Yeah, I suppose I do," she agreed. "I actually lost one of my favorite ones' last semester. It was a silver one with elephant charms... It was different, but my grandmother gave it to me, so I loved it."

Dee just stared at her. "Oh wow, that's a shame," she sympathized. "Anyway, I gotta go finish unpacking... See you."

Sidra nodded before walking out of the bathroom, shutting the door behind her.

Alex, who was unpacking some items from a plastic bag, looked at her, "Our neighbors are back, huh?" she quipped.

Sidra rolled her eyes. "Unfortunately," she muttered, sitting on her bed. "Another semester of trifling-ness."

Alex giggled; she knew all too well Sidra's disdain for their neighbors, especially Dee's roommate Dominque.

"Well, maybe it'll be better this time around."

Sidra shrugged. "You went to the bookstore, I see," she observed, changing the subject.

"Yeah, had to get first dibs on some of my books," Alex replied, holding one of the heavy texts in her hands. "I swear, each semester they get more expensive… I've just about blown through the money I saved over winter break."

"Tell me about it," Sidra agreed. "I spent damn near a hundred dollars on my Criminology textbook… I better be able to pass the damn bar with it."

Alex laughed, then gasped. "Crap! I forgot to get index cards," she griped. "I guess I'll head back over." She grabbed her coat from the bed and pulled it on. "You need anything while I'm over there?"

"No, I'm fine," Sidra replied.

Alex hurried across campus, hoping to grab the least expensive cards; they always sold out first. Passing by the apartment complex, she spotted a familiar figure in the parking lot, standing next to a car. Alex stopped walking and headed over.

Alex smiled as she tapped the person's shoulder. "Emily," she beamed.

Startled, Emily spun around. "Hey," she smiled, giving Alex a hug.

"I thought you were gonna call when you got back."

"I planned on it, but um… *She's* here," Emily muttered.

Alex nodded. "Ahhh, yeah I get it," she said, catching on. "Well, when she leaves, come over to the dorm." She shoved her hands in her coat pockets. "Everybody's back and we're gonna hang out later tonight."

The words in Emily's mouth wouldn't come out; her mother called her name from the stairwell. Emily's pleasant demeanor gave way to a scowl. Still facing Alex, she rolled her eyes. "Yes, Mommy?" she answered.

"Girl, come on with that last bag so you can get settled,"

Ms. Harris hissed.

Emily sighed as she retrieved her last duffle bag from the car.

Alex shot Emily a sympathetic look, then smiled up at Ms. Harris. "Hi," she waved.

Ignoring Alex, Ms. Harris turned and headed back up the steps.

"Wow," Alex scoffed. "She *still* hates us, huh?"

Emily slung the bag over her shoulder as she closed the car door. "I'm sorry, Alex," she mumbled.

"You don't have to apologize for her behavior." Alex assured her as Emily looked down at the ground. "Go ahead and get settled. See you later."

"Okay." Emily watched Alex walk away, wishing that she could go with her, instead of back into that lonely room with her mother.

She'll be leaving soon enough, Emily reminded herself, heading to the steps.

Chapter 4

"What y'all got in here to eat, bee?" Mark asked, rifling through Malajia's mini-refrigerator.

Malajia darted from her bed and smacked his hand off the door. "Get your nasty self away from my fridge," she hissed.

"You ain't got shit in there but frozen pickles *anyway*," Mark sneered, moving away from it.

Malajia looked confused as she grabbed the jar from the shelf. "Damn it!" she yelped, examining the frozen contents. "This damn thing is freezing everything again."

"Cheap ass fridge," Mark laughed.

"You two *stay* at each other's throats," Alex commented, amused. "Guys, now come on, we interrupted Jason and Chasity's alone time because we're trying to figure out what to do tonight."

Later that same evening, as Alex had told Emily earlier, the group met up at Chasity and Malajia's room to make plans. But as always, trying to get everyone to focus was proving to be difficult.

Chasity frowned as Jason put his hand over his face and shook his head. "I was putting software on his laptop," she explained.

"*Sure*, you were," Mark teased. "More like he was putting *his* software in *your* laptop."

"Really bro?" Jason ground out, tossing a pillow at a laughing Mark. *When are they gonna stop with the jokes?* he wondered.

"That was actually a good one," Malajia approved. "I have to use that one day."

Chasity glared at Malajia. "Fuck you *and* your frozen pickles," she bit out; Malajia flopped down on the floor and whined.

"Are there any good movies out?" Sidra asked, examining the polish on her nails.

"Nothing worth sitting in a cold ass theater for *two hours* for," Chasity answered, placing a pillow behind her back as she sat back on her bed.

"We could go bowling," Josh suggested.

"Been there, done that, *bored* with it," Malajia sneered.

Mark sucked his teeth. "I don't know about *y'all*, but I'm hungry," he complained. "Let's go out to eat."

"Mark, I'm not going out to eat with you unless you have money for food," Josh stipulated. "Nobody has time for you and that 'I got y'all later' mess that you always pull."

"Oh shut up." Mark threw back. "You always bitchin'. You don't say nothin' when I pay for *your* food."

Josh looked puzzled. "When have you *ever* paid for my food?"

"Man, ain't nobody tryna hear your bullshit. Just pick something to do and let's *do* it," Mark threw back, flagging his hand at Josh dismissively.

"Yeah, that's what I thought," Josh retorted.

Alex sat on Malajia's bed and ran her hands through her hair. "Why is it always a battle with you guys?" she whined. "Can we—" she immediately grabbed her ringing cell phone from her jeans pocket and put it to her ear.

"You hype as shit you got that old ass flip phone," Malajia teased. "It probably don't even have caller ID on it."

Alex flipped Malajia off as she turned away from her,

talking on the phone.

"Malajia, somebody is gonna slap you one of these days," Sidra concluded.

Ignoring the commotion behind her, Alex spoke into the phone. "Yeah Em, we're just sitting around trying to figure out what to do."

Emily glanced at the door. "How's that going?" she asked.

"Like pulling teeth, as *always*," Alex joked.

Emily sat on her bed and giggled. "I can't wait to see you guys, I miss everybody."

"When are you coming over?"

Emily sighed loudly, "As soon as my mom leaves," she replied. "It's like seven o'clock, she's been here since three something."

"She's stalling huh?" Alex assumed.

"Big time," Emily confirmed, scratching her head. "Anyway, I think I hear her in the hallway, I'll be over soon."

"All right sweetie." Alex hung up the phone and faced the group again.

"We figured out what to do while you were talking on that dinosaur," Malajia put out, earning snickers from around the room.

"And what is that?" Alex asked, ignoring Malajia's comment about her phone.

"We're gonna play truth or dare," Malajia answered.

Alex looked surprised as she glanced around the room. Some of the faces looked unenthused. "*Everybody* agreed to this?"

"*No*, but we're gonna play *anyway*," Mark chortled, grabbing a fast food menu from Malajia's desk. "First, let's order some damn food."

Emily drummed her fingers on the wooden nightstand by her bed. *Will you just go?!* she screamed to herself as her mother flipped through a takeout menu.

"Hey honey, do you want some dinner?" Ms. Harris asked.

"Um, no I'm fine," Emily replied, tone dry as she looked at her short, unpolished nails. "Mommy, it's getting late, you should probably go before the rain starts."

"I'm not worrying about the rain sweetie," Ms. Harris replied. "I'm not heading out until the morning."

Emily felt her stomach drop. "Um...huh?" she stammered.

Ms. Harris looked at her. "I'm spending the night," she confirmed. "I'm tired and I can get a fresh start tomorrow."

Emily's light-brown face turned red and her mouth fell open. "Mommy, it's gonna be packed on the road tomorrow," she rambled. "I mean, you'll be stuck with all of those um...Sunday drivers."

Ms. Harris stared at her daughter. "Are you trying to get rid of me?"

Emily's eyes widened. *Yes!* "No ma'am," she lied. Emily was in a panic, if her mother stayed, she would never get away to go see her friends. "I just—Um, I think—"

"That's enough, I'm staying the night and that's that," Ms. Harris told her, voice stern.

At least tell her to go stay in a motel Emily! Despite the voice screaming in Emily's head, she couldn't bring herself to say what it wanted her to say.

"You sure you don't want dinner?" Ms. Harris pressed, unaware of what Emily was thinking.

No, I want a drink right now. Emily felt like crying as she shook her head. "Yes... I'm sure," she muttered.

"Who placed the order for this food?" Mark charged, flipping open the box pizza.

Chasity put her head in her hands and groaned. The sound of Mark's voice was like nails on a chalkboard to her. "You already know *you* did," she snarled.

"Then how come they didn't hear me order half cheese, half peperoni?" Mark asked. "They gave us all cheese and shit."

"Please…*please* just eat the pizza and shut up," David pleaded, agitated.

Mark looked at David. "What*chu'* mad for?"

David leaned forward in his seat and regarded Mark with shock. "Did I *not* just spot you money for your share of the food?"

"I told you I got you when we get back to the room," Mark threw back, grabbing a slice. "It was five dollars, damn."

"Yeah? And that's the last time you'll get even a *penny* from me," David promised, reaching for a slice of pizza.

Alex barged through the door in a huff. "Well, Emily isn't coming over," she fussed, tossing her hand which held her phone, up in frustration.

"Why, what happened?" Sidra frowned.

"Her mother didn't leave," Chasity dryly assumed.

"*Exactly,*" Alex confirmed, folding her arms. Having just gotten off the phone with Emily, who had called her practically in tears as she expressed her frustration about her unexpected overnight guest, Alex was both sad *and* angry for her friend.

"Her mom needs a life," Malajia stated matter-of-factly. "Or at least a damn *man.*"

"That miserable hover-board isn't gonna back off until Emily cusses her ass out," Chasity put in. "But when I tell her that, *I'm* the bitch."

"No, *that's* not the only reason," Malajia joked, then dissolved into laughter when Chasity made a face at her. "All right, let's get this game going," Malajia began, clapping her hands. "Sidra, truth or dare."

Sidra rolled her eyes. "I'm not playing."

"Yes you *are*, don't start your prissy shit tonight," Malajia hurled.

Sidra sighed loudly. *Might as well.* "Fine, dare."

"I dare you to punch Alex in the boobs," Malajia said, earning laughter from the room.

Sidra, nor Alex found it amusing. *"Seriously?"* Alex huffed.

"I'm not going to hit her in the breast," Sidra scoffed.

Malajia sucked her teeth. "I didn't say 'hit her in the breast'," she mocked, mimicking Sidra's haughty voice. "I said, punch her in the goddamn boobs. And you'll *do* it, or you're gonna have to do truth, and I *promise* you I'll ask you if you masturbate and you'll *have* to answer."

Sidra's mouth fell open. Her brown face became flushed; she was mortified. Shifting her eyes, she locked them with the guys, who were staring at her, smiling. "You guys are perverts," she snarled, stomping her foot on the floor. She looked over at Alex and shot her an apologetic look.

Alex put her hands on her ample breasts and gasped. "Sidra!"

"I'm sorry Alex, I don't want to do it, I *really* don't," Sidra replied, remorseful.

"Sidra, there's nothing wrong with telling the truth—"

"Shhhh, shush," Sidra hissed, interrupting Alex. The last thing that she wanted was to have her personal business broadcasted in front of her friends, *especially* the guys.

"Yeah Sid, go ahead and tell us how you play with yourself while reading those porno books you got in your nightstand," Mark teased, opening a bottle of soda. Josh, who was in the middle of taking a sip of his, nearly choked.

Malajia roared with laughter. "Wait, you found them *too?*" she shot at Mark, who in turn nodded emphatically.

Sidra sucked her teeth. "See, nobody's trying to deal with that nonsense," she fussed. "It's not going to be hard Alex, I promise." Alex watched Sidra raise her fist before gently hitting her in her left breast.

"Ow," Alex grimaced.

"I barely touched you," Sidra said. "I'm sorry though."

"Yeah, yeah," Alex jeered at Sidra's departing back. "Malajia, you're gonna pay before the night is over."

"Alex, truth or dare?" Mark charged.

"Boy, I just got punched in the chest. Skip me!" Alex wailed.

"Nope, no skipsies," Malajia taunted.

Alex sighed. "Truth," she grunted.

Mark thought for a moment, then smiled slyly. "Out of the guys in this room, who would you sleep with, if you didn't know us?"

Alex's eyes widened as the four guys turned and looked at her, eager for her response. "I'm *not* going to answer that question!"

"Come on Alex, what's the big deal?" Mark asked, flexing his muscles.

Alex sucked her teeth at his blatant flaunting. "Definitely not *you*," she spat.

"You lyin' like shit," Mark boasted. "You know you want this chocolate thunder."

Chasity busted out laughing hysterically; Malajia made a face of disgust. "Please," Malajia scoffed. "Don't nobody want your ashy ass."

Sidra reached for a slice of pizza. "Did you just call him ashy?" she laughed.

Mark clenched his jaw as laughter filled the room. "Just answer the damn question, Alex."

Alex tossed her hand up in surrender. "Fine," she huffed, looking around at the handsome men. "*If* I didn't know you guys...and this will *never* happen, you guys are like my brothers—"

"Just answer the goddamn question!" Malajia snapped, slapping her hand on the floor. This game was taking much too long for her liking.

Alex rolled her eyes. "David," she muttered. Her answer was met with shock and amusement.

"The *nerd*?!" Mark wailed.

"I guess I have a thing for men with glasses," Alex shrugged, looking at David, whose brown face was flushed.

"Why thank you," David smiled, pushing his glasses up

the bridge of his nose.

"Don't get all cocky David," Mark teased, "She only said that out of pity. *Nobody* likes glasses."

"Let's move this shit along," Malajia hissed. "Jason, truth or dare?"

"Why is it that you and Mark are the *only* ones making people do stuff?" Sidra asked.

"'Cause the rest of y'all are dry as shit," Malajia barked. "Jase?"

Jason sat up in his seat. "Dare," he replied full of confidence.

Malajia tapped her cheek with her finger as she pondered what to make him do. She glanced over at Chasity, who was looking at her cell phone. A sneaky look formed on Malajia's pretty face. "Jason, I dare you...to grab Chasity's boobs and give her a kiss."

"What the fuck, Mel?" Chasity snapped, head jerking up from her phone. Jason shook his head as he pinched the bridge of his nose, trying not to laugh.

"What is with you and *boobs* today?" Sidra scoffed.

Jason looked at Chasity and shrugged. She returned his look with wide eyes. "Seriously?" she bit out.

"I'm sorry," he laughed. "It's not my fault."

"Oh Chaz, get over it. It's not like he hasn't grabbed them *before*," Mark taunted.

"I'm not grabbing her in front of you guys," Jason refused, knowing how uncomfortable it would make both of them.

"Fine, grab 'em later, but just kiss her *now*," Malajia huffed. "And make it a good one. My porno DVD broke and I need some visions for later," she joked.

Josh buried his face in a pillow and laughed.

Sidra poked his arm. "Don't encourage her," she chided.

Chasity ran her hands through her hair. The last thing that she wanted to do was kiss Jason in front of everybody, especially knowing how fast she could get worked up just by him looking at her. "Just come on," she mumbled to him.

Facing each other, they leaned in.

"You cool?" he whispered.

No, she screamed internally, but simply nodded. Chasity closed her eyes as Jason's lips touched hers. Jason touched her face, then her hair as their kiss deepened. In that moment, they forgot that they had an audience. The kiss spoke volumes to each other and to the others in the room. Snapping back to reality, Chasity put her hand on Jason's chest and nudged him away. The room was silent as the two caught their breath.

"Well…damn," was all Alex could say as she fanned herself. *That was intense.*

"Can y'all film that?" Malajia teased.

Embarrassment resonated on Chasity's face as Mark clapped his hands loudly. "Damn, y'all want us to leave?" he joked.

"Knock it off, asshole," Jason demanded through clenched teeth.

Chasity narrowed her eyes once she regained her composure. "Malajia," she called, tone eerily calm.

"What's good, boo?" Malajia smiled.

"Don't call me that," Chasity spat.

"Call you *what*, boo?" Malajia mocked.

I'm about to slap her. "Truth or dare?" Chasity challenged.

"Oh, you think I'm scared?" Malajia threw back.

"You *should* be."

"Bitch, bring it. *Truth.*"

"Do you wanna fuck Mark?" Chasity asked.

"Oh shit," Jason laughed.

Malajia's mouth dropped open as Mark got in her face, eagerly waiting for a response. "I'm not answering that, you vindictive jackass!"

"What's the problem?" Chasity taunted. "You must *want* to if you're so adamant about answering."

"Let me find out you want me and shit," Mark boasted.

"Boy, you *wish*," Malajia scoffed.

"You don't want to answer? I got a dare for you," Chasity goaded.

"Get her Chaz," Alex urged, waiting in anticipation.

Malajia looked nervous. *Shit!*

"I dare you to kiss Mark...for thirty seconds."

Alex jumped up from her seat and darted over to Chasity. "*My* girl!" she raved, giving her a high five.

Malajia looked like she wanted to crawl into a hole as her friends laughed at and taunted her. "This...is some cruel shit," she complained.

"You think I want your big ass lips touching *me*?" Mark griped.

Malajia looked at Mark with disgust when he belched loudly. She turned back to Chasity. "Chasity," she pleaded to unfazed ears. "*Please*, don't do this to me. I'm your *roommate*."

"I don't *give* a fuck," Chasity threw back. "Do it."

Reluctantly, Mark and Malajia moved in close to one another, eyeing each other with disdain. Mark threw his head back. "Malajia, did you brush your teeth today? Damn," he jeered, loud as ever.

"I swear to God, I hate you," Malajia fumed to him. "And don't put your damn hands on me either."

They leaned in closer and finally let their lips touch. Both tried their best to block out the hollering and teasing that was happening in the background. Malajia closed her eyes tight as she felt Mark's tongue slide into her mouth. *He's a pretty damn good kisser, I just wish it wasn't him!*

"Is it over? Please tell me its over," Sidra whined, covering her eyes. Watching two of her oldest friends kiss each other as if they actually enjoyed it, wasn't something that Sidra wanted to see.

"Nope, still going," Josh laughed.

Mark moved his hand from his side and placed it on Malajia's chest as their kiss continued, Malajia immediately slapped it away, then pulled away from him. "I told you not to touch me," she barked, slapping his hand again.

Mark held his hands up. "Don't flatter yourself, it's a force of habit," he explained. "You ain't got shit to grab *anyway*," he teased. *Damn, she's a good kisser,* he thought, shaking his head to rid the thoughts.

"Yeah whatever," Malajia seethed. "I think my tongue is about to fall out."

"You know you liked it," Mark boasted as Malajia began to dry heave.

"That…was disturbing," Josh chortled.

Chapter 5

Waiting in one of the offices of the Education Department, Emily sighed and ran her hand along the back of her neck. *Oh my God, this class is going to kill me*, she thought, eyeing the syllabus for her Philosophy course.

Emily awoke that Monday morning, already feeling low. As if her mother constantly throwing up her poor grades and threatening to pull her out of Paradise Valley University if they didn't improve wasn't bad enough, getting called into the office by her department head had her nearly in tears.

She shoved the papers back into her pink book bag as the office door opened. Glancing up to the department head, she forced a smile. "Hi Dr. Walker."

"Good morning Miss Harris," the stern-faced man said, taking a seat at the massive desk in front of Emily. "Do you know why I wanted to meet with you?"

She fidgeted in her seat. "Um…to go over my classes?" she sputtered.

Looking at the paper on his desk, he pushed the glasses up on his nose. "Yes, and more *importantly*, your grades," he confirmed.

Emily lowered her head. "I know that I didn't do my best last semester."

"I would love to know *why?*" Dr. Walker pressed. "You were doing well when you first started. Then you hit your sophomore year and your grades just took a nosedive."

"I know," Emily mumbled, looking down at her hands. "I'm just dealing with—I um..." Emily shook her head. How could she sit in front of the department head at her university and explain to him that she, at almost nineteen years old, was failing because she was letting her mother stress her out, without sounding like a complete loser. "I'll do better," she said, tone unconvincing.

Dr. Walker fixed a stern gaze upon the meek girl in front of him. "Miss. Harris, I want you to be aware that if you don't pull at least a C average in all of your classes this semester, you *will* be put on academic probation at the start of next year."

His words hit Emily like a ton of bricks. "Ac—academic probation?" she stammered.

"Yes," he nodded. "Once you're added to that list, and you fail to pass your classes, the next step is academic dismissal."

Emily put her hands over her face and let out a heavy sigh; this was all too much for her to hear. *What am I gonna do if I get kicked out of school?*

"Do you understand?"

"Yes," Emily murmured. She understood the ramifications of not passing, but she also understood how hard that would be, given her course load. "Can I please go? I have to get to my next class."

Dr. Walker gave her the okay to do as she'd asked. "Miss. Harris, I'll set up another meeting with you after midterms to see how you're improving," he said as she headed for the door.

Emily just nodded as she walked out, closing the office door quietly behind her. Resting her back against the closed door, she stared up at the ceiling, processing the conversation that had just taken place. Sighing again, she glanced at the pink watch on her wrist and made a beeline for the hallway.

"This semester is going to be hell," Sidra griped to Josh as they walked the path heading for the student lounge. "I can safely say that I'm going to hate every single one of my classes."

Josh placed his arm around her shoulder and chuckled. "Even Criminology?"

"*Especially* Criminology," she fussed. "That damn syllabus is ridiculous. They expect me to have to understand some stupid theories to explain crime... How should *I* know why people do the dumb stuff they do?"

"Because you'll *have* to, if you want to become a lawyer," Josh teased, rubbing her shoulder. He, of all people, knew of Sidra's desire to become a lawyer. It was something that she'd been talking about ever since she was a little girl.

Sidra rolled her eyes. "Yeah, I know, I know," she grumbled. "You know how I get when I'm stressed."

"Yes, yes I do," Josh agreed, recalling the many times that the normally reserved Sidra cracked and exploded under pressure

Sidra leaned her head on his broad shoulder. A move that Josh, unbeknownst to Sidra, relished. But his happiness was short-lived; she lifted her head once she heard her cell phone ring. "Sweetie, can you hold this?" she asked Josh as she dug in her purse for her phone. He gladly obliged, holding onto the blue pocketbook while Sidra unzipped a small pocket. He rolled his eyes as he saw Mark dart pass him.

"Nice purse, Joshua," Mark laughed, in his hasty passing.

"Shut up," Josh hurled back.

Shaking her head at them, Sidra retrieved the phone. The smile that lit up her face could have replaced the sun. She eagerly put it to her ear as she grabbed her purse from Josh.

Josh stared, wondering who could have shifted her mood so quickly.

"Hi James," Sidra beamed.

Josh rolled his eyes. *Great, just great.* Just what he needed, for Sidra to get a phone call from the fancy, older lawyer that she met in New York. He wished, if only for a moment, that *he* could be the reason for such enthusiasm. *Why is she still talking to him anyway?* he wondered as they continued to walk through the crowds of students. He waited while Sidra spoke on the phone, seething quietly.

"Was that your boyfriend?" Josh hissed, once she ended the call.

Sidra's smile was still plastered to her face as she placed the phone back into her purse. "Come on Josh, you know that James isn't my boyfriend," she answered. "He's just a friend."

Please, you don't smile at me that way, he thought. "Uh huh," he muttered.

Picking up on Josh's sudden change in attitude, Sidra glanced at him. "Is something wrong?"

Josh shook his head. "No," he grumbled.

"Are you sure?"

No. Josh sighed. "Yeah, just a little drained from this morning's classes," he lied. The lie satisfied Sidra, who just shrugged as they kept walking.

Malajia hurried into her room and slammed the door. She tossed her book bag on the floor, and kicked it with her foot. "Ow!" she howled when her foot hit the corner of one of her books.

Removing her coat and high-heeled boots, she examined her sore toe, then sat on the bed and rubbed it. She let out a sigh. Then, hearing her cell phone ring, she retrieved it from her purse and put it to her ear. "I hope you're calling me to tell me that you got Dad to put more money in my account," she barked into the line.

"Chick, you already know Dad isn't gonna give you another dime for another month," Geri Simmons returned, laughter in her voice.

Malajia broke into a giggle. Despite her initial greeting, she was happy to hear from her older sister. "What's up, crazy?" she said, sitting back on the bed.

"Girl nothing, just left that stupid job," Geri replied.

"Yeah? Well I just left my second class," Malajia grunted, twirling some of her hair around her finger. "I swear, it's only the first day of classes and I have all of this damn work... I gotta read like six chapters in my History class *alone*." She let out a huff, still reeling from the assignment given to her. "The professors are trippin' *hard* this semester."

"Get over it," Geri teased. "You're always complaining about something."

"Yeah a'ight," Malajia ground out. "That's why you be bored as shit at work. With those old, ugly ass dudes."

"God, I knoooow," Geri whined. "Sis, you gotta set me up with one of those fine ass men on your campus... What's up with Mark?"

Malajia was disgusted. "Girl—Mark? Eww! No!" she bellowed.

"What's wrong with me dating Mark? He's cute," Geri teased.

"I'll punch you in your freakin' neck muscle if you ever say Mark and cute in the same sentence again," Malajia jeered.

Geri was enjoying Malajia's discontent, laughing hysterically.

"You done made my stomach hurt," Malajia griped. A notification sound made Malajia pull the phone from her ear and look at it. She frowned at the number flashing across the screen. *Whose number is this?* She wondered. "Geri, I gotta call you back," she announced.

"You always tryna rush me off!" Geri wailed. "I *just* called you—"

"Geri, don't nobody got time for your shit, get off my damn phone," Malajia barked back, before clicking over. "Hello?" her tone was skeptical.

"Hello? Malajia?" the male voice on the other end questioned.

"Yeah?" Malajia frowned.

"Hey it's uh...its Tyrone."

Malajia's face went from confused to angry. The last time that she spoke to the Prime State University football player and potential love interest Tyrone Edmonds was weeks before she left school for winter break, after he'd snapped on her.

"*Who?*" she snapped, sitting up straight on her bed. The line went silent. "Tyrone? As in the same Tyrone who treated me like shit when I was only calling to say 'hi'?"

"Malajia, can you just let me talk?" he requested.

"Oh *now* you wanna talk? Only when *you* want to, huh?" Malajia mocked. After the morning that she had, she couldn't believe he was on her phone. She looked at the screen. "Whose number is this anyway?"

"It's my friend's," Tyrone informed. "I've been trying to call you and text you for weeks. You wouldn't answer."

"That's because I blocked your ass," Malajia sniped.

"I figured that, so I decided to call you from another number."

Malajia rolled her eyes to the ceiling. "What the fuck do you want Tyrone?"

There was hesitation. "Malajia...I want to apolo—"

"I'm not trying to hear that bullshit dawg!" she erupted, jumping up from her bed. After the heartache that Tyrone put her through in the short time that she'd known him, Malajia had no interest in any apology. "You made me feel like shit. *After* I gave your ass another chance *after* you disrespected me in the *first* place."

"I know that," he said. "I know that I was wrong, I'm trying to make amends."

Malajia sucked her teeth. "Man, amend my fine *ass* and

get off my damn phone," she spat.

Tyrone sighed. "Look, I know you're mad right now, but I would like a chance to make things right," he pleaded. "I'll hang up, but can you *please* unblock my number?"

Malajia once again rolled her eyes as she let out a loud sigh. "Bye Tyrone," she muttered, before ending the call. Malajia stared at the phone for seconds, then tossed it on the bed behind her. "I need a damn drink," she vented.

Alex slung her book bag on her shoulder as she headed out of the English building. *A paper already, sheesh,* she thought, navigating the steps. Glancing at her watch, she reached the bottom of the steps. A loud screech in her ear made her jump and nearly stumble on the step. Spinning around, she saw Mark standing close to her, laughing.

"You are an asshole!" she screamed, nudging him away from her. "Damn near gave me a heart attack...What's wrong with you?"

"I wanted to get your attention," he explained.

Alex vigorously rubbed her face. "You could've just called my name," she hissed, pushing some of her wavy tendrils back up into her bun. "You didn't have to scream in my damn ear."

Mark's laughter became a chuckle as he placed his arm around a fussy Alex. "My bad thickums," he teased of her thick frame. "What are you about to do?"

Alex shook her head as she calmed down. She playfully backhanded her silly friend in his toned abdomen as they ambled along the path. "I'm about to hit this library," she informed. "I have a five-page draft due in a few days."

Mark winced. "Damn," he commiserated. "Yeah, I got a bunch of homework that I *ain't* doin'."

Alex shook her head. "Slacking already, huh?"

"Yup," Mark chortled, nodding to a fellow classmate as they passed each other. "So, when are you gonna start back at that pizza place?"

"You mean the Pizza Shack?" Alex questioned, scratching her head.

Mark sucked his teeth. "That *is* the only place you worked at, right?"

"Boy, what's your attitude for?"

"'Cause I'm tryna get a free pizza and shit and you asking stupid questions," Mark jeered.

Alex stared at him in disbelief. "You are certifiably stupid; do you know that?"

Mark dissolved into laughter. "Yeah, I know," he agreed. "Soooo, when can I get that free pizza?"

Alex stared at the wide smile on his face and gritted her teeth. Even though Alex was somewhat excited about starting back her part-time job as a waitress at the popular college hangout, her mind was far from it as she began brainstorming about the paper that she needed to write. "I start next week," she huffed.

Mark clapped his hands. "Yeeeesss," he rejoiced, parting ways. "I'm about to go play some ball, we meeting for dinner later?"

"Yeah, more than likely," Alex called after him, glancing at her watch. "Don't you have Financial Accounting now?"

"Fuck that class," Mark threw back, continuing on his way. She waved her hand at him dismissively, then continued on her way.

Chasity walked into her room to see Malajia pacing the carpeted floor. Chasity dropped her book bag and folded her arms as she watched Malajia keep her steady pace, mumbling something to herself. It was when Malajia didn't make eye contact that Chasity realized she had headphones in.

Chasity walked over and tapped Malajia on the shoulder, inciting a loud scream from her roommate as she quickly removed her headphones. "Damn it Chasity," Malajia fussed, putting her hand on her chest. "You scared the *shit* outta me."

"I sure hope that's not true," Chasity smirked; Malajia made a face. "How long have you been burning a hole in the carpet?"

Malajia wrapped her ear buds around her finger before tossing them on her dresser. "I lost track of time after like fifteen minutes," she answered, tone sullen. Malajia hadn't left her room since she received her unexpected phone call from Tyrone. She spent the time seething, lying in bed and listening to music, before jumping up and pacing the floor. "I swear I never noticed how hard this damn carpet is," she said at an attempt at a joke.

Chasity glanced down at the carpet, then back at Malajia. Folding her arms yet again, she studied the troubled look on her roommates' face. "What's the matter with you?" she asked.

Malajia sighed as she looked at Chasity. "Guess who called me today?"

"Do I really want to know?"

"Probably not, but I'm gonna tell you *anyway*," Malajia replied. "*Tyrone's* raggedy ass."

Chasity frowned. "*Who?*"

Malajia rolled her eyes. "You remember the guy that—"

"Treated you like shit, yeah I know who you're talking about," Chasity sniped, putting her hand up. After Malajia revealed to Chasity over winter break about how Tyrone acted towards her and how her feelings were hurt by it, Chasity had hoped, for Malajia's sake, that she would never speak to him again. "What the fuck could he *possibly* want? Didn't you block his number?"

"I *did* block it," Malajia assured her. "That sneaky bastard called from someone else's phone."

"How stalkerish," Chasity bit out.

"Yeah, right? And *after* he called *me* a damn stalker," Malajia griped, running her hand over her hair. "He was trying to say sorry. Talking about wanting to make amends and shit."

Chasity shot Malajia a skeptical look. "You told him

where to shove that shit, *right*?"

"Yeah, I did," Malajia confirmed, tone low. She then glanced down at her hands. Truth be told, hearing from Tyrone after all this time stirred something in her that she wasn't sure could go away.

Chasity shook her head as she came to a realization. "Malajia, don't," she warned.

Malajia lifted her head, confusion written on her face. "Don't *what*?"

"You look real unsure right now," Chasity pointed out. "Don't you give that piece of shit another chance."

Malajia rubbed her face with vigor. *Damn her perceptive ass!* "Look, trust me, I'm pissed all the way off at him," she swore. "But...if he knows he was wrong and apologizes—"

"Mel!" Chasity exclaimed in disbelief.

"I mean..." Malajia shook her head. "Nothing, never mind. I'm not gonna talk to him anymore."

Chasity didn't know if she could believe Malajia or not, but she didn't have time to argue about it any longer. "Yeah, okay," she muttered, heading for the bathroom, leaving Malajia standing there.

Retrieving her phone from her pocket, she looked up Tyrone's phone number and stared at it. *Don't Malajia, don't do it*. Sighing and ignoring the voice in her head, Malajia hit the unblock button and shoved the phone into her back pocket.

Just two more problems and you're finished, Jason thought, rubbing his eyes. Two hours of homework later, Jason was mentally drained and desperate for a break.

A knock at his door was a welcomed distraction. "Come in," he called.

"Hey Jase," Josh said, walking in, leaving the door cracked behind him.

Jason spun around in his seat. "Hey what's up?" He glanced at his watch. "It's not time to go to dinner yet, is it? I want to finish these last two problems first."

Josh shook his head as he sat on the edge of Jason's bed. "No, not yet," he assured.

Jason shrugged as he reached for the bottle of soda on his desk. As he took a sip, he noticed that Josh was just sitting quiet. "Something wrong?" he wondered.

"No, nothing's wrong but… Can I talk to you about something?"

Jason eyed him skeptically. "Sure."

"I was gonna talk to David, but he's at the library and Mark… Well, Mark's an asshole, so…"

Jason held a blank expression on his face at Josh's hesitation. "Soooo, what's the question Josh?"

"Okay well, do you remember that guy that Sidra met in New York?" Josh quizzed.

"Vaguely," Jason recalled.

"Yeah well—" Both Josh and Jason were startled when Mark barged through the door.

"Dude, *knock*," Jason barked.

"The shit was open, what's the point of knocking?" Mark threw back. Josh rolled his eyes as Jason shook his head. "Jase man, don't let Josh talk to you. Trust me, you don't wanna hear that shit."

"Mind your damn business," Josh hissed. "Get the hell out of here."

Mark scoffed. "This ain't your room dawg, you can't kick me out."

Fed up with the bickering, Jason put his hands up. "Hey, chill out," he demanded. "Josh, what were you trying to talk to me about?"

Before Josh could answer, Mark stepped in. "Josh has been bitchin' all day long because Sidra got a phone call from that damn lawyer James Grant—"

Josh sucked his teeth. "Did you *have* to say his last name?"

Mark looked at him, perplexed. "What the fuck does a *last name* have to do with anything?"

Jason tried to suppress his laugh, while Josh looked like he wanted to punch Mark in his mouth. "Josh, is that true?" Jason asked.

Josh rolled his eyes. "I wasn't *bitchin'*," he mumbled. "I just wanted your opinion on the guy, that's all."

"We don't really know anything about him," Jason shrugged.

"Yeah, go ask the girls," Mark grunted. "Hell, *we* probably won't hear shit until she starts dating him."

"Who said anything about *dating*?" Josh snarled. "They're just friends."

"No, *you're* just a friend," Mark mocked, pointing at Josh.

Jason winced at the remark. *Damn!* he thought as Josh's brown face held a scowl.

"*James* ain't gonna be no damn friend to Sidra," Mark added, folding his arms.

"Why can't you shut the hell up for *once*?" Josh seethed, clenching his fist.

"You mad you a friend and shit," Mark taunted.

Having had enough, Josh stood up and stormed out of the room. "Jackass," he hissed at Mark as he shut the door behind him.

Jason laughed. "You're wrong for that, bro."

"Ain't nobody's fault that he too damn scared to tell Sid that he likes her," Mark griped. "Hell, everybody knows *but* her... Now he got a damn attitude 'cause she like somebody else."

"True," Jason nodded. He spun around in his chair and picked up his pencil. "All right, get out so I can finish my homework."

Mark stood there as Jason began to write on his notebook. "Yo, when you and Chaz gonna bang again? 'Cause I ain't been liking *your* attitude neither," he jeered.

Jason slammed his pencil down and pointed to the door. "Out!" he boomed.

Mark laughed. "Fine, I'm going," he promised, walking to the door. "See you at dinner."

Jason put up his middle finger as Mark closed the door.

Emily rushed into her room just as her room phone was ringing. "Please be Daddy, please be Daddy," she wished, dropping her books. She'd called her father earlier that morning before class, but he was in a meeting. Emily hoped that he was calling back. She darted for the phone, but wasn't fast enough; the call went to the answering machine.

Emily shrugged out of her coat. Prepared to pick the phone up mid-message, she jerked her hand back when she heard her mother's voice on the line.

"I don't feel like this," she sighed to herself, deciding to let her mother talk to the machine. Sitting on the bed, she listened.

"Emily, it's Mommy, I've called you five times in the past few days... Why aren't you answering? I was calling to check in on you. I know you started classes on Monday and I wanted to see how they're going so far."

Emily rolled her eyes. "It's only Wednesday, get off my back," she hissed to the machine.

"I'll just come down there on Friday then—"

Emily's eyes widened and she snatched the phone. "Hello? Mommy, I'm here," she said, voice panicked. She sighed yet again at her mother's stern voice. "No, I know— Classes are okay, I just started—But...why are you coming here? You just left Sunday." Emily didn't know when it happened, but she had hung up the phone while her mother was still ranting at her.

Furious, she raised the phone and prepared to throw it across the room, then decided against it. Clutching the pink cordless phone in her hand, she felt tears prick her eyes. *Why? Why won't she leave me alone? Why is she coming here this weekend? I haven't been gone a week yet?!* Feeling the walls close in on her, Emily jumped up from her bed and darted out of the room, leaving her coat on the floor.

Emily stormed out of her apartment complex, folding her arms to her chest. The cold didn't hit her at first; her adrenaline was on high. Wiping her tears with the back of her hand, she proceeded to make a beeline for Paradise Terrace in search of comfort from her friends, but something caught her eye. Better yet, some*one*. Seeing the familiar person strolling in her direction, she forced a smile.

"He—hey Praz," she stammered, waving.

The handsome, dark-skinned senior smiled back at her. "What's up, little lady? Aren't you cold?" he asked, noticing her lack of a coat.

Emily shook her head. "Um, can I ask you a question?"

He shifted his books from one arm to the other and nodded.

Emily ran her hand along the back of her neck, the cold biting at her skin. "Um….do you still make those um…." She glanced down at the ground, trying to find her words. "Do you still make those…drinks?"

Praz smiled. "You mean my special 'red hurricane'?" he asked. "Not as often, but I *could*. Why, is Malajia looking for some?" Praz was known around campus for his alcoholic drinks. They were always a hit at parties. Malajia was no stranger to requesting them.

Emily gave a nervous laugh. "Uh…no it's not for Malajia," she muttered. "It's for…me."

Praz looked confused. He had known the group since their freshman year, and was under the impression that Emily didn't drink.

Picking up on his skepticism, Emily immediately shook her head. "No, not for me *per se*," she amended. "It's for my um..." *think, think!* "My housemate said that she would tutor me in my Spanish class, if I bought her a drink." Praz stared at her with a blank expression. "I mean I'm not twenty-one yet so I can't go buy some so—so I figured I'd ask *you*."

He hesitated. "Uh...o-kay,"

Emily dug into her pocket, fishing for some cash. "I can pay you, if you want."

Praz put his hand up. "No, you're cool. Any friend of Malajia's gets drinks on *me*," he smiled. Emily smiled back. "You going to her room? I can drop it off there on my way to see a friend."

Emily's eyes widened. "No, I'll just meet you to get it," she panicked. The last thing that she wanted was for the girls to know that she had asked for alcohol. "As a matter of fact, I'd appreciate it if...you didn't mention to Malajia that I asked you for it."

Praz shrugged. "Hey, I make it a point to stay out of people's business," he assured. "I'll drop it off to you."

Emily provided her room information, and Praz headed off, leaving Emily smiling. A wave of relief came over her as she anticipated the arrival of her stress reliever.

Chapter 6

Chasity glanced at the silver watch on her wrist as she headed out of Paradise Terrace. "Fuckin' eight o'clock classes," she hissed. She was trying to mentally prepare herself for her Advanced Computer Language class. As much as Chasity loved computers, she could do without hearing her professor drone on about them first thing in the morning.

She ignored the chatting students and headed for the path across from Court Terrace. Fixing her gaze ahead of her, she saw one person she couldn't ignore.

"Hey Jason," she smiled.

Jason walked up, stopping right in front of her.

"Morning," he returned, cheerfully.

"You seem extra happy this morning," she teased, pushing her hair behind her ears.

Jason chuckled. "Yeah, well, I got a good night's sleep," he explained.

"Must be nice," Chasity muttered. Her ability to sleep peaceful was almost non-existent, Chasity's busy mind kept her up most of the night.

"Heading to the science building?" he asked.

Chasity nodded.

"You want company?"

Chasity nodded again, prompting them to start on their way.

"We almost made it through our first week back on campus," Jason mused, adjusting the black gloves on his hands. "How's it been for you, so far?"

"Fine, I guess," Chasity shrugged, looking over at him. "I called you yesterday to see how your laptop was working with the software add."

He paused for a moment. "Yeah, I saw your missed call. I'm sorry I didn't get to return it," he apologized. "Numerical Analysis had my attention all night."

Chasity just focused ahead of her, not bothering to respond. Jason's laptop was not the real reason she called, Chasity just wanted to hear his voice. She had gone the entire day without seeing or talking to him and that didn't sit well. She was disappointed that he didn't answer, and that he hadn't bothered to return her call; he had never done that before.

Jason, picking up on Chasity's silence, and wanting to say what was on his mind, looked at her. "Look, I know we haven't talked as much—"

"It's fine, you're busy," she quickly interrupted. "I don't expect you to call me or hang out with me."

Jason, hearing sarcasm in her tone, frowned. "I'm sure you *don't*," he grumbled.

Chasity rolled her eyes. Not at Jason, but at herself. She'd gone and turned a pleasant walk to class into a sniping session, all because she was battling her feelings. Reaching the steps of their building, Chasity faced Jason. "I'm sorry," she said.

Jason looked at her, stern. "For?"

"For getting an attitude just now," she replied, adjusting her book bag. Jason's facial expression hadn't changed. "Didn't get much sleep, so I'm cranky."

Jason took a deep breath. While her response was normal, he knew something else was up. "You didn't start off cranky. What changed just now?"

Chasity stood there, caught off guard by his question. She'd almost forgotten how in tune to her emotions Jason was, even when she wasn't. She wanted to just come out and ask him the question that had been on her mind—the question that had kept her up all night. "Um… Jason are we okay?" she hesitantly asked.

Her question took him by surprise, and it showed on his face. "Yes. Why would you ask me that?"

"I don't know, I just—" she shook her head. "Never mind, I'm about to be late."

Jason gently caught her by the arm to stop her from walking off. "No, don't run off," he said, tone calm. "Why would you ask me that?"

"I just… I don't know." She ran her hand through her hair as she tried to compose her thoughts. Expressing emotions other than anger was never her strong suit. "I mean, I know we said we would go back to being friends after everything that happened, but I just… I feel like it's still weird."

Jason looked away momentarily. *She's right*, he thought. He had to admit that trying to put their friendship back to where it was before they slept together was proving to be more difficult than either intended. There were too many feelings there. "Look Chaz, I'm *trying*, here."

Chasity just looked at him as he refused to make eye contact.

"You already know how I feel, and how *you don't*," he added.

Chasity frowned slightly. "So we're *not* okay," she concluded, bite in her voice.

Jason finally looked at her. "I didn't say that," he replied. "We're good… I'm just trying to give you some space, *while* being your friend."

I don't need space! I need you! She hollered to herself. "Okay, that's fine," she answered. "You're right, I want space."

"I'm not upset with you," he promised.

"Uh huh," Chasity sneered.

"I'm *serious*," he insisted, adjusting his book bag.

"I *heard* you," Chasity ground out, a cold look in her eyes as she fixed her gaze on him.

Jason shook his head. He kicked himself for pushing her to say anything. *Shit, you went and pissed her off, stupid. You just took two steps back.* Sighing, he reached for her hand. "Come on, let's get to class."

Chasity moved her hand out of his reach, using that hand to rub her forehead. "Go head, I'll go in a minute."

Without saying another word, Jason headed for the door. Chasity stared at his back until he disappeared inside.

"Idiot," she chided herself.

Malajia stood in the dorm hallway, staring at her phone. "God, stop, *stop*," she hissed at the phone.

Alex walked out of her room. "Girl, who are you fussing at?" she asked, shutting the door behind her.

Malajia sucked her teeth. "Nobody important." *Just Tyrone's stupid ass texting me again.* She'd just got finished reading the fourth "please talk to me" message that he'd sent her that day. "You *finally* ready to go?" Malajia snarled, fluffing her curls with her hand. "What took you so damn long?"

"I couldn't decide which shirt to change into," Alex shrugged.

"Alex, all those ugly ass shirts you got look the same," Malajia snapped. "You didn't have to take that damn long."

Alex gritted her teeth, then plucked Malajia on the arm. "Stop talking about my damn clothes," she chided. "I've already told you about that."

Malajia rubbed her arm. "Alex, that was childish."

"Shut up and come on," Alex barked, grabbing Malajia by the arm and nudging her toward the elevator. "We have to go meet Emily, so we can walk over to the SDC."

"I still don't even know *why* you wanna go over there," Malajia griped as they stepped onto the elevator.

"They added some new games to the game room over there," Alex explained. "I thought it would be fun to go."

"Do I *look* twelve?" Malajia sneered, folding her arms.

Alex rolled her eyes. "No, but you *act* like it," she threw back.

"Funny," Malajia smirked. "Those boots you got on, look like you had 'em for *twelve* hard years,"

Alex glanced down at her brown cloth boots. "I really hate you sometimes," she spat after a few seconds of seething silence.

Walking out of the building, the girls headed for Emily's apartment building. "I haven't talked to Emily all damn week," Malajia declared.

"*I* have, *briefly*," Alex informed. "She seems pretty down. I think her mother plans on coming down here this weekend."

Malajia glanced at Alex in disbelief as they continued walking. "Eww. For *what*? To sit in her damn face?" she scoffed.

Alex shrugged. "I guess."

"Yo, Kelly Harris is trippin'. Em needs to tell her to back off," Malajia fussed. She was tired of Emily's overbearing mother. She only wished that Emily would get tired enough to do something about it.

"I agree with you Mel, but you know how Em is when it comes to her mom," Alex placated. "She doesn't want to disrespect her, and in some way, I feel her on that… I would never disrespect *my* mother either."

"*Your* mother ain't up your ass every damn weekend," Malajia pointed out. "*Your* mother isn't treating you like you're five." She folded her arms. "I woulda cussed my mom out."

"And she would've beat you with that shoe of hers," Alex teased, laughter in her voice.

"Yeah well... I'da had a shoeprint on my ass, but I would've gotten my point across," Malajia joked, folding her arms.

"True," Alex laughed as they approached the front of the building. Opening the door, they stepped into the gloomy common area.

"Ugh, do these damn people know how to open blinds?" Malajia scoffed, looking around. She couldn't put her finger on it, but the apartment living space looked even darker than last semester. The lack of sunlight peering through the small windows, paired with the dark furniture, made the place uninviting. "This grey ass furniture is ugly as shit... It smells like loneliness in here."

"Mel, chill," Alex sighed as they stood in front of Emily's door. Alex gave the door a knock. She glanced over at Malajia, who quickly brushed something off her coat. "Girl, will you be still?"

"There was a bug on me," Malajia complained. "Knock again so we can get the hell out of here."

Alex did as Malajia asked. "I wonder if she's out or something," she said when Emily didn't answer.

"Did you even call her to tell her that we were on our way?" Malajia asked, voice not hiding her agitation.

"Well...no," Alex admitted shamefully. "I guess I just assumed that she'd *be* here."

Malajia stared at Alex, aggravation written on her face. "You know what," she mumbled. "Let me call her now."

"*I'll* do it," Alex volunteered, reaching into her brown satchel.

"Bitch don't you pull that damn Stone Age flip out that raggedy ass bag," Malajia barked, earning another pluck to her arm from Alex. "Ow! Stop plucking me with those fat ass fingers!"

"Just hurry up and call," Alex demanded.

Malajia dialed Emily's number and held the phone to her ear. Both girls heard Emily's phone ring on the other side of the door.

Malajia shrugged when the machine picked up. "She's not here, let's get out of this dungeon," she said, hurrying to the door, with Alex reluctantly trailing behind.

Emily's eyes fluttered open Saturday morning. Sitting up, she grabbed her pounding head with both hands. *God Emily, the whole bottle?* Emily barely remembered opening the bottle of Praz's Red Hurricane the night before. Receiving a phone call from her mother stating that she'd come down Saturday instead, Emily, angry that she was coming at all, grabbed the large, glass bottle from under her bed and drank it all after her last class.

She drifted off to sleep soon after, only waking up briefly when she heard Alex and Malajia outside of her door. Unable to get out of bed, she laid there, willing the spinning room and the ringing phone to stop.

A hard knock at the door made her wince. "Coming," she muttered, gingerly standing from the bed. She tripped over the bottle in her quest to the door. Letting out a yelp, she retrieved it from the floor. Getting a whiff of the alcoholic remnants, Emily felt sick to her stomach. Hearing another knock, she buried the bottle under some papers in her trashcan before opening the door.

Emily took a step back, allowing her mother to walk in. "Hi," she mumbled. Even though her tone was calm, Emily was panicking on the inside. *Please don't smell this liquor on me.*

If Ms. Harris smelled anything, she didn't let it be known. She just folded her arms, studying Emily's appearance. The tired look in her daughters' eyes, combined with her disheveled hair, and the fact that she looked like she'd slept in her day clothes, made her frown.

"Emily are you sick?" she questioned.

Emily's eyes shifted. *I'm hungover.* "Um, yes, a little," she sputtered, trying to run her hand through her tangled hair. "I think I ate something bad last night."

Ms. Harris shook her head, then moved pass Emily in a huff to get to her window. "I knew I should've come down here last night," she fussed, snatching open the blinds.

The bright light didn't help Emily's headache; it made it worse. Emily put her hand in front of her face in an effort to block out the sun. "Please shut those," she begged.

"I could've taken you to get some *real* food," Ms. Harris ranted, ignoring Emily's request. "Where's your course work? I want to have a look at it."

Emily felt her stomach turn as her mother continued talking. She put a hand over her midsection. "I um... I have to go to the bathroom," she announced, darting for the door. Ms. Harris let out a loud sigh as she proceeded to make Emily's bed.

"I swear I haven't been on a damn treadmill in like forever," Malajia said, taking a sip of soda.

Chasity, who was jogging on the treadmill next to Malajia's machine, shot her a quick glance before focusing back on the screen in front of her. "How are you drinking a soda when you're supposed to be working out?" she panted.

"'Cause I'm not doing shit but *walking*," Malajia returned, slow walking on her treadmill. "I don't even feel like *being* in here, I'd rather be watching TV...or drinking. Either one."

Chasity shook her head as she checked her stride. "Then why did you ask to come here with me?"

Malajia took another sip of soda. "'Cause I wanted to spend some time with your evil ass," she ground out.

"Do we *not* live in the same damn room?"

"Yeah, but you been acting dry, so I figured working out with you would force you to talk," Malajia countered, reaching for a small bag of chips in a compartment on the treadmill.

Chasity looked confused. Malajia's comment made no sense. "I'm not acting dry," she grunted.

"You *are*," Malajia insisted. "And I *don't* like it, what's your problem?"

Chasity continued her jog, not answering right away. She knew that Malajia had a point. Ever since her conversation with Jason nearly a week ago, Chasity couldn't think about anything else. Every feeling that she had for him was at the forethought of her mind, and without a way to release them, she found herself withdrawing into her silent shell.

"I don't *have* a problem," Chasity bit out, finally.

"Bullshit," Malajia sneered, stuffing a chip into her mouth. "That's okay, you don't have to say something now...you *will* eventually."

Chasity rolled her eyes. "Yeah, whatever," she mumbled. "Look, either do an actual work out or get away from me."

"Fuck this treadmill," Malajia hissed, causing Chasity to snicker. "I don't need to work out anyway." Malajia's loud ringtone made Chasity groan.

"Girl, go away," Chasity barked.

Malajia's eyes widened at the number. "Shut up," she threw back, before hopping off the treadmill. She hurried to a corner and answered the call. "What do you want?"

"Where are you?" Tyrone asked, point blank.

Malajia looked at the phone in disbelief, before putting it back to her ear. "Excuse me?" she fussed. "You don't get to ask me *shit*."

"It's not like that," Tyrone placated. "I'm on your campus and I wanted to know if you could meet me somewhere."

What the hell is he doing on my damn campus? He goes to school in the next town over. Everything in Malajia told her to hang up the phone, but she didn't. "Meet me outside of the gym," she huffed. After giving Tyrone directions and checking to make sure that Chasity was still engrossed in her workout routine, Malajia slipped outside.

Within minutes, Tyrone was in front of her, smiling.

She'd almost forgotten how tall and attractive he was. And that she'd always had a thing for dark-skinned men. "What are you doing here?" she snarled, folding her arms to her chest. "I thought I told you not to contact me."

"You unblocked my number, so I figured that was your way of saying that you still *wanted* me to," Tyrone returned.

Malajia rolled her eyes. "No, I hit the unblock button by accident," she lied. "Why are you here?"

"I wanted to see you," he answered honestly.

Malajia looked confused. "So you drove over here just to see someone who clearly wants *nothing* to do with you?" she fussed. "Are you crazy?"

Tyrone shrugged. "Maybe," he replied; she made a face. "Look, me texting and calling you wasn't working, so I figured a face to face might make a difference."

"Well, you thought wrong. Bye, boy," Malajia sneered, then turned to walk off.

Tyrone grabbed her arm, stopping her. "Hold on a second."

Malajia jerked away from him and faced him once again. "You don't get to touch me, asshole."

Tyrone ran his hands down his face in an effort to keep calm. *I hate being called names*, he thought. Despite the venom that she was spewing at him, her attitude turned him on. He pictured himself grabbing her, pushing her against the wall and planting a kiss on her. "My apology still don't mean shit, huh?" he asked after a moment.

"Nope," Malajia ground out, examining the red polish on her nails.

Malajia was proving to be more stubborn than he thought. It was clear to him that winning her over with words wasn't going to work. "Well, since my words aren't getting through to you… How about my actions?" he proposed.

Malajia looked unfazed. "If your actions are anything like they were months ago, you can keep *those* too."

"I want to take you on a date."

"Ha," Malajia spat out. "You mean like the one where

you took me to your place and expected me to fuck you?" Malajia was seething as she recalled their first outing together.

"No," Tyrone replied after a brief pause. "I mean a *real* date. A date that I should've taken you on in the *first* place."

Malajia was silent as she pondered his proposal. A real date with him was something she'd wanted since she met him. But she kept going back to how he disrespected her on more than one occasion. She shook her head. "No, it's too late for that."

"I don't think that it *is*," Tyrone contradicted. "I think that you *want* to give me another chance, but you don't think that I'm serious."

Malajia looked away, not saying anything.

"I *am* serious. I really like you, and I want to get to know you better," he said.

The deepness of his voice, paired with the words that Malajia had been wanting to hear, was starting to wear on her. But still she remained silent.

"I can show you that I'm a good guy, just give me a chance," he pressed. "Let me prove it. Let me take you out."

In Malajia's mind, she was smiling. She played out her dream date with him in just those few seconds. "I'll think about it," she replied, finally. Her tone was sharp.

"I'll take that," Tyrone replied, a hint of a smile in his voice. "Can I call you later?"

"Maybe," she muttered.

"Will you *answer*?" he chortled.

"Maybe," she repeated, forcing herself to keep her smile contained.

"Fair enough," he replied. He took his hand and brushed her soft cheek before walking off, leaving Malajia feeling like her heart skipped a beat. She put her hand on her chest and held it there as she watched him walk away.

Chasity, relieved that Malajia had left so that she could

finish her workout in peace, grabbed her towel and water bottle from the treadmill and headed to the weight room. She saw Jason off in a corner near one of the machines.

Slowly walking inside, her eyes were fixed on him. His back was facing her, so she went unnoticed. But Chasity certainly noticed the young woman sitting on the machine in front of him. If Chasity's eyes could shoot lasers, they would have burned a hole straight through Jason's back to the girls' face. She watched while he helped the girl on the machine, as they enjoyed what seemed to be an engrossing conversation. Chasity felt herself about to snap when she saw the pretty, perky girl put her hand on Jason's arm, then held it there as she laughed.

Girl, leave before you choke her, Chasity urged herself. Listening to the voice in her head, Chasity turned and slipped out of the room. As she hurried towards the exit, she nearly collided with Mark who was heading inside.

"Damn Parker, you tryna feel me up?" he joked.

Chasity turned her lip up. "Never," she hissed.

Mark laughed as he adjusted the gym bag on his arm. "You look like you had a good workout," he observed of her glistening appearance.

"It was fine, I gotta go," Chasity quickly put out, moving around him.

"Is Jase in here yet? I'm supposed to meet him."

"He's here," Chasity threw over her shoulder, as she walked away.

Chapter 7

Chasity, laying on her bed, dipped french fries in a pool of ketchup on her plate. After leaving the gym with haste, Chasity spent the rest of the day in her room, lying in bed, sulking. It was now evening, and she was trying to enjoy her takeout food, but not surprisingly, her appetite was scarce.

Malajia walked through the door, sighing in the process. "I hope you got enough food to share, 'cause I'm starving," she said, eying the abundance of fries on Chasity's plate.

Chasity rolled her eyes as she sat up on her bed. "Here, you can have these," she offered, handing the plate to an eager Malajia.

"Yeeeeessss," Malajia rejoiced. "You got salt and pepper on these?" She fixed an intense gaze on Chasity.

Chasity narrowed her eyes. "Just eat the damn fries," she bit out.

Malajia chuckled. Plate and plastic bag in hand, she walked over and sat on the floor near her dresser. Silence filled the room as both women sat, allowing the noise in their heads to consume them. Malajia, not being good with staying silent for too long, was the first to speak.

"You want to have a drink with me?"

Chasity looked at Malajia like she had ten heads. "No,

alchy," she sneered. "You keep trying to get me to drink with you."

"*So*? Take it as a damn compliment," Malajia threw back, retrieving a bottle of wine from the plastic bag next to her. "Come on, this is supposed to be the good stuff. I got it from a senior."

"Is that supposed to persuade me?" Chasity scoffed.

Malajia let out a sigh as she ran a hand through her hair. "Chaz, I got some shit that I wanna tell you, and I think you'll be less inclined to be judgmental if you drink first," she revealed.

Chasity frowned. She was curious as to what Malajia possibly felt the need to tell her. She sucked her teeth. "I'll get some cups," she relented, standing from her bed.

Malajia clapped her hands and let out a squeal of delight as Chasity handed her one of the plastic red cups. Chasity sat on the floor in front of her roommate, while Malajia filled both cups to capacity.

Chasity put the cup to her lips. "This shit just *smells* hot," she complained.

Malajia giggled. "Just shut up and drink it." After sipping on some of the bitter, warm wine, Malajia began to feel a little relaxed.

"What do you want to tell me?" Chasity wondered.

Malajia looked up from her cup as she took yet another sip, making a face at the taste. "You promise not to judge?"

"I can't make that promise, because I don't know what you're about to tell me," Chasity stated.

Malajia took a deep breath. "Fuck it," she said, tossing a hand up. "Tyrone came to see me today."

Chasity paused mid-sip. "Came to see you *where*?"

"Here on campus," Malajia revealed. "He met me at the gym earlier."

"So *that's* why you left," Chasity recalled.

Malajia nodded.

Chasity stared at her. "You unblocked his number, *didn't* you?"

"Details, honey, just focus," Malajia ground out, running her hand down the front of her jeans.

"I *knew* you were gonna do that shit," Chasity hissed, shaking her head. "So what the hell was he saying? The same old bullshit?"

"*Kind* of," Malajia muttered, giving the contents of her cup a long look. "He really wants to make things up to me… He wants to take me on a date. A *real* date." Malajia looked up. "And… I'm thinking about letting him."

Chasity stared at Malajia for a long moment. She couldn't believe what she'd just heard come out of the girls' mouth. She opened her mouth to speak.

"Don't start," Malajia spat out, interrupting her.

"Bull*shit*," Chasity countered, tone not hiding her agitation. "Are you crazy?"

"Chasity," Malajia warned.

"*Malajia*," Chasity shot back.

Malajia rolled her eyes as she sat her cup down. "Look, yeah, he made some mistakes, but he wants to make it right… Nobody's perfect, and if he's willing to try, then I don't see why I shouldn't *let* him."

Chasity was completely confused and it showed on her face. "I don't get what this boy has over you."

Malajia looked down at her hands and shrugged. "I guess, I just feel some kind of connection to him for some reason," she admitted. "The times when we talked *before* he acted stupid… I enjoyed it… I feel like he's someone I can really get to know on a deeper level, you know?"

Chasity stared at her. Even though her mind told her to cuss Malajia out for giving someone who clearly didn't think highly of her a second chance, she realized that she wasn't exactly the pillar of good decisions herself. She decided to refrain. "Look, it's *your* life, *your* feelings, *your* heart," she said, tone sincere. "Just be careful."

Malajia smiled. Although Chasity's calmer demeanor took her by surprise, she was grateful for her advice. It let her know that Chasity cared. "I will, and what you said is noted."

As Malajia took another sip of her drink, Chasity felt like it was a good time to get what she was dealing with off her chest. "Okay, since we're sharing and shit. I guess I should tell you that I saw Jason with a girl today."

Malajia nearly choked on her drink. She coughed as she sat her cup down. "It went up my nose," she grimaced of the wine. Finally gaining her composure, she patted her chest, looking at Chasity wide-eyed. "The fuck you *mean* you saw Jason with a girl?" she exclaimed. "Do we gotta stomp a bitch?"

Chasity resisted the urge to laugh. "No, it wasn't like that," she explained.

"Oh," Malajia replied, calming down. "I was about to say…Jason betta not get slapped."

"That's just the thing, Jason can see whoever or do whatever he wants. He's not my boyfriend," Chasity said.

"He's yours, don't even play."

"No…he's *not*," Chasity insisted, voice sullen. Malajia took notice of the change in tone and listened intently. "I saw him and even though he was just helping her… I got mad. I got jealous. But I have no *right* to be."

Malajia processed what was said. "You may not have a right *per se*, but you're entitled to feel how you *want*," she pointed out. "My question to *you* is, the fact that he's not your boyfriend…is it your fault or his?" she asked, already knowing the answer to that question.

Chasity sighed, "It's mine."

"Why *is* that?" Malajia pressed. "Do you just not feel for him that way?"

Chasity was silent.

Malajia studied her face to see if she could find the answer. "Do you want to be with Jason or *not*?" she asked. "Do you care about him at *all* in that way? I mean, I thought you *did*. You slept with the guy after all. But it's hard to read you sometimes."

Chasity looked like she was struggling to answer. She hated expressing her feelings, but since she brought it up, she would need to talk about them.

"Well? *Do* you?" Malajia pressed.

Chasity took a deep breath. "Yes… I have feelings for him. *A lot* of them."

A huge smile crossed Malajia's face. "About time you admitted it, damn you."

Chasity sighed. She was telling the half-truth. Yes, she had feelings for Jason, but she didn't reveal exactly how deep they went. "Yeah," she mumbled. "I just don't know what to do with them."

"Oh heffa, you know *exactly* what to do with them," Malajia contradicted, "Get your ass up and go tell him." She was brimming with excitement

Chasity shook her head. "It's complicated."

"No the hell it *isn't*," Malajia argued. "You have feelings for him, now go get your damn man."

Chasity ran her hand through her hair. "I think I put him through too much. I don't even think he wants me anymore."

"Are you crazy or just stupid?" Malajia barked.

"*Neither*," Chasity frowned.

"Yeah well, you're fooling me right now," Malajia countered, grabbing Chasity's hand.

Chasity tried to yank her hand away. "Do you *have* to touch me?"

Malajia held on to it. "Yes, 'cause I need for my common sense to flow to you, 'cause you talking crazy right now," she jeered. "You think that Jason telling you that he loved you was some shit talk?"

"That was like—"

"Not that long ago when he said it, cut it the hell out," Malajia interrupted. "Jason's feelings for you didn't change. You're making excuses because you're too damn scared to put your big girl drawls on and go get him."

Chasity opened her mouth to protest, but Malajia jerked her hand up to silence her.

"You *will* get slapped tonight," Malajia warned.

Chasity smirked. "Uh huh."

Malajia tilted her head. "All jokes aside sis… You need to go tell him how you feel," she advised. "As much as he loves you, he's not gonna wait for you forever… Don't mess around and watch him *really* end up with someone else."

Chasity looked away. The mere thought of Jason ending up with another woman was something that she couldn't handle. "Okay," was all that she said after a long pause.

Malajia watched as Chasity made a move to get up from the floor. "You're gonna talk to him *now*?"

"Uh huh," Chasity replied, grabbing her coat from the back of her chair.

"Good, then I can have the rest of your wine," Malajia mused, grabbing Chasity's cup from the floor. Peering inside, she frowned once she made a discovery. "Your cup is still full!"

Chasity glanced at her as she headed for the door.

"You were *pretending* to drink this nasty shit the *whole* time?"

"Uh huh," Chasity confirmed, walking out the door.

Malajia smiled to herself. "Smart bitch," she said, amused.

Chasity slowly walked up to Jason's door and stood in front of it. "Just knock," she whispered to herself, closing her eyes. Giving the door a tap, she waited. When Jason didn't answer right away, she was almost relieved. But the relief was short-lived when she heard his voice on the other side of the door.

"Who is it?"

Chasity didn't say anything right away; she was still deciding if she should run or not. "It's Chasity," she said finally. Upon being told to come in, Chasity opened the door.

Jason, who was standing over his TV, plugged something in and glanced up at her, surprise written on his face. "Hey." He couldn't remember the last time that she'd been to his room. Not to mention the fact that they hadn't been alone together or had a real conversation for nearly a week.

"Hey," she returned. "Are you busy?"

Jason looked down at the game system on his TV stand and shook his head. "Not really. I was just gonna play this game for a little bit."

"Oh," she replied. "Can I talk to you about something?"

Jason looked at her. "Um, yeah sure," he put out, turning the TV off. "Judging by the sound of your voice, it sounds important."

Chasity removed her coat and slung it over the back of his chair. "It kinda *is*," she confirmed, walking over to him. "Can you sit down please?"

Sitting on the edge of his bed, Jason was both curious and nervous. "Okay so… What do you have to talk to me about?" he asked as Chasity sat down next to him.

Chasity ran her hand through her hair, then down the front of her jeans. She tried to calm her nervousness, but to no avail. She tugged at her black long-sleeved shirt. "Is it hot in here?"

"No," he replied. "Chaz, what's up?"

"Um…" as Chasity tried to decide how to start this overdue conversation, her leg began to bounce up and down. "So… After our talk in New York, I've been doing a lot of thinking," she began.

"*About?*" he asked. Jason looked down at her bouncing leg. He knew that tell. "Why are you nervous?"

His question caught her off guard. "Huh?"

"You're bouncing your leg," he pointed out.

Chasity glanced down; she wasn't even aware that she was doing it. She immediately stopped.

"What were you thinking about?" he asked.

She hesitated. His question threw her off and she needed to regather her thoughts. "Um… *you*," she replied. He just stared at her intensely, patiently waiting for her to finish. "*Us* and um… How we left things. I know that you wanted to—" *Fuck! I can't form my goddamn sentences!* Chasity took a

deep breath as she locked eyes with hm. She felt a desperate
need to convey her feelings, but part of her was fighting to
keep them in. "Jason...do you still love me?" she blurted out.

Jason frowned at her question. "Is that a joke?"

"No," Chasity shook her head. "I'm asking you
because... I need to know."

Jason was confused by her behavior, and it showed. Why
was she asking him this? What was the point in him saying it
again, if it wasn't going to change anything? Jason ignored
the questions in his head and gave her a long look. "Yes, I
love you," he said. "That hasn't changed, Chasity."

"I'm sorry," Chasity quickly put out, noticing the
intensity in his tone. She got the feeling that she had insulted
him by questioning him. "I didn't mean to—I just..." *You're
torturing yourself, just tell him!* "I...love you too," she
slowly revealed.

Jason had the look of pure disbelief and shock on his
face. He wondered if he'd heard her correctly. "You *what*?"
he stammered.

Chasity felt completely vulnerable. She wished that she
could run and hide, but she couldn't. "Yeah...I love you,"
she confirmed.

He just continued to sit in stunned silence.

"I knew that I felt something for you even before we
slept together. I just didn't know what it was...or, I didn't
want to know," she revealed. Her fingers fidgeted as she
continued. "I finally *knew* after we talked in New York, and I
just couldn't say anything."

Jason felt like he had held his breath until he just spoke,
"Why *not*, Chasity?"

She shook her head as a wave of emotion overcame her.
"I didn't know how to tell you that...that I want what *you*
want—that I want to be with you, but I'm terrified."

Jason fought the urge to put his arms around her. That
would only stop her from talking, and he needed her to talk.
He needed her to say what she was feeling. "Terrified of
what?"

"I don't want to be hurt," she admitted.

"Have I given you reason to believe that I would hurt you?"

Chasity slowly shook her head. "No," she answered truthfully. "But I just feel that if you're in a relationship with me, that...eventually you'll get tired of me, or just realize that I'm not really what you want." She sighed. "I'm afraid that the reality of being with me will outweigh the fantasy of being with me, and when that happens...I know that I won't be able to make you stay."

Jason shook his head as he ran a hand over his hair. He knew that Chasity had reservations about being in a relationship. He had a feeling that she was scared, but he never knew to what extent. He never knew how deep her fear went, and he wished that he could make her see how much her reservations were unwarranted when it came to him.

"I don't know if I'm enough to make you happy," she said. "I *want* to be, but I don't believe that I *am*."

Jason faced her. "Why do you, as great as you *are*, feel that you wouldn't be able to make me happy?" he asked. "I've told you before that you already *do*."

Chasity took a deep breath. A burden that she had been carrying around for years was now at her surface, and she wasn't sure if she wanted to let it out. "Nothing," she said.

"No, you're not going to 'nothing' me, Chasity," Jason chided, voice stern. "You need to be honest with me." He grabbed her hand and held it. "What makes you think that you're incapable of making me happy?"

She hesitated for a moment. "When the people that raised you made you feel like everything you did was wrong, that your presence brought unhappiness, that you were a burden...unwanted...it tends to stick with you," she revealed.

At the sight of the pain and uncertainty in Chasity's eyes, Jason held a sympathetic gaze as he held her hand.

"I just—I still carry that with me. And I avoided relationships in the past because I felt that eventually, whoever I was with would feel the same way that *they* did."

Jason couldn't take it anymore. He reached his arms out and tried to hug her, but she moved away.

"No don't," she said. "If you hug me right now, I'm gonna cry, and I don't want to do that."

Jason did as she asked and refrained; instead he just held onto her hand. "Listen to me," he began. "How you were raised was fucked up…so I can understand why you feel the way you do." He placed her hand on his chest. "I'm telling you right now, you don't have to be afraid when it comes to being with me… I already see the reality of you, and as complicated as it can be, I'm in love with it."

Chasity let a few tears build in her eyes. "You sure about that?" she questioned, eyes searching for certainty in his.

Jason nodded. "Absolutely," he promised. "I already knew what I wanted when I first met you, attitude and all… I'm not going anywhere, baby."

Chasity managed a smile through her tear-streaked face. The release of everything that she had been holding on to for so long made her feel lighter. In that moment, she truly felt that she could be happy with Jason, and she was proud of herself for allowing them both the opportunity to be just that.

Jason wiped a tear from her face with his hand, smiling. "Does this mean I get to call you my girlfriend now?" he hoped after a moment.

She let out a little laugh. "I would say it's safe to say that," she confirmed.

Relieved, Jason finally pulled Chasity into his arms. They held on to each other as if they were both trying to make sure the other was real. Moving his head, Jason planted a kiss upon Chasity's lips. He deepened his kiss, and she returned it with full passion. Jason moved his lips to her neck. He relished the feeling of her in his arms and expressed his happiness with his kisses and his hands as they roamed her body. Pulling away momentarily, he glanced up.

"Did you lock the door?" he asked, panting.

"Do you *care*?" she returned. Her hormones were in overdrive, and at that moment Chasity couldn't care less about a locked door, even though she *did* lock it when she walked in. She just wanted him to take her, like she knew he could.

"Hell no," Jason groaned against her lips as he laid her back on his bed. As the new couple undressed each other, Chasity felt different. She wasn't nervous like she was when they first had sex. She wasn't unsure of her feelings for the man who was pleasing her with his mouth and his hands. She knew exactly what she wanted and how she felt, and that made her feel uninhibited.

Jason relished the sounds of pleasure coming from Chasity as he showed her just how much he loved her. Her reaction to him only made him hotter and more eager. As he prepared to take her body for the second time, he knew that it would not be the last, because she was finally his, and he made sure to claim her as such.

Chapter 8

Alex dutifully jotted down notes while her professor spoke with enthusiasm.

"Last class, we were discussing the behavior of individuals in social situations, and that our purpose is to understand them," the short, bubbly woman stated, pacing the front of the classroom.

Alex lifted her head from her notebook and stared at the professor intently while she continued to speak. Over the past two weeks, Social Psychology had started to become one of Alex's favorite classes of the semester. The study of behaviors was something that she was in to.

"Dealing with different personalities and behaviors in a social setting is something that you should be experts at by now, being here at college." The professors' attempt at a joke was met with a few giggles.

Alex nodded in agreement. She chuckled, thinking of her personal experience with the group that she had grown close with since coming to college. She raised her hand.

"Yes, Alexandra?" Professor Devlin called, gesturing for her to speak.

Alex cringed at the use of her full first name. *Ugh, I hate that name.* "Professor Devlin, if you're dealing with behaviors that you think aren't necessarily…*normal*, do you think that instead of just trying to understand them, that one should try to *change* them?"

Professor Devlin sat on her desk, pondering Alex's question. "What do you mean by *normal*?"

Alex was silent as she tried to think of an educated answer.

"Are you saying that the behavior isn't normal, as in you think that there is something *wrong* with the individual? Or is it just that it's not a behavior that you *yourself* are used to?"

Alex was stumped, and it showed on her face. "Well... I wouldn't say that there is anything *wrong* with them per se, but I think that certain behaviors could use some improvements. At least *I* think so."

"Why do you think that?"

Alex scratched her head. "Well... the way that these *behaviors* are coming off to people—being *perceived*—isn't that great," she answered honestly "And I—"

"Sometimes the people who have these behaviors don't exactly know how they're coming off to the world," Professor Devlin cut in. "Maybe they already think that what they are doing is normal."

"But what if they are *told* how they come off?" Alex wondered. "And still continue to do the same things?"

"Some people don't listen to what they are told, because in *their* mind, they think nothing is wrong with what they're doing," Professor Devlin returned. "Some people need to be *shown*."

Alex sat back and pondered what her professor had just said to her. *How can you show someone how they act when you can't switch bodies with them? You can't walk in someone else's shoes.*

Professor Devlin stood from her desk and headed over to the black board. "So, it's project time," she announced, earning groans from her classroom. "Ah, excitement, I love it," she joked. "I want all of you to create and follow through on a social experiment involving your peers."

Alex raised her hand. "You said create, so you mean that we have to come up with our own type of experiment?"

"Yes, that's correct." Professor Devlin wrote something on the board. "You must come up with the type of experiment, list the details, subjects that you used, and I want details on how the behaviors of the subjects were affected and what *you* learned from the experiment... Its due two weeks from now." She glanced at the clock on the wall. "And that is it for the day. See you next class."

Alex's mind was focused on the assignment as her classmates packed up their belongings. *What the hell am I going to do for an experiment? And who the hell is gonna let me do it on them?* Shaking her head and letting out a sigh, Alex grabbed her books from her desk and made a beeline for the door.

Malajia sauntered through the campus quad in route to class. Checking herself out in a hand mirror, she fluffed her burgundy curls with her hand. "Hey sexy," she cooed to herself, before putting the mirror in her purse. She slowed her walk and folded her arms, when she noticed her roommate heading in her direction.

"Well, well, well, look who it is," Malajia jeered as she and Chasity stopped in front of one another. "Someone gets a boyfriend and acts like she don't know no-damn-body."

Chasity's mouth fell open. "That's not even *true*," she threw back.

"Yeah, sure, okay Mrs. Adams," Malajia teased. "I barely seen your ass in damn near a week."

Chasity rolled her eyes. She wasn't surprised that Malajia would have something smart to say. Ever since she and Jason made their relationship official a week ago, she had been spending a lot of time with him, even opting to spend nights in his single room, as opposed to her shared room with Malajia.

"Can't sleep in your own bed, huh?" Malajia harped. "You think you grown now?"

Chasity narrowed her eyes at Malajia. "Are you finished?"

Malajia's taut face gave way to a smile. "Yeah, I'm just messing with you," she assured, giving Chasity's arm a tap. "It's good to see you guys spending so much time together," she approved.

Chasity folded her arms, sighing happily. "Yeah, it's been good."

"Shit, you look happy finally...*and* relaxed," Malajia added. "Been getting that back cracked, huh?"

Chasity's smile gave way to a scowl. "Really?" she hissed as Malajia started gyrating near her.

"Get it Jase, get it Jase. Crack that back, crack that back," Malajia sang as she continued her hip gyrations in front of an unenthused Chasity. "I'm surprised you can *walk*."

"Get away from me," Chasity snarled, giving Malajia's arm a pinch.

"Ow!" Malajia screeched, laughter in her voice. "Childish."

Chasity waved her hand dismissively at Malajia. "You're stupid, I gotta go to class."

"Very well," Malajia returned as Chasity started to walk off. "Hold on bitch, one more thing," she called.

Chasity turned around. "What?"

"You have your ass back home today, you hear?" she ordered. "I kinda sorta miss your ignorant self."

Chasity smirked. "Oh *really*?"

"Yeah, don't get all big headed," Malajia jeered. "But you're kinda like my favorite person to talk to."

Chasity was touched, but didn't let it show. "You can talk to the *other* girls, you know," she pointed out.

"Who? *Alex*?" Malajia scoffed. "You want me to talk to *Alex*?"

Chasity laughed.

Malajia too laughed. "Naw, but come on, I need you to help me find something to wear tonight. I'm going out with Tyrone and I don't need no fashion advice from the queens of ugly shirts, pencil skirts, and baggy ass sweaters."

Chasity's smile faded. She completely ignored Malajia's dig at the other girls' fashion choices, and focused on the fact that Malajia just confirmed that she was going to see Tyrone again. *Ugh, she's really going out with this fool.* "You made that call, huh?"

Malajia nodded. When Chasity left the room to talk to Jason after their sharing session, Malajia made the final decision to let Tyrone take her out. She called him that same night. "I'm a little skeptical, but excited at the same time," she said.

Chasity took one look at the hopeful look on Malajia's face and kept her true feelings about the situation to herself. "Okay Malajia, I'll be back tonight," she promised.

Malajia clapped her hands and pointed at Chasity. "*My* girl," she beamed.

Chasity just shook her head and walked off; Malajia headed off in the opposite direction.

Emily glanced down at the paper in her hand, feeling tears well up in her eyes as she focused on the big red D in the corner. "Another quiz down the drain," she sniffled to herself as she sat the paper down on the library table. When Emily woke up that morning, she decided to spend some much-needed time at the library. But after receiving yet another bad test score from one of her classes, the disappointment ruined her motivation to study. Instead, she sat at the small wooden table, sulking.

Emily glanced at the paper once more before putting her face in her hands, fighting to keep the tears from overtaking her.

"Emily?"

Emily's head jerked up at the sound of Sidra's voice.

"Hey Sid," she stammered, quickly placing her badly graded paper inside of a textbook.

Sidra eyed Emily with skepticism. "You okay?" she asked, placing her hand on the table. "Your eyes are all red."

Emily frantically wiped her eyes. "Yeah, I'm fine," she lied. "Allergies."

That explanation seemed to satisfy Sidra, who just nodded. "Haven't been seeing you lately sweetie," she said. "And Alex said she's been stopping by, but you're never there."

Emily glanced down at the table. She knew of every time that Sidra spoke of. She was usually in her bed with the covers over her face, waiting for the knocking to subside. "I'm sorry, I know I've been MIA... I've been studying a lot, that's all."

"I can understand that," Sidra replied, running a hand over her ponytail. "I'm in here to get some work done *myself*." Sidra took a seat. "Well, since you haven't been around, I guess I'll fill you in on some news."

"What's that?" Emily asked, intrigued.

"Jason and Chasity *finally* got it together and they're a couple now."

Emily's mouth opened in a wide smile as she sat back in her seat. "That's awesome," she mused. Knowing their history, she was elated. "I'm happy for them."

"Yeah, we *all* are," Sidra replied. "I swear, when we were bowling last Sunday and they announced it, Mark damn near slid down the aisle with the ball in his hand."

Emily's smile faded as she recalled what she was doing that day. Sitting across a restaurant table from her mother, listening to the woman grill her about homework. *I keep missing out on fun.*

"I have to go find a book for my English Lit class," Sidra announced, standing up. "If you need a break from studying later, come over to our room, we'll probably watch a movie."

Emily tugged at the sleeve of her faded pink sweatshirt. "Um...I'll try to stop over," she put out, voice low. Emily's mood was sour and all she wanted to do was crawl in bed and sleep the rest of the day away.

Sidra shrugged. "Well, if you don't make it, will you at least call Alex?" she requested. "The girl has been talking about how much she misses you, and I think she's starting to get on people's nerves," she joked.

Emily forced a smile. "Yes, I'll call her," she promised.

"Cool... We *all* miss you by the way," Sidra amended. Emily just nodded. Adjusting the pocketbook on her shoulder, Sidra walked off.

"Malajia just keep the fuckin' dress on," Chasity barked, her hand over her face while clutching a dress in her other hand.

Malajia examined herself in the full-length mirror. "I mean, I don't want to come off as trying too hard, you know?" she said, tugging at the short, red sleeveless dress that she had on.

Chasity pulled her hand down her face, trying to calm herself down. "You *say* that, but every time you put on another outfit, you change *back* into that same damn dress." After trying to help Malajia complete her date look for over an hour, Chasity was regretting her decision to help.

Malajia spun around, her hands on her hips. "Look here cranky, you're supposed to be helping me."

Chasity shot daggers at Malajia with her eyes. "What the fuck do you think I've been *doing* all this damn time?" she exclaimed.

"You've been *yelling* at me," Malajia threw back, stomping her foot on the floor.

"'Cause you won't make a goddamn decision!"

Malajia let out a loud sigh. "I'm trying to convey a message here," she explained. "I want my outfit to say that 'I'm sexy', but 'I'm mad at you, so don't touch me'."

"That dress you got on *now*, that's damn near showing

your ass, isn't saying nothing but 'let me bend over for you,'" Chasity sneered.

Malajia's mouth fell open in astonishment. Then she smiled slyly. "Is that what you do for Jason?" she teased.

Chasity made a face and flipped Malajia off as a knock sounded at the door.

"Come in," Malajia called at the same time that Chasity hissed, "What?"

Sidra walked in, clutching a DVD case in her hand. "Here Chaz," she said, handing it to Chasity. "Thanks for letting me hold it."

"Sure," Chasity grunted, still agitated with Malajia's antics.

Sidra paused on her way out, catching eye of Malajia's attire. "And just *where* are *you* going with all of your snacks and goodies showing?" she demanded.

Chasity looked confused. "Did you just say snacks?"

"And *goodies*," Malajia chuckled.

Sidra pointed her finger at Malajia. "Don't change the subject, girl," she chided. "Where are you going with that on?"

"Well, *Mom*, I'm going on a date," Malajia jeered.

Sidra was unimpressed. "You *do* know that it's still winter, right?" she ground out. "And that you can almost see your..." Sidra cringed as she gestured to Malajia's privates, which luckily for her were concealed in black underwear. "Naughty bits, in that dress."

"You mean my vag?" Malajia mocked.

"I know the proper word!" Sidra snapped. "I just hate saying it. Don't tease me."

Chasity put her hands up. "You're freakin' weird, Sidra," she laughed.

Malajia flagged Sidra with her hand. "Whatever," she huffed, pulling the dress over her head. "Chaz, can you toss me that black dress in your hand? And Sidra, take yourself, that bun, and those kindergarten ass words out my damn room, so I can finish getting ready," she dismissed.

Sidra ignored Malajia's request and sat on the bed next to Chasity. "So…who are you going on a date with?"

Malajia caught the dress that Chasity tossed to her in mid-air and proceeded to step into it. "Just a guy," she vaguely responded.

"Do we know him?" Sidra pressed.

"Uh, not really." Malajia pulled the dress up her slender frame. "You might've heard of him before though."

Confused, Sidra glanced at Chasity, who shook her head. "Don't ask me shit, I'm minding my business," Chasity immediately put out.

Sidra glanced back at Malajia, "You're keeping secrets from me, Mel?" she pouted.

Malajia sighed as she fixed the spaghetti straps on her dress. "It's not that—" She paused, grabbing a pair of silver dangle earrings from her dresser. "I'm going out with Tyrone, Sid."

Sidra jerked her head back at the news. "You mean the guy that you went out with last semester?" Malajia nodded. "The one that had you looking like you were about to cry on *more* than one occasion?"

"Mmm," Chasity muttered.

Malajia shot Chasity a warning look. Although Malajia never went into detail with anybody besides Chasity about the many times that Tyrone had upset her, the girls were aware of when Malajia was upset. "Look, don't worry about all that. We're good now," she bit out. "So please refrain from bringing up old stuff."

Sidra shrugged. "I mean, if that's what you want," she complied. "I hope for your sake he really *has* changed."

"He ain't change shit," Chasity mumbled under her breath. The side comment, although low, wasn't missed by Malajia, who just rolled her eyes at her.

"Girl, you already know that Alex is gonna grill you *and* him when you tell her," Sidra grinned.

Malajia spun around as she placed an earring into her ear. "Which is why I don't want her to know right now," she said. "I don't have time for Alex and her ten thousand, million questions." She placed the other earring into her ear. "At *least* not until I know exactly where this is going."

Sidra and Chasity both agreed. Malajia stepped into her black high-heeled shoes, then grabbed her phone when it sounded. Eyeing the message, she took a deep breath, placing her hand over her flat midsection. "He's here," she breathed. "He's on his way up."

"You nervous?" Sidra asked, smiling. She may have had her reservations about Tyrone, but Malajia seemed happy, and that made Sidra happy for her.

"A little," Malajia admitted.

Chasity didn't say anything. She just stood from her bed and walked over to Malajia, then fixed a tag on the back of Malajia's dress. "Thanks," Malajia said.

Sidra jumped up to get the door when she heard a knock. Malajia turned to face Chasity. "You gonna say anything smart?" she asked.

Chasity shook her head, remaining silent. Malajia smiled, then grabbed her purse from the dresser.

Sidra opened the door. Tyrone stood there, dressed in a pair of black dress pants, red button down shirt and black tie; holding a dozen of red roses in his hand. Sidra moved aside as Malajia walked to the door. "You look beautiful," he crooned.

Malajia blushed as Sidra handed her her coat. She waved goodbye to the girls, and Tyrone gave them a nod before walking out and shutting the door.

Sidra and Chasity both stared at the closed door. "Um... despite that nonverbal head nod that he gave to us, he seemed okay," Sidra commented.

"I don't like him," Chasity declared, voice not hiding her contempt.

Sidra looked at her and laughed. "I thought you weren't going to say anything smart," she recalled.

"To *her*," Chasity clarified.

Sidra shrugged.

Adjusting herself in her seat, Malajia, smoothed her hands down the front of her dress. She glanced around the restaurant. *This is pretty fancy. So far so good,* she thought of the ambiance. The dim lights, overhead chandeliers paired with the soft candle light flickering in the crystal candle holders on their intimate table, were enticing. The soft music playing in the background added to the sultry mood.

"This is a nice place," she mused as she glanced at her menu.

"Yeah, I've been past here once or twice before," Tyrone replied.

Malajia sat her menu down and looked at him. "I can honestly say that I haven't been to this part of Virginia," she said. When Tyrone let it be known during their ride that he was taking her to a restaurant in his part of town, she was intrigued. "Most of us PVU students stay away from these parts... School rivalry and all," she joked.

Tyrone smirked, then put his hand on top of her menu when she reached for it again. "You don't have to look at that," he stated.

Malajia frowned. "Why not?"

"Because I already pre-ordered your food," he explained.

Malajia was initially annoyed. "You ordered for me?" she questioned. He nodded. "How do you even know that I'd want what you ordered?"

"Because its steak and shrimp, and I figured that you would want that since you mentioned that you liked those two things during our first phone conversation."

Malajia ignored the sternness of Tyrone's voice when he explained himself. She even let go of the fact that he hadn't even asked her what she wanted to eat. That he took it upon himself to basically *tell* her what she wanted. She could only focus on one thing at that moment.

"You remembered our first conversation?" Her smile could have illuminated the entire block.

"Of course," Tyrone replied, confident.

You get another point, she mused. "Well...that's been noted," she smiled.

"I hope *so*," Tyrone chuckled.

Malajia didn't know where the time went. She looked up and they had been eating and conversing for almost two hours. He was attentive, he was engrossed in their conversation, and he was funny. This was the Tyrone that she longed to see again, the Tyrone that she enjoyed.

"I'm stuffed," Malajia breathed, sitting back in her seat.

Tyrone wiped his mouth with his cloth napkin as he eyed the half-eaten steak on her plate. "Too much for you, huh?"

She pinched her fingers together. "Just a little."

Tyrone nodded. "I guess, next time I'll let you order your *own* dinner," he joked.

Malajia leaned forward in her seat and touched his arm. "No, it was a nice gesture and I appreciate it," she cooed.

Tyrone, grabbed her hand and held it as he stared at her. "I really like you," he declared.

Malajia blushed. "I like you too," she admitted. "Just not when you act funny towards me."

"I get that, and I'm sorry," Tyrone apologized. "I'm not perfect, but I'm trying to be better."

"I can see that you're trying," Malajia assured him.

Tyrone rubbed her hand with his fingers. "Come on, let me take you home," he offered.

Malajia nodded as he signaled for the check. *He's not even trying to take me back to his place. He gets another point.*

The ride back to Paradise Valley Campus was even more relaxing than the ride leaving. The conversation was easy, the music was good, and Tyrone even held her hand during the ride. Malajia was on cloud nine as he walked her to the entrance of her dorm.

Digging into her purse for her keys, she faced him. "This was nice," she smiled. "Thank you."

"You're welcome," Tyrone returned.

Malajia glanced down at her shoes as Tyrone touched her face. *Please kiss me, please kiss me,* she thought, hoping that her words would be transferred to his brain somehow. As if on cue, Tyrone stepped forward, eliminating any personal space that she may have had, and touched his lips to hers.

Although she wanted it, Malajia was shocked at how deep he was kissing her. The initial shock then wore off, allowing her to enjoy it. Feeling a wave of heat come over her, she moved her head back.

"Okay Tyrone, I gotta go," she breathed. The last thing that she wanted to do was to get him worked up; this was only the first date after all. Tyrone wiped Malajia's lip gloss from his mouth as he watched Malajia trot inside the dorm and close the door. Smiling to himself, he walked off.

Chapter 9

Alex tapped her notebook with her pen while she laid across her bed. "What is my experiment going to be on?" she asked herself, looking up at the ceiling. Her Social Psychology assignment had made a prominent mark in Alex's brain. Drawing a blank, Alex let out a whine and flopped her head down on her pillow. "I'm gonna fail this project," she said aloud, voice muffled by her pillow. Hearing a knock, she hopped up from the bed and darted for the door.

Alex immediately reached out and hugged the visitor. "Emily," she beamed, pulling her into the room. "What brings you by?"

Emily shoved her hands into the pockets of her coat. "Um, I needed a break from studying, so I figured I'd come visit," she answered. After staring at her textbooks for most of the evening, Emily realized that none of the words were sticking in her mind. Missing her friends, she decided to do a pop up visit.

"Well, I'm glad you came," Alex replied. "We miss you."

"I miss you guys too," Emily smiled, then glanced at the books sprawled across Alex's bed. Her smile faded. "I'm sorry Alex, are you studying? I didn't mean to bother you."

Alex grabbed Emily's arm as she went to leave. "No no, you're not bothering me," Alex giggled. Emily turned around. "Fact *is*, I wasn't doing much of anything. My mind is on strike right now."

Emily nodded. *I know the feeling.*

"Are you hungry?" Alex asked, glancing at the clock on her nightstand. "It's almost seven, they're still serving dinner in the cafeteria. I can call the others and have them meet us there."

"Sounds good," Emily agreed. She raised her eyebrows as Alex grabbed her coat. "You're not gonna change?" she asked.

Alex looked down at her yellow and white printed pajama pants, yellow tank top, and brown slippers. "Nope, this is college. I've seen people leave their rooms with much worse," she laughed, gesturing for Emily to walk out.

Mark did a dance in his seat as he took a bite of his taco, drawing looks of agitation from his friends.

"You hype as shit its taco night," Malajia mocked, pouring sauce on her own.

"You minding my business real hard," Mark shot back, before taking another bite.

Alex shook her head, reaching for her cup of juice. It took less than fifteen minutes since she made the calls to the group for them to congregate at their usual booth in the crowded cafeteria. "Can't make it through one meal without sniping, huh?"

"Alex, shut up. Nobody says 'snipe'," Malajia quickly dismissed, waving her hand in Alex's direction.

Chasity snickered at the frustrated look on Alex's face. Sidra, choosing to ignore Malajia and her silly remarks all together, focused her gaze upon Emily. "Taking a break from the books I see," she said.

Emily nodded as she swallowed her water. "Yeah, the room was starting to close in on me," she joked. "Besides, I missed hanging out with you guys."

"We miss you too Em," Alex smiled, reaching across the table for the salt shaker, "But we understand if your need to study has to keep you away." Alex looked around the table when she heard groans coming from Sidra, Malajia, and Chasity. "What?"

"Girl please, we've been hearing you whine all week about not seeing Emily," Malajia recalled. "Don't act all nonchalant now that she's sitting here... Cryin' ass."

Emily laughed.

"Malajia, stuff a damn taco in your mouth so it can stay shut," Alex grunted.

"That ain't gonna stop shit," Malajia returned, unfazed. "You know I have no problem talking with my mouth full."

Emily shook her head. The banter was something that she missed. "Oh, I almost forgot. Chaz and Jase, I heard the good news," she grinned. "I'm happy for you guys."

"Thanks Em," Jason smiled, then gave Chasity a longing glance.

Mark, catching the interaction, sucked his teeth loudly. "God, don't get them started," he groaned. Jason flashed Mark a glare. "I swear they been sucking face all damn day."

"If you wasn't in our damn faces, you wouldn't notice," Chasity sneered.

"Right," Jason cosigned. "Mark, worry about what you do with that imaginary woman *you* have."

Mark scoffed. "*First* of all, I don't *have* no imaginary woman," he spat, grabbing another taco off his plate. "I got a *real* one...*plenty* of them, to be exact."

"Bullshit," Chasity hissed.

"Boy, stop lying," Malajia barked, pointing at Mark. "Other than that snaggle tooth girl who sucked you off last year, you ain't been messin' with anybody." Mark stared at Malajia, fuming. "I already told you, nobody wants your ashy ass."

"Hey, stop calling me ashy," Mark hurled, plucking a balled-up tissue in her direction. "And your lonely ass don't need to talk about *nobody*. I don't see anybody taking *your* skinny, spaghetti noodle looking ass out."

Malajia tossed the soiled napkin back at him, hitting him in the chest with it. *That's what you think, you stupid bastard.*

Once the laughter at Mark's remark subsided, it was quiet for a few moments. Emily folded her arms on the table top and glanced around at the group. "So um…is anybody planning anything fun for this weekend?"

"Why? Isn't your mom coming down?" Chasity blurted out. Malajia almost choked on her food, laughing.

Alex looked at Chasity like she wanted to slap her, while Emily looked down at the table in embarrassment. "Really Chasity?" Alex condemned. "How long were you holding *that* in?"

Chasity sat back in her seat and folded her arms. "I told you when her mom came down here *last* week that I wanted to say something to Emily about it."

"And *I* told *you* that Emily doesn't need to hear any more comments from us about her mother," Alex argued. "She feels bad enough."

Chasity frowned. "You *do* know she's sitting right there and can talk on her own, right?"

"Alex, it's fine," Emily mumbled. Chasity's approach might not have been nice, but she had a point. Emily knew there was no point in making plans because her mother already ruined them, either in person or by being stuck in her head.

"No, it's *not*," Alex fussed. "Chasity, I swear your mouth is freakin' ridiculous."

"And your point is *what*?" Chasity challenged.

Malajia picked up her cup of soda and took a sip, eagerly looking back and forth between the arguing Alex and Chasity. If there was something that peeked her interest, it was a good argument that didn't involve *her*.

Sidra, uncomfortable with the bickering, put her hands up. "Hey Malajia, why don't you tell us about your date from last night?" she blurted out.

Malajia's eyes widened as the unaware group members, including Alex, stopped and looked at her. "I thought I told you not to say anything, Sidra," Malajia fumed, slamming her cup down.

"I'm sorry, I just wanted Chaz and Alex to stop arguing," Sidra explained.

"So the *only* way for that to happen was to tell my damn business?" Malajia snarled.

"Hold up, who did you go out with?" Mark asked, curious. After accusing Malajia of not having any dates, he wondered why she didn't mention anything.

Malajia stared at Sidra, giving her eyes, telling her to keep her mouth shut.

"Tyrone," Sidra revealed, ignoring Malajia's silent warning.

"Tyrone?" Alex reacted with disbelief.

"Who the hell is *Tyrone*?" Mark barked.

David, who was sitting next to him, frantically wiped his hand. "You spit on me," he groused.

"Shut up," Mark returned, then focused his gaze back on Malajia, "Who's Tyrone? *I* don't know a damn Tyrone."

"Some jerk that she doesn't need to talk to," Josh mumbled, eyes fixed on the taco that he was creating on his plate. Sidra quickly shook her head at him, telling him to be quiet.

Josh glanced up, nervous. "Oops."

Malajia folded her arms as she stared at Sidra. "Oh, so you were bad-mouthing my man to Josh?" she hissed.

"Oh so he's your *man* now?" Chasity charged, before Sidra had a chance to respond. Malajia rolled her eyes to the ceiling, quietly seething. Chasity looked Malajia in her face. "So after *one* bullshit date, he's your man?" she pressed.

Malajia took a deep breath. "Look, Chasity don't—"

"I don't even understand *why* you went out with him again, anyway," Alex cut in. "He seemed to always upset you last semester. Why would you put yourself through that again?'"

Malajia drummed her finger nails on the table, furious at Sidra. "You see what you and your lopsided-ass bun started?" she snapped.

Sidra's hand instantly jerked up to feel her hair. "It's *not* lopsided," she muttered.

"And Alex, don't start your shit *either*," Malajia scowled, pointing at Alex.

"I'm just concerned about you, Malajia," Alex explained.

"Concern yourself with finding your *own* dick and stop worrying about *me*," Malajia spat.

Alex was taken back. "What was *that* rude ass comment for?" she bristled.

"Oh, so you slept with him *too*?" Chasity scoffed. It was bad enough that Malajia went out with the guy in the first place, but if Malajia went as far as giving him her virginity, Chasity didn't know if she could ever respect her again.

"No, I *didn't*," Malajia assured, voice filed with attitude. "But I'm sure *you're* getting enough for *both* of us, since you barely sleep in your own damn *bed* anymore." Malajia then turned to Alex as she pointed to Chasity. "Alex, you wanna know why you can't find Chasity at night? She's been sleeping in Jason's room...now judge *that*."

Chasity's eyes widened as Alex shot Chasity a look of judgment. Jason pinched the bridge of his nose and sighed.

"Way to go man," Mark celebrated, giving Jason a pat on his back.

"Don't touch me," Jason replied, voice eerily calm.

"You're so fuckin' petty Malajia," Chasity fumed.

"Yup," Malajia agreed, examining her nails.

Josh quickly gathered the mess on the table and placed it on to his tray. He and the guys were used to being quiet spectators during one of the girls' arguments, but the glances from nearby students as the girls' voices became louder made him realize it was time to leave. "Okay, I'd say it's time to go," he suggested.

"I second that," Jason agreed, standing up.

"I still don't know who the hell *Tyrone* is," Mark grunted.

Upon approaching the front of Paradise Terrace, the guys parted ways from the girls, whose bickering was still going on.

"Why are you still talking to me, Alex?" Chasity snarled, stepping off the elevator along with the other girls.

"Look, I'm just saying that you shouldn't get so engrossed in your new relationship. You don't want to start neglecting your common sense," Alex argued.

Chasity paused from unlocking her door, spun around, and faced Alex. "What the fuck do you mean 'common sense'?" she hissed. "You trying to call me stupid?"

"*She's* the one who sounds stupid," Malajia cut in, interrupting Alex's explanation.

"*You* shut up. I'm arguing with this bitch because of *you* in the first damn place," Chasity hurled at Malajia.

Malajia rolled her eyes. "Just open the damn door," she ordered.

"Over this shit," Chasity huffed, pushing the door open and walking into the room.

"Chasity, I'm not calling you stupid," Alex clarified, walking in behind her.

"Why am I *not* surprised that you followed us in here?" Chasity mocked.

"Look, all I'm saying is that sometimes when people get into new relationships, it consumes them. It ends up getting all of their attention," Alex said.

"I don't get it," Chasity fussed, clearly trying to refrain from snapping. "You were up my ass about me *not* being with Jason when everyone thought that I *should* be, and now that I *am* with him, you have a problem with it?"

"No, that's *not* it," Alex maintained, stomping her foot on the floor. "I'm happy for you and Jason. Trust me, I *am*. But face it, you haven't experienced *any* of this before, so you may be diving in too fast."

Chasity was confused by Alex's words. "Are you referring to me having *sex*?" she slowly put out. Alex rolled her eyes. "Are you concerning yourself..." Chasity took a minute to compose herself, "with *my* sex life?"

Alex let out a deep sigh. *She's missing my point.*

When Chasity didn't get a response from Alex, it just confirmed her accusation. "I'm not fucking *you* Alex," she bit out. Alex's mouth fell open. "That being *said*, don't worry about what I do and how often I *do* it."

"Chasity, that was uncalled for," Sidra scoffed.

Malajia shot Sidra a side-glance. "Oh shut up," she spat, still annoyed that Sidra spilled her secret. "What? Did the fact that Chasity used 'fucking' instead of 'love making' make your little snotty ass cringe?"

Sidra put her hand up. "Don't start with me, Malajia," she warned.

"That little hand in my direction don't scare me," Malajia threw back, pointing. "You started this whole damn thing."

"How?" Sidra challenged, hands on her hips. "I didn't tell Chasity's business to Alex, *you* did."

"Yeah?" Malajia argued. "And if you hadn't told *my* business, none of this would've happened. So *your* sneaky ass is to blame."

Emily, who was standing quietly with her back to the door, was nervous. The argument was getting even more heated and she was thinking about trying to stop it. *Would they even listen to me?* She wondered.

"I'm *far* from sneaky, sweetheart," Sidra protested, tone confident. "I may have had one lapse in judgment, but *you're* the one sneaking around on dates, dressed like a floosy, with a guy who, I might add, seems *very* questionable," she spat. "That idiot promised you an expensive dinner and you went running, with all your assets just hanging out... How did you thank him for that, huh?"

Malajia clenched her jaw as she processed what Sidra just threw at her. "You saying I hoed myself for a meal?" she questioned, tone filled with fury.

Sidra shrugged, a smug look on her face. "I didn't say that, *you* did."

Emily put her hands over her mouth in shock. She never heard Sidra be so nasty before, especially not to her friends.

Malajia slowly took a step forward. "You stuck up ass bitch," she hissed. Sidra fixed an angry gaze. "You spittin' that bullshit *knowing* the type of person that I am," she stopped within inches of Sidra's face. "Despite what you or anybody *else* thinks of me, I know what I do and *don't* do. But everybody knows for a *fact* that you're a *whole* fuckin' snob. All you do is look down your damn nose at people, and you wonder why *everybody* hates your ass."

"You two cut it out," Alex ordered, seeing the pained looks on both Malajia and Sidra's faces as they stared each other down. "All of those insults were uncalled for."

"Try minding your fuckin' business Alex," Chasity barked, still seething from Alex's prodding into her personal business.

"Oh what? So I'm not allowed to tell you guys what I think?" Alex questioned loudly.

"Not when nobody *asks* you," Chasity argued. "After all this time, you *still* don't get that."

Alex rolled her eyes. "I get that just *fine*," she groused. "However, no matter *what* you say, I'm still going to let you know how I feel. So just get over it and take the damn advice."

Chasity wanted to shake Alex. "God, you are so fuckin' *annoying!*" she erupted. "*Nobody* wants your worthless advice Alex. It don't even work for *your* stupid ass half the time."

Alex regarded Chasity with a stern look as she shook her head. Chasity's mouth was too much. "You know what I always wondered?" she began, Chasity shot her a challenging look. "I wonder if how you were treated growing up, wasn't just about everyone picking on poor little Chasity. I wonder if it was all *you*," she mocked.

Chasity looked at Alex in disbelief.

"I'm starting to think that maybe, just *maybe,* that screwed up ass attitude of yours is what made people treat you like shit," Alex spewed with a venom that had not been seen before.

Chasity took a moment to compose herself. She already struggled with the memories of her troubled upbringing, but to hear one of her friends throw what she went through up in her face made her see red. "You know what *I* wonder?" she began.

Alex folded her arms, standing there in anticipation. "What's *that*?"

"I wonder how pathetic you feel knowing that your loser ass boyfriend fucked your hoe ass best friend," Chasity hissed.

Alex looked like the wind had been knocked out of her. "Chas—How could you say that to me?!" Alex screamed. "You're a horrible person!"

"You think I give a shit about your feelings after what *you* just said to *me*?!" Chasity yelled back.

Emily had had enough. "Oh my God, stop it!" she wailed, stepping forward. "I can't believe you said all that stuff to each other." Her voice quivered. Emily looked around at her friends, who stood in seething silence. All of them looked as if they could bust out crying at any moment. "This has gone too far."

"Not far *enough*. Get the fuck out my room, Alex," Chasity barked, gesturing towards the door.

"Gladly," Alex returned, wiping a tear from her eye. Upon leaving, she grabbed Sidra, who was too angry to say another word, by the arm and pulled her along.

When the door slammed, Emily watched as Chasity and Malajia shot each other a glare, before Chasity stormed into their private bathroom, slamming the door behind her. Malajia, feeling mentally drained, flopped down on her bed and put her head in her hands.

Emily, not knowing what else to do or say, just solemnly walked out of the room, closing the door behind her.

Chapter 10

Emily paced the lobby of Paradise Terrace the next afternoon in slow fashion. Letting out a long sigh, she glanced at the elevator doors for the third time.

"You keep looking at that door Em, expecting someone?" Malajia hissed as she sat, legs crossed on one of the lounge chairs.

Emily fidgeted with her fingers as she halted her pace. *Please come on girls*, she thought. Emily awoke earlier that morning feeling both groggy and troubled. The latter due to the fact that she had witnessed one of the nastiest arguments between the girls. Feeling upset, Emily decided to try to rectify the situation.

"Emily, you called us to meet you in this raggedy lobby for *what* exactly?" Chasity asked, folding her arms and fixing a stern gaze upon Emily. "I don't have time for whatever this is, I have shit to do."

Emily glanced at the door once more.

"Emily, I swear to God, if you don't tell me what's going on, I'm marching my sexy ass back upstairs," Malajia barked, pointing to the elevator. Upon hearing Chasity suck her teeth, Malajia turned to her. "You got something to say, Parker?" she goaded.

Chasity fixed Malajia with an angry stare, but said nothing.

"Oh really? Nothing?" Malajia taunted. "'Cause your ass sure had *plenty* to say *last night*."

"Don't fuckin' start with me, Malajia," Chasity snarled.

Emily lurched forward and stood in between the two chairs where the girls sat across from each other. "Please, stop," she urged, bringing their bickering to a halt. Emily nervously pushed some of her hair behind her ears. "I just—I called you here because I hated how things ended last night," she stammered.

"We weren't arguing with *you*," Chasity pointed out, tone full of frustration.

"It was *still* horrible to watch," Emily replied, voice trembling. She would give anything to have Alex and Sidra in the lobby with them. *I wasn't expecting the two mean ones to show first.* "I just... I think that you all should try talking—" Emily took a step back as Malajia and Chasity started yelling obscenities at her.

"I ain't talking to Sidra's rude ass, okay," Malajia snapped. "You got me chopped."

Emily sighed. "I'll be right back," she mumbled before taking off for the elevators. She paused and faced the girls. "Please don't leave."

Chasity rolled her eyes as Emily scurried off. "This is some bullshit," she spat.

"Who you tellin'?" Malajia agreed, leaning her elbow on the arm of the chair as she played with strands of her hair. "I got this damn Spanish homework to do."

Chasity looked at her nails, not bothering to say a word.

Malajia looked at her and leaned forward. "Chaz," she called.

"What?" Chasity ground out, still focusing on the shiny black polish.

Malajia sighed. "Look, before anybody else gets here I just want to tell you that...I shouldn't have put your business out on front street like that," she said. "You just pissed me off."

Chasity just looked at her.

"But, I want you to know that I *am* seeing Tyrone again," Malajia informed. "And while he's not my boyfriend *yet*, I'm gonna keep dating him. I know you have your opinions—"

"I shouldn't have made those comments in front of everybody," Chasity interrupted. "That was a very 'Alex' thing to do."

Malajia chuckled.

"My hypocritical ass should've kept my opinions to myself," Chasity added.

"Chasity, I value your opinions. I don't want you to keep them to yourself," Malajia admitted. "But I just don't want you to treat me like I'm stupid when it comes to him... I know what I'm doing."

Chasity put her hands up. *It's your life*, she thought. "Okay," she replied.

"So...are we good?" Malajia asked.

"We're good," Chasity confirmed.

Malajia smiled, then rose from her seat and walked over to Chasity. "Aww, come here boo boo, give me a hug," she teased. Her outstretched arms were met by Chasity's hand.

"Why do you always have to touch me?"

Malajia giggled, sitting down next to Chasity. She playfully nudged her. "Okay *we're* good, that's all that matters. Fuck *them*," Malajia jeered, waving her hand in the direction of the elevator. "We need to be a united front against them." Malajia held her fist out for Chasity to bump, and after a few seconds, Chasity did. "Roommates against roommates."

Within minutes, the elevator door opened and Emily emerged with a reluctant Alex and Sidra in tow. Malajia and Chasity held their stern gazes as the other girls sat down on the couch across from them. Emily took a seat on the coffee table in between the two couches. She looked around at her friends, who were clearly on the defense.

Emily took a deep breath. *I hope this comes out right.* "Last night…you ladies really hurt each other's feelings," Emily began, voice low. "And *my* feelings were hurt just *watching.*"

"So?" Chasity muttered, earning a stern look from Alex.

Emily looked down at her hands. This was harder than she thought. Emily was never one for playing a peace maker, she never had much to say for fear of being ignored or jumped on. "At the end of the day, you're friends and I think that you should um…apologize to each other." Emily's eyes shifted nervously as each girl looked at her like she had completely lost her mind. After a few moments, Emily was shocked that no one stood up and walked off. They instead sat there staring at each other.

Malajia and Sidra stared each other down. Malajia leaned in close to Chasity. "No backing down," she whispered.

Sidra's angry gaze gave way to a sad pout. She missed her friend. Even if it was only for a day. "Mel, I'm sorry," Sidra pouted. Malajia looked at Sidra wide-eyed. "I don't think that you're a hoe. I was wrong for even *suggesting* that." Sidra smoothed her bangs out of her face. "You know I love you… I'm sorry."

Malajia tried to stay angry, but seeing her childhood friend break and apologize sincerely, broke her too. A smile formed across her face. "Awww, I love you *too*, my ponytail," she gushed, standing up, with her arms outstretched.

Alex fought the urge to chuckle at the two as Chasity shook her head. "Punk ass," Chasity jeered to Malajia.

"Shut up," Malajia threw back, as she and Sidra embraced. Malajia parted. "I didn't mean what I said *either.*" She put her hands on Sidra's shoulders. "I mean, you *are* stuck up," she clarified.

Sidra poked her on the arm. "See?"

Malajia laughed. "But I don't hate you. Never *could*."

Emily beamed with delight at the scene. *Two down, two more to go.* As Malajia and Sidra returned to their seats, all eyes fixed on Chasity and Alex. "Ladies?" Emily coaxed, hopeful. "Can you *please* make up?"

Alex tried to fight it, but realizing that it was taking more energy to be mad and the fact that she hated the tension, she let out a sigh. "I'm sorry, Chaz," she put out, leaning forward. "I can only imagine how hard growing up was for you."

Chasity looked away briefly.

"And I um..." Alex paused momentarily. "I didn't mean what I said. I know none of that stuff was your fault. Abuse, no matter *what* kind, is *never* a child's fault."

Chasity didn't speak right away. Her expression then softened. "I'm sorry that I threw the whole Paul/Victoria thing in your face," she said.

 Malajia's head snapped towards Chasity. "Did you just apologize?" she joked.

Chasity held her middle finger in Malajia's face as she continued to face Alex. "You pissed me off, but you didn't deserve that."

Alex was emotional as she nodded. "Are we okay?" she asked, voice quivering.

"Yeah," Chasity answered. She made a face when she saw tears form in Alex's eyes. "Oh God Alex, don't do that," she complained. Ignoring Chasity's snide remark, Alex walked over and hugged her.

"Ol' cryin' ass," Malajia teased.

"Hush," Alex chided, wiping her eye. She fluffed her hair with her hand. "Look Chaz, about getting all up in your business about Jason... I don't mean to come off nosey—"

"You *don't*?" Malajia mocked.

Alex cut her eye at her, but refrained from hurling a retort. "I was just trying to give you advice. I know what it's like when a new relationship consumes you—"

"Alex, I'm not *you* and my relationship is *not* the same," Chasity cut in.

Alex nodded. "I know that," she agreed. "I was just…" she took a deep breath. "Look, I just try to look out for everybody, and I guess my intentions don't come off that way. I know it comes off…*momish*." Alex chuckled at the word.

"Yeah well, sometimes how we see ourselves is not how *others* see us," Sidra pointed out. "And as much as we try, we're never really going to know unless we walk in each other's shoes."

Emily giggled. "Can you imagine if we could all see what everyone else sees?"

"What? You mean like switch places?" Sidra asked, unsure.

Emily nodded.

"Nope," Chasity answered nonchalantly.

Malajia smugly folded her arms. "Ha, y'all heffa's wouldn't last a day as *me* honey."

Alex sat, ears perked as her friends chatted around her. Suddenly something clicked in her head. *Oh my God, this is perfect!* "Ooh, I have the perfect idea," she put out enthusiastically.

"Nobody wants one of your fussy bus ideas," Malajia griped, putting her hand up.

"Still trying to make that phrase stick, huh Mel?" Sidra teased. Malajia shrugged.

Alex put her hands together. "No wait, just hear me out," she pleaded. "It's actually a favor that I need."

"What is it Alex?" Chasity huffed. She just wanted to go back to her room and finish her dreaded homework.

"So, I have this project that I have to do for my Social Psychology class," Alex explained. "And I was thinking that maybe, we could all…walk in each other's shoes for the next few days."

Alex's suggestion was met with confused looks. "You want us to wear each other's shoes?" Sidra asked.

"Man, ain't nobody wearing those big ass brown boats *you* wear, Alex!" Malajia exclaimed, tossing her hands up. She then looked at Chasity and said, "Let me hold a pair of *yours*."

"Fuck you and no," Chasity threw back.

"No, no that's not what I mean," Alex jumped in. "I think we should *be* one another. Let us see how we come off to each other." She glanced around at her perplexed friends. "Please ladies, this will really help me get a good grade."

"Alex this is stupid, nobody wants to—"

"I'll be Chasity!" Malajia shouted, interrupting Chasity's protest.

"Why am I *not* surprised?" Chasity sneered.

"No, no, I think we should pick names out of a bag," Alex proposed. The girls watched as she jumped up from her seat and darted out of the lounge.

The remaining girls exchanged glances. "Is she serious?" Sidra asked.

"Um… I'm not sure," Emily replied, scratching her head.

Alex soon returned with a gift bag containing five small pieces of paper. She smiled as she walked over with the bag open. "Okay, pick a name and keep it to yourself," she urged.

Sidra shrugged as she reached into the bag. Her eyes widened as she read the name on the paper in her hand. "Oh my God!" she exclaimed. "This is the *last* person that I should be portraying."

"Shhh Sid, don't give it away," Alex giggled. "It'll be more fun if we try to guess."

Malajia eagerly dug her hand in the bag and closed her eyes. "Please give me somebody with cute clothes, please give me somebody with cute clothes." She pulled the name out and stared at it. "You know what! ILL," she hollered.

Emily put her hand over her mouth and snickered. Malajia certainly didn't seem pleased with her pick. Alex held the bag in Emily's direction, allowing her to choose. Glancing at her paper, Emily winced. *It doesn't even matter who I picked, I'm never gonna pull this off,* she thought.

Alex then looked at Chasity, bag outstretched. "Come on mama, *your* turn," she smiled.

Chasity sucked her teeth as she leaned forward. "You're lucky it's for your grade. Otherwise I'd tell you to kiss my ass," she hissed.

"Yes, I know," Alex chortled as Chasity picked.

Chasity's mouth dropped open as she eyed her paper "Oh *hell* no, I quit," she immediately put out, trying to throw the paper back in the bag. "I don't wanna do it."

Alex moved the bag out of Chasity's reach. "No Chaz, you have to keep it." Alex's voice was filled with amusement.

"Man," Chasity whined.

Alex smiled as she grabbed the last name. She busted out laughing. "Oh this is gonna be good," she mused. "Okay ladies, I say we begin this tomorrow."

"How far can we go with this?" Malajia asked, staring at her paper.

"As far as you want to take it," Alex answered, excited. "The point is to really *portray* your person."

"We have to dress like them too?" Emily wondered.

Alex shrugged. "Sure, if it would help you channel your person better."

"In that case, I need to go to the store," Sidra announced. "Anybody wanna come with? I just have to run up and get my purse."

"I guess I'll go," Chasity sulked, standing up. "I don't have shit in my closet that's gonna make me look like my damn person."

"That bad, huh?" Sidra chortled as both girls headed for the elevator.

"You have *no* idea," Chasity returned.

Oh, I got this bitch, Malajia thought, amused. "Hold up, I'm coming too," she called after Chasity and Sidra.

Alex let out a happy sigh as she looked at Emily. "I really appreciate this; you have no idea."

Emily smiled and nodded. "How long do we have to do this?"

Alex pondered that question. "I guess three days will be good enough."

Emily took a deep breath. "Well…okay then."

Chapter 11

Alex gave herself a long look in the bathroom mirror Monday morning. She ran her hand through her pressed locks, which fell to her chest. She touched up her black eyeliner and tinted lip gloss, then smiled. "This should be fun," she mused, gathering her items from the sink.

As Alex placed her primping items back on her dresser, she heard keys jiggle in the door. She spun around to see Sidra walk in. Her mouth immediately dropped open. "Sidra?!" she wailed, amusement in her voice.

Sidra put her finger up and shook it in Alex's direction. "No, no honey," she denied.

Alex glanced down Sidra's length as she removed her coat. Sidra ditched her trademark sophisticated attire for a short, tight red, sweater dress, paired with high-heeled red boots and large costume jewelry. Sidra's brown hair was dyed burgundy. She wore it down and curled. "Malajia?" Alex corrected.

"*Malajia*," Sidra confirmed. "Heeeeyyy bitch!"

Alex fought to contain her laugh. Sidra already had Malajia's loudness down. "Fuck off," Alex hissed.

Sidra pointed at Alex and laughed. "Chasity?"

Alex nodded. "You really dyed your hair?" she asked, breaking character.

"Girl *no*," Sidra chortled. "This is just a rinse that I'll be *happy* to wash out in three days." She tugged at her dress. "This thing keeps riding up my damn thighs. How does Mel maneuver in clothes like this?" She adjusted the large gaudy necklace on her neck. "I walked with my damn coat open so people can see this skimpy thing."

"At least it's not as cold out," Alex shrugged. The weather that week felt like early spring. Pretty unusual for February.

Sidra shook her head, then gestured towards Alex's hair. "Black hair looks good on you," Sidra complimented. She walked over and touched the pressed locks. "And it's really long too."

"Girl, when I tell you, I will *never* put a flat iron to this mess again," Alex joked. "This took me all damn morning to do. I don't see how y'all do it… And don't let me get started on what I went through putting this damn black rinse in my hair."

"Well, it looks good," Sidra reiterated, adjusting the abundance of gold bangles on her arm.

"You know Malajia is gonna kill you, she doesn't wear that much jewelry," Alex laughed.

"Ain't nobody thinkin' 'bout her damn feelings," Sidra sneered, waving her hand wildly.

Alex nodded. *She just went back to Malajia, I love this.* She grabbed her book bag and headed for the door. "I am apologizing *now* for all of the f-bombs that I'll be dropping over the next few days."

"Noted," Sidra chuckled.

"Be out my fuckin' room when I get back," Alex barked, opening the door.

"Ain't nobody scared of you," Sidra threw back, heading for the bathroom.

Closing the door behind her, Alex giggled. She headed for the elevator, but paused when she heard a door open.

Ooh! That must be Chasity or Malajia, I can't wait to see who they're portraying. Alex's musings were cut short when she spun around, coming face to face with Malajia. All traces of smile left her face as she fixed an angry gaze. "Malajia! What the hell?" she exclaimed.

Malajia stood there, unfazed by Alex's reaction. "I take it you're Chasity," she assumed. "Nice boots, *finally*," she teased of the black high-heeled ankle boots that Alex had on.

Alex was too taken aback by the atrocity that Malajia had on to even respond. All Alex could focus on was the long brown sheet that Malajia had cut holes into for her arms. Malajia had tied an unstylish yellow belt around the unshapely garment. Alex's eyes moved down to the grey furry ankle boots that covered Malajia's feet, then zoned in on her head. "Is that a damn mop on your head?"

Malajia smiled and nodded emphatically, causing the mop strings to dangle.

Alex folded her arms. "So what, this is supposed to be *me*?" she fumed, Malajia held the same goofy smile on her face. "I do *not* dress like that. Malajia, this is just plain disrespectful."

Malajia put her finger to her lips. "Shhh, use your indoor voice," she whispered, then walked off.

Alex spun around to face her departing back. Malajia was swinging her arms in dramatic fashion as she bobbed her head. "Girl! You—"

Malajia turned around. "Now, now Chaz—can I call you Chaz?" she mocked. "You look mad. You wanna talk about whatever your issue is so I can give you advice that you didn't ask for?"

Alex was too offended by Malajia's antics to be in character. She just stomped off.

"You shouldn't stomp like that, you could sprain a muscle!" Malajia yelled after her. She laughed to herself, then stopped when a dorm mate shot her a skeptical look. "What?" Malajia sneered. "It's for a project, mind your business."

Chasity let out a groan as she walked through the math building, holding the strap of her book bag with one hand and tugging at the baggy pink sweatshirt she had on with the other. *These clothes have no fuckin' shape whatsoever.*

Catching the eyes of fellow students as she headed towards the building exit, she glared back. "What?" she hissed, not in the mood to be in character. "You never seen anybody in a baggy ass sweat suit before?"

"Not *you*," a girl laughed.

Realizing that the girl had a point, Chasity rolled her eyes and headed out of the building. She came to a sudden stop and her eyes widened. "Shit," she whispered to herself, seeing Jason head up the steps. *I look like shit!* She covered one side of her face with her hand and tried to walk past him.

"Chaz?" Jason called, turning to face her departing back.

"Huh?" she answered, facing him, eyes wide.

Jason gave her a once over. She didn't look like her normal self. The pink unshapely sweat suit that she had on certainly wasn't her style, and neither were the two low ponytails in her hair. "Hey, what's up?" he asked, approaching.

"Um...nothing," Chasity slowly put out. She then sighed. "Why? Is something wrong?" she stammered, voice noticeably lower.

Jason frowned in confusion. "No," he answered. "But you seem kind of...different," he added. "*Cute,* but different," he amended.

Yeah, you better not say I look like shit. "I'm sorry Jason, I don't know what you're talking about...I *always* dress like a baggy fashion reject," she whispered, looking down at the ground.

"Wait, what did you say?" Jason asked, leaning in close.

"I said my clothes are ugly," Chasity whispered again, completely avoiding eye contact.

"Huh?"

"I said, I look like trash." She glanced at Jason for a split second, and tried not to laugh at the confused look on his face. "My mommy is gonna call me in five minutes, I gotta go."

"Why are you whispering?" Jason asked, scratching his head. "Baby, what's going on with you?"

"See you later Jason." Chasity held her laugh until she was far enough away from Jason. "I'm gonna kill Alex for this," she said to herself.

Stepping out of her apartment complex, Emily took a deep breath. She clutched her books to her chest while walking along the path. She winced when she stumbled in her black pumps. "Ow," she whined, reaching down and rubbing her ankle. "How do they walk in these things?"

Passing a building, Emily paused and looked at her reflection in the glass door. She touched the top of her head to make sure that her extension enhanced ponytail was straight. *I hope this thing doesn't fall out*, she thought. She switched her stance to examine the dark blue pencil skirt and matching blazer that she elected to wear. As she fixed her collar, she noticed Mark, Josh, and David standing on the steps of the library across the path. She had every intention of scurrying to class without them noticing, but decided against it. *You promised Alex you'd do this.* "Here goes nothing," she prompted herself.

Emily did her best saunter as she headed over to the guys. *Crap,* she thought when she stumbled again. She stood behind them and waited for them to turn around.

"You're so full of crap," David laughed at Mark.

"Mark, you know that never happened," Josh added.

Emily cleared her throat to get their attention, but they were so engrossed in their conversation that they didn't hear her.

"Yo, no bullshit," Mark replied, confident. "She was all

rubbing on me and shit and I was about to hit it and—"

"Hey guys," Emily interrupted.

The three guys turned and looked at her. "What the hell?" Mark commented, initially startled by her change in appearance.

"Emily?" David questioned, pushing his glasses up on his nose.

Emily smiled.

Mark looked her up and down. "Wow Em, I can *actually* see a shape today," he mused. "You look good."

Emily looked down at the ground momentarily as she blushed. She had to admit, although the outfit wasn't her style, it did allude to her slim figure. Clearing her throat, she jerked her head back up and flipped her ponytail over her shoulder. "Thank you," she beamed.

Josh was about to say something when someone caught his eye. His eyes nearly popped out of his head and his mouth fell open. "Oh…My…God," he gasped, voice filled with awe. He grabbed Mark's collar to get his attention as Emily and David focused on what had him so awestruck.

"Why you got your hands on my damn shirt, Joshua?" Mark barked, snatching Josh's hand off of him. Mark then spotted the same person. "Damn!" he bellowed.

Sidra smiled a seductive smile as she moseyed up to them. "Hey boys," she crooned, then struck a seductive pose. Josh was speechless.

"Wow Sid, I've never seen you look so—"

"Stank?" Sidra quizzed, interrupting David. "What? You've never seen a girl in a slinky dress before?"

"Not *you*?" Mark mumbled, taking the words right out of David's mouth.

Sidra shrugged then focused on Josh who was staring at her. "What's wrong, Josh?" she teased.

"Uh nothing," Josh stammered. *You look so freakin hot right now.* He ran his hand along the back of his neck. "You look—"

"Cold?" Emily cut in.

Sidra was so focused on the guys that she hadn't noticed that Emily was standing there. She fixed her eyes on Emily. "So, I take it you're me?" it was more of a statement than a question.

Emily held a smug look, remaining in character. "You don't look very ladylike," she criticized.

Sidra narrowed her eyes as Emily flung her ponytail in dramatic fashion. "I don't even *do* that," she hissed. Her eyes widened at Emily's jacket. "Are those shoulder pads?!"

Emily's hand reached up and patted her shoulder. "Maybe," she answered.

"Since when have you *ever* known me to wear shoulder pads?" Sidra fussed, folding her arms. "*Nobody* wears those."

Emily's hand fell to her side. "All the *cute* jackets were too expensive," she muttered. The money that her father placed into her bank account the previous week certainly couldn't all be used on the kind of excessively priced clothing that Sidra wore. *Stay in character.* "Yeah well, you need to stop showing your um...*assets*," Emily hurled.

The guys stood there completely confused at what was going on. "What the hell are y'all *on*?" Mark slowly put out.

"Shut up, jackass," Sidra spat at a shocked Mark.

"Huh?" Mark frowned, astonished by her outburst. "Damn Sid, why I gotta be a jackass?"

Emily turned her nose up as she flung her ponytail once more. "Ugh, so ghetto," she scoffed, walking away.

Sidra stomped her foot on the ground. "Emily, I don't even sound like that," she fussed, darting off to catch up to her.

The guys looked at each other. "They're acting weird," David pointed out.

Mark glanced at Josh, who was focused on Sidra's departing figure. "Dude she's gone," he mocked. "Focus, before you nut on yourself."

Josh snapped out of his trance and backhanded Mark in the ribs. "Shut up, asshole," he snapped, then hurried off in embarrassment.

Malajia sat on an accent chair in Paradise Terrace's lounge, listening to two of her dorm mates have a conversation.

She inched her chair closer, grinning as the conversation continued. She'd gotten close enough, without them initially noticing. She held a creepy smile on her face as one of them turned around, startled.

"Malajia!" the girl exclaimed, placing her hand over her heart. "What are you doing? And what are you *wearing*?"

Malajia sat there momentarily, not saying a word before suddenly getting up and walking away, leaving the girls even more confused by her behavior. Malajia laughed to herself as she proceeded for the door. Chasity walked in and both girls stared at each other for a long moment, before busting out laughing.

"Alex?" Chasity laughed, pointing to Malajia's makeshift ensemble. "Ewww!"

"Emily?" Malajia laughed back, approaching.

"*Unfortunately*," Chasity returned, laughter subsiding.

"I was knocked out when you left the room this morning," Malajia said, adjusting her belt. "You look quite baggy today, I might add," she teased. "You're lucky Emily stopped wearing those curtain dresses and started in on those old-ass sweat suits."

Chasity tugged on her shirt. "This shit itches," she complained. "But what the fuck do *you* have on?"

Malajia laughed. "Some shit that I *literally* threw together." She moved one of the mop strings out of her face. "Alex was pissed when she saw me earlier."

"Yeah *I* would be too," Chasity chuckled. "Nice touch with the mop though."

"Thanks, I think it adds the finishing touch, don't you think?" Malajia boasted, striking a pose.

Chasity shook her head, then noticed Alex coming out of the elevator. Watching Alex approach, she made a face.

"So this is supposed to be *me*, huh?" Chasity charged, gesturing to Alex's look of black form-fitting skinny jeans, paired with a black long-sleeved top. The silver jewelry completed the look. The entire outfit accentuated Alex's full figure. "I didn't think you owned anything tight in your closet...or black."

Alex smirked as she ran her hands through her hair. "Mind your fuckin' business about what the fuck I got in my fuckin' closet," she snapped, taking Chasity by surprise.

"I don't even *do* all that," Chasity hissed.

"*Yeah*, you do," Malajia laughed, earning a side-glance from Chasity.

"Yeah, 'cause this outfit cost more than your *entire* wardrobe," Alex continued, staying in character.

"Not that dollar store ass jewelry you got on," Chasity snarled, not bothering to channel her character. Malajia snickered loudly.

Alex sucked her teeth. "Why are you even talking to me?" she goaded. "You're not good enough to be in my conceited ass presence, you poor, insignificant, whiney bitch,"

"Oh for real?" Chasity spat. "You know what—"

Malajia nudged her. "You're supposed to be Emily," she whispered. Chasity nodded as Malajia focused on Alex. "Alex, why are you talking to poor Chasity like that?" she chided, pointing. "You know that she is an innocent, sweet child. You are heartless and cruel."

"Fuck off, mop head," Alex barked.

Malajia sighed. "Aww you don't mean that," she placated, holding her arms out. "Come on, hug me, my hostile sister."

Alex jerked her hand up. "Touch me and I'll snap you in half." She looked at Chasity. "God, I just want to punch somebody in the face. I don't know *why* I always have that urge...It's like I'm just *always* angry, and sometimes for *no* good reason."

Chasity fought the urge to fire off a smart retort. Instead, she turned to Malajia. "Malajia *why* is she so mean?" she sulked, then put her hands over her face. "She hates me, everybody hates me because I'm so annoying."

Malajia put her hand over her heart. "Don't you pay her any mind, she's just on her monthly cycle," she said.

Alex put her hand on her hip, trying not to lose her temper. *I'm gonna choke her,* she thought of Malajia.

Chasity pretended to cry. "Why am I so awkward?"

Malajia grabbed Chasity and hugged her. "Oh no, don't cry," she consoled. "You are *not* awkward. You are the sweetest thing in the world."

"I want my Mommy!" Chasity wailed.

"Oh *I'll* be your Mommy, I'll be your Mommy." Malajia hugged Chasity tight, while vigorously rubbing her back.

"Malajia!" Alex snapped, unable to hold in her agitation.

Malajia put her finger up to silence Alex. "Don't you *dare* try to justify talking to her this way, you big meanie," she retorted.

Alex gritted her teeth. "You know what?" she huffed, heading for the door. "Fuck you two bitches."

"Say that with some *feeling* next time," Chasity hurled at her. "If you're *gonna* be me, don't half-ass it."

Alex flipped her off in retaliation.

"Alex, don't give people the finger. If you do, that finger will fall off and crawl up your behind!" Malajia yelled after her, much to the confusion of both Alex and Chasity.

"What the hell, Malajia?" Chasity questioned.

"Oh what? You telling me that Alex would never say some shit like that?" Malajia countered.

Chapter 12

Alex pushed her hair over her shoulder as she stood by her classroom, waiting for the early class to let out. She glanced at her watch and rolled her eyes at Mark, who was standing next to her.

"You hype as shit you early for class," Mark jeered.

"Shut the fuck up," Alex grumbled.

Mark shook his head. "Yo, I've heard you cuss more in the past two days than the damn near two years I've known you," he chortled.

Tell me about it, Alex thought.

"I swear, you sound just like—"

"Chasity?" Alex finished.

Mark looked at her and pointed. "Yeah, *exactly*."

Alex giggled. Day two of her social experiment with the girls was in full swing, and although it was fun tapping into her chosen alter ego, she was starting to miss her own personality…and her natural hair. "God, I can't take this straight stuff anymore," she complained, flipping hair over her shoulder once again. She then grabbed a few strands and stared. "Ugh, I need my ends trimmed."

"What the hell are you talking about, yo?" Mark grunted. "You've been running your mouth about nothing for like a half hour."

Alex turned her lip up. "*First* of all," she began, facing him. "I was minding my business when *you* came over here and stood next to *me*. Second, you started talking to *me first*. *Third*, we haven't even been standing here a half hour, you butthole."

Mark laughed as he adjusted his book bag.

Alex sucked her teeth. "Anyway, what are *you* waiting for?"

"Man, my Accounting professor talkin' 'bout he wanna talk to me about my last test," he replied.

"Why?"

"'Cause I failed that shit," Mark admitted.

Alex couldn't help but laugh. "Boy, you better stop playing around in your classes."

"Man, fuck that class," Mark grumbled, looking at his phone. "Let me get going before he start bitchin'."

"Bye crazy," Alex chuckled, as Mark headed off. Within another moment, students filtered out of the classrooms and into the hallway. Alex held her post against the wall and waited for the crowd to subside. As she prepared to head into her class, she caught sight of Malajia and immediately scowled.

"Hey, my sister," Malajia smiled, approaching. "I think I'm liking the 'Chasity' look on you. You should keep it."

"It's not *me*," Alex ground out.

Malajia looked shocked by Alex's tone. "Why are you so angry?" she teased. "Are you cramping sweetie? Do you need a hug?"

Alex folded her arms, the frown frozen on her face. "So you're really going to pretend you don't know why I'm mad?"

Malajia shrugged.

Alex stomped her foot on the floor. "Malajia, you're wearing the same crap that you had on *yesterday*!" she wailed.

Malajia successfully concealed a laugh, while staring at Alex with a blank expression. Deep down, Malajia was doubling over with laughter. She knew exactly what she was doing when she elected to wear the same brown sheet, boots and mop wig that had Alex feeling insulted from the day before.

"You think this is funny?" Alex ranted.

"I'm not even *laughing*," Malajia pointed out, tone calm.

Alex was livid. "You're not taking this seriously."

"*Sure* I am."

"No you're *not*," Alex threw back. "You didn't pick a real outfit. You're walking around with that damn sheet on, trying to insinuate that that's how I dress."

Malajia rolled her eyes. "I have no idea what you're talking about." She then began to swing her head from side to side, sending the mop strings swerving.

"See?" Alex fumed over Malajia's deliberate attempt to annoy her. "My hair has *never* looked like that cheap mop that you have on your head."

Malajia laughed. "Awww, calm down honey. You're gonna give yourself a yeast infection,"

"Oh *come* on! I don't say things like that."

"Alex, you're so tense." Malajia held her arms out. "Come on, talk to me. Share your feelings. Hug me. Let me love you."

Alex's eyes were drawn to the middle of Malajia's ensemble. "Is that a mustard stain?"

Malajia eagerly nodded, then glanced over at two classmates talking. Much to Alex's agitation, Malajia slowly leaned close to them, a crazy smile plastered to her face, listening to their conversation.

Alex sucked her teeth and gave Malajia's arm a yank. "Girl, will you stop it," she barked. Alex looked at her watch. "Damn it! I'm late for class, messing around with you."

Satisfied with getting Alex in an uproar, Malajia

shrugged and walked away, swinging her head around in the process.

Alex followed her progress, angry. "Asshole," she seethed before storming off to her class.

Emily tugged at the white blouse that she had on as she headed out of the bathroom of the Math and Science building. *This ponytail is killing me*, she thought, giving the top of the extension an adjustment. The black pencil skirt that she wore was making it hard for her to maneuver as she normally did.

Carefully tip-toeing in her pumps out of the building, she nearly collided into Chasity. "Sorry," she immediately put out.

"It's fine, Emily," Chasity returned.

Glancing down Chasity's length, Emily smiled. She could tell by the look on Chasity's face alone that she had grown tired of her Emily-esq attire. The baggy jeans and grey sweat jacket didn't complement Chasity's figure at all.

I wonder if I look this shapeless in my clothes, Emily wondered. Getting into character, Emily swung her ponytail over her shoulder in dramatic fashion. "Ugh, I am in major need of some coffee," she scoffed. "But only the *good* coffee, I don't drink that cheap instant stuff."

Chasity smirked at Emily's haughty, dramatic interpretation of her former roommate. "You drink coffee?" Chasity asked, eyes wide. "I've never had it."

Emily blinked. "Really?" She could have sworn that she saw Chasity drink coffee on more than one occasion.

Chasity nodded, pushing her straight hair behind her ear. "My mommy never let me have any," she added, voice low.

Emily's face fell. *Ooooh, she's being me right now.* "Um...you need to tell your mom to let you try some," she sputtered, frazzled.

"Well..." Chasity began, glancing at the ground, clutching her books to her chest.

God, she even has my movements down. Emily just stood there, waiting.

"I *would* but I have absolutely *no* backbone *whatsoever*," Chasity taunted, voice sullen. "*Mommy* controls *everything* that I do, that I *wear*, that I *say*...I'm weak."

Emily felt like a ton of bricks just hit her right in the face. Even though she knew that Chasity was trying to poke fun, she knew that this was exactly how her life was and the reflection wasn't funny. "Well Emily—I mean Chasity, you...."

Chasity waited, a sly smile forming on her face. She wondered if she would get a Sidra inspired comeback, or the teary-eyed retreat that she *normally* received from Emily. "I know there's a snide remark in there *some*where," she goaded.

Emily clutched her books to her chest. No longer in the mood to play, she lowered her heard and scurried off.

Chasity shook her head. "Spineless ass," she commented to herself.

Sidra sighed, sticking her key into her door. The walk back from her last class of the day was irritating. All the unwanted attention from her temporary wardrobe change was making Sidra contemplate dropping Alex's little experiment a day early. Realizing that her door was already unlocked, she opened it. Walking in, she was startled to see Malajia sitting on Alex's bed, eating fruit snacks.

"Malajia!" she screeched, dropping her coat and books to the floor. "What are you doing in here?"

"I'm Alex and this is my room," Malajia smirked, placing another fruit-shaped gummy candy into her mouth. Upon seeing the annoyed look on Sidra's face, Malajia busted out laughing. "What? Your door was unlocked so I decided to come in and steal some of these fruit snacks that you were trying to hide."

Sidra shook her head. "Girl, why do you have that damn

sheet on again?" she chuckled. "Alex is gonna choke you."

Malajia stood from the bed. "Ain't nobody scared of no damn Alex." Malajia gave Sidra's outfit a once over. "You actually look cute in my 'inspired' clothes," she mused, examining the form-fitting burgundy dress that barely concealed Sidra's slender figure. "Let me borrow that when you're done with it."

"Honey, you can *have* this thing when I'm done with it," Sidra promised.

Malajia tossed her head back. "Yeeeessss!" she rejoiced, then spun around when the mop fell off of her head.

Sidra put her hand over her face and shook her head as Malajia scrambled to retrieve it. "Something is wrong with you," she concluded.

Malajia shrugged, sitting it back atop her head. "Oh and I don't appreciate all that big ass jewelry you got on either," she jeered, pointing to the abundance of bracelets on both of Sidra's wrists. "You know I'm *not* that gaudy."

"Aren't you supposed to be *Alex* right now?" Sidra challenged.

Malajia thought for a moment, then gasped. "Sidra!" she exclaimed.

"What?" Sidra panicked, looking behind her.

"Why do you *always* have to wear clothes that leave nothing to the imagination?" she scolded.

"Oh," Sidra replied. She flipped her hair and struck a pose. "Jealous much?" she crooned.

Malajia twisted her lip up at the exaggerated pose.

"I'm just too sexy for words and you *wish* you could wear what I wear," Sidra added, rolling her neck and waving her hand excessively. "Whatchu' all in my business for *anyway* witcho' ugly shirt wearing ass?"

"Really Sidra?" Malajia grunted, breaking character. "You know I don't even do all that extra shit when I talk."

Sidra signaled for her to throw something back.

"Tsk tsk tsk," Malajia replied, pointing her finger. "You

should really cover up. It's cold outside. Do you know that your titties could get frost bite?"

Sidra frowned in confusion. "Huh?"

Malajia smiled and walked out, just to come face to face with Alex. Alex let out a loud groan as Malajia took off slow running down the hallway. "Can you at least *wash* the thing?" she fussed. Alex sucked her teeth when Malajia's ill-fitting boot slipped off her foot in mid-run. Alex held her gaze as Malajia ran back, picked it up, and started jogging again.

"You're an idiot Malajia!" Alex stormed into the room and slammed the door. "Sidra, I can't take how that damn girl is portraying me," she vented.

Sidra rolled her eyes. "Alex, I don't want to talk about *anything* that isn't about *me*," she scoffed.

Alex put her hands up. "I want to talk to *Sidra*, not Malajia," she stressed.

Sidra laughed. "Okay."

"I mean, *you've* seen her," Alex huffed.

"Yeah, the whole *campus* has," Sidra nodded, amused. "But you know she doesn't care about what anybody says."

"I'm not concerned with what people are saying about *her*," Alex spat. "I'm pissed that she's portraying *me* like that." Alex removed her shoes. "I mean, I may not have much, but I *don't* wear the same clothes every day and I certainly don't dress like *that*."

Sidra giggled. "Well Alex, this was *your* idea," she pointed out. "You already know how silly she is… Are you really surprised?"

Alex rolled her eyes. "I mean, I *get* it, but—" She paused when she heard a tap on the door. She headed over and opened it to find Malajia standing with her ear to the door. Alex sucked her teeth.

"What? You saying that I'm nosey?" Alex growled.

Malajia looked at her, then without saying a word, turned and walked back down the hall. "You make me sick!" Alex hollered after her.

Sidra busted out laughing.

Alex adjusted the towel around her freshly washed hair before jotting something down in her notebook.

"When do you have to turn that raggedy ass project in?" Malajia asked, opening a bag of microwave popcorn.

"Tomorrow," Alex replied, not looking up from her notebook. Her social experiment now over, Alex was in the process of putting her information together for submission first thing in the morning.

"I tell you what, I love you ladies, but I never want to play any of you ever again," Sidra said. "*Especially* you, Malajia. I swear, every guy I walked pass stared straight at my breasts."

Malajia waved a popcorn filled hand Sidra's way. "Girl, you know I'm here for the attention."

Sidra shook her head. She, like the other girls, was glad to be back to her normal self. "So, what did you learn from all of this Alex?"

Alex wrote something else in her book. "Well…I learned that how we think we're being perceived might not necessarily be how others see us," she concluded. She glanced at Malajia. "And that *some* of us can't take *anything* seriously."

"Oh I was *very* serious," Malajia threw back. "*You're* just mad because I played you to a damn T."

"You lie," Alex countered. "You know damn well, I don't act like that."

Malajia laughed. "Okay, maybe I exaggerated a little…a *lot*," she amended, catching the stares of the girls. "But it was worth it to see your face every time I had that damn sheet on."

Alex rolled her eyes.

"Alex, don't act like you didn't exaggerate either," Chasity added.

"Exaggerate *what*?" Alex wondered, perplexed.

Chasity shot Alex a knowing look. "I don't go around cussing people out for no damn reason," she denied. "And I don't cuss *that* much."

"Bitch *please*," Malajia scoffed. "Your mouth can put a *sailor* to shame...ol' potty mouth having ass."

Chasity flipped Malajia off. "Whatever," she muttered.

"And Emily was pretty upset over your portrayal of her, Chasity," Alex informed, pointing her pencil in her direction. "I think you hurt her feelings."

"*Everything* hurts that damn girls' feelings," Chasity dismissed. "She can either fight me or get over it."

Alex shook her head. She was sure that Emily was still reeling, which would explain why she neglected to come over and hang out with them. "Yeah...*my* version of you was *so* exaggerated," Alex drawled sarcastically.

Malajia grabbed more popcorn from the bag. "Yo, the guys thought we lost our minds," she recalled, amused.

"Yeah, I'm glad we finally told them what was going on, that second night," Sidra added, shaking a bottle of nail polish in her hand.

Malajia glanced at Sidra. "Ooh, do my nails when you're done," she ordered.

"Girl no," Sidra refused, twisting the top off the silver polish.

Alex laughed at the banter. "Look, I appreciate you girls doing this for me, I'm almost sure I'm gonna pull an A on this assignment." she gushed. "You know, this also taught me that even though we get on each other's nerves, when any one of us is in need, we rally together to help." She smiled. "I love you girls."

"We love you too, Alex," Sidra returned the same time that Malajia sneered, "always on some mushy shit," and Chasity griped, "shut up."

Alex couldn't help but laugh. *Gotta love them.*

Chapter 13

"Babe I swear, these damn classes are kicking my ass," Malajia complained, laying across her bed with her cell phone to her ear.

"These professors must *all* be on the same shit," Tyrone returned into the line. "*My* classes are hell *too*."

Malajia nodded. Talking to Tyrone was something that Malajia looked forward to every day. Ever since her dream date with him over a month ago, he'd begun showing her the attention that she craved from him.

"I can't *wait* until break," Malajia replied, twirling hair with her fingers. "You gonna come see me before then?"

"Absolutely," Tyrone assured her. "I know I haven't seen you in like a week, but tests got me trippin',"

"I understand," Malajia sighed. Malajia realized that she had a need to not only talk to him, but to be in his presence.

"I promise, I'll make some time for you real soon."

"You *better*," she crooned. "I mean talking is good, but I need that face to face time…I need to *see* my man."

Tyrone chuckled. "Oh so you're finally admitting that I'm your man, huh?"

Malajia put her hand over her face. She'd been holding out on confirming that title with Tyrone until he proved himself. But, satisfied with what he'd shown thus far, she figured it was time. "Uh, yeah I guess," she replied coyly.

"That's just what I wanted to hear," he said.

Malajia blushed, and glanced at the door when Chasity walked in. "Ty, let me call you right back."

"Why?" he pressed, tone changing. "Who's in there with you?"

Malajia paid his paranoia no mind. "My roommate just walked in."

"Oh? Tell her I said what's up."

Malajia sat up. "Chaz, Tyrone said what's up."

Chasity flagged Malajia with her hand as she sat a grocery bag on her desk.

Malajia shook her head. "She said 'hey'," she lied. "I'll call you soon."

"You *better*, bye."

Malajia ended the call and gave Chasity a stern look. "Why do you have to react so stank every time I say he's on the phone?"

"Why do I have to answer this same damn question every time you hang *up*?" Chasity threw back, removing items from the bag.

Malajia rolled her eyes. "Whatever. You don't like Tyrone, I get it," she replied, standing up. "But can you at *least* keep your attitude to yourself?"

"Nope."

Malajia tossed her hands in the air. "Whatever, bitch." She knew it was pointless to go back and forth on the matter. Malajia walked over and peered in the bag. "Did you get my noodles?"

Chasity grabbed the back of Malajia's shirt and pulled her away from her desk. "I didn't get you *shit*," she sneered.

Malajia jerked away from Chasity. "How you gonna go to the store and not bring back my noodles?" she barked, smoothing her tank top down. "I told you I ran out two days ago."

"Then you should've taken your ass to the *store* two

days ago," Chasity retorted, unfazed by Malajia's reaction.

Alex walked through the door after knocking twice. "Hey girls," she quickly greeted. "Chaz, did you pick up my noodles?"

"I told your fat ass about just walking in our damn room," Malajia huffed.

Alex frowned, then dismissed Malajia with a wave of her hand. An argument was not on her to-do list.

Chasity pointed to her dresser. "They're over there."

"My girl," Alex smiled, trotting over. "Thank you for grabbing these for me."

"It's fine," Chasity uttered.

Malajia watched as Alex retrieved the small pack of instant noodles and headed for the door. "Hold on," she said, halting Alex's departure, who spun around. "Why the hell did you get *her* broke ass, noodles?" she asked, looking at Chasity.

Alex placed a hand on her hip. "Really Malajia?" she fumed. "Was it necessary to call me broke?"

Malajia shot Alex a confused look. "Bitch you *know* you're broke. Don't act all sensitive *now*."

Alex sucked her teeth and walked out of the room.

"Chaz, I don't appreciate that shit," Malajia harped, folding her arms.

Chasity threw her head back and groaned. "Oh my God, go away for like *five* minutes, *please*."

Malajia rolled her eyes. "Fine, *fuck* your noodles," she spat, heading for the door. "I'm gonna get some of *Alex's*." She punctuated her announcement by running out the door.

Josh stared at Sidra while she focused on the Advanced Algebra book in her lap. With a test on the horizon, both she and Josh elected to study together. However, what seemed like a good idea was proving to be too much for Josh to handle. His focus wasn't on the formulas in his book, but on the woman sitting next to him.

She's so perfect, Josh mused internally.

"Josh, do you have the notes from last class?" Sidra asked, glancing up at him.

Josh quickly looked down at his book. *I hope she didn't catch me staring.* "Um, let me check," he sputtered, grabbing his notebook.

"Thank you. I wrote them down, but I must've mixed some stuff up." Sidra flipped a page in her notebook. "These formulas aren't coming out right."

Josh let out a sigh of relief. *Good, she didn't notice.* "Here you go." He handed her the book.

Grateful, Sidra smiled. After jotting the notes down, Sidra stretched her neck. "God, I could use a break," she sighed.

"Yeah, I hear you," Josh replied, fixing his gaze on her as she ran her hand along the back of her neck. He pictured himself taking his hand and rubbing it for her. He then imagined giving her a full body massage.

Sidra's ringing cell phone interrupted his fantasy. "Sorry Josh, hold on a sec," she said, reaching for it. Looking at the caller ID, she smiled. "Hi James," she gushed.

Josh rolled his eyes and jumped from the bed. *I hate this guy!* he seethed, standing against the dresser with his arms folded like a child. Then Mark barged in, startling him from his petulant behavior. "*Knock* damn it!" Josh snapped.

Mark squinted at him. "Shut your punk ass up," he shot back, flagging him in the process. He headed to Josh's refrigerator and opened it. "Whatchu' doing?"

"We're *trying* to study," Josh huffed, gesturing towards Sidra.

Mark looked up from the contents of the fridge and focused on Sidra, who seemed to be engrossed in her conversation. "Man y'all ain't studying; she's on the phone," he observed. "Hey Sid."

Sidra turned around, and waved before going back to her conversation.

Mark focused his attention on the scowl on Josh's face.

"What the hell is *your* problem?"

"Nothing," Josh lied. "What do you want?"

"I'm hungry," Mark answered, rubbing his stomach. "David hid all his damn snacks."

"Good for him," Josh hissed.

Mark rolled his eyes. "Anyway, what you got to eat? Got any noodles?"

"Not for *your* greedy ass," Josh grunted, walking over to his closet.

Mark's mouth fell open when Josh retrieved a cup of instant noodles from the top shelf. "Oh so you just gonna make noodles right in my face?" he quibbled.

Josh carefully poured some bottled water into the Styrofoam cup. "You don't have to watch," he spat.

Annoyed, Mark walked over as Josh was about to place the cup into the microwave. "Come on, let me get that real quick," he demanded, grabbing for the cup.

"Get out my face!" Josh hollered, holding the cup out of reach.

"Just give me the fuckin' noodles dawg!" Mark wailed, taking hold of the cup.

Sidra turned around and witnessed the commotion taking place. "Guys, can you stop?" she huffed. "I'm on the phone, you're so rude,"

"That's *Josh* making all that noise," Mark blamed, tugging at the cup.

"You're breaking it," Josh barked. The cup split in half, spilling the contents to the floor. "See what you did, you stupid jackass?"

"Now *nobody* gets the noodles," Mark mocked, brushing seasoning from his shirt. "You should have gave 'em to me when I *asked* for it, you fuckin' fool."

Josh watched as Mark started making faces and taunting noises at him, and lost it. "Get out!" he boomed, pushing Mark towards the door.

"He's grabbing my ass! He's grabbing my ass," Mark joked as he was forced out the door.

Josh slammed it shut and locked it for good measure.

Alex put her hands on her face and pulled down as Malajia's mouth ran non-stop. Fed up, Alex snapped. "Malajia!" she yelled, slapping her bed with each syllable of Malajia's name.

"What are you yelling for?" Malajia wondered.

"You've been running your mouth for like an hour straight," Alex fussed. "I don't want to hear anymore."

"You just mad 'cause I'm talking about Tyrone," Malajia accused.

"*That*," Alex declared. Malajia confirming her relationship status with Tyrone over the phone earlier wasn't something that was of interest to Alex. "*And* I'm *trying* to work on this draft of this damn English paper. Now get out."

"How you gonna act all rude when *you* invited me over?" Malajia threw back, folding her arms. "I don't appreciate this shit."

Alex grimaced. "I didn't invite you over here," she recalled. "You followed me over here to steal some of my noodles."

Malajia sat there, a dumb look on her face. "*Maybe* that's true," she admitted. "Whatever, what class is that for anyway?"

"English Comp."

Malajia's eyes widened. "Wait, you said English Comp?" she asked, "Dr. Bolding's class?"

Alex let out a loud sigh. "*Yes* Malajia." She put her head in her hands. "The draft is due tomorrow."

Malajia jumped up. "Shit! I have that class at four tomorrow," she panicked. "I didn't know that draft was due so soon."

"Malajia, she gave this assignment a *week* ago," Alex pointed out.

Malajia grabbed her slippers from the floor and shoved them on her feet. "Nobody asked you all that," she sneered, running for the door. "Why you hold me hostage over here with you? I got work to do."

Alex buried her face in her pillows. She was done with Malajia's nonsense.

"I didn't even *start*," Malajia complained, running out.

Alex glanced at the ceiling. "Thank *God*," she rejoiced.

"I hope I didn't miss my show," Sidra muttered, flipping on the television. Thanks to her due diligence in her studies, Sidra finished her test promptly and was allowed to leave class early. She was pleased to have some extra time to herself for a change.

Finding her channel, she grabbed a small bottle of iced coffee from her refrigerator and twisted the cap. "Damn it," she complained when coffee dripped on her hands. "Did they *have* to fill it so high?"

She immediately headed for the bathroom. Upon entering, her mouth dropped open. "Are you freaking kidding me?" she seethed.

Despite having just cleaned her side of the bathroom before leaving that morning, her neighbor's mess of paper towels, make up smudges, toothpaste droppings and sanitary napkin wrappers had grown, spilling over to her side.

Fuming, Sidra snatched open the bottom cabinet door, and from it retrieved a pair of rubber gloves and cleaning products. "Sick of this shit," she fussed.

For the next twenty minutes, with glove-covered hands, Sidra scrubbed, swept, and mopped the entire bathroom. She placed all items that weren't hers or Alex's into a plastic bag and tossed it on the neighbors' side of the sink.

"Freaking poor excuses for women," she vented to herself. Glancing down at her hand, she groaned when she noticed a tear in her glove. She took off the ripped glove and slammed it on the counter. Sidra removed the blue and silver, heart-shaped crystal ring from her slender finger and sat it on the counter. "Damn thing must've ripped it."

Placing a fresh glove on her hand, she grabbed the bag of her neighbors' contents from the counter and gave their door a hard knock.

Seconds later, Dee opened the door. "What's up, Sidra?"

Sidra was in no mood for pleasantries. "You and your roommate left your mess in here... *Again*," she bit out, shoving the bag in Dee's face.

Grabbing the bag from Sidra's hand, Dee scowled. "Sidra, it's a damn bathroom. This stuff is *supposed* to be in here."

"Not laying all over the *floor*, it's not," Sidra snapped, placing a hand on her hip. "And not when it spills over to *my* damn side."

Dee rolled her eyes. "Do you ever get tired of hearing yourself whine about the same thing?" she threw back. "I know *I* do."

Sidra made a face. "That's real cute," she hissed.

Dee sucked her teeth.

"Look Deidre, I don't mean to sound like a nag—"

"Oh, you *don't*?"

Sidra wanted to slap Dee in her face. "This is *really* getting ridiculous," she asserted. "I just spent my free time cleaning this *entire* bathroom—"

"*Nobody* asked you to do that," Dee interjected.

"Cut me off again," Sidra warned, shooting Dee a death stare. "Now look, it doesn't matter if I was *asked* or not, okay." She snatched the gloves from her hands. "The *point* is that I *cleaned* it. And since you seem to be having a hard time acting like you have home training, just be sure to keep your shit on your *own* side."

The anger was noticeable on Dee's face. "I don't know *who* you think—"

"Thank you," Sidra spat, turning on her heel and sauntered out of the bathroom. Dee slammed her door the same time that Sidra slammed hers.

Chapter 14

Feeling a light breeze caress her face, Alex closed her eyes. "Spring is finally in full effect," she gushed. After what seemed like a long winter, Alex, Jason, Chasity, and Malajia were taking advantage of the pleasant weather as they journeyed through campus.

Alex, hearing her stomach growl, placed her hand there. "I'm starving," she declared. "If I don't get some food in my system before I go to Spanish class, I'm going to fall out."

"You ain't gonna fall *no*where," Malajia mocked, adjusting her purse strap on her shoulder. "Always exaggerating."

"No, that would be *you*," Alex threw back.

"How are you liking Spanish?" Jason asked Alex, hoping to stop an impending argument.

"It's okay," Alex shrugged. "I took it in high school, so I'm not *completely* new to it."

Malajia sucked her teeth. "Man, to hell with stupid ass Spanish," she griped. "I had that mess last semester."

"And you have it again *this* semester," Chasity revealed.

Malajia's eyes widened as Jason laughed.

"Malajia, you had to repeat Spanish 101?" Alex charged, disappointment in her voice. "One of the *easiest* classes here?"

"Look, failing that class wasn't my damn fault," Malajia argued, pointing to herself.

"How the hell do you figure *that*?" Chasity laughed.

"Shut up, snitch," Malajia hurled, giving Chasity's arm a poke. "Anyway, the professor was on some dumb shit last semester." She glanced at the others, who stared at her, unconvinced. "You know what, save your judgments okay. I don't give a damn. Why should I have to learn how to say *rice* in Spanish huh? I speak *English*."

"Regardless of that pointless argument, foreign language is a *requirement*," Jason pointed out.

Malajia made a face at him. "Nobody asked you, jock brain."

"Yeah? *I* passed Spanish 101 though," Jason boasted. Salty, Malajia made a face at him.

"Pendejo," Chasity muttered.

Malajia's head snapped towards her. "Don't nobody care that you speak Spanish, you bilingual bitch," she barked.

Alex shook her head. "Malajia, chill out, will you?" she turned to Chasity. "Not that I want to feed into this, but Chaz what did you say to her?"

"I called her stupid," Chasity returned, nonchalant.

Malajia flipped the middle finger. Glancing ahead as they continued their walk, Malajia spotted Mark making his way towards the fitness center. "Look at this fool," she mumbled to the others. "Hey dirty!" she called. She busted out laughing when Mark stopped and looked in their direction.

"At least he knows his name," Alex laughed, approaching him.

"I knew that was *your* loud ass," Mark grunted at Malajia. "What are y'all up to?"

Jason had a thought. "Mark, shouldn't you be in your Business Applications class right now?"

"Man, *fuck* them apps," Mark snapped.

Jason shook his head.

"I need to get in a workout before this party tonight," Mark added.

Malajia perked up. "Party? *What* Party?"

"The one that's going to be at the gym," Mark informed, fixing his gym bag on his shoulder.

"Who's gonna be at the door?" Malajia interrogated.

Alex was confused. "Why?"

Malajia shot Alex a glare. "I wanna get in for free," she snapped. "Damn, all up in my business." When Alex opened her mouth to retort, Malajia jerked her hand up, silencing her. "Anyway, who's gonna be at the door, dirty?" she directed to Mark.

"Mitch, I think."

"Oh *hell* yeah. That's my buddy," Malajia beamed. "I'm in there like swim wear."

"A'ight, we gonna be out like lights on school night. Feel me, bee?" Mark added, giving Malajia a high five.

Alex threw her hands up in the air. "I don't have time for these two," she grumbled. "I'm starving. Chasity, let's go."

"All right," Chasity chuckled. She gave a quick kiss to Jason before walking off with Alex.

"Later baby," Jason called after her.

Malajia and Mark eyed Jason with disgust. "You two are sickening," Malajia scoffed.

"*Ain't* they?" Mark added, nudging Malajia. "Later baby," he mocked Jason's voice.

Jason laughed a little. "That's okay, say what you want," he goaded. "You *wish* you had what we have."

Mark waved his hand at him. "Whatever yo, you coming to the party later?"

"Don't think so, I have a late practice," Jason responded.

"Man *fuck* practice!" Mark erupted.

"Keep yelling at me dawg, I'm gonna choke the shit outta you," Jason warned, pointing at Mark.

"They corny," Malajia complained as Jason walked off.

"Forget 'em," Mark dismissed. "I'll meet you at your room like ten. We can roll together."

Malajia turned her lip up. "I'm not going with *you*."

Mark stared at her for a moment, salty. "Forget you then."

"Oh boy, shut the hell up; I was joking," Malajia amended.

Mark let a smile come through, holding his hand up for a high five. "All right, we gonna be cooler than a penguin ice skating with shades on."

Malajia dropped her hand. "See, never mind," she huffed, walking off.

"What I do?" he called after her.

"You always gotta take shit overboard," she threw over her shoulder. "Why would a fuckin' penguin be wearing shades?"

Mark laughed. He knew that what he said sounded stupid, even for him. "'Cause he cool, bee!" he yelled after her. Malajia ignored him, and Mark headed into the fitness center.

Emily sat on a bench near the library, staring up at the clear sky, silently wishing that it would open and suck her in. The warm sun or gentle breeze didn't feel pleasant to Emily; she felt numb.

Emily played back the four messages that her mother had left between the previous evening and that morning in her head. The pestering, prodding words had Emily on edge. She was so lost on her thoughts; she didn't even hear Alex call her name.

"Em?" Alex called once more, sitting next to her on the bench.

Emily looked at Alex, a blank look in her eyes. "How are you, Alex?"

Alex took note of Emily's somber mood. "You okay sweetie?" her voice failed to mask her concern.

No, no I'm not. "I'm fine," she lied. "Just not feeling too well."

Alex winced. "I'm sorry to hear that," she sympathized, giving Emily's shoulder a rub.

"Thanks," Emily mumbled, looking at the ground.

Alex sighed. She felt like she knew why Emily was being standoffish. "Em, we didn't forget your birthday last weekend," she said. "We tried calling but—"

"I know, don't worry about it," Emily sulked. "I was home anyway." Turning nineteen merely a week ago didn't give Emily the happy feeling that she hoped for. Besides being pressured to spend her weekend at home, her birthday was just another reminder that no matter how old she got, her mother still had a hold on her.

"No, I feel like we should still do something for you," Alex insisted. "How about—"

"Alex it's okay, really," Emily cut in. She was in no mood for any celebrations. "I appreciate you *wanting* to do something though."

Alex nodded, resisting the urge to press the issue any further. "Okay, if that's what you want," she relented. "Well," she began after a moment. "Do you at *least* want to come over and watch a movie with us later?"

Emily forced a half-smile. As nice as spending time with the girls sounded, Emily was depressed and didn't want to bring the vibe down with her mood. She shook her head. "I can't, I have homework to do."

"I hear you, but its *Friday*." While Alex understood that school work was important, everyone deserved a break, especially on the weekend.

Emily retrieved her book bag from the ground. "I know, but I have a lot of it, so I really want to get started."

Alex looked disappointed. "Okay," she replied, watching Emily hurry off.

Emily continued her hurried pace into her apartment complex. As she walked through the living space in route to her secluded bedroom, she stopped suddenly; her eyes were drawn to a half-empty bottle of liquor on the floor.

Emily stared at it, remembering the party that her suite mates had the night before. She recalled it vividly, because the noise kept her awake for most of the night. *I guess they forgot to clean up the mess.* Emily couldn't care less about the mess, or the fact that if an RA walked in, she could be blamed for the mess *and* the alcohol. All she saw was a bottle of something that would take her mind off of her mother, her classes, *everything.* Emily glanced around the room in search of open doors. Finding none, Emily snatched up the bottle and ran into her room, shutting the door behind her.

"What movie are we about to watch?" Alex asked, grabbing a bag of freshly popped popcorn from the microwave.

"Some crap that Sidra picked out," Chasity griped, adjusting a pillow behind her back.

After the long week, instead of going out, Chasity, Alex, and Sidra elected to spend the night in, watching a movie.

Sidra regarded Chasity with shock. "Wait a minute, I asked your opinion on which movie we should watch and you said that you didn't care," she reminded.

"That's because I don't like *any* of them," Chasity shot back, opening her bag of popcorn.

Sidra flagged Chasity with her hand.

Alex put some popcorn in her mouth, then reached for the remote just as Malajia barged in.

"Chasity, where did you put the curling iron?" Malajia asked, voice hurried.

Chasity looked at her. "You mean *my* curling iron?"

Malajia rolled her eyes. "Who *else's* would it be?" she sniped. "You already know mine broke last week."

"Which is why I hid *mine* from you. You break shit too much," Chasity retorted.

"*No*, the shit I buy is just *cheap*," Malajia clarified.

Chasity shrugged. Malajia, annoyed by Chasity's blatant disregard for the need for her belongings, stomped her foot on the floor. "Stop being a bitch and tell me where the curlers are."

"Kiss my ass," Chasity threw back.

"Malajia, where are you going anyway?" Alex asked, trying to diffuse the confrontation. "I thought you were going to watch the movie with us."

"I never said I was gonna watch some corny ass movie," Malajia spat out, gesturing towards the television. "I told you earlier that I'm going to that party in the gym."

Alex fixed an annoyed gaze. "Why do you always have to have an attitude?" she questioned. "It was just a damn question."

Malajia put her hand up in Alex's direction and focused her attention on Sidra. "Anyway, Sidra can I use *your* curlers, since Chasity is being an asshole?"

Sidra laughed. "Girl, go ahead." She pointed to her nightstand. "Look in the bottom drawer."

Happy, Malajia darted over to the nightstand, grabbed the curlers, and hurried out of the room. "Enjoy your dry ass night," she threw over her shoulder.

Alex shook her head when the door slammed shut. "Now that surround sound is gone, let's start this movie," she suggested, hitting play.

As the opening credits played, Sidra opened her bag of popcorn. "I heard they have a new DJ tonight. He's supposed to be really good," she informed. "How much is it to get in?"

"Like three or four dollars, I think," Alex replied, tone dry.

It was silent as the images flashed on the screen. Chasity was frustrated. "Sidra, what the fuck do you have us watching?" she sneered, pointing to the screen.

Sidra put her head down and laughed. "I've never seen it, it's one of my mother's DVD's."

Seeing something silly play on the screen, Chasity stood up from her seat. "I can't do this. I'm going to that party," she announced.

"Girl, me too." Sidra jumped up and sat her popcorn bag on her microwave.

Alex looked up at both girls, hesitating momentarily as she watched them head for the door. Sitting up on her bed, she sighed loudly. "Me three."

Chapter 15

Jason practically skipped down the steps of the Math building, addressing fellow classmates on his way to the bottom of the concrete steps. "Hey ladies," he beamed to Chasity and Alex, who were waiting.

"Happy birthday, Jase," Alex smiled, giving him a pat on his arm.

He adjusted the book bag on his shoulder. "Thanks," he returned, enthused.

"Was I the first one in the group to wish you a happy birthday?" Alex wondered, adjusting the gold hoop earring in her ear.

Amused, Jason shook his head. "*She* was," he said, gesturing with his head to Chasity; she was the first person that Jason saw when he opened his eyes that morning.

Alex waved her hand. "Of *course* she was," she joked.

Ignoring Alex, Chasity turned to Jason. "Did you pass your Programing test?" she asked him.

"*Hell* yeah," Jason grinned. His birthday not only had his mood at an all-time high, but the fact that he found out in the beginning of his Programming 3 class that he'd passed a test that he was stressing over for the past week, only heightened his mood. "So I'm *extra* happy today."

"Good, 'cause I'm taking you out after my last class," Chasity announced, much to Jason's delight.

Alex pouted; she enjoyed spending birthdays as a group. She felt that it was important for one to be surrounded by friends on their special day. "Aww, I figured we could all hang out together for your birthday, Jase," she put in. "I mean, it's a big one for you, turning twenty-one and all."

Chasity shot her a glare, then nudged her. "Girl, stop blocking."

Jason chuckled at the salty look on Alex's face. He put his arm around Chasity. "I appreciate the thought Alex, but I'm just gonna chill with Chaz today."

"Well, suit yourself," Alex shrugged. "I'll still pick up dessert for you guys later."

"Alex please," Chasity sneered. "Nobody wants that *one* cookie that's sitting in that dusty ass jar at your job."

Alex couldn't help but laugh. "You make me so sick," she joked, pointing at Chasity.

Jason glanced at his watch. "I gotta get to English."

Waving, the girls made their way down the path as Jason headed off in the other direction. "You are so stingy with him," Alex teased.

"Shut up," Chasity hissed.

"I'm just messing with you, cranky," Alex placated, continuing her stride. "How's your Public Speaking class going?" she asked. "Mel told me you were practicing a speech yesterday."

Chasity shot Alex a sideways glance. "You already *know* that I'm miserable," she grimaced. "I hate speaking to *one* person, let alone a whole room *full* of them."

Alex giggled; she knew all too well. "Come on, it's not so bad," she said. "What's your assignment for this week?"

Chasity rolled her eyes. "We have to find *or* write a poem based on some dumb topic and recite it in front of the class... My face is irked."

Alex gave Chasity's shoulder a pat. "Aww, I'm sorry,"

she sympathized. "I had that class last year and I actually loved it."

"No surprise there. You *love* to run your damn mouth," Chasity sneered; Alex sucked her teeth. "You got a poem I can have?"

"No, I *don't*," Alex threw back. "Nice try."

Coming up on their destination, Alex spotted Emily walking slowly down the steps. Concern froze on her face. She grabbed Chasity's arm, halting both of their progress. "Do you see Emily? She looks terrible," she observed. "I wonder what's going on with her."

"Why don't you go ask her, Alex?" Chasity spat, glancing at her watch. "You know you want to."

"Let's go," Alex demanded, pulling Chasity along. The girls stood at the bottom of the stairs as Emily reached the last step.

Emily, already feeling off balance, stumbled and nearly bumped into the girls. "I'm sorry," she murmured, steadying herself. She placed her hand on top of her head.

"It's okay," Alex assured, smoothing hair from her face.

"I didn't see you," Emily claimed, voice low, slow.

Alex reached out and touched Emily's arm. "Sis, you look sick," she said, worried. "Do you have a cold?"

Emily sighed and shook her head. "I'm tired." It was the truth in more ways than one. Having just found out that she had failed yet another exam in one of her classes, she was both physically and mentally spent.

"Sweetie, maybe you should take a day and just rest," Alex urged. "You've been looking tired a *lot* lately. You can't push yourself too much."

Chasity listened as Alex gave Emily a lecture about taking care of herself, all the while she was giving Emily a once over. Something didn't seem right. Emily was disheveled. Her speech was low, slurred. Her focus was off, the sluggish way she moved—Chasity knew she'd seen this before.

"What's the matter with you?" Chasity abruptly asked, bringing Alex's pacifying words to a screeching halt.

Emily didn't make eye contact with Chasity, while Alex's head snapped towards her.

"Chaz, she just said that she's tired," Alex barked.

"Yes I *heard* that. *That's* not what I am asking about," Chasity threw back, eyes not leaving Emily. "Emily," she called. Emily hesitantly locked eyes with Chasity. "Are you drunk, or hungover?"

Emily's eyes widened slightly. *How did she know?* She panicked; she thought that she was doing a pretty good job of masking her hangover.

Alex became angry. "What kind of question is that to ask her, Chasity?" she fumed, hands on her hips. "You *know* she doesn't drink."

Chasity let out a loud, angry sigh. "You're mad at me, *why?*" she directed at Alex.

"Because you're being ignorant."

"I asked the girl, who has a fuckin' mouth of her *own,* a question," Chasity argued. "You don't see that something's off with her? *I* do."

Emily ran her hand along the back of her neck. Her head was pounding and she felt that she might vomit at any given moment. She was regretting finishing off another one of those Red Hurricanes last night. What she wouldn't give to crawl into her bed and sleep the rest of the week away.

Alex angrily flagged Chasity with her hand, then turned back to Emily. "Emily, can you *please* tell the Devil that you *haven't* been drinking and that you're just *tired*, like you *said*?"

Emily looked down at her hands "Um…I'm just tired," she reiterated after a moment.

"See?" Alex snapped at Chasity, who in turn glared daggers at her.

"Yeah, okay," Chasity hissed, walking off. She didn't have time to argue with Alex over being oblivious to Emily's issues.

Alex faced Emily once again. "Ignore her."

Emily nodded, then lowered her head. "I have to go," she muttered, walking away.

Sitting across from Chasity at an ice cream parlor, Jason grabbed a scoop of his sundae. "I wish they sold ice cream like this in the store," he mused, taking a bite.

Chasity grabbed some with her spoon. "You're real hype about this ice cream," she mocked.

Jason chuckled at her attitude. "You still mad you had to cook for me?"

Chasity shot him a glare. To her surprise, Jason elected not to go out to an expensive restaurant for his birthday as Chasity had planned on. Instead, he asked if she could just make him dinner. A request that she was none too happy about.

She pointed her spoon at him. "Do you have *any* idea the shit I went through to cook that damn dinner you wanted?" she hissed. "Between dealing with the grocery store, cooking in that small ass kitchen in the dorm, and having to damn near fight Malajia's greedy ass to keep her from stealing it…you're lucky I didn't throw it in the trash."

Jason found her irritation with the events amusing. "Well, I appreciate you for doing that," he placated.

"Yeah, yeah," Chasity muttered.

"That seafood alfredo you made was so damn good," he mused.

"Yeah, thanks."

The couple took several more bites of their shared sundae before Jason leaned back in his seat. "So, I talked to my dad earlier," he began. "He told me that he, my mom, and Kyle are coming down on Saturday…for a belated birthday visit."

Chasity nodded. "That's nice." She knew how much Jason's family meant to him and understood his excitement. "I hope you have a good time with them."

"I'm sure I *will*," he replied, then took a short pause. "Especially if *you* hang out with us."

Chasity stared at the hope glittering in his brown eyes. "Nah, not happening baby," she declined.

Jason sucked his teeth. "Why *not*?"

"You really want to know the answer to that question?" she challenged.

Jason narrowed his eyes at her. "Why *wouldn't* I?"

"I'm almost sure that your mother doesn't like me."

Her response shocked him, and it showed on his face. "What do you mean?"

"What I *said*," Chasity returned.

Jason rubbed his forehead with his hand, recalling on a few occasions where his mother made remarks and assumptions about Chasity when they were just friends. But ever since he told his parents about his new relationship, he hadn't heard one snide remark come from his mother's lips. "That's not true," he assured her.

Chasity leaned back in her seat. "Yeah, okay," she rebuffed. "Jase come on, I grew up not being liked. I think I can tell when it happens."

"Why do you think that?" he wondered. His mother never said anything to Chasity directly.

"Every time I've been over your house, I get this vibe from her," Chasity said. "It's like she wants to be *mean*, but can't, so she pretends to be nice."

Yep, it sounds like her, Jason admitted to himself. He leaned forward and grabbed hold of her hand. "Baby listen, any vibe that you got from my mom…I'm sorry for it," he stated. "But I promise you that you have nothing to worry about now."

Chasity just stared at him.

"I really want to spend the day with the most important people in my life, so…can you please come?"

"I reeeaaaallly don't want to," Chasity slowly put out.

Jason sighed. "Can you just think about it?" he pleaded.

Chasity let out a sigh, then nodded. Her response seemed to satisfy him; he went back to eating his ice cream. Chasity lost her appetite, electing to stick her spoon in it and lean back in her seat.

Chasity sat on her bed Saturday afternoon staring at the wall, leg bouncing in a nervous rhythm. She glanced at her watch and sighed. *Why did I agree to this?* Hearing a knock on the door, she closed her eyes and said a silent prayer. "It's open."

"Hey lady," Sidra announced, walking in.

Chasity turned around. "Thank God," she breathed.

Sidra chuckled. "Happy to see me, huh?"

"Somewhat."

Sidra studied Chasity's face. "What the matter? You look nauseas."

"I wish I *was*, so I wouldn't have to leave the damn room," she griped.

Sidra was confused. "Um, you want to tell me what's going on?" she pressed, sitting on the bed next to Chasity.

Chasity took a deep breath. "Jason's on his way over here…with his parents," she revealed.

Sidra shot her a confused look. "Um…o-kay," she wasn't sure what the nervousness was about.

"I'm supposed to be hanging out with them today." Upon returning from the parlor on Jason's birthday, Chasity did some thinking. After pondering his request for most of that evening, she decided to put aside her reservations and concede to his wishes. It didn't mean that she was happy with her decision.

A smile broke across Sidra's face. "He wants you to spend the day with him and his family?" she gushed. "Awww, that's so sweet."

"No 'awww, that's so sweet'," Chasity hissed.

Sidra giggled. "What's the problem?"

"I don't want to go," Chasity vented. "I'm just—I don't want to."

Sidra rolled her eyes to the ceiling and shook her head. "Chaz, stop whining and enjoy your time with your man and his family," she urged.

"I don't think his mom likes me," Chasity confided, pushing her curled hair over her shoulder.

"You don't think *anybody* likes you," Sidra pointed out.

"That's because most people *don't*," Chasity stated matter-of-factly

Sidra let out a quick sigh. "Sweetie, you're being paranoid," she dismissed. "Every time I've seen Ms. Nancy, she's been a sweetheart."

"To *you* maybe," Chasity grumbled, playing with the fabric from her bedspread.

Sidra was about to say something when a knock was heard. "Come in," Chasity called. Both girls stood up. They greeted Jason and his family as they entered the room.

Mrs. Adams stared at Chasity, folding her arms. "So young lady, I heard that you'll be hanging out with us today," she said.

"Um, yeah…looks like," Chasity returned, tone polite.

A noticeably phony smile appeared on Mrs. Adams's light brown face. "How nice," she sneered.

Chasity, noticing the snide response, just kept her composure.

Sidra smiled. "Well, I'll just leave you to your day." As she went to leave, she felt Chasity grab hold of her shirt. Sidra glanced at her. "What are you doing?" she whispered to her.

"Don't leave," Chasity whispered back.

"Oh stop it, you'll be fine," Sidra reassured, trying to pry Chasity's hand from her shirt. When Chasity wouldn't budge, Sidra tapped her hand. "You're wrinkling it," she hissed. Chasity reluctantly released the shirt and watched as Sidra walked out of the room.

While his family conversed amongst themselves, Jason walked over to Chasity and stood in front of her. "You look nervous," he said in a quiet aside. "Everything will be fine, don't worry."

Chasity wanted to tell Jason that she was backing out, she had every intention to. The vibe that she was getting from his mother wasn't something that she felt like being subjected to all afternoon. Nevertheless, she knew how important this was to Jason, and somewhere in the back of her mind, she hoped that Sidra was right, that she was just being paranoid.

"Okay," she returned.

"Is everybody hungry?" Mr. Adams asked, excited.

"*I* am," Jason's fourteen-year-old bother Kyle announced, hands tossed in the air.

Jason shook his head. "As always," he chortled.

Chapter 16

"Look, don't get the wrong idea about me calling you to go to lunch with me," Mark stated, playfully poking Malajia on the arm.

"Boy please," Malajia sneered, lips turned up. "You should count yourself lucky that I've graced you with my sexy ass presence."

Mark rolled his eyes. With Jason being off campus with Chasity and his family, and both Josh and David preoccupied, Mark called Malajia to have lunch with him. "Whatever," he ground out as they continued walking.

Malajia, hearing her phone ring, reached into her purse and grabbed it. Mark snatched it from her hand. "Boy! Give me my damn phone!" she hollered, trying to grab it back.

Mark laughed and held the phone out of her reach. "No calls when hanging with Mark," he teased. As Malajia continuously slapped his arm, Mark looked at the caller ID. "Who the hell is Booskie?" he mocked, hitting the answer button and placing the phone to his ear. "Hello, you've reached dumbass's phone."

"You play too damn much!" she wailed, snatching it from him. She gave Mark's arm, one last slap. "Jackass."

"Oh shut up and talk to Booskie," he laughed.

"Hey Ty," she breathed, fixing her hair with her hand. "Oh that was nobody. Just my idiot friend, Mark." The smile left her face and was replaced by a frown. "What are you talking about? ...No, he's just my friend... Are you *serious* right now? Hello? Hello?!"

Mark frowned as he watched Malajia angrily toss the phone back into her purse.

"Everything cool?" he asked.

"No, everything's *not* cool," she barked, jerking the purse strap on her shoulder. "My damn boyfriend just caught an attitude and hung up on me."

"Was he mad because I answered the phone?"

Malajia was seething; she couldn't believe that Tyrone had gotten so angry. "Judging by the way he questioned me about who the fuck you *were,* I'd say *so,*" she bit out.

"Damn, tell him to stop being a bitch," Mark scoffed. "I was only playing."

"That's the problem, you play too damn much," Malajia fumed, glaring at him. "How would *you* feel if a man answered *your* girlfriend's phone?"

Mark sighed as he rubbed the back of his neck. "Look...my bad, Mel," he apologized. "You want me to talk to him?"

"No, you've done *enough,*" Malajia sulked, shaking her head. Folding her arms to her chest, Malajia continued on to the cafeteria in silence.

Chasity poked at her chicken salad as she listened to the chatter around her. She had only been at the restaurant for an hour, but it seemed much longer.

"Chasity, did Jason ever tell you that he was the star football player on his pee wee football team?" Mr. Adams gushed.

Jason put his hand over his face and shook his head. "Dad, don't start," he grimaced.

"Oh, don't get all embarrassed son," Mr. Adams threw back, amused. "There is nothing wrong with me bragging."

"Bragging about *what*?" Jason asked, confused. "They barely let me on the field back then."

"They were afraid that you were taking all of the shine from the other players, that's all," Mr. Adams boasted.

Jason held a blank expression. "Dad, I couldn't catch the ball," he recalled, earning a deep laugh from his father. "You *know* you remember all those times I got hit with it."

Mr. Adams directed his gaze at Chasity. "He was great, don't let him tell you otherwise," he insisted.

Jason rolled his eyes to the ceiling. The doting he was used to, but it still embarrassed him at times.

Chasity rubbed Jason's back and giggled. "Yeah, I—"

"Jason, I heard that the school is going to be building a new stadium," Mrs. Adams cut in, interrupting Chasity.

Chasity found it hard to hide her frustration. That had been the third time that Mrs. Adams had cut her off while she was in the middle of talking. She dropped her hand from Jason's back, gritted her teeth, and glanced out of the window.

"Is that true, Jason?" Mrs. Adams asked, glancing at him.

Jason fixed a stern gaze upon his mother. He'd noticed what she was doing. "No Mom, that's *not* true," he replied, bite in his voice.

She shrugged. "Oh, well I must've heard that about *another* school," she chuckled, going back to the salad on her plate.

As Jason's father and brother began another conversation, Jason reached under the table and took hold of Chasity's hand, which was sitting on her lap, balled into a fist. Even though she didn't remove her eyes from the scenery outside, he hoped that the gesture was comforting to her.

"Jase, did you change your mind about wanting to go pro after college?" Kyle asked, reaching for his soda. He'd always looked up to his big brother for many things, his football skills were just one of them.

Jason shook his head, "No, I still don't want to go pro," he answered. "Football is paying for my education, that's all."

"I support that," Mr. Adams approved. "But… You'd look good in our home teams' jersey… I'm just saying."

"Not gonna happen, Dad," Jason chortled.

Mrs. Adams shot her husband a side-glance. "Stop pressuring him to play pro," she hissed, then directed a loving gaze at her eldest son. "I'm happy that you're concentrating on your education. You'll make an excellent software engineer."

"Thanks Mom," Jason replied. "Chaz and I *both* will end up in the computer field when we graduate," he added, giving Chasity a soft nudge, forcing her to bring her attention back to the table.

Mrs. Adams glanced down at her food, while her husband seemed intrigued.

"Oh really?" Mr. Adams inquired, enthused. "What field of computers are you into, Chasity?"

"Web design," Chasity answered. "I like the—"

"I mean, what is that exactly?" Mrs. Adams jumped in.

The table went silent.

Jason pinched the bridge of his nose with two fingers. *I swear to God Mom, chill the hell out!*

Chasity frowned slightly. "What is *what*, exactly?" she asked, trying to keep her rising temper and tone in check.

"Web design?" Mrs. Adams clarified. "I mean, it doesn't seem that hard. Not like being a *programmer* or *software engineer*, like my baby is going to be."

Chasity tilted her head slightly as she listened to the condescending words come out of Jason's mothers' mouth.

"I mean, what do you do, draw out designs and have a computer expert do all the work?"

Chasity stared at the woman. If it was anybody else, she would have thrown her plate at her, followed with a punch to the face. For Jason's sake, she knew she couldn't react, but she knew that she'd had enough.

When Jason opened his mouth to protest, Chasity put her hand on his shoulder to silence him.

"Yes, Ms. Nancy, that's *exactly* what I do. I draw pictures and let someone *smart* do the work," she sneered, a smile on her face. She pushed herself back from the table. "It was really nice seeing you all again, and thanks for lunch. I need to go."

Kyle's face fell as he watched Chasity pull her purse strap onto her shoulder. "Aww do you *have* to?" he pouted. "We're about to go to the arcade. Jase said you were good at the racing games."

Chasity smiled slightly. She thought Kyle was adorable. "Maybe next time."

As Jason stood up to allow her to move, his father said, "You don't have to leave, Chasity."

"No, I *do*," she returned, respectful.

Jason ignored the wide-eyed look from his mother as he guided Chasity to a corner. "Chaz, I—"

"I'm fine," she assured. "Go enjoy your time with them,"

"I'll talk to her," he promised. "Can you just stay?"

"No, I *can't*." She touched his arm. "Don't worry about it."

Jason sighed, running his hand over his head. He regretted asking her to hang with them in the first place. "Wait here, I'll tell them that I'm taking you back to campus."

"No you're not. I'm a big girl, I can get back on my own," Chasity declared. "That's what cabs are for." She smiled to ease Jason's guilt. "Go back over there," she ordered, before giving him a quick kiss. "Call me later."

Jason followed her progress to the door with his eyes. "Love you," he said to her as she walked out.

She glanced back inside. "Love you too."

Once the door closed, Jason clenched his jaw. Afraid of

what he might say to his mother if he went right back to the table, he made a beeline for the men's room.

Chasity walked to the edge of the sidewalk, retrieved her cell phone from her purse, then dialed a number. "Hey Alex...you still at work? ...When do you get off? ...I'm like ten minutes from your job, so I'm about to come there... No, I don't want you to make me a pizza... No, my lunch with them is over... Nope, just me...You gonna keep asking me questions or let me tell you when I see you? Thought so... See you soon."

Chasity sighed, then put her phone back into her purse. Just as she was about to head off, she heard Mrs. Adams's voice call her name.

Chasity spun around, a confused look on her face. *What the hell does she want?* "Yes?" she questioned, folding her arms.

"I figured since I won't be seeing you again before we head back home, I might as well have a little chat with you, one on one," Mrs. Adams said.

Chasity eyed the woman skeptically. "About?"

Mrs. Adams folded her arms. "Look, it's apparent that my son has some feelings for you—"

"Oh, *some*?" Chasity sneered, amused.

"Yes, *some*," Mrs. Adams bit back. "And as his mother, I just want to talk about where you see this relationship going."

Chasity was confused. After this woman had practically isolated her all day, even going so far as to insult her intelligence, Mrs. Adams had the nerve to want to have a relationship talk with her. "Isn't this something that you should be asking your *son*?" Chasity asked.

"No, I want to ask *you*." she hissed. "Because *you're* the one who had my baby all upset and not himself last year, so I want to know exactly what you're doing with him."

Chasity stared at her, disbelief written all over her face.

"Are you *serious* right now?"

"*Very.*" Mrs. Adams's tone had gotten nasty. "From what I know, he's been chasing after you since his freshman year and *now* suddenly you decide to be in a relationship with him?"

"What's your point Ms. Nancy?" Chasity spat out.

"I want to know what made you decide that *now* he's good enough for you."

Chasity's eyes widened. *Oh my God! Is she seriously asking me why I didn't fuckin' jump on him when I first met him?!* Chasity had formed every explicit word combination that she could think of in her head, and wanted more than anything to spew every single one of them.

Chasity stared daggers at the woman in front of her. She might have been able to control her mouth, but her face was another issue. "With all due respect, *ma'am*, I'm not going to stand here and discuss details about *my* relationship with *your* son with *you*," she stated matter-of-factly.

Mrs. Adams gritted her teeth as she shook her head. "I *knew* you were bad news when I first met you last year," she sneered. Chasity rolled her eyed and glanced away. "That damn attitude."

Chasity looked back at the woman; dead in her face. "Well, you seem to have formed an opinion about me based of off things you know *nothing* about. And you know what, that's fine, you're entitled," Chasity said. "Just like *I'm* entitled to not have to stand here and talk to you anymore."

Mrs. Adams's eyes flashed as Chasity went to leave. "No, you're going to listen—"

"Enjoy the rest of your day," Chasity interrupted, sauntering away.

Jason hit the punching bag over and over until he felt pain radiating up his arms. He paused to shake the feeling free for a moment, before striking the bag again.

The conversation that he had had with his mother before

his family left earlier that evening had Jason's mood at a low.

I can't believe she acted like that, he fumed, giving the bag another one-two punch. Having had words with his mother over her treatment of Chasity, Jason learned of her little pop-up conversation with Chasity while he was cooling off in the men's room. He could only imagine how upset Chasity had been. When he called Chasity and she didn't answer, that only confirmed his suspicions.

Delivering one last punch to the massive bag, Jason removed his gloves and headed over to the bench. He glanced up as Mark approached.

"Taking advantage of the empty gym, huh?" Mark quibbled, sitting on the bench next to him.

Jason sighed. "I *was*."

Mark made a face. "Ain't nobody tryna bother you, dawg," he barked.

"Man, calm your ass down. I was joking," Jason returned, reaching for his water bottle.

"Oh a'ight," Mark muttered, adjusting the towel around his neck. "Your family rolled out?"

Jason wiped his face with his towel. "Yep," he grunted.

Mark nodded. "I figured Chaz would still be with you, but I just saw her walking back from the campus fast food joint with the other girls," he informed.

Jason concentrated on drinking the water from his bottle as Mark took a long pause.

"Yo, have you met Tyrone?" Mark asked out of nowhere.

"*Who?*"

"Mel's dude," Mark clarified.

Jason shook his head. "No."

Mark scratched his head. "Me neither," he mumbled. "Why?"

Mark paused for a moment as he thought back to Malajia's mood after she'd been chewed out by the guy. Although hours had passed, and Malajia seemed to have forgotten about it, he hadn't. Deciding not to harp on the subject, he quickly shook his head. "Just wondering," he replied, standing up. "I'm about to go hit these weights."

"Have fun," Jason threw out as Mark nodded and walked off, leaving him to his thoughts.

"Alex, quit offering me those nasty ass wing dings!" Malajia hollered, standing in front of Alex and Sidra's door.

Alex stuck her key in and acknowledged Malajia with a frown, "What's the damn attitude for?" she barked.

"'Cause, that's the fourth time that you asked me if I wanted some," Malajia threw back as Alex pushed the door open, allowing her to storm through.

Alex looked confused as she sat her container of fried chicken wings on her dresser. "I only asked you *once*," she pointed out. They had just gotten back from the campus fast food diner, and Alex was looking forward to enjoying her meal while hanging with the girls. She didn't expect to get into an argument with Malajia over it.

Sidra removed her purse and sat it on her bed, laughing. "Malajia, you're always exaggerating," she said. "The girl asked you *one* time if you wanted some."

Malajia sucked her teeth. "So what," she admitted, directing her attention to Alex. "Alex, you know those are the same wings that were in the cafeteria *last* night, and you offering them to people all hype."

Chasity sat on a chair and listened to the pointless argument. Although she found it amusing, it was the furthest thing from her mind. She was focused on the text messages that she was sending.

"*First* of all, those aren't the same wings from the cafeteria," Alex ground out, pointing to the container.

"*Yes*, they are," Malajia maintained. "One of 'em had a bite mark in it."

Alex dismissed her with a wave of her hand. "Something is wrong with you," she resolved. "And I won't offer your ungrateful butt another thing, *that's* for sure."

Malajia watched as Alex opened the container and took a wing out. "How you mad at me 'cause I don't want them old ass wing dings?" she argued.

"I'm not even mad!" Alex snapped. She was over Malajia's nit-picking.

Chasity stood up from her seat and headed for the door. Malajia pointed to Alex, while looking at Chasity. "Why she got an attitude over *wings* though?" Malajia pestered.

Alex tossed her hands in the air in frustration.

Chasity spun around, confused. "What?" she ground out. "Malajia, leave that girl alone."

"I didn't say anything else *about* the damn wings!" Alex yelled. "Malajia, you're gonna have to leave if you don't shut up."

Chasity walked out of the room, shaking her head.

Sidra pointed to a chair, trying to keep from breaking out into another fit of laughter. "Mel, chill out and have a seat," she ordered, voice calm. "You're upsetting my roommate."

Malajia folded her arms in a huff and sat down on the chair. "I'll spit on those dry ass wings," she mumbled.

Alex pointed to the door. "Get out!"

Chasity sat on a bench outside of her dorm and looked at her phone. Not more than a minute later, Jason sat down beside her.

"Thanks for meeting me," he said, setting his gym bag on the ground.

"Sure," she replied, putting her phone into the pocket of her jacket. "My ringer was off earlier, that's why I didn't answer when you called."

Jason nodded. That was a relief to him; originally he had thought that she had ignored his call. When he saw a text from her while he was finishing up his work out, he immediately texted back, asking her to come out so they could talk.

"So...about what happened earlier—"

"Jason, it's okay," Chasity immediately cut in. This wasn't something that she wanted to harp on.

"It's *not* okay," Jason maintained, voice stern. "It's *not* okay that my mother kept interrupting you, it's *not* okay that she was throwing digs at you, and it's *not* okay what she said to you when you tried to leave."

Chasity looked at him. "She told you about that?" she asked, tone even.

"Yep," Jason nodded. "One thing about her, she's honest about what she does. Even if it *is* completely wrong."

"What did you say to her?" Chasity asked, curious

"That she was out of line and needs to apologize to you."

Chasity folded her arms and leaned back in the seat. "Yeah, I don't see that happening," she ground out.

Jason shook his head. "Yeah well, she *needs* to," he muttered. "I love my mom, but I don't like that shit."

"She thinks I'm bad for you."

"I don't care *what* she thinks," he stood firm.

"I know you don't." Chasity sighed, adjusting the watch on her wrist.

Jason turned and faced her. "Chaz, I don't want you to feel like you have to prove anything to her," he said. "Because you *don't*."

"Okay."

Jason put his arm around her and drew her close. "She'll just have to get over it," he bit out.

Chasity leaned her head on Jason's shoulder as they enjoyed the night air. "At least your dad and brother like me," Chasity chortled after a moment of silence.

Jason chuckled, nodding in agreement. "Oh, they *love* you."

"Yeah, winning over guys was never my problem," she joked.

"Funny," Jason returned, sarcastic.

Chasity giggled.

Chapter 17

Sidra searched through organized piles of bracelets, rings, and necklaces in her glass jewelry box on her dresser. "Where the hell *is* it?" she muttered to herself, closing the box.

Scratching her head, she stepped away from the dresser and sat on her bed. Having a thought, she headed into the bathroom. Sidra took a moment to glance around the shared space. *Still neat. I must have gotten through to them.* Searching a small drawer under the sink counter, she heard the door open.

Great, she thought, seeing Dee walk into the bathroom, makeup bag in hand. "Sidra," she bit out.

"Deidre," Sidra returned, just as much bite in her voice. Ever since her last confrontation about the messy bathroom, Sidra had only been on one word speaking terms with Dee. That didn't faze Sidra; she wasn't looking to be friends with Dee. As long as the bathroom was neat, Dee nor her roommate had to speak.

Dee began applying makeup to her glowing dark skin in silence while Sidra continued digging through the drawer. Dee glanced at her. "Looking for something?"

Sidra closed the drawer and smoothed her white blouse with her hands. "Yes, a ring," she answered.

"Hmm," Dee shrugged. "Hope you find it."

"Thanks," Sidra threw over her shoulder, walking out of the bathroom.

Applying liner to her eyes, Dee rolled her eyes. "Bitch," she hissed to herself as the door closed.

Sidra tossed her hands in the air in frustration. "Where the hell is my damn ring?" she fussed to an empty room. The heart-shaped crystal ring was one of her favorites. Glancing at her watch, she let out a huff, "Great, now I'm about to be late," she complained. She slipped on her grey pumps, grabbed her matching jacket, and book bag from her bed, then headed for the door.

Upon exiting her room, Sidra was startled when her name was called in an aggressive manner. She spun around, coming face to face with the culprit. "Why are you yelling my name like that, Dominique?" she barked.

Sidra's neighbor and Dee's roommate Dominque stormed over to her. "You *still* talking shit, Sidra?" she spat out.

Sidra tossed her book bag and jacket to the floor. "I've warned you *before* about getting in my damn face."

Dominique sucked her teeth.

"What shit did you hear *this* time?" Sidra questioned. "More stuff about the bathroom?" she goaded when Dominique didn't respond. "If so, then yes, I said it. You and your roommate are nasty."

"I don't give a shit about you whining over that bathroom," Dominique bit out. "*I'm* not even the one who's leaving shit in there, that's *Dee*."

"Then what the hell is this *about*?" Sidra fumed. She was already late for class and had no time for pointless arguments.

"You called me an ugly, ghetto trash bag," Dominque accused. "And said that my man is only with me 'cause I give good head."

Sidra's mouth fell open. "What? I *never* said that shit!" she denied. "I don't give a shit about what you do with your damn boyfriend. I didn't even need to *hear* that shit."

"Yes, you did!" Dominique pointed her finger in Sidra's face. "I swear I'll beat—"

"You better get that finger out of my face," Sidra warned.

Dominque went to say something, when Chasity and Malajia walked out of their room. "Sid, we heard you yell. What's going on?" Malajia charged, heading over and standing next to Sidra.

Sidra didn't take her eyes off Dominque, who put her finger down. "This *thing* wants to fight me."

"Oh *does* she?" Chasity challenged, standing on the other side of Sidra. "You really want this problem, Dominque?"

"Dom, you ain't done nothing to me personally," Malajia put out, shaking her hand in Dominque's direction. "But Sidra is my girl, so if I gotta drop you, I *will*."

Dominque folded her arms and stared Sidra down. "Oh, so you need *backup*?" she taunted.

"Trust me, I *don't*," Sidra boasted.

Dominque glanced back and forth between the three girls, who looked like they could pounce at any moment. "Whatever, just keep my damn name out your mouth."

"I already *told* you, I don't talk about you, so stay out my face," Sidra spat.

"You *heard* what I said," Dominique threw over her shoulder as she stomped off.

"Yeah you *better* go!" Malajia yelled after her.

Chasity turned to Sidra. "You okay?"

"No, I'm late for class," Sidra fussed, retrieving her belongings from the floor.

"What was that all about?" Malajia asked, adjusting an earring in her ear.

Sidra slung the bag on her shoulder. "She keeps saying that I talk about her, but I'm *not*."

"You don't even *talk to* the girl," Malajia pointed out, confused.

"I *know*," Sidra agreed. "Where would she get that shit from?"

"Well she's hearing it from *some*where," Chasity concluded, rubbing her lower back with her hands. "Watch that sneaky ass roommate of hers."

Malajia shot Chasity a glance, "Dee?" she asked.

"Dee, Deidre, Dumbass, *whatever* the girls name is," Chasity hissed, then walked back to her room.

"All right girl, call me if you want me to trip one of them heffas, or something," Malajia joked.

Sidra laughed as she nudged her. "Will do."

Malajia stuffed some items into an overnight bag, then headed over to her dresser for some personal items. Realizing that she had too many, she placed some back. "Girl, you don't need all these damn lotions," she said to herself. The door opened and she glanced behind her. "Hey sunshine," she beamed to Chasity.

Chasity walked over to her desk and pulled the chair out. "What are *you* so cheerful for?"

Malajia narrowed her eyes at Chasity's tone, while placing a bottle of lotion into her bag. "Didn't you just leave Jason's?"

"Yeah?" Chasity was confused by the question.

"Then you shouldn't have that attitude," Malajia jeered.

Chasity chuckled as she sat down. "I *don't* have an attitude," she assured, turning her laptop on.

"Yeah well, even if you *did*, I won't be here to deal with it," Malajia returned, spraying herself with perfume.

"Why? You moving out?" Chasity asked, tone dry as she focused on her screen.

"*No*." Malajia made a face. "You're stuck with me as your roommate, so get over it."

Chasity flagged her with her hand. Having to finish a

paper, Chasity left Jason's earlier than she wanted to. If Malajia's going out for a while gave her quiet, she welcomed it.

Malajia sat on the bed and stared at Chasity's back. "So um…I'm spending the night at Tyrone's."

Chasity spun around in her seat and flashed a skeptical glance her way. "Oh, okay."

Malajia rolled her eyes. "What?" she hissed.

"I didn't say anything." Chasity pointed out.

"You forget, I *know* you," Malajia reminded. "That look, and that fake response? What do you want to say?" She folded her arms. Malajia already knew that once she revealed her plans to Chasity, she would receive a less than enthused reaction.

"Malajia, I have work to do," Chasity replied, voice tired. "And you already know that you don't want to hear *anything* that I have to say about him, so…have fun."

Malajia rolled her eyes when she heard a notification on her phone. Reaching for it, she sucked her teeth. "I'm not going there to sleep with him, if *that's* what you're implying," she snarled, checking her message.

"I didn't imply *anything*," Chasity returned, going back to her work.

"I know what you're thinking," Malajia ground out, tossing the phone into her bag. "He just wants to spend time with me," she insisted. "He already knows that I'm not ready for sex."

"Uh huh," Chasity muttered. "Did you tell *him* that?"

"He *knows*," Malajia spat, grabbing her bag from the bed and standing up. "Couples spend nights together even when they're *not* sleeping together."

"Okay," Chasity shrugged.

Malajia shook her head. "Whatever," she grumbled under her breath. "He's downstairs, I gotta go," she threw over her shoulder, walking out of the room. Malajia punctuated her departure with a sharp slam of the door.

Chasity shook her head as she hit the keys with her fingers. "Be careful, stupid," she sighed.

The loud ringtone of Jason's phone stirred him out of his deep slumber. Rolling over towards his nightstand, he glanced at the clock. *Three in the damn morning.* It had taken him forever to get to sleep after finishing up the loads of homework for three of his five classes.

Grabbing the cell phone, Jason groaned. Focusing, he noticed that his home number was flashing across the screen. Letting out a sigh, he answered. "Hello?" his voice was tired.

Jason frowned when he heard the panicked voice on the other end. He sat up in bed. "Wait, Mom… Mom, calm down," he urged, turning his light on. "What happened?" Jason's eyes widened. "Wait, *what*?"

Chasity, still sitting at her desk, put her head down and ran her hands through her hair. *I fuckin' hate writing papers*, she fumed to herself. She'd been trying to get through her ten-page paper ever since Malajia left hours ago. If she could've thrown her laptop and the professor who assigned the paper out of the window, she would.

Jerking her head back up, Chasity hit the laptop screen with her hand. "Who *gives* a fuck about overpopulation in some damn country that I *don't* live in?" she barked of the topic that she was assigned. "Fuckin' waste of time." She pushed herself away from the desk, intending on getting into bed.

She was confused when she heard a knock at the door. Chasity glanced at the clock. *Three fifteen? Who the hell wants to get cussed out this early?* she thought, walking to the door. The scowl on her face changed to surprise when she saw Jason standing there, clad in sweatpants and a sweatshirt, a blank expression on his face.

"Jason?" she questioned, moving aside to let him in.

"What are you doing here? Why are you up?"

Jason didn't say a word, he just stared at her.

Chasity studied him. He looked like he wanted to speak, but couldn't. "What's wrong with you?" she asked, point-blank.

Jason took a long breath. "My dad is in the hospital," he revealed, tone somber.

Chasity was shocked. Jason had just spoken to his father while she was over his place earlier that day. "What? Why? What happened?" she sputtered, grabbing his arm and directing him to sit down on her bed.

Jason ran his hands over his head and down his face. "My mother said that he ha—" he took a pause as he fought to maintain his composure. "He had a h—heart attack."

Chasity sat down next to him and rubbed his shoulder. "I'm sorry Jason," she sympathized.

"I just talked to him earlier and he was fine, I don't understand," he stammered. Feeling tears prick the back of his eyes, he rubbed them in an effort to keep them in.

Chasity, seeing the fear in him, put her arms around him and pulled him to her. She knew how much his father meant to him. "He's going to be fine, don't worry," she pacified. Chasity was trying to stay calm for him, but inside, she wasn't sure if the words that she spoke would reign true.

"He's in the emergency room," Jason said. "Mom said he's not conscious... I have to go see him." He stood up. "I can't stay here while he's lying in a hospital bed."

"I understand," Chasity said to him. "You want me to take you home?"

Jason looked at her. "I can't ask you to do that," he said. "I was going to take the train."

Chasity stood up. "You didn't ask me, I'm offering," she pointed out, heading to her closet. "We can leave now."

Jason watched as Chasity grabbed her purse and jacket. He was amazed at her generosity. He could only imagine how tired she was, and to offer to drive four hours to get him to his father's side, only made his adoration for her grow. "Chasity I—"

"It'll be okay," she assured him, holding her hand out. "Come on, let's go."

He grabbed her hand and held it. "Thank you," he sighed.

Malajia stormed into her room the next morning and threw her overnight bag against the wall. "Stupid bastard!" she vented, kicking out of her shoes and slamming them into her closet door. Flopping down on her bed, she wiped the tears that had fallen down her cheeks.

After the night that she had with Tyrone, she was seething. On top of that, she missed her first class of the day and as much as she loathed Foreign Politics, she didn't want to miss any of the notes, especially with midterms coming up.

She heard her phone ring. Snatching it out of her bag, Malajia jerked it to her ear. "What?" she snarled.

"You left your jacket in my car," Tyrone barked.

"Fuck that jacket," Malajia spat out.

"Yo, you better calm your dramatic ass down," Tyrone scolded.

Malajia sat there in shock. "*Dramatic?*" she fumed. "After how you treated me last night because I refused to sleep with you, you want to call me dramatic? Fuck you."

"Time out, *you* got all defensive," he argued.

"After *you* caught a damn attitude!" Malajia yelled. She couldn't believe that he was placing the blame on her for their argument. When she made herself comfortable in Tyrone's bed the previous evening, she thought nothing of him being overly affectionate towards her while they watched a movie. She welcomed the attention, even welcoming his passionate kisses. But it wasn't until Tyrone's hand went up her skirt that she brought their make out session to an abrupt stop. "All I said was that I wasn't ready for that, and your whole damn attitude changed."

"Damn right," he admitted, angry. "You're my woman now; why *wouldn't* I expect us to have sex? This is not the first date Malajia. We've been together for almost two months now. There's no reason why we shouldn't be having sex."

Malajia's mouth fell open. She was shocked and livid at what was coming out of his mouth. He was being such a jerk about it. "I'm not *ready*, you asshole," she maintained, voice filled with fury.

"How long are you gonna play that virgin card Malajia?" Tyrone hissed after a moment of strained silence.

Malajia gasped.

"How long am I supposed to wait? A week, a month, a *year*? How long are you gonna play with me?"

Malajia pulled the phone from her ear and stared at it, breathing heavy. She wished that he was standing in front of her so she could shove her phone down his throat. He always had a way of making her feel like she was the worst person in the world. She placed her phone back. "Go to hell," she hurled, then abruptly ended the call before he could get another word out. She held the phone in her hand, staring at the wall in front of her. Too angry to cry, she just sat in silence.

Emily sat up in bed, groggy. Running her hand through her disheveled hair, she glanced at the clock on her desk and did a double take. "Oh my God!" she exclaimed, jumping out of bed. She had slept through her alarms; she was about to be late for class.

Emily readied herself within record time and ran out of her apartment. She jogged all the way to the English building and up to her classroom door, just in time to see the English Comprehension professor shut the door in her face.

"No, no please," she begged, knocking on the door.

The professor opened the door and regarded Emily with

a stern look. "Miss Harris, you're late,"

"I know Dr. Bella, and I'm so sorry." Emily was practically in tears.

"You already know the rules, at five minutes after, I shut the door. Especially on the days when I'm giving an exam."

Emily put her hand on her head. *Crap, I forgot about the test!* "Dr. Bella, please—"

"No exceptions," Dr. Bella maintained, unfazed by Emily's emotional state.

Emily wanted to break down in tears when she watched the woman close the door once more. Emily was beside herself. That had been the second class that she missed that week. With her grades being what they were, she couldn't afford to miss *any*, let alone a test. Sighing, Emily turned and slowly walked away.

Emily let the tears flow as she reached her room. Dropping her books to the floor, she staggered over to her bed and fell on to it. Curling into the fetal position, Emily laid there, staring at the wall in front of her. *I'm going to fail.* Those words boomed through Emily's head as she curled her position more. Hearing her phone ring didn't even budge her. "I already know who that is," she said to herself, voice low and monotone.

When the machine turned on and she heard her mother's voice, Emily jumped up, grabbed the cordless phone and its machine holder from her nightstand, and threw it across the room. She watched as the phone hit the wall, breaking. She grabbed one of her pillows, buried her face in it, and screamed.

Chapter 18

Malajia closed her textbook and pushed it to the floor. Still reeling from her argument with Tyrone earlier that morning, Malajia was finding it difficult to concentrate on her studies. She laid her head to her pillow and closed her eyes, hoping to wake up with Tyrone no longer on her mind.

Not more than a few seconds later, Malajia's eyes popped back open. She sat up. *I need to talk,* she thought. "Where the hell is Chasity?" she asked aloud. She grabbed her cell phone and looked at the time. *Four o'clock. She would've at least stopped in by now. I haven't seen her ass all day.* Malajia quickly dialed Chasity's number.

"Hello?" Chasity answered after the fourth ring.

"Bitch, where the hell are you?" Malajia spat out.

Chasity smirked at her roommates' tone. "I'm in Philly,"

Malajia was confused. "*Philly*? What the hell are you doing *there*?"

"Jason's dad is in the hospital," Chasity revealed, much to Malajia's shock. "I drove him here."

Malajia held her hand on her chest, forgetting about her own problems. "Oh wow," she breathed, worried. "Is he gonna be all right?"

Chasity sighed as she rubbed the back of her neck. "I honestly don't know," she answered. "I don't know any details. Jason and his family have been in there since we got here."

"Well, how is Jase holding up?"

Chasity glanced back at the emergency room doors. "As well as he possibly *can* right now."

"Yeah, I hear you," Malajia replied, somber. "Do the others know?"

"No, we haven't spoken to anybody since we left."

"Want me to let them know what's going on?" Malajia asked.

"Yeah."

Malajia nodded, even though Chasity couldn't see her. "I'll let them know," she promised. She took a brief pause. "So, how is his mom acting towards you?" Malajia knew of Mrs. Adams's treatment of Chasity, since Chasity vented to her the night of the visit.

"I haven't seen her," Chasity answered, then rolled her eyes a second later. "Damn, spoke too soon," she mumbled to Malajia when she heard Mrs. Adams call her name. "I gotta go."

"Keep me posted," Malajia ordered.

"Yeah," Chasity muttered, then ended the call. She spun around to find Mrs. Adams approaching. Feeling sympathy for the woman because of her husband's condition, Chasity successfully held her ill feelings. "Hi."

Mrs. Adams folded her arms. "Hello," she returned. "Listen, I wanted to express my gratitude for you bringing my son here."

"Okay," Chasity replied, trying to feel her out.

"So...thanks for that," she added.

"You're welcome."

Mrs. Adams glanced back at the doors, then faced Chasity once more. "So, again, thanks for bringing my son home... You can leave now."

Chasity stared at her, slowly shaking her head. *And there it is.* "Um...I'm not leaving," she declared.

Mrs. Adams glared daggers at her. *Who the hell does this*

girl think she is? "What do you *mean*, you're not leaving?" she hissed.

"Exactly what I *said*," Chasity maintained. "I'm not going anywhere until I know that Jason is okay."

"He's not going to be *okay* anytime *soon*," Mrs. Adams fumed. "His father had a heart attack."

"Exactly, so that means that unless *he* tells me to leave, I'm not *going* to."

"There is *no need* for you to be here!"

"Ms. Nancy, I'm not bothering you," Chasity pointed out, exasperated. "I've been in this waiting room since I got here. I'm not trying to be up under anybody. I'm just here to support Jason. If you weren't out—" Chasity cut her words short; she was on the verge of going too far.

"If I weren't *what*?" Mrs. Adams goaded. "What little smart assed thing were you going to say to me? Huh?"

"Not a thing," Chasity spat out.

Mrs. Adams stood close to Chasity's face and pointed her finger. Chasity glanced at her finger, then back to her face. "Look, my son has his family here," she sniped. "He doesn't need *you*. So just go—"

"Mom," Jason barked.

Both women turned around to see Jason approaching. "Jason," Mrs. Adams stammered, eyes wide.

Jason fixed an angry gaze on his mother before turning to Chasity. "Can you excuse us for a minute?"

"Gladly," Chasity complied, walking away.

Jason followed Chasity departure for a moment, then focused his attention back to his mother, "What's wrong with you?" he charged.

She put her hand up. "Now look—"

"Instead of being in the room with Dad, finding out what the doctors are saying, you're out here harassing my girlfriend?" Jason was furious. "And you think that's okay?"

She frowned at him. "Don't be disrespectful."

"I'm *not* being disrespectful."

"You *are*," she stood firm. "I *know* what the damn

doctors said. I was with him even before *you* got here."

Jason ran his hand over his head. "That's not the point," he argued. "Leave Chasity alone," he ordered, voice stern. "She's here for *me*, *not* you."

Mrs. Adams grabbed Jason's arm as he went to walk away. "Jase, wait a minute."

He spun around. "Mom, I love you and I know that you're upset," he put out. "We *all* are. But that doesn't give you the right to do what you're doing... Stop."

Mrs. Adams stood, stunned as her son pulled away from her and walked off.

Chasity sat on one of the cushy chairs in the hospital lobby, fiddling with her hands. She was on edge from the words that she had had with Jason's mother. She wondered if her being there was doing more harm than good. She glanced over when Jason sat next to her.

"You okay?" she asked.

"No, not really," he answered honestly.

Chasity held her gaze. "You want me to leave?"

"Absolutely not."

She sighed. "Look, I don't want to cause problems between you and your mom," Chasity said. "I mean, your dad seems to be in pretty bad shape, and he doesn't need that tension around him."

"*You* didn't cause that, *she* did," Jason stated bluntly.

"I know, but still—"

"Look Chaz," he cut in. "My mother doesn't get to dictate who I'm with. I'm a grown ass man. If she doesn't like it, then she can stay away from me."

Chasity put her hand on his leg. "You don't mean that."

"Yes, I do."

"Okay," she relented, putting her hand up in surrender. She took a deep breath. "Look, I'm gonna go—"

"Chasity, please don't go. I need you here," Jason pleaded.

Chasity shot him a sympathetic look. If she could've taken away his pain right then and there, she would've. "I'm not leaving," she promised, touching his face. "I'm just going to go get us something to eat."

He managed a smile. With everything that was going on, it didn't dawn on him until just then that he hadn't eaten all day. "Thanks, I guess that's a good idea," he agreed. "I'm starting to feel light-headed."

She kissed him on his cheek then stood up. "I'll be back," she assured, walking away.

"Thanks baby," he called after her. She turned around. "For everything."

Chasity smiled and nodded, before continuing on her way.

"Man, that's rough," Mark commented. "Damn, Jason's dad is cool peoples."

"I know," Josh added. "I hope he pulls through."

Having found out from Malajia moments prior about what she learned about Jason's father, the gang sat in Paradise Terrace's lobby, somber.

"Malajia, has Chasity called you back with any updates?" Sidra asked.

"No, not yet," Malajia answered, as she played in her hair with her hand.

"Well, she's probably waiting until she has more concrete information," David pointed out. "I'm sure Jason is in no mood to talk. I know how that is."

Sidra reached over and patted David on the shoulder. "We know sweetie," she sympathized.

David patted her hand and looked at her. "It's okay," he mouthed, a small smile on his face.

Alex leaned back in her seat and sighed. "Has anybody told Em?"

"I tried calling, but the phone just keeps ringing," Malajia ground out. "She probably wouldn't be over here *anyway*. The girl acts like she barely knows us nowadays."

"Mel, let's just focus on Jason, okay?" Sidra advised, voice calm.

Malajia just nodded in agreement.

"I can't imagine what he's going through," Alex said, ignoring Malajia's comment about Emily. While she agreed with her about Emily's behavior, she knew this was not the time to discuss it. Alex looked at Malajia. "Did Chaz say when they were coming back?"

"No, she didn't," Malajia answered, tone dry. "I'm guessing Jason will be there until his dad is out of the woods."

"Well did she say when *she's* coming back?" Alex pressed.

Malajia let out a loud huff. "No Alex, damn!" she exploded, startling the group with her loudness.

Alex was stunned. "What is your problem?" she hurled back.

"You all hype asking me ten thousand damn questions and shit," Malajia fussed, waving her hands. "You *just* heard me tell Sidra that I don't have any updates...I only talked to Chaz *once*, for a few minutes."

Alex glared at her. "That was uncalled for," she chided. "I'm just concerned."

Malajia flagged Alex with her hand. Truth was, although Alex's many questions were irritating to Malajia, that wasn't the reason for her bad mood. Besides being worried about her friend, she was still upset about Tyrone. She needed to vent, but the person she normally did that with was at Jason's side, hours away.

"We should try to do something nice for Jase," Mark suggested, trying for once to be the one to cut an impending argument short.

Sidra straightened up in her seat. "Yeah, we could send a card and some flowers," she suggested.

"Sending flowers reminds me of a funeral," Malajia pointed out.

"Good point," Sidra agreed, thinking. "Well, we can get a nice basket with fruit and muffins or something. We can have it delivered to his parents' house."

"That's cool, food is always good," Mark approved. "I'll even put to it," he joked.

"Like you had a damn *choice*," Malajia muttered.

Mark rolled his eyes at Malajia, but decided not to argue. "When he gets back, we should take him out and do something fun."

"I like that," Alex beamed.

Malajia cleared her throat as she looked at a message on her phone. "Chaz just texted me," she announced. "She said that she's at her house in West Chester. Jason is still at the hospital with his family and that his father might need surgery."

"Oh no," Alex panicked. She could only imagine the desperation that the family felt. "We should try calling Jase now. He needs to know that we're all here for him."

"Let's do it," David agreed.

As Malajia began to dial Jason's number, Alex leaned in close to her. "Do you have speaker so that he can hear us all?"

Mark looked confused. "Why *wouldn't* she?" he asked.

Alex shrugged and caught Malajia staring at her, angry. "What did I say *now*?" she exclaimed.

"Just 'cause *your* dollar store flip phone don't have the speaker button, doesn't mean that everyone *else's* doesn't," Malajia snapped, slapping the arm of the couch with her hand. "And *why* are you so close to my damn face?"

"Just shut up and make the call," Alex commanded.

Jason sat in the quiet waiting room with his head in his hands. Hearing the doctors confirm that his father would need to have cardiac surgery had Jason's head filled with worry. Seeing his mother and brother break down was almost too much for him to take.

Leaning back in his seat, staring at the cold, white wall in front of him, he regretted sending Chasity home to sleep. He needed her presence, but knew it would be selfish of him to keep her there in uncomfortable conditions. The vibration of his cell phone stirred him.

Recognizing the number, he put the phone to his ear.

"Hey Mel," he tiredly answered.

"Hey Jason," Malajia greeted in unison with the others.

Jason chuckled at the sound of his friends loud, animated voices. "How's it going?"

"Don't worry about us, how are *you*?" Alex returned, voice caring.

Jason rubbed his eyes, "I'm okay."

"How's your dad doing?" David asked, concerned.

Jason pinched the bridge of his nose and sighed. "Um…he has to have surgery tomorrow."

"Damn man, sorry to hear that," Mark commiserated. "He'll pull through it. You gotta believe that."

"Yeah, I know," Jason returned. As much as Jason wanted to believe that, he had to admit that he was unsure.

"Jase man, we're not gonna hold you up," Josh cut in. "We just wanted to let you know that you and your family are in our prayers."

"Look at Josh tryna be all profound," Mark teased.

"Look at *you* knowing what profound *means*," Malajia joked, causing the others to laugh.

"Right!" Alex chimed in, laughing.

"Shut up," Mark threw back.

Jason shook his head and laughed, "Y'all are crazy."

"All right Jase, we love you. We'll talk to you later," Sidra said.

"Love you guys too. See you," he replied.

"Bye," they replied in unison. Jason hung up the phone, and for a moment, smiled to himself.

Chasity ran her hand through her hair as she sat in the

den of her West Chester home, gazing out the window. With her mind in another space, she didn't hear the door open, nor the footsteps coming closer.

"Chasity."

Chasity jumped and turned around to find her aunt Trisha standing there. "Damn it," she hissed, annoyed that she was startled.

Trisha tied the belt on her plush white robe and sat on the ottoman in front of Chasity. "Sweetie, it's one in the morning; what are you still doing up?"

"I can't sleep," Chasity declared.

"I figured that," Trisha chortled. She was pleasantly surprised when Chasity arrived at their home a few hours prior. She hadn't seen her niece since she left for school after winter break. Her happiness changed to concern once she learned the reason for Chasity's impromptu visit. "How's Jason's father?" she asked.

Chasity sighed. "He has to have surgery in the morning," she said, voice tired. "I feel like I need to be there."

"You *will* be, in the morning," Trisha assured, putting her hand on Chasity's arm. "But you couldn't sleep there and Jason wouldn't even want you to."

"Yeah, I know," Chasity agreed. She sighed. "I just feel bad… His dad is like his best friend and—" she shook her head. "He's being so strong for his family, when I know he just wants to break down."

Trisha lowered her head momentarily. "His father will be okay," she promised, seeing the worry in Chasity's eyes. "And so will *Jason*."

Chasity just nodded, then glanced back out the window.

"Are *you* okay?" Trisha asked after moments of silence. "I know how hard it is for you to handle emotional situations."

"I'm fine," she answered, pulling the throw blanket up to her waist. "I just keep trying to imagine what he's going through."

"I know you are," Trisha consoled. "Having a parent

who's sick is a hard thing to deal with, trust me."

"Yeah, but I don't feel for *my* parents what he feels for *his*, so... I can only *try* to imagine," Chasity put out, tone somber. "If you can even *call* Brenda and Derrick parents."

Trisha felt her heart drop as she squeezed Chasity's arm.

Chasity, feeling the squeeze, looked at her aunt. "Trisha, I'm fine," she assured. "I was thinking, that's all."

"I know," Trisha muttered, looking down at the cream-carpeted floor. "This may not be a good time to ask, but...have you spoken to—"

"Brenda?" Chasity frowned.

Trisha quickly shook her head. "No, I know you wouldn't talk to her again."

"Nope," Chasity agreed.

"I was talking about...Derrick."

"Nope," Chasity repeated. Just like her adoptive mother, Chasity had no desire to speak to her adoptive father either. She hadn't heard from him since her dinner meeting with him in New York months ago, and that was fine with her.

Trisha frowned. "I don't understand why he hasn't called you, especially after he *claimed* to miss you."

"Are you really surprised?" Chasity sneered. "Your sister and brother-in-law are incapable of doing anything they *should* do when it comes to me, so—" Chasity pinched the bridge of her nose. This was the last thing that she wanted to talk about. If she couldn't sleep, then talking about her estranged adoptive parents certainly wasn't going to help her get any rest. "Can we drop this? It's giving me a headache."

"Sure," Trisha relented. Truth was, it was giving her a headache too. "I just want to say that... I'm sorry for the way that you were raised."

"Why are *you* apologizing?" Chasity wondered. "It's not your fault."

Trisha bit her lip. "I just...I feel like I—" she paused as she tried to gather her thoughts. "I should've done more—"

"Trisha, you're *not* responsible for what your sister did," Chasity assured her.

Trisha ran her hand over her hair and sighed. No matter what Chasity said, she couldn't help but feel guilty. She opened her mouth to speak, but was interrupted.

"Stop," Chasity ordered, sensing another apology. "You were there for me when you didn't *have* to be," she reminded. "You treat me like your daughter and I'm not even your *blood*, so you've done *more* than enough."

Trisha stared at Chasity. *No, I haven't done nearly enough. You deserve so much more.* Regardless of what she wanted to say, she just nodded and patted Chasity's hand. "You need some rest," she said, standing up. "You want some tea to help you relax?"

"Sure," Chasity replied, then returned her attention to the window as Trisha headed to the kitchen.

Chapter 19

Malajia flicked the TV remote with her finger as she sat on her bed. Upon hearing the key turn in the door, she bolted up. "My friend is back," Malajia beamed, jumping from the bed.

Chasity was taken back when Malajia nearly tackled her with a hug. "Girl—" she didn't have the energy to even throw out a smart remark. She just gave Malajia two pats on her back. That seemed to satisfy Malajia, who released her from her embrace. Chasity left Philadelphia earlier that morning after being gone for two days. She was exhausted after the long drive.

Malajia moved her hair from her face as she sat back down on her bed. "How's Jason's dad holding up after the surgery?" she asked as Chasity sat a bag on her chair.

"He's in recovery," Chasity answered. "They'll continue to monitor him for complications, but for now he seems to be doing okay."

Malajia put her hand over her chest. "Thank God," she breathed. "Everybody was pulling for him."

Chasity smiled slightly as she sat down and removed her shoes. "Jason knows that, and he appreciates it."

"Did he come back with you?"

Chasity shook her head. "He's gonna stay up there a few more days," she answered. "I would've stayed with him, but he told me to come back."

"Yeah, I'm sure he didn't want you to miss anymore classes," Malajia said.

"Fuck those classes," Chasity muttered.

Malajia laughed. "You sound like *me*." She glanced at her finger nails. "So... How did his mom act?"

Chasity shot Malajia a knowing look. She'd neglected to tell Malajia about the woman's behavior during her visit; she didn't want to dwell and wanted to keep her focus on her boyfriend.

"That bad, huh?" Malajia assumed, picking up on the look.

"Yep," she replied, removing some items from her bag.

Malajia shook her head. "Damn shame, she's a fool."

"Yep," Chasity repeated. "But it is what it is."

"Yeah, I hear you," Malajia mumbled before sighing. "Can I talk to you about something?"

Chasity tossed her now empty bag in the closet. "Now?" she asked. All Chasity could think about was laying her head to her pillow for some much-needed rest.

Malajia narrowed her eyes. "Yes, *now*," she hissed.

Chasity put her hands up. "Fine," she relented. "What's up?"

Malajia took a deep breath. "Okay so…remember when I went over Tyrone's? The night that you left?" she asked.

Chasity nodded.

"Well, as you probably suspected, he tried to have sex with me," Malajia revealed. Chasity rolled her eyes. "And when I told him no, he caught a major attitude with me. The whole night was so damn awkward, I ended up sleeping on the couch." She pushed hair behind her ears. "After he dropped me off the next day—"

"Why did you even stay the night after that?" Chasity hissed, unable to hold her tongue any longer.

"How was I gonna get home?" Malajia countered, angry.

"Take a damn cab, take a *bus*," Chasity pointed out, tone not hiding her frustration. "Hell, you could've called Sidra or Mark, *both* of them have cars."

"At damn near midnight? No, I wasn't gonna do that," Malajia scoffed. "Anyway, after he dropped me off, we got into an argument. He had the nerve to ask me how long I was gonna play the virgin card."

"He's an asshole Malajia, I've already told you that," Chasity spat.

"I *know* you have," Malajia grunted, looking down at her hands.

"Why are you surprised by *any* of this?"

"Because I thought he was past *acting* like this," Malajia answered truthfully. "I thought—he was doing so well."

"In *what* world?!" Chasity exclaimed. "He fuckin' disrespects you *all* the time."

"No, he *doesn't*."

"And you're defending him, *that* doesn't surprise me either," Chasity argued.

"I'm not defending him—" Malajia tossed her hands up in the air. "You know what, you're right. He's an asshole… I'm done with him."

Chasity shook her head; she'd heard that before. "No you're not."

"I *am*," Malajia insisted, looking Chasity in the eye.

"If you say so," Chasity threw back, standing from her seat.

Malajia watched as Chasity walked into the bathroom, before putting her head in her hands and letting out a long sigh.

Jason opened his room door and tossed his bags to the floor. Letting out a sigh, he held his phone to his ear, shutting the door behind him. It'd been four days since his father's surgery and five since he'd gotten the phone call that he had his heart attack. Jason was tired, both mentally and physically. Although he wished he could have stayed back home until his father was out of the hospital, he was relieved to be back on campus.

Sitting on his bed, he ran his hand over his face as he talked to his mother. "Yeah I'm back on campus now... The train ride wasn't so bad. It gave me time to clear my head...Yeah I know... Mom, please call me and give me updates everyday... If I have to come back up there I will... All right, tell Kyle I'll talk to him later...love you too... Bye."

Jason stared at the phone after he ended the call. His mind was racing. He hadn't had a decent night's sleep in days. His father nearly died, and although he was speaking to his mother, he had not forgotten the way that she behaved.

Pinching the bridge of his nose and taking a long sigh, he dialed another number.

"I swear that cafeteria food gets nastier every time we go," Malajia complained as she, Chasity, Alex, and Sidra were making their way back to the dorm from the cafeteria.

"It does *not*," Sidra laughed. "You just keep picking the grossest looking stuff on the menu."

As the other girls were talking, Chasity heard her phone ring. "Hello?" she answered "Hey Jase."

"Oh, he's back!" Alex exclaimed, trying to grab the phone from her.

"Get your dumb ass away from me," Chasity barked, moving away. Alex was stunned by the comment.

Malajia busted out laughing as Chasity continued her conversation. Sidra shot Malajia a side-glance.

"Was that necessary Chasity?" Alex fussed when Chasity ended her brief conversation.

Malajia grabbed her stomach. "Oh my God, my stomach! Pleeeaaasssseee," she screamed with laughter.

"Yes it *was*," Chasity shot back. "You don't try to snatch my phone from me, are you stupid?"

"I just wanted to check on him, damn!"

"Then you call him on that game prize phone *you* got," Chasity retorted. Malajia screamed louder.

"Mel come on, you're being embarrassing," Sidra commented, looking at her.

"Shut the fuck up Sidra!" Malajia shouted through her laughter.

Sidra sucked her teeth and moved away from Malajia.

As they approached their dorm, Chasity proceeded to walk across the path to Court Terrance. "Where are you going?" Alex called after her.

Malajia shot Alex a confused look. "Where do you *think* she's going?"

"*That's* why I called her a dumbass," Chasity threw over her shoulder as she continued walking.

Alex sucked her teeth. "You know what? I am over you both insulting me. It's getting ridiculous," she fumed.

"Then stop saying dumb shit," Malajia retorted, causing Sidra to snicker. Alex glared at Sidra as Malajia continued, "and get a new damn phone! I'm sick of that old ass flip."

"I'm not wasting money on a new phone," Alex ground out. "If it bothers you so much, then *you* buy me a new one."

Malajia made a face. "Shiiit, I ain't buying you a phone," she refused. "I'll put some *minutes* on that bitch though."

Alex let out a loud huff, then stormed inside their dorm, leaving her and Sidra standing outside.

"Malajia will you leave that girl and her phone alone?" Sidra wondered, amusement in her voice.

"She know I love her old, throwback flip phone having ass," Malajia joked, walking inside along with Sidra.

Jason opened the door to find Chasity standing there. He smiled brightly as she stepped inside the room. "I missed you," he said, hugging her tightly.

"I missed you too," she returned as they parted. Jason closed the door and Chasity removed her jacket. "Why didn't you call me to come pick you up from the train station?" she asked, sitting down on his bed.

"I just wanted some time alone to clear my head."

"Understandable," Chasity replied. "When is he going to be able to go home?"

Jason sat down next to her. "Hopefully in a few days," he replied. "They're still monitoring him... Mom said she'll update me every day."

Chasity watched as Jason continuously rubbed his hands down the front of his jeans. "Oh okay," she replied.

Jason nodded as he ran his hand over his head. "You hungry?" he asked her.

Chasity stared at him, concerned look on her face. "No, I ate already."

Jason rubbed his face. "Okay."

"Are *you*?" she asked, eyes fixed on him.

He shook his head. "No."

Chasity continued to observe him. To her, it seemed that he was desperately trying not to break down. As Jason ran his hands over his head yet again, Chasity reached out to touch his shoulder. "I'm okay," he stated with a nervous chuckle. As he felt Chasity's hand touch him, he found it harder to remain composed. "No really, I'm okay," he insisted.

Chasity, knowing what he needed, didn't say a word. She just wrapped her arms around him, pulling him to her. It was in that moment that Jason felt every wall that he had up fall. He wrapped his arms around her and broke down crying.

He had been strong for his mother, his brother, his father and the rest of this family. Everything happened so fast, Jason was never able to deal with his own feelings, his own grief, and his own worry. He had to be the rock, just like always.

Chasity understood all too well what it felt like to have to keep emotions bottled. She didn't judge him, she didn't say anything, she just held him as he let go.

Malajia gave herself a once over in her full-length mirror, late Friday evening. With her mind so preoccupied with Tyrone, whom she hadn't spoken to since she'd hung up on him nearly a week ago, Malajia was ready for a party. She was elated when Mark called her almost two hours ago, telling her about an off-campus party that he and Josh were headed to.

"Looking sexy as usual, girl," she mused of herself, eyeing the black shorts, red halter top and red high-heel sandals. Her hair was curled, her makeup was flawless, and she was ready to dance until her feet hurt. Grabbing her purse from a nearby chair, Malajia's cell phone rang. "Yeah Mark?" she answered.

"Where you at?" Mark replied.

"I'm coming, just grabbing my purse," she said, fixing a wayward curl with her fingers. She paused. "Wait, I'm not carrying this thing to the party," she said of her purse. "I'm just gonna carry my phone, lip gloss and ID."

"Oh my God I don't caaaaarrrree," Mark complained, loud. "Just come ooooonnnnn. You always gotta take extra long to get ready."

"Boy shut up," Malajia threw back, unfazed by his attitude. "Do you have pockets?"

"What kinda shit is that to ask?" He barked. "*Yes*, I have pockets."

"Good 'cause my stuff is going in there. I'm coming down now."

"Hurry up."

"Yeah, yeah." She hung up, then glanced in the mirror once again, doing a little dance. "Boobs not falling out, I'm good." Darting for the door, she opened it and let out a scream. "What the hell?!" she bellowed, seeing Tyrone standing there.

"Sorry to scare you," he replied.

Malajia stared at him, both disbelief and anger written on her face as he moved around her to enter her room. "What the hell are you doing here?" she fumed, slamming the door behind him.

Tyrone spun around to face her, a frown forming. "Where the hell are you going with *that* on?"

"That's *none* of *your* damn business," Malajia wailed, waving her hand in his direction. "What the hell are you *doing* here?"

"I've been trying to call you. You don't answer," Tyrone stated, a stern gaze fixed on her.

"Duh," she sneered. "I blocked your freakin' number."

"Which is why I'm *here*," he returned, adjusting the fitted cap on his head. "I came to say I'm sorry."

Malajia could have slapped him right across his face. "Sorry?!" she erupted. "After what you said to me? After how you *treated* me? You think that 'sorry' is gonna cut it?"

"Hey, you need to calm that screaming shit down," he ordered, voice stern.

Malajia folded her arms and turned away from him. "Look," she began, tone lowered. "You don't get to show up to my room after how you treated me and expect me to be calm," she pointed out, facing him. "You made me feel like I was wrong for not being ready for sex."

"I didn't mean to make you feel that way," he said. "I was just frustrated. I thought that maybe we were at that place where we could take that next step."

"Tyrone, I never gave you the impression that I was ready," Malajia argued. "And I don't want to be made to feel like shit because I'm *not*."

Tyrone lowered his head and nodded. "You're absolutely right," he agreed, taking a step towards her. "I'm sorry."

She took a step back. "That's not gonna cut it," she sneered.

Tyrone took another step, reaching for her hand. "Let me make it up to you," he pressed.

Malajia held her frown as he moved closer. "I'm mad at
you," she pouted. Malajia tried to resist, but when he
wrapped his strong arms around her, she just melted.

"I won't disrespect you again," he promised.

"You better *not*," she muttered against his chest. Tyrone
pulled away and leaned in for a kiss when the door busted
open, startling them both.

"Boy!" Malajia hollered at Mark as he and Josh walked
into the room. Tyrone held a fiery gaze on both men.

"What the fuck are you still doing up here, yo?" Mark
charged. "We've been down there for like a half hour waiting
on you."

Just as Malajia was about to respond, Tyrone pointed at
Mark. "Yo, don't be talking to my girl like that," he raged.

Mark looked at him as if he was crazy. He then looked at
Malajia, while pointing to Tyrone. "Who the fuck is *this*?"

Shit! Malajia panicked, knowing Tyrone's temper all too
well. Malajia grabbed Tyrone's arm. "Mark, Josh this is my
boyfriend Tyrone," she stammered. "Ty babe, these are my
friends."

Mark and Tyrone stared each other down, neither one
interested in an introduction.

"You the same Mark who answered Malajia's phone?"
Tyrone hissed.

"You the same Tyrone who acted like a bitch
afterwards?" Mark threw back, unintimidated.

Tyrone's eyes widened with fury as Malajia stood in
front of him, hoping that would stop an impending fight.
"Mark stop," Malajia pleaded.

Mark continued to glare at Tyrone as Josh, hoping to
diffuse the tension, stepped forward and extended his hand
for Tyrone to shake. "Hey man, nice to meet you."

Tyrone just looked at Josh, not saying a word, and not
shaking his hand. Josh, offended, frowned and put his hand
down.

Malajia was embarrassed by Tyrone's behavior. "Babe,
chill, these are my *friends*," she reiterated. "They were

waiting for me to come down so we could go to a party."

Tyrone switched his gaze from Mark, to Malajia, back to the guys. "You were going to a party with *them*?"

Malajia frowned, "Yes," she answered, wondering where he was going with his questioning.

"Well then you won't mind if I go *with* y'all," Tyrone proposed. "*Do* you Mark and Josh?"

"Yes the hell I *do* mi—"

"Naw man, we don't. It's cool," Josh cut in, putting his arm in front of Mark to halt his angered response.

"Babe, you don't *have* to come," Malajia stated. She didn't need Tyrone hovering over her all night.

"Naw, I *do*," Tyrone insisted, before walking pass the guys and out the door. Malajia shook her head and followed him, leaving Mark and Josh standing there perplexed.

After a few seconds, Mark turned to Josh. "Man, how you gonna try to shake his dumb ass hand?" he scolded, smacking Josh on the arm.

Josh hit him back. "What did you *expect* me to do?" Josh shot back. "That's Mel's dude, I was trying to be respectful."

"Man, fuck that dude," Mark spat out, walking out the door. "That's why he left your hype ass hanging."

"Whatever dawg," Josh returned, following him out the door.

Chapter 20

Chasity searched through Jason's piles of DVD's while she waited for him to return from the library. Having arrived nearly a half hour ago to a messy room, Chasity took the liberty of straitening up for him.

Jason walked through the door and dropped his book bag to the floor. "Hey," he grunted.

"Hey," Chasity returned, ignoring his tone. "Did you get a lot done at the library?"

Jason shrugged. "I guess," he replied, removing his shirt. "It still feels like I have a lot to do."

"Yeah well, you're trying to catch up on a weeks' worth of classes in a few days," Chasity consoled.

Jason sighed as he glanced at the floor. "Yeah," he muttered. He was stressed, to say the least. Between trying to catch up on his missed classwork, trying to keep tabs on his father, who was still in the hospital, and receiving call after call from his extended family looking for updates when his mother wouldn't answer their calls, Jason felt like he could lose his mind at any moment.

Jason searched the floor for something, then frowned.

Chasity glanced over at him "You okay?" she asked, when he started looking under his bed.

He looked up at her. "What did you do with the pile of clothes that was next to my bed?"

Chasity was taken back by the bite in his tone. "I put them in your laundry basket."

Jason frowned. "Why did you do that?" he hissed, standing from the floor.

"Um, I thought they were dirty," she returned, confused.

He rubbed his face. "They *weren't* dirty."

This time Chasity frowned. "What is your problem?"

"My *problem* is that what I was looking for was *in* that pile," he barked. "And because you threw them in the damn hamper with the dirty stuff, *now* it's dirty."

Chasity tried to remain calm. "Well *baby*, *wash* them," she suggested. "I don't understand what the big damn deal is."

"That's not the point!" he exploded.

"Well what *is* the point?" Chasity hollered back, tossing the DVD's that she was holding to the floor. "Why the fuck are you snapping at me over a pile of clothes?"

He pointed to the spot where the pile was. "Why the hell did you touch it in the *first* place?"

"I was *trying* to be nice and straighten up your room for you," Chasity explained, furious. "I figured that you had too much on your mind to do it yourself. I thought I was helping you. Best believe I won't do *that* shit again."

Jason rubbed his tired eyes. "Look, my father's college jersey was in that pile and I wanted to sleep in it and now I *can't* 'cause it's dirty."

"So just wash the damn jersey!" At this point, Chasity was too annoyed to be sympathetic.

"I hadn't planned on washing *anything* tonight," Jason shot back. "I didn't ask you to come in here touching stuff. You just do whatever you want without checking with people first."

Chasity put her hands up. "*First* of all, your fuckin' tone is unnecessary," she bit out. "*Second*, I don't know why you're trippin; it was *clearly* a mistake. I didn't mean to throw your dad's jersey, which was lying in a pile on the *floor*, in the basket."

Jason rolled his eyes at her mocking tone.

"You're being ridiculous, and frankly you're pissing me the hell off," Chasity added.

"I really don't care about what pisses you off right about now," Jason threw back. "I deal with you and your bad moods every damn day, and I don't complain. I get angry at you *one* time and it's the end of the freakin' world for you. Grow up."

"Screw you Jason," Chasity snapped back, pointing at him. "I get you're worried about your dad, but why are you snapping at *me*? *I* didn't cause his heart attack."

"Shut up!"

"*You* shut up!"

"You don't know what to say out your fuckin' mouth," Jason fumed, "That was uncalled for."

"No, your pissy ass *attitude* is uncalled for." Angry, Chasity stormed towards the door. "I'm leaving."

"Fine, leave," he hurled, following her progress to the door. "That's all you do when things get rough anyway."

Chasity spun around, facing him, eyes flashing. "Really? You just said that shit to me?" she fussed. "I *didn't* leave when things got rough. I was there when you needed me. I took you home; I stayed with you for *two* days."

"Look—"

"No," she abruptly cut in. Chasity wasn't interested in listening to anything else that Jason had to say. "You don't get to say that to me after everything. I even put up with your mothers' bullshit, *just* so I could be there for *you*. You want to talk about what was uncalled for to say? *That* was uncalled for."

Jason ran his hands over his hair; it was clear that he had hurt Chasity's feelings. He tried to walk up to her, "Chasity—"

"No, kiss my ass you ungrateful bastard," Chasity spat, storming out and slamming the door.

Jason looked at the ceiling and let out a long sigh. "Shit," he huffed.

"Oh my God, it's so damn hoooottt," Malajia complained, fanning herself.

"Hush up and keep going," Sidra demanded, moving along to her workout DVD. "Come on, it's not that hard."

"Can we get some water?" Alex asked, out of breath. She was regretting allowing Sidra to talk her and Malajia into working out in the room with her. After nearly forty minutes of non-stop movement, Alex was ready to call it quits.

"You'll get a water break after this segment," Sidra panted.

Malajia stomped her foot on the floor. "Come on, my tracks are sliding out," she barked. The out of nowhere complaint caused Alex to bust out laughing.

Sidra halted her movement and regarded Malajia sternly. "Aren't they sewn in?"

"So? Thread can slide too," Malajia threw back.

Sidra rolled her eyes. "Were you *not* the one who came to me and complained that you put on a few pounds? Did you *not* ask me to help you out?"

"Bitch I didn't put on no damn pounds, you're lying out your ass," Malajia griped, wiping sweat from her brow. "That must've been *Alex's* wide ass."

Alex sucked her teeth. "Leave me out of this," she muttered, still moving to the rhythm of the beat on screen.

"Was all of that necessary?" Sidra scolded.

"Yep, every last word," Malajia returned, unfazed.

Sidra waved her hand at Malajia. "Well you must've been drunk or something, 'cause you asked me to help," she maintained, scratching her damp scalp. "You don't like what I'm having you do? Go work out with Chasity."

"Hello *no* I'm not working out with that ninja," Malajia protested.

"Well then, stop whining and keep moving," Sidra

ordered, getting her momentum back up. "You won't get fat on *my* watch."

Alex stopped moving. "I'm *already* fat, can I stop?" she joked, placing her hands on her knees to catch her breath.

Malajia snickered, earning a backhand from Sidra. "Alex you're not fat. Stop it," Sidra chided.

As Alex and Malajia's complaining resonated throughout the room, the door opened and in walked Chasity. "I need to talk. *Now*," she announced, shutting the door behind her.

"Yes! A break," Malajia rejoiced, flopping down on Sidra's bed.

"Don't get excited," Sidra cut in, sitting down next to Malajia. "We *will* finish this workout today."

Malajia rolled her eyes.

Alex grabbed a bottle of water out of Sidra's refrigerator. "What's wrong Chaz?" she asked.

Chasity began pacing back and forth. "Jason and I got into an argument," she revealed.

"Really?" Sidra questioned, full of surprise.

"I never thought I'd see the day that Jason would argue with you after y'all became a couple," Malajia mocked.

Sidra looked at Malajia. "And why is *that*?" she chuckled.

"Come on, y'all know he's all like 'Chasity is my earth, my moon and my stars. I would give my life before I upset her'," Malajia teased in a dramatic fashion.

Alex and Sidra both snickered before breaking into full on laughter.

Chasity slowly folded her arms, eyes fixed in an angry stare; she was not amused. "That's not funny," she hissed.

"We're sorry," Alex replied, wiping her face with her damp t-shirt. "What happened?"

"So, you know that he's been all distracted lately," Chasity began. "Well, I went over to his room to chill and I saw that the place was a mess. That's not like him, so I straighten up, trying to be a helpful, thoughtful girlfriend."

She began pacing again as she felt her temper flare. "This bastard had the *audacity* to snap at me because I moved a pile of clothes from his floor to the laundry basket."

Malajia frowned in confusion. "Why? They were dirty, weren't they?"

"*I thought* so," Chasity explained. "But apparently, his dad's jersey was in the pile, so he caught a whole damn attitude."

Alex placed her hand to her chest. "Aww, he wants to feel close to his dad," she sympathized.

"Okay, fine whatever," Chasity bit out, tossing her arms in the air. "He didn't have to yell at me over it... Telling me to grow up and talking about I always leave when things get rough," she continued to vent, folding her arms. "I wanted to punch him right in his goddamn face."

"Chaz, he didn't really say that to you after everything, did he?" Malajia questioned, in disbelief.

"Yep," Chasity confirmed.

"Well...he's just upset and he needs to vent," Alex pointed out.

"No, he wasn't *venting*. He was being a snappin' jackass," Chasity contradicted, tone not masking her frustration.

Alex sighed. She understood Chasity's irritation, but she felt that as friends to both her and Jason, she was obligated to present Jason's side. "Sweetie, he *is* dealing with a lot right now," she calmly stated. "Maybe he just needed to let his frustration out."

"No, Chasity's right," Malajia argued, moving wet hair from her face. "Venting is one thing. But he *didn't* have to snap at her for moving a pile of damn laundry. He was being an ass."

"That's what *I'm* saying," Chasity muttered.

"Who leaves clean clothes on the floor *anyway*?" Malajia scoffed.

Sidra looked at her, "Are you sure you want to ask that question?" she challenged. "'Cause I've seen plenty of *your* crap on the floor in your room."

Malajia tossed her head back in frustration. "I don't leave clean clothes on the floor Sidra," she groaned.

"Hey, bring the focus back, okay," Chasity ordered, halting their bickering.

"Look sis, I understand why you're upset. Granted he shouldn't have gone off on you for something so small," Alex cut in, adamant on making Chasity see her point of view. "But you have to understand that he's going through something very traumatic right now. I mean, his father almost *died*," she reminded. "I can't even *imagine* going through that. As his girlfriend, it's *your* job to be there for him and support him."

Chasity let out a frustrated sigh as Alex continued.

"And to be honest, how he reacted is *nowhere near* as bad as *you* react when *you're* upset," Alex bluntly stated. "Through *all* of your moods, he's still there for you. You have to do the same, it's only fair."

Chasity rolled her eyes as she pondered what Alex just said to her. Meanwhile Malajia was looking at Alex with an agitated look frozen on her face. "Alex shut up!" Malajia snapped.

"Excuse me?" Alex frowned at Malajia.

"Nobody asked you to be captain save-a-dick—" Malajia began, causing Sidra to spit some of the water she had been drinking out. "We *get* he's going through something, but the bottom line is that he was being an asshole."

"Whatever Malajia, you and *your* boyfriend-of-five-minutes haven't gone through any *real* issues yet, so you have no room to comment," Alex argued.

"And *you* have room?" Malajia shot back.

"Yes, I *do*," Alex boasted, folding her arms. "I *am* the *only* one who has been in a long-term relationship."

"Yeah and that turned out to be *soooo* successful," Malajia jeered, rolling her eyes.

Alex tossed a pillow at her. "You know what—"

"I didn't come over here to hear y'all argue," Chasity

barked, interrupting the bickering.

"So are you going to talk to him?" Sidra asked, retrieving the throw pillow from the floor.

"No," Chasity fussed. "I don't want to see him for the rest of the week…day."

"I say you make him suffer as long as you can," Malajia advised, combing through her tangled hair with her fingers. "Don't cave when he comes crawling."

"What, you mean like *you* did, with Tyrone?" Chasity goaded, examining her finger nails.

Malajia paused her finger combing and narrowed her eyes at Chasity. When she hesitantly revealed to Chasity that she was giving Tyrone another chance, just three days ago, her news was met with silence. She knew it was only a matter of time before Chasity made a snide comment.

"Real cute," Malajia hissed, then rolled her eyes.

Sidra put her hands up. The tension in the room was too much. "You know what we need?" she asked, standing up. Her question was met with anticipation. "We need to release some stress. Let's get back to this workout."

"Come *on*," Malajia whined, flopping back on the bed and stomping on the floor.

"Sidra, my hips hurt," Alex moaned.

"Shut it up—Chasity, I see you trying to sneak out," Sidra barked, pointing to Chasity who was trying to tip toe out the door.

"Damn it," Chasity griped.

"Go get your workout clothes and get back here," Sidra demanded. "Time to work off those brownies we ate last night."

"I didn't even eat any—"

"Get your clothes!" Sidra ordered, interrupting Chasity's protest.

"Okay damn," Chasity relented. "I'm just getting hollered at all day today," she muttered, walking out the room.

"Those damn brownies was hard as hell anyway," Malajia scoffed.

Chasity pulled her pajama top over her head. After working out for an hour with the girls, she'd retreated to her room to take a shower and had planned on enjoying a moment of quiet while Malajia was still in Sidra and Alex's room.

She sucked her teeth when someone knocked on the door. "Damn Malajia, stop forgetting your fuckin' key," she fussed, yanking the door open. She rolled her eyes when she saw someone who she was equally irritated with. "What are you doing here, Jason?"

Jason adjusted the zipper on his jacket. "I came to talk to you," he declared.

"Sucks for *you*, 'cause I don't wanna talk to you right now," she threw back, then tried to shut the door.

"I'm not leaving until we talk," he insisted, putting his hand on the door, preventing her from shutting it on him.

Sucking her teeth, Chasity jerked the door open, allowing him to walk in. "What is it?" she sneered, closing the door.

Jason faced her, sincerity on his face. "I'm sorry."

"Sorry don't mean shit to me, try again," Chasity huffed, turning to walk away.

Jason gently grabbed her arm to stop her. "No, I mean it. I'm sorry baby," he insisted. "My snapping wasn't about the clothes. I appreciate you trying to help, I really do."

Chasity looked at him. She had every intention of showing him the door. But in taking what Alex said into consideration, as well as Jason's difficulties, she decided not to make things more difficult for him. "Did you hear anything else about your dad?"

Jason sighed. "That's actually the reason why I lost it earlier," he admitted. "I hadn't gotten an update from my mom about how he was doing for two days...so I was worried, and frustrated." He ran his hand along the back of his neck. "I took it out on you and I shouldn't have."

"No, you *shouldn't* have," Chasity agreed. "But I'll give you a pass...*this* time."

Jason smiled as he moved in close, wrapping his arms around her small waist. "You know I appreciate you," he said.

She found it hard to resist him, finally letting a smile come through. "I know," she replied, wrapping her arms around his neck. "Did you ever hear from your mom?"

Jason nodded, expression relaxed. "Before I came over here," he revealed. "It looks like he's on his way to a full recovery. He'll be going home in a few days."

Chasity hugged him tightly. "That's great baby."

Jason buried his face into her sweet-scented neck as he held on to her. For the first time in what seemed like forever to him, Jason felt like a weight had been lifted from his broad shoulders. He lifted his head and moved his lips to hers.

Malajia barged in just in time to witness the couple engaged in a passionate kiss. "Eww, get out with that mess," she grunted, interrupting them.

Jason chuckled as Chasity shot Malajia a warning glance. "Can't you go annoy someone *else* for like ten minutes?" she hissed.

"No horny, I *can't*," Malajia mocked, removing her sneakers. "Oh Chaz, Sidra's gonna come over here and ask you why you broke her workout DVD."

Confusion showed on Chasity's face. "Huh?"

Before Malajia could answer, Sidra stormed through the door, holding a broken DVD in her hand. Malajia quickly darted into the bathroom as Sidra began her tirade. "Chasity Taj-Mahal Parker!" she boomed.

Chasity frowned, "Taj-*Marie*," she corrected.

"I don't give a damn *what* your middle name is," Sidra wailed. "You broke my DVD!"

"I didn't *touch* the thing," Chasity argued. "After the workout, I left right out."

"No, Malajia said she saw you with it," Sidra accused.

Chasity raised an eyebrow and folded her arms. "*Yeah?*"

Sidra thought for a moment. "Malajia!" she stomped over to the bathroom and started banging on the door. "You broke my damn DVD, you liar," she yelled. "You owe me fifteen dollars!"

"That stupid ass DVD wasn't worth no fifteen dollars," Malajia exclaimed from inside the bathroom as Sidra continued to bang.

Chapter 21

Alex wiped the last table in her serving area. Stretching her neck from side to side, she tried to stifle a yawn, but was unsuccessful. "I'm gonna hit that pillow *so* hard when I get home," Alex mumbled to herself. After finishing another five-hour shift at the Pizza Shack, Alex couldn't wait to get back to campus. Hearing the door open, Alex glanced up to see one of her classmates walking in.

"Hey Alex," the girl waved.

Alex walked over and stood by the front counter. "Hey Monica, what's up?"

"Just stopped in to pick up my roommate's order," she replied with a wave of her hand. "Midterms got us eating everything in sight."

"I don't blame you," Alex laughed. "At least we only have two more weeks before spring break."

Monica nodded as she adjusted her book bag. "You about to leave?" she assumed.

Alex adjusted her ponytail. "Yes, thank God," she chortled. "I gotta go hit these books...then my pillow."

"Before you go," Monica began as Alex went to walk behind the counter. "Do you know Brandon Hendricks?"

Alex frowned, "Um, can't say that I *do*," she answered honestly. "Why?"

"He died last night."

Alex's eyes widened, "Oh my God," she gasped. That certainly wasn't news that she'd expected to hear. She's been at school for almost two years and not once had she heard of a fellow student passing until now. "What happened?"

"Apparently, he was drunk and stumbled out into oncoming traffic in town," Monica revealed, somber. "It's really sad."

Alex rubbed the back of her neck. "Wow, that's a shame. I feel for his family," she sulked. "They're definitely in my prayers."

"Yeah, the school is going to hold a candlelight vigil for him tonight outside of the SDC," Monica informed. "You should come. I mean you may not have known him, but he *was* a fellow classmate."

"I agree, I'll be there," Alex replied. "I have to get out of here, but I'll see you later." Alex walked to the back office, grabbed her book bag and purse, then made a beeline for the front door.

"Ouch! Damn Sidra, that hurt," Malajia wailed, vigorously rubbing her eyebrow.

"Girl, did you think that having your eyebrows tweezed would feel *good*?" Sidra shot back as she moved her tweezer-filled fingers away from Malajia's face.

Malajia had walked into Sidra and Alex's room twenty minutes earlier, begging Sidra to tweeze her eyebrows. She was due for a wax and didn't feel like taking the journey to the salon off campus.

"You don't have to be so hype with it," Malajia argued. "You know you don't treat your *own* face like this."

Sidra rolled her eyes; Malajia's flinching and whining was getting on her nerves. Sidra always broke out after having her eyebrows waxed, so she learned to do her own.

She was used to the pain. "Malajia, you're exaggerating as usual," she griped, placing her tweezers to Malajia's brow.

Malajia jerked her head away. "I'm *not* exaggerating," she spat back, adjusting herself in her seat. "I think you're doing it extra rough 'cause you really don't wanna do them."

"No I *don't* feel like doing them," Sidra agreed, annoyed. "But I'm *not* doing it extra rough. It just *hurts*. Get over it and move your damn hand so I can finish."

Malajia let out a quick sigh. "Yeah okay, just hurry up," she ordered.

"Just be quiet," Sidra ground out, focusing. She pulled a few more hairs before yanking a long one, causing Malajia to jump.

"Bitch! You know what—"

"Malajia, this is the last time that you're going to call me a bitch," Sidra warned. "Now, either you stop whining and let me finish, or you can do them your-damn-self. I don't have time for this shit, I have to study."

Malajia pointed her finger in Sidra's face. "You already *know* I don't know how to tweeze my own brows," Malajia hissed. Sidra gave Malajia's finger, which was practically touching her nose, a long stare. "Now you gonna *do* them and they *better* be right," Malajia barked.

Sidra directed her venomous gaze to Malajia's face, before taking her tweezers and snatching several of Malajia's brow hairs out at once.

"Ow!" Malajia screamed, jumping up from the chair.

"Now pencil it in, bitch," Sidra hissed, tossing her tweezers on her dresser. She was over it.

Malajia stared in the mirror. "Sidra, you fucked up my eyebrow," she fumed, eyeing the small part in her brow. She tried to fix it with her finger. "You ain't even have to do that. You take shit too damn far."

"You put your damn finger in my face," Sidra defended. "*That*, and you're just on my nerves in general."

Malajia eyed Sidra with disgust as she watched her sit on her bed and grab her textbook. "Let me get your brow pencil," she demanded.

"No," Sidra spat.

Alex walked into the room, halting any response that Malajia was about to give. "Hey girls," she sighed, shutting the door.

"Hey Alex," Sidra muttered, eyes focused on her book.

Alex focused on Malajia, who was just staring at her. "Malajia, what's up with your eyebrow?" she wondered.

"Your roommate is an ignorant asshole, *that's* what's up with it," Malajia sneered, much to Alex's confusion.

"Leave me alone, Malajia," Sidra grunted, running a highlighter across a page.

"Yeah okay, I'm two seconds from slicing that ponytail right off the top of your small ass head," Malajia mumbled.

Alex shrugged. The girls bickered so much, she couldn't keep track of what their reasons were. "Where's Chasity?"

"In our room studying," Malajia answered.

"Can you go get her? I wanted to tell you all something," Alex requested, letting her wild ponytail down.

Malajia walked to the door, "Girl, I'm not walking all the way over there," she refused. She stuck her head out. "Chasity! Come over to Alex and Sidra's room, Alex wants to tell us something!" she yelled at the top of her lungs.

Sidra and Alex stared at Malajia as she pulled her head back inside. "Really Malajia?" Alex quibbled, as Sidra shook her head.

Malajia shrugged as Chasity walked into the room. "Why the fuck do you have to be so damn loud?" Chasity fussed. Her eyes were fixed on Malajia's face. "What the hell's wrong with your eyebrow?"

Malajia made a face at her. "Shut up."

"Okay Alex, what did you have to tell us?" Sidra wondered, sitting her book on her bed.

"Do you know Brandon Hendricks?" Alex asked, removing her work shirt.

"I have a class with him, but I don't really *know* him," Sidra replied the same time that Chasity said, "No."

"No not really," Malajia answered. "Why?"

"I heard that he died last night."

Sidra's mouth fell open. "Oh no, that's such a shame," she commiserated. "What happened?"

"He'd been drinking and stumbled into oncoming traffic," Alex informed. "He was struck and killed."

"Damn, that's sad," Malajia responded, sitting on Alex's bed.

"Yeah I know," Alex agreed. "They're having a candlelight vigil for him tonight at the SDC, we should all go."

"Why?" Chasity asked, tone nonchalant.

Alex frowned. "What do you mean *why*?"

"Look, it's a shame that he died, really," Chasity began, putting her hand up. "But I didn't know him. Why should I go mourn for someone I didn't know?"

"She has a point," Malajia shrugged.

"No, no she *doesn't* have a point," Alex argued, fixing an angry gaze upon Malajia. "Stop agreeing with her on everything."

"Why you *mad* though?" Malajia shot back. "'Cause nobody agrees with *you*?"

"Ladies," Sidra interjected, clapping her hands to grab their attention. "Granted we didn't know him, but he was our classmate. It just shows respect," she pointed out.

"*Thank you*, Sidra," Alex approved.

"Fine," Chasity huffed, before walking out the door.

Malajia tossed her hands up in frustration. "How you get mad at *me* for agreeing with Chasity, but Sidra agrees with *you* and all is okay?"

"*You* agree with ignorant stuff," Alex ground out, folding her arms.

Malajia made a face, then walked out.

Alex shook her head. "I'm gonna call Emily," she announced, reaching for the room phone. "She should come too."

"Do you think she'll even answer?" Sidra asked. Based

on Emily's reclusive behavior over the past few weeks,
Sidra, like the rest of the group, hadn't heard from Emily.
They had only seen her in brief passing, while out and about.

"If she *doesn't*, I'm walking my tired butt right on over
to her room," Alex promised. "She needs to stop hibernating
and spend time with us." She placed the phone to her ear. "If
it takes this unfortunate incident to bring her out, then so be
it."

Later that evening, the students gathered outside of the
Student Development Center to pay respect to their fallen
classmate. The girls were standing in the back, holding their
lit candles, as a student said a prayer.

Alex sighed as the light from the candle flickered.

Sidra, noticing the somber look on Alex's face leaned
close. "You still disappointed that Emily didn't come?" she
whispered.

Alex glanced at Sidra and nodded. She was more than
disappointed. Her calls to Emily had once again gone
unanswered. Even her walk to Emily's apartment was
pointless; the girl didn't answer.

"I miss her you know," Alex sulked. "I feel like in times
of tragedy we should all be together."

Sidra put her arm around her roommate. "I hear you,"
she agreed. "Maybe we should take a day and go drag her out
of that room. Make her remember that we're her friends."

Alex once again nodded. "You know, I'm for it," she
approved.

Malajia hadn't heard a word of what Alex or Sidra said.
She was too busy staring at a girl who was crying
hysterically next to her. As a few students began saying kind
words of the deceased, the girl started howling; "I can't take
it. It's too much!"

Malajia held a blank expression as the girl wailed on.

"I just saw him the other day. It's too much," she
rambled, before being hauled away with the help of some

nearby students.

After a few seconds, Malajia turned to the girls. "Um…I don't mean to be smart but…" she rubbed her forehead with her hand. "She didn't even *know* him."

Chasity closed her eyes and snickered. Focusing on the candle in her hand, hoping not to burst out into full laugher.

Alex, on the other hand was not amused. "Malajia, for real? *Now*? You do this *now*?" she hissed, trying to keep her voice down.

"Naw really," Malajia maintained, shaking her hand in Alex's direction. "Like, she over here all hype, *crying* and shit and she never even talked to him before," she continued, making Chasity snicker again, this time louder.

"How the hell do *you* know that she didn't know him?" Alex questioned, agitated.

Malajia rolled her eyes. "'Cause I know that girl and she never hung out with or mentioned his name *once*."

"She said that she just saw him," Alex argued.

Malajia became annoyed. "She saw his ass walking across campus," she pointed out in animated fashion. "She *didn't* know him, *nobody* really did."

"I really hate you sometimes," Chasity said to Malajia, tone even.

"Malajia, you're going to hell," Sidra declared, cupping her flame with her hand to keep it from blowing out.

"Oh what? I'm the *only* one who thinks that she's full of shit?" Malajia spat.

"Girl, we're supposed to be paying our *respects*, not making fun of others who are trying to do the same. No matter *how* they do it," Alex scolded, facing forward.

Malajia rolled her eyes and faced forward. She then leaned close to Chasity. "I don't care *what* the mop says, she ain't know him to be acting all extra like that," she whispered.

Chasity put her hand over her mouth to try to keep her laugh silent.

"Malajia," Alex warned.

Malajia sucked her teeth and mumbled something under her breath when the guys walked up, candle in hand.

"Hey guys, I'm glad y'all came," Alex smiled. She was proud of her friends for showing up and supporting, no matter how foolish some of them were acting. She only wished that Emily did the same.

"I wouldn't have missed it," Josh said. "I spoke to Brandon a few times and he seemed pretty cool. It's a shame."

Mark sucked his teeth. "Man, you never spoke to him," he contradicted. Josh flashed a scowl his way. "You just want to get in the mix."

"I did *so* talk to him a few times—why am I even *explaining* anything to you?" Josh wondered.

"'Cause you lyin'," Mark goaded, earning a laugh from Malajia.

"Well, *I've* spoken to him and Josh is right, he was cool," Jason put in. "He kept to himself mostly, but he was nice." He looked at Mark, who was giving him the side-eye paired with a twisted mouth. "Go ahead and call me a liar," Jason challenged.

Mark was silent. Until he sneezed. "Liar."

Jason mugged Mark in the back of the head in retaliation, causing him to bust out laughing.

"Y'all are so disrespectful," Alex scoffed.

Chapter 22

Chasity jogged down the hallway towards her room. Glancing at her watch, she sucked her teeth. As she pushed open her door and stepped in, she tripped over something and fell to the floor. Turning over, she eyed the item. "Damn it Malajia!" she yelled at Malajia's book bag which was laying right near the door.

Picking herself up from the floor, she rubbed her sore ankle. "Fuckin' idiot," she fumed. It hadn't been the first time that Malajia left her bag close to the door.

Grabbing her needed textbook from her desk, Chasity limped out of the room. She stepped out of the elevator and proceeded to make her way towards the door. Not even stopping when she heard someone call her name.

"I don't have time to talk to whoever that is," she hissed, grabbing the door handle.

"Not even your favorite person?" a familiar voice chortled.

Not picking up on the voice, Chasity let out a huff. "Who the f—" she paused her profanity laced reply when she saw the owner of the voice. "Trisha?" she amended. "What are you doing here?"

Trisha and Chasity approached one another. Trisha put her hands on Chasity's shoulders, halting their would-be embrace. "Why are you limping?" she asked, concerned.

Chasity rolled her eyes. "I tripped over my soon-to-be dead roommate's book bag," she ground out.

Trisha shook her head and let out a chuckle as she gave Chasity a hug.

"How long have you been here?" Chasity asked.

"I just got here a few minutes ago," Trisha answered. "I was about to call you, but I saw you come out of the elevator."

"So..." Chasity began once they parted. "What are you *doing* here?" she repeated, confused. She'd just spoken to her aunt the day before, and Trisha never mentioned that she would be popping in for a visit.

Trisha adjusted the strap of her designer bag on her shoulder. "Well, I'm here in Virginia on business and I figured, why not come visit my baby and take her to dinner," she replied.

"Um...O-kay." Chasity eyed Trisha skeptically. It wasn't like her to do pop up visits. She'd normally call ahead.

"What?" Trisha asked, noticing Chasity's look.

"What are you up to?" Chasity asked, raising an arched eyebrow.

Trisha giggled. "Nothing," she insisted. "I wanted to check in on you." She laughed when Chasity folded her arms, still holding her gaze. "Chasity, really, I finished up my meeting early and wanted to see you before I catch my flight later tonight."

Chasity relaxed her face. "Okay, if you say so," she relented.

Satisfied, Trisha smiled. "How about I pick you up after your last class?"

"Um, I have a study group after, so I'll just call you when I'm done," Chasity said, heading for the door.

Trisha looked surprised. "*You're* in a study group?" she teased. "As mean as you are?"

"I know, but I don't have a choice. The professor is making us do it," Chasity scoffed. "What are you gonna do while you wait?"

"Go do some damage at that mall," Trisha chortled.

Chasity shrugged. "Okay, see you," she threw over her shoulder.

Trisha stood, watching with pride as Chasity walked out of the dorm.

Malajia reached for a piece of her burger. "Sid, do you still remember anything from your Spanish 101 class?" she asked, before taking a big bite.

Sidra stirred her chicken noodle soup around in her bowl. "Yeah, enough for me to be able to take Spanish 102, *this* semester," she chuckled.

Malajia sucked her teeth. After finishing up a few midterms, Malajia and Sidra met up for a quick lunch before diving back into the books. "Nobody asked you about 102," Malajia griped, in between chews.

Sidra shook her head as she opened a small pack of crackers. "That's a damn shame that you had to repeat that class," she chided. "You're smarter than that."

"Oh, come up off your high horse," Malajia hissed, reaching for a french fry. "You act like *you've* never repeated a class."

"That's because I *haven't*," Sidra stated, staring daggers at Malajia.

"Whatever." Malajia waved her fry in Sidra's direction. "Save your judgments. I hate foreign languages. How am I supposed to know what a biblioteca is?"

"Simple, you *study*," Sidra replied, tone sharp. "And ask for help if you need it. Your roommate can speak Spanish fluently. There is no excuse why you didn't pass."

Malajia flagged her with her hand. She was in no mood for Sidra's lecture. With her midterm the very next day, Malajia's mind was focused on trying to pass. "What does biblioteca mean anyway?"

"Library," Sidra answered, taking a bite of a cracker.

Malajia rolled her eyes and let out a loud sigh, "Sidra, I'm not trying to go to the library right now. I'm trying to find out what *biblioteca* means," she barked.

Sidra held a blank stare on Malajia for a few seconds. "Wow," she slowly put out. Hearing her name called, Sidra spun around to see Dee approaching her table.

"Yes?" Sidra answered with a twinge of annoyance.

Malajia held a stern gaze on Dee. Knowing the issues that Sidra had with her, Malajia was no fan of hers. *Well if it isn't the dirty bathroom chick,* she thought, taking a sip of her drink.

Dee and Sidra both shot Malajia a glance as she took a loud sip through her straw.

"Really?" Sidra scoffed.

Malajia put her hand up. "What? Is my straw sipping *bothering* you?" she spat out.

Sidra shook her head at Malajia, then focused her attention back on Dee. "Can I help you?"

"I take it that you've noticed that the bathroom has been clean lately," Dee said.

Malajia looked confused. "You came over here to say *that*?" she quibbled. "You could've knocked on the bathroom door for all that."

Sidra shot Malajia a glance. "Malajia," she warned.

Malajia, taking that as "be quiet", put her hands up in surrender before going back to her food.

"Yes, Dee. I've noticed," Sidra replied. "I'm glad that we can live in peace now."

"I know, right?" Dee smiled. "'Cause I'd hate to hear about you and my roommate having another argument in the hallway."

"That happened *weeks* ago, why even bring that up?"

Sidra bit out, confused.

Dee shrugged. "No reason." She adjusted her bag on her shoulder and Sidra fixed her eyes on what was on her wrist. "Anyway, see you later."

Sidra followed Dee's progress through the cafeteria before snapping her head towards Malajia, a shocked expression on her face. "That chick has my charms!"

Malajia squinted. "*What* charms?"

"The silver elephant charms from the bracelet," Sidra informed, Malajia still looked confused. "The one that I asked you about last semester? ...The one that I said I might've left in the bathroom?"

"Sidra...*way* too much shit has happened since then for me to remember some damn elephants," Malajia sniped.

Sidra sucked her teeth. "She took the damn charms off my bracelet and put them on that cheap one she had on," she fumed, pushing her bowl away from her.

"Now hold on Sid, how can you be sure that those are from *your* bracelet?" Malajia asked. "You think you're the only one who likes elephants?"

"I know what my damn belongings *look* like Malajia," Sidra fumed.

"Hey, I get you're pissed about losing your stuff," Malajia sympathized, pointing at her. "But you need to be *sure* before you go accusing her of *taking* it,"

"Whatever," Sidra ground out, slamming her hand on the table. "Ever since I moved into that damn room last semester, things that I've left in the bathroom have mysteriously disappeared."

"Stuff like *what*, drama queen?" Malajia jeered, picking up another fry.

"My cell phone case, that bracelet, my crystal ring—"

"Stop leaving your shit in the bathroom!" Malajia exclaimed, cutting Sidra's list short.

Sidra narrowed her eyes at her. "Bite me."

"No thank you," Malajia threw back. "Now look, you

need to get proof that it's yours before you go off on that girl."

Sidra folded her arms and sat back in her seat, sighing loudly.

"Now if we gotta choke slam a bitch for stealing from you, I'm down," Malajia added. "But just be *right*."

Sidra pondered Malajia's words. "I guess you're right," she admitted, tone low.

Malajia reached across the booth and patted Sidra's arm to comfort her. "Now, tell me what biblioteca means," she ordered.

Sidra's eyes became slits. "I'm about to slap you."

Chasity limped down the library steps, then let out a groan when she reached the bottom. *I'm gonna kill Malajia,* she thought, bending down to rub her sore ankle.

"You all right Chasity?" a member of Chasity's study group asked in passing.

"Sure, why not?" Chasity hissed, standing upright. She rolled her eyes in the girls' direction as she trotted away. The girl had singlehandedly caused the group session to surpass its normal hour time with her pointless questions. At least they were pointless to Chasity. "Does the house being red symbolize anything from the characters past?" she muttered to herself, recalling a question that the girl put out regarding their required book reading. "No bitch, it's just a fuckin' red house." Her solo fuss session ceased when she noticed Emily a few feet away. Chasity tilted her head as she watched her walk. Emily's gait was sluggish.

Chasity had every intention of letting the girl continue on her way, but when she noticed that Emily actually locked eyes with her, then quickly put her head down as she tried to hurry pass, Chasity became suspicious.

"Emily," she called. Emily stopped and hesitantly turned around. "Come here," she ordered, signaling her with her hand.

Emily slowly walked up. "Yes?" she meekly put out.

Chasity folded her arms as she adjusted her weight to her good ankle. "You actually saw me looking at you and you were just gonna keep walking, huh?" Chasity spat out, eyes fixed in a stern gaze.

Emily looked at the ground. "I guess I didn't notice you," she stammered.

Chasity rolled her eyes. The girl was a terrible liar. "Nice try," she hissed. "What the hell is going on with you?"

Emily clutched the books to her chest as she continued to stare at the ground. "Nothing, I'm—I've just been studying a whole lot." She hoped that Chasity believed that, but she knew it wasn't true. Emily could barely concentrate long enough to finish homework, let alone study for midterms.

Chasity frowned at Emily's behavior. "I'm not on your shoes Emily. Look me in my face when you're talking to me," she challenged.

Emily lifted her head up and looked at her. "I'm sorry," she sputtered.

Chasity shook her head. Unlike Alex, Chasity wasn't going to baby Emily. "So, you're *still* on this 'I don't know anybody' bullshit?" she spat. "Not answering your phone, your door, acting like you can't speak to people when you *clearly* saw them looking at you."

Emily lowered her head as Chasity continued to scold her. *Since when does she care?* She thought. "Chasity, I've had a lot on my mind," she admitted, voice somber. She sighed. "I didn't think anybody cared."

"*I don't, they* do," Chasity sneered. She immediately felt bad for saying that, the sadness on Emily's face didn't help. "Okay, maybe that's not entirely true," she amended. "I care...a *little*."

Emily pushed hair behind her ears. *I don't believe that because I don't even care about me anymore.* "I don't know what...to say," she muttered.

Chasity frowned as she studied her movements. "Are you drunk?" she asked.

I want to be. Emily shook her head. "I don't drink," she replied. She'd had a few sips before leaving for her Algebra midterm. But she knew she was nowhere near drunk, at least she didn't think so.

Chasity was frustrated; she was getting nowhere with the slovenly looking girl in front of her. "I don't have time for this," she muttered as if she was the only one standing there. "You can go now," she ordered, then watched as Emily scurried off.

"Yo, what the hell are you doing?!" Mark yelled as Malajia picked up a stack of cards from the small coffee table in front of them.

Malajia stared at him as if he had completely lost his mind. "What the hell are you yelling for, fool?" she threw back, adjusting herself in her cushy seat. After playing cards with Mark in Court Terrace's lobby for the past half hour, Malajia was regretting agreeing to the game in the first place.

"You keep taking my damn cards," he fussed, slamming one on the table.

Malajia scratched her head as she regarded him with confusion written on her face. "We're playing *War* dumbass," she spat. "I'm *supposed* to take the cards when I win." She sucked her teeth when Mark sat there with a silly look on his face. "I swear, I don't know why the hell I keep playing cards with you. You piss me off each and every time."

Mark flagged her with his hand. "Shut up," he hissed, not having any other comeback. After playing another hand in silence, Mark began to speak once again. "So Mel."

"What, boy?" Malajia answered, tone even.

"What's the deal with you and that damn Tyrone?"

Malajia studied her cards intensely. "What do you mean

'what's the deal with him'?"

"You still messin' with him?"

Malajia finally glanced up from her cards, frowning. "He's my boyfriend, of course I'm still *messing* with him." She was confused as to where this topic of conversation came from. "Why are you all up in my business?"

Mark made a face. "Yeah well...I don't like him," he bluntly declared.

"*And*?" she sneered.

"He's a bitch," Mark hurled.

"And so are all the girls *you* mess with, but you don't see *me* commenting on them," Malajia threw back.

Mark thought for a moment. "You do *so*," he contradicted.

"Yeah well, maybe on a few 'cause they were just nasty," Malajia amended. "And Ty is *not* a bitch," she barked, delivering a slap to Mark's arm. "Don't be disrespectful."

"Ow!" Mark howled, rubbing his arm. "Look, the dude always be on some ol' whining shit," he stated, examining his arm. "Point is, I don't like him, like I said."

Malajia rolled her eyes.

"And as much as you get on my fuckin' nerves...which you do every single damn *day*," Mark griped, looking at her. "You can do better than that asshat."

"Well now that that's been established, can we just finish the damn game please?" Malajia hissed, over the conversation.

Mark shrugged as he went back to picking a card from his hand. "Just don't bring him around me," he grunted.

"Can you drop it?" Malajia barked. "And what the hell are *you* gonna do if I *do*?"

"I'll punch that dumb ass hat off his head," Mark mumbled.

Malajia sucked her teeth. "Just hurry up and throw out a

damn card," she demanded, pointing to the table.

"So how are midterms going?" Trisha asked, slicing into her freshly-prepared chicken breast.

Chasity reached for her glass of water. "They're okay," she answered. "Ready for them to be over."

Trisha nodded. Having just received their ordered dishes at the quiet restaurant in downtown Paradise Valley, Trisha was enjoying the one on one conversation with Chasity. "I'm sure you'll pass with flying colors," she gushed. "You always *do*."

"Yeah well, I've been losing sleep studying my ass off, so I *better* pass," Chasity joked, twirling some pasta around on her fork. "So how much damage did you do at the mall today?"

Trisha chuckled. "Girl, too damn much," she admitted. "My damn credit cards took a hard hit." She took a sip of her red wine. "I have a few bags in the car for *you* by the way."

Chasity just smiled. Trisha hardly ever went major shopping without including items for Chasity in her budget. Which is something she had always been grateful for. "I'll have to hide whatever you bought me because my damn roommate sniffs shopping bags out like a damn dog."

Trisha laughed. "You leave Malajia alone," she teased. "You pretty much wear the same shirt size; you might as well give her one of the shirts I bought."

Chasity looked at Trisha as if she was crazy. "I wish I *would* give her anything of mine," she sneered. "Hell, after everything she puts me through, she should be giving *me* stuff."

Trisha shook her head. "Still mad you tripped over her bag earlier, huh?"

"My *ankle* is," Chasity jeered.

Trisha stared at her smiling. "You know what, I just want to say that I'm glad that you and those girls are friends," she put out.

Chasity looked confused. "*That* was out of nowhere."

"I wouldn't say that it was exactly out of *nowhere*," Trisha stated, leaning back in her seat. "Truth be told Chaz, *that* and you *in general* have been on my mind a lot lately."

"You mean more than usual?"

Trisha nodded. Truth was, Chasity had been weighing heavily on Trisha's mind ever since they had their first major fight during Thanksgiving. When Chasity came to her, expressing her determination to find her birth mother after a stay in the hospital the previous semester, Trisha practically threatened to disown her if she went through with it. Trisha, knowing how much she'd hurt Chasity, hated herself and with much work, was able to earn Chasity's forgiveness. Even though the fight was behind them, and even though Chasity had decided not to go ahead with her search, Trisha still felt guilty and that feeling, among others had kept Chasity on her mind.

"You know, it hit me," Trisha began, leaning forward. "You're twenty years old."

Chasity stared blankly. "I know, my birthday was almost two months ago," she joked.

"I'm being serious," Trisha giggled, tapping Chasity's hand. "It seems like just yesterday you were a baby, and now you're a grown woman." She took a deep breath as she tried to contain her emotions. "As time passes, I watch you grow and…you're in college and doing *amazing*. You have *friends* and a *boyfriend*—"

"Why are you saying it like you never expected me to have those things?" Chasity asked, voice filled with amusement.

Trisha gave Chasity a knowing look. "Come on girl, you know how evil you are," she joked.

Chasity shrugged, she couldn't argue that fact.

"It's just…even though you were raised in a crappy environment, you're not letting that stop you from growing," Trisha added. "You've already surpassed where *I* was at your age. I just love and admire you…that's all."

The amusement left Chasity's face as she focused on Trisha, who seemed to be filling with emotion right in front of her. "You're not about to cry, are you?"

The question caught Trisha off guard, causing her to chuckle. She wiped a forming tear from her eye. "If I *do*, it's only because I'm happy," she said.

Chasity just concentrated on her food as Trisha continued.

"I want you to know that if I never have a—" Trisha paused for a moment as she tried to gather her words. "If I never have any children of my *own*, you are the best daughter figure that I could ever ask for. I just want you to know that."

"I know that," Chasity assured her. "You've *always* made me feel like I was yours."

Trisha wiped more tears from her eyes. *God, this is getting to be too much,* she thought. "I'm glad that I was able to do that," she smiled.

"Me too," Chasity smiled back. "Are you finished acting weird now?" she asked after a few moments.

"Yes smart ass, I *am*," Trisha laughed. "Let me get back to this food before it gets cold," she added, picking up her fork.

Chapter 23

Malajia opened the door to leave her classroom. "I swear to God, if I failed that Spanish midterm, I'm gonna spit right on Professor Michaels desk," she griped to a classmate once her midterm ended.

"Did you say something, Miss Simmons?" Professor Michaels, who was at the blackboard, asked.

"Huh? No," Malajia lied, hurrying out of the room.

"Girl, he's about sick of you," the girl laughed as the door closed behind them.

"Ain't nobody scared of him," Malajia dismissed, moving hair from her face. "Let me get out of this damn building before I lose my mind."

After waving to her classmate, Malajia proceeded towards the exit. She stopped when she saw Emily in a corner, leaned over a chair. She headed over and stood in front of her. "Miss Harris," she spat out.

Emily was startled, and it showed on her face as she bolted upright. "Hey Malajia," she sputtered, placing her hand on her stomach.

Malajia looked Emily up and down. "You look like you didn't even *bother* to match this morning," she observed, placing her hand on her hip.

Emily glanced down at the baggy yellow T-shirt that she had on, paired with orange yoga pants and pink and grey sneakers. "I was in a rush," she groaned, moving her hand from her stomach to her chest.

Malajia held a look of disgust on her face. "What's the matter with you?" she asked. "You look like you're about to throw up."

Emily felt a dry heave coming on, but successfully contained the urge. "I'm fine," she lied. The hangover that she was suffering from was worse than she'd had in a while. *Please leave so I can go to the bathroom.*

Malajia shook her head. "I don't believe you," she replied, folding her arms. "What did you eat? Did you mix eggrolls and ice cream again?" she wondered, recalling Emily's bout with nausea their freshman year after combining the same food.

Emily just shook her head. "I'm fine," she reiterated.

"Yeah whatever," Malajia hissed. She wasn't exactly happy with Emily and her behavior. "Look, when you start feeling better, you need to bring your ass around more," she stated. "Or at *least* answer when someone calls your ass. I'm sick of hearing Alex bitch about you."

Emily stood there, blinking slowly as Malajia continued to scold her. She almost wished for Chasity to be standing there instead of Malajia. Chasity's rants may have been harsher, but they weren't nearly as long or animated. Feeling the urge to vomit once again, Emily moved around Malajia. "I'm sorry, I gotta go," she put out before darting for the bathroom.

Malajia shook her head. "I can't with her," she mumbled, before heading for the exit.

About halfway through her journey back to her dorm, Malajia saw another familiar face. "Hey Praz," she beamed as she approached her friend.

Praz returned her smile with one of his own as he gave

her a quick hug. "Hey sexy," he cooed. "Haven't seen you at any of my parties lately. Where've you been hiding?"

Malajia waved her hand in his direction. "My whole entire *face* has been in these damn textbooks," she returned. "I hope it was enough to pass these stupid midterms."

Praz chuckled. "I'm sure you did fine."

"I'm sure I bombed on at least *two*," she uttered. "I think it's about time I had you make me one of your drinks to lift my spirits."

Praz rubbed the back of his neck and sighed. "Unfortunately, I don't think I'll be making drinks anytime soon," he stated.

Malajia eyed him with shock. "What?" she barked. "How you gonna just take away our drinks like that? Don't be selfish."

Praz shrugged. "I don't know, ever since I heard about what happened to Brandon, I just don't feel right supplying drinks to people."

Malajia, feeling somber, nodded. "I get that," she said. "Was he drunk off one of *yours* when he died?"

"Nah," Praz shook his head. "I never gave him one. Hardly knew the man. But it's sad nonetheless."

Malajia nodded as she adjusted the purse strap on her shoulder.

"So, tell Emily that I won't be supplying her with anymore...at least for now."

Malajia frowned in confusion. "Emily?" she asked. "Emily *who*?"

Praz gave Malajia's arm a playful poke. "You know what Emily I'm talking about," he hinted.

Malajia was still confused. "Who? *My* Emily?" she questioned, pointing to herself. Praz nodded. "You must be confused."

"No, I know who I'm talking about," Praz assured. "Light-skinned girl, baggy clothes, always quiet—"

"Yeah, I get it," Malajia cut in, putting her hand up. She couldn't believe her ears.

"Yeah, I've been making drinks for her for *months* now," he revealed. "In fact, I just gave her one last night."

Malajia's eyes widened. *That's why she looked sick when I saw her.* "I don't get it," she sputtered, still in disbelief. "Emily doesn't drink."

Praz gave Malajia a long look. "Yes, she *does*," he confirmed. He patted Malajia on her arm. "If you didn't know, you may wanna holler at her."

"Oh I'll *holler* all right," Malajia grunted as Praz walked off. Malajia took a deep breath and began jogging the rest of the way towards Paradise Terrace.

"Can you just taste it, please?" Alex asked Chasity, pushing a spoon full of soup in her face.

Chasity pushed the spoon away from her, spilling some of the liquid on the floor. "I told you, I'm not tasting that nasty ass soup," she snapped.

Sidra laughed as Alex let out a sigh. Having microwaved too much soup, Alex along with Sidra walked over to Chasity and Malajia's room moments ago to offer up some extras. A gesture that Chasity was not interested in accepting.

"I put seasoning in it," Alex explained, yanking tissue from a small box on Malajia's desk.

"I don't give a shit *what's* in there," Chasity griped. "I'm *not* eating it."

"So damn picky," Alex grunted, wiping the soup from the carpet.

Sidra pushed her ponytail over her shoulder. "Alex, you *did* ask the girl like five times if she wanted some," she teased. "Even *after* she told you 'no' the first time."

Chasity spun around in her seat. "Exactly," she agreed. "Like asking me again was gonna change my mind."

Alex waved her hand at Chasity as she tossed the soiled tissue into the trash can.

Malajia barged through the door, panting. "Eww, what smells like old boots?" she jeered, looking at Alex.

"Alex's nasty ass soup," Chasity answered nonchalantly.

Alex couldn't help but laugh. "I hate you both," she joked.

Malajia winced as she carefully stepped out of her high-heeled sandals. "Remind me never to run in those shoes again."

"Why *were* you running?" Sidra asked, eyeing the red strap marks on Malajia's bare feet.

Malajia sat on her bed and grabbed one foot, giving it a rub. "'Cause I got some stuff to tell y'all that couldn't wait," she vaguely put out.

"Stuff like *what*?" Alex ground out. "There's a party in the clusters that you want to drag us to?"

Malajia shot Alex a side-glance. "*No,*" she spat. "It's about Emily…Yo, that girl has been drinking."

All eyes were fixed on Malajia. Alex was confused. "Drinking what? Juice?"

Malajia pinched the bridge of her nose in agitation. She could've slapped Alex. "Why would I rush back here to tell you that she was drinking *juice*?" she barked.

Alex folded her arms in a huff. "What *else* could you *possibly* be talking about when it comes to Emily?" she threw back.

"*Alcohol* dumbass!" Malajia snapped. Her feet hurt; she worked up a sweat and she was not in the mood for Alex's nonsense.

Chasity pointed at Alex, who stood there in disbelief. "I *told* you," Chasity hurled.

"No wait, that can't be right," Sidra cut in, holding her hands up. "Malajia, where did you hear that?"

"Praz," Malajia revealed. "I ran into him and we got to talking. He mentioned that he'd been making drinks for Emily for *months* now. Even as recently as last night."

"What?" Alex whispered to herself as she placed a hand on her head.

"I saw her earlier and she looked rough," Malajia continued. "Like she had a *serious* hangover."

Chasity shook her head. "Alex, I told you," she reiterated. "I *knew* there was something off about her."

"I don't understand why she would be drinking like that," Alex sputtered, taking a seat on a chair. "What is she *doing*?"

"She's obviously going through something serious," Sidra said.

"And she thinks that drinking is gonna fix whatever her issue is?!" Alex boomed, pounding her fist in her other hand.

"Why are you yelling at *us*?" Chasity wondered.

Alex vigorously shook her head. "No, I can't take Praz's word for it."

"Alex, why would he lie? What *purpose* would that serve?" Malajia pointed out.

"She has a point," Sidra added.

"No, I know Emily and she would never do that," Alex declared. "I saw how regretful she was after her first experience with liquor *last* semester."

"This isn't *last* semester," Chasity argued. "And you obviously don't know her like you *think* you do."

Alex flashed a scowl Chasity's way. "Oh and what? *You* know her?"

"I know what *alcohol* is doing to her," Chasity flashed back, folding her arms.

"Even if she *was* drinking, that doesn't mean she's gonna turn out like *Brenda*, Chasity," Alex fumed.

"Don't get your feelings hurt again, *Alex*," Chasity warned.

"Whatever," Alex hurled back. "I don't even know *why* you're commenting on Emily. It's not like you care about her anyway."

"Don't do that Alex," Chasity hissed. "I may not care for how she *acts*, but I *do* care about her."

"Alex, you're mad at Chasity because you know that she has a point," Malajia interjected.

Alex tossed her hands in the air in frustration. "There you go agreeing with her again," she bit out. "No opinions of your own, huh minion?"

"Kiss my *entire* black ass, Alex," Malajia barked.

"No, no everybody just chill out," Sidra jumped in, standing from the bed.

"This isn't about agreeing with me just to spite *you*, Alex," Chasity hissed, ignoring Sidra's urging. "You keep making it seem like nobody cares about her the way *you* do."

"That's not what—"

Chasity jerked her hand up to silence Alex. "But since you think you're the *only* friend she has, you're not being a good one because you're turning a blind eye to what she's doing," she scolded.

Alex rolled her eyes and looked away in anger.

"Alex, I agree with *them*," Sidra calmly stated. "Emily…she's not herself. And we should've seen this a long time ago."

Alex stood from the bed after a few seconds. "We need to see her, *now*," she ordered.

Emily rolled over in bed, pulling the covers up over her head in the process. She couldn't fall asleep. On top of still feeling the effects of her hangover, the answers to her Spanish midterm swirled in her head. *You failed that midterm, just like the others.*

The minute she closed her eyes, a loud bang jerked them back open.

"Emily, its Alex. Open the door," Alex demanded, banging again.

Emily was startled by Alex's angry tone. Jumping out of bed, she glanced around her messy room. Ignoring the piles of clothes, crumbled up paper and soiled dishes, she focused on the empty glass bottles on the floor by her bed. "Coming," she muttered when Alex banged again. Giving the bottles a quick kick under her bed, she ran to the door and opened it. Emily's eyes widened when she saw not only Alex, but the other girls standing there, sternness on their faces.

"You gonna invite us in?" Malajia hissed.

Emily moved aside. "Sure," she replied, as the girls moved inside.

"Oh my God girl, this room is disgusting," Sidra complained, looking around. "It looks like you haven't cleaned in *weeks*."

"I'm sorry for the mess," Emily put out, embarrassed. "I wasn't expecting any company."

"*Clearly*," Chasity spat.

"*Damn* the mess," Malajia barked. "What's up with not sharing your drinks with us?"

Emily's mouth fell open. "Um, I don't know what you're talking about," she stammered.

"Emily, stop," Sidra cut in, tone stern. "Just stop, we know what you've been doing."

"Yeah, getting drunk without us…Without *me*," Malajia grumbled.

Alex shot Malajia a stern look before turning back to Emily. Disappointment was written on her face. "Praz told Malajia that he's been supplying you with his drinks for a while," she revealed. "Is that true? Emily…have you been getting drunk?"

"Without *me*," Malajia clarified, earning a stiff backhand to the arm from Sidra.

Emily felt like the walls were closing in on her. She feared the day that they would find out. She couldn't find the words to say as her eyes shifted to each girl. "Um, I don't know—"

Chasity glanced at the floor, then back at Emily, who had slowly sat down on her bed. "Before you open your mouth to lie *again*, keep in mind that there are two empty bottles on the floor," Chasity pointed out, gesturing to the bottles peeking from under her bed.

Emily felt tears fill her eyes. *Busted.* "I'm sorry," she sniffled.

The sternness left Alex's face as she sat down next to Emily. "Sweetie…" she moved some of Emily's disheveled hair from her face. "What's going on with you?" she asked, tone soft. "Why are you doing this?"

Emily sucked in a breath as she tried not to completely break down. "I'm stressed out," she sobbed.

Chasity rolled her eyes; she was not for the pity party. "Get over it," she snapped.

Emily put her hands over her face and broke.

"You're *not* the only person who's stressed," Chasity chided, unfazed by Emily's tears. "You need to find a better way to deal with it."

Sidra sighed. "Sweetie, we're not upset at the fact that you had a drink, we've *all* had one at some point in time," she clarified. "What upsets us is the fact that you're obviously doing it because you think it's going to solve whatever it is that you're dealing with… If you don't watch it, you'll become an alcoholic."

"I'm *not* an alcoholic," Emily argued through her sobbing.

"Maybe not *now*," Sidra agreed. "But if you continue on like this…You *will* be."

"I just… I just wanted to forget about everything for a little while," Emily explained, rubbing her arm. "I don't even *like* it, I just…for a little while, I don't feel."

"Yeah well, I'm sure you feel those *hangovers*," Malajia jeered. "You *look* like you do."

"Em, what's stressing you?" Alex asked, ignoring Malajia's comment.

Emily wiped her face with the sleeve of her shirt. "I'm not doing well in my classes," she said. "I can't concentrate on anything because my mom—"

"Your *mom*?" Chasity cut in, agitated. "You're in danger of becoming an alcoholic because of your fuckin' *mother*?"

"Chaz," Alex warned.

"No, 'Chaz' *nothing*," Chasity snapped, frowning at Alex. "I told you, I wasn't coming here to baby this bitch." She focused her piercing gaze to Emily, who couldn't even look Chasity in the eye. "You're grown, and instead of putting that lonely ass, crazy person in her place, you're letting her dictate what you do. From *miles away*, she runs you. You're *letting* her run you."

"I know," Emily admitted through her tears.

Malajia shook her head. "Look Emily, jokes aside...you need to stop this," she advised. "We want to help you. We really *do*. But until you deal with your mother...you're *never* gonna be okay."

"That woman has a vice grip on you...and you're choking from it," Sidra added. "You can't even hang out with us without wondering what she's gonna say or do... It's not right. It's not *healthy*."

Alex put her arm around Emily. "The girls are right," she admitted. "Your mother is just—" Alex took a deep breath. "Look, maybe you don't want to hear this but...you might need to move in with your father."

"Wait, that's an *option*?" Malajia asked, surprised.

Emily managed a nod. Alex was the only one whom she told about her father's offer to have her come live with him.

"Then what the hell is the damn issue about?" Malajia asked, confused.

Emily sniffled. "I just *can't* do that. I can't move out... It'll crush my mom," she explained, voice trembling. "And as much as she drives me crazy...I love her and I don't want her to hate me."

Chasity tossed her hands in the air. "You know what, I can't do this with her anymore," she sneered, heading for the door.

"Chaz, don't leave," Malajia pleaded.

"Yeah come on, she needs our support," Sidra added.

Chasity spun around. "No, what she *needs* is to have some sense slapped into her weak ass," she barked. "I'm over it, I'm done, I'm *leaving*."

Alex just hugged Emily as Chasity stormed out of the room.

Malajia let out a huff. "Let me go calm this girl down so I ain't gotta deal with that mood later," she complained, heading for the door. "Take care of yourself Emily," she sincerely said before walking out.

Alex pulled away from Emily and looked at her. "Emily, please stop trying to drink your problems away," she begged. "I'm scared for you. I just imagine what happened to Brandon…happening to *you*."

Emily shook her head. "I know what I was doing was wrong," she said. "I just—I needed an outlet."

"Talk to *us*, let *us* be your outlet," Sidra urged. "Bottling things up hasn't been good for *any* of us… If you don't want to hear what *we* have to say, then talk to a counselor… *someone*."

"You can talk to Ms. Smith," Alex suggested. "I'll even go *with* you."

Emily managed a small smile. But she knew that no matter if it was her friends or a stranger, nobody was going to solve the issue with her mother. "Okay," she promised.

Sidra headed for the door. "Alex, come on. Let's let her get some rest," she ordered. "She looks like she could use it."

Alex stood up. "Call me later," she said, voice stern. "I mean it. No more hiding. We're your friends and we're here for you."

"*All* of us, even Lucifer," Sidra chortled, earning a small chuckle from Emily. Emily nodded and both girls left the room. Emily reached down and grabbed the two empty glass jars. After giving them a long stare, she tossed them in the nearby trashcan.

Chapter 24

Trisha chuckled as she jotted notes down on the notepad in front of her. "Chasity, you already knew this was going to happen," she said into her phone. "No need to give yourself a headache because of it."

Chasity tossed a small suitcase into her trunk and slammed it shut. "This is your fault, you know," she hissed, walking over to the passenger's side of her car. "You should've told her ass no."

"You know I can't say no to Malajia," Trisha replied, amusement in her voice. "Come on, having her here for spring break will be fun." Trisha had a feeling that when she accepted Malajia's request to stay with her and Chasity in West Chester for spring break, that Chasity wouldn't be pleased. But knowing that Chasity would just spend practically the entire break held up in her room, she figured that having Malajia around would force her to have fun.

"For *you* maybe," Chasity griped. She rolled her eyes when Malajia trotted up to the car, a small suitcase in hand.

"Heeeey boo," Malajia sang. "You ready to spend break in that big ass house of yours?"

Chasity held her angry gaze as Malajia did a dance in a circle. "You know what Trisha, let me call you back," she said into the phone.

"Don't choke the girl," Trisha joked.

"I'm not making any promises," Chasity jeered.

Trisha shook her head and giggled to herself once she ended the call. Glancing at her expensive watch, she tapped her pen on the wood desk. "One more meeting and I can get out of here," she sighed to herself. Knowing that she was having an extra guest for the week, Trisha couldn't wait to leave her Philadelphia office and begin planning some fun things for the girls to do. Hearing a beep on her intercom, Trisha pressed a button. "Yes Deb."

"Ms. Duvall, your three o'clock is here," the woman's voice announced through the speaker.

"Send them in," Trisha ordered. Shifting some papers on her desk, she mentally prepared herself for a face to face with a new potential mansion buyer. She stood from her swivel chair and smoothed her jacket down. When the door opened, the smile that Trisha held gave way to shock. "What the hell?" she ground out as the door closed.

"Long time no see, Patrisha," Derrick Parker returned, straightening his tie.

Trisha felt the blood drain from her face. Of all people, she never expected to see her ex-brother in law walk through her office door. "What are you doing here?"

Derrick strolled over to the chair across from Trisha's. "May I?" he asked, pointing to it.

Trisha nodded, as she too sat down.

"Derrick," she said, trying to keep her composure. "Why are you here?"

"Well, since you haven't been answering any of my phone calls, I figured I'd take a trip from New York to come see you face to face."

Trisha frowned. "So you making up some phony name, pretending to be a damn client, having me do all this freakin' research on a house that you have no *intention* of buying was just so you can *visit*?" she hissed.

"I was desperate," Derrick explained, tone calm. "I know you've seen that I've been calling."

"I'm a busy woman, Derrick," Trisha returned. "Unless it's about business, I don't answer."

"I know, and I promise I won't take up too much of your time," he replied. "But this is important."

Trisha fiddled with her hands. "*What* is?"

Derrick leaned forward. "I need to talk to you about your sister."

"You know that Brenda and I don't talk."

"I know that, but this has to do with what she said to Chasity," Derrick clarified. "What she's going around saying to *everybody*."

Trisha's eyes shifted. "Um…I don't—"

"After Chasity told me a few months ago that Brenda told her that she was adopted, I've been trying to talk to my reclusive, alcoholic ex-wife to figure out why the hell she would tell our daughter that." His tone was angry as he spoke of Brenda.

Trisha glanced at the desk. She felt her chest tighten. She knew that Derrick would eventually come to her for answers. Ever since she learned from Chasity about her conversation with her father in New York over winter break, Trisha had been on edge. She hoped that avoiding his calls would send him in another direction, but his presence in her office proved otherwise. "Um, did you ever get in touch with Brenda?" she wondered.

Derrick sighed. "Briefly," he admitted. "I asked her why she would say that, and what the hell her problem was…she told me to ask *you*," he spat, fixing a skeptical gaze. "Then she hung up and is now blocking all of my calls."

Trisha pinched the bridge of her nose as Derrick continued. *Fuck!*

"Look, I already know that what Brenda said was completely absurd," Derrick concluded. "I mean, I know the woman spews garbage when she's been drinking, but to lie like that to our daughter is disgusting."

"Derrick," Trisha began, looking at the ceiling momentarily, as if the words that she needed would be up there. "Brenda didn't lie, Chasity *is* adopted."

"That's not possible," he contradicted.

Trisha frowned. "It *is* possible," she maintained. "You remember, you were gone for a whole year. And…look, Chasity is adopted, Brenda hid it from you… It is what it is."

Derrick shook his head. "That's bullshit," he spat. "You know how I know that?"

"*How* Derrick? How do you know that?" Trisha was tired, she wished that he would stop arguing with her and leave.

"Because I'm her *biological* father," he informed, angry.

Trisha's eyes widened. "Wait, how—"

"I had a paternity test done on Chasity when she was three years old," he revealed.

Trisha sat back in her seat, unable to speak. *What? He did what?!*

"When Chasity was a baby, things were fine between me and Brenda. We were getting back to where we were, before—" He paused momentarily as he rubbed his forehead, Trisha looked down at her hands. "Anyway, a few years passed and Brenda and I started fighting again…more than usual. It's like something in her triggered. And every time I spent time with Chasity, it was like she hated it, like she didn't want me to bond with her," he added as Trisha remained silent. "I thought that maybe while I was gone…that she cheated on me and that Chasity wasn't mine…so I had the test done."

"Did you *tell* Brenda?" Trisha asked, finally able to speak. Even though her words were calm, Trisha was screaming on the inside.

Derrick shook his head.

Trisha looked confused. "How could you have done that without her knowing?"

"My friend worked at the DNA department in Tucson; he did me a favor."

Trisha felt her heart drop to her stomach. "As angry as Brenda was at you…and as fucked up as she *is*….she would never cheat on you."

"I figured that maybe she wanted to get back at me for what *I* did," Derrick shrugged.

"Could you blame her if she *did*?" Trisha asked point blank.

Derrick once again shook his head. "No."

Trisha ran her trembling hands through her hair. "I don't understand," she muttered. "If…if you knew that you were Chasity's father, that you *are* her father…why haven't you been reaching out to her?" she hissed, feeling a wave of anger come over her. "Why hasn't she heard from you? Why do you act like she doesn't exist?"

"Look, I'm not proud of how I was when she was growing up," Derrick argued. "I let my misery with Brenda keep me detached from my child, and I want to make that right," he reasoned. "But I don't want to go back to Chasity until I get this shit—this *lie* straightened out."

"That sounds like more excuses for why you're not being a damn father to her," Trisha fumed.

"I *am* her father," Derrick countered. "And despite what *you*, your *mother*, *Brenda* or anybody *else* in this damn family thinks, I *do* love her," he insisted. "And you lashing out at me still doesn't take away the fact that your sister lied to her."

Trisha shook her head. "Derrick…Brenda wasn't lying," she maintained, pausing for a moment "She *isn't* Chasity's mother."

Derrick was fed up. After everything that he just said, Trisha was still lying to him. "I just told you that I'm her *father* Patrisha," he barked.

"I *know* that Derrick," Trisha assured him.

"If you know that, then *why* are you keeping up with that bullshit story?" he fumed. "How can Brenda *not* be her mother? That's ridiculous."

Trisha leaned forward as she tried to control her breathing. "Derrick listen—"

"No, there is no way *possible* that Brenda isn't Chasity's mother," Derrick protested. "She's the only woman who *could* be."

Trisha locked eyes with him. "You sure about that?"

"Yes, yes I'm *sure*," Derrick returned, confident. "I never fathered a child with anyone else. Hell, except for that *one* indiscretion; I was faithful to her." He pounded his fist on the desk. "No child resulted from me cheating that *one* time. Brenda is a liar."

Trisha held her gaze even as tears glassed over. "You sure about that?" she repeated.

Derrick fixed an angry stare at Trisha. When she didn't speak, his look changed to confusion. Then as realization set in, sickness. He leaned back in his seat and placed his hand over his head. "Oh my God," he stammered, before closing his eyes.

Trisha felt a tear fall as silence filled the room.

Chapter 25

Emily poked at the sandwich on her plate as she listened to her mother talk from across the small bistro table. She would give anything to be in her room, with her door locked, under the covers.

"When do you get your midterm grades?" Ms. Harris asked, taking a sip of her wine spritzer.

Emily shrugged, staring at the chilled glass. "Probably in a few weeks," she answered, tone dry. She'd just returned home for spring break that morning, and her mother was already pestering her about midterm grades.

"You already know that I'm going to want to see them," Ms. Harris declared.

"Yes, I know." Emily's tone hadn't changed. *God, shut up!*

"Did you pass?"

Emily refrained from rolling her eyes at her mother's interrogation. She shrugged. "I hope so," she mumbled. Emily didn't even believe her own words.

Ms. Harris sat her glass back down, annoyed at Emily's indifference. "Look, if I knew you weren't going to talk, we could have stayed home."

"Mommy, I said *earlier* that I wanted to stay home," Emily replied, tired. "You told me to stop whining and come on."

Ms. Harris fixed a stern gaze. "I *remember* what I said."

"Then why—" Emily put her hand over her face as she fought to keep her agitation from showing. The last thing that she wanted was to upset her mother more than she already was and run the risk of suffering an earful for the rest of the day. "Okay, I'm sorry," she amended, reaching for her glass of water.

Ms. Harris picked her fork up, the apology seemed to satisfy her. "You know, this place is really nice," she mused of the restaurant.

Emily just sat there in silence, trying to keep her focus off of the spritzer sitting in front of her mother. *Stop it Emily, you promised yourself that you wouldn't touch another drink.* "Oh yeah?" she answered, unenthused.

"Yes," she nodded. "It's close to the Community College too," she informed.

Emily gave a blank stare. "Uh huh," she muttered. She knew it was only a matter of time before her mother brought up another college.

"I figured, if you transferred, we could meet here for lunch some days."

Emily felt like she was trying to catch her breath. The mention of transferring, paired with knowing that her midterm grades would not meet her mother's requirements, made Emily feel a panic attack coming on. Her mother's warning from last semester rang in her head. *She's gonna make me transfer.* "I'll be right back," Emily quickly put out before bolting from her seat, leaving her mother perplexed.

Emily made a beeline for the bathroom and once inside, ran water in the sink and splashed some on her face. As she stared at her reflection in the mirror, Emily steadied her breathing. She would give anything to be able to talk to one of the girls.

Sidra applied one final coat of silver polish to her nails, before giving the nails a long blow. "That nail polish smells like straight chemicals," Josh jeered, fanning his hand in front of his face.

Sidra giggled as she screwed the top on the small glass container. "So dramatic," she teased. Sidra had been home on spring break for two days before Josh popped in for a visit. While her family was out, the two friends were enjoying some one on one time. "So, what do you plan on doing for the rest of the week?" she asked, fanning her hands.

Josh shrugged. "Nothing much really," he answered, leaning back on the couch. "I'll probably help Dad out in the car garage."

"How is that going by the way?" Sidra asked, adjusting her legs on the couch. "The car maintenance business."

"It's okay, I guess," Josh replied, switching his position to face her. "It pays the bills."

Sidra nodded as she blew her cool breath on her fingertips. She glanced back up to find Josh staring at her. "What?" she smiled.

"What?" Josh wondered.

"You're staring at me like a crazy person," she teased.

Josh immediately turned his head. He hadn't realized that he was doing it. *Way to go dumbass.* He glanced at the clock on the wall in front of him. "Listen, when I get off work later, you want to go to a movie?"

Sidra shrugged. "Sounds good," she agreed. "Mark and David coming?"

Josh ran a hand over his head. "Um…no," he muttered. "I thought it would be kind of nice if you and *I* just hung out." He glanced at her, eyes hopeful. "You don't think so?"

"No sweetie, I wasn't implying that," Sidra assured with a wave of her hand. "I was just asking, that's all."

"So it's a date then," Josh smiled.

Sidra went to respond, but was interrupted by the ringing phone. "Hold on," she said to Josh who just nodded. She reached for the phone and once it was at her ear, she smiled. "Hi James," she beamed.

Josh sucked his teeth. *He's not dead yet!* He hopped up

from the couch. "I gotta go to work," he grunted.

Sidra, unaware of the change in Josh's mood; waved to him as he walked out the door. "How have you been?" she asked into the phone.

"Good, just taking a quick break," James replied. "Decided to check up on you. How's your break going?"

"It's fine. I haven't done anything yet," Sidra sighed. "But I guess that's a good thing."

"Yeah," James agreed. "Listen, besides checking in on you, I wanted to ask you something."

Sidra waited in anticipation. "Ask me what?"

"I'll be taking a trip up to Delaware in a few days, and I was wondering if you'd allow me to take you to dinner while I'm there."

She was smiling so much that her cheeks started to hurt. She'd only been out for coffee with him when they first met, and although they had been talking on the phone quite often, Sidra hoped that she would get the opportunity to see him face to face again. "I'd love that," she crooned.

"Great." The tone of James's voice, made it clear that he was smiling too. "Listen sweetie, I have to jump on a conference call, but I'll call you later tonight with the details."

Sidra was fighting to contain her building excitement. "Okay," was all that she could get out. It was when she ended the call that she let out a high-pitched scream of excitement.

Trisha gave the doorbell to her mother's house a ring before crossing her arms to her chest. Hearing a voice yell from inside, Trisha glanced up at the night sky. "It's Trisha, Mom," she replied.

"It's open!"

Trisha sighed as she twisted the door knob, finding it unlocked. Stepping into the living room, she regarded her elderly mother with a stern look. "Mom, what have I told you about leaving your door unlocked?"

The salt and pepper haired, distinguished woman waved her hand dismissively at her youngest child from the comfort of her couch. "Child, nothing happens in this neighborhood," she assured.

Trisha crossed the hardwood floor, removing the purse from her shoulder. "That's not the point," she chided.

Grandmother Duvall grinned. "All right Patrisha, I'll make sure to lock the door from now on," she promised as Trisha flopped down on the couch next to her.

"Thank you," Trisha mumbled, pinching the bridge of her nose.

Her mother studied her; Trisha looked tired. "What brings you by?" she wondered. "I know you're usually working."

Trisha turned in her seat to face her mother. Work was the last thing on her mind. Ever since Derrick's visit days ago, Trisha felt like her world was caving in around her. She couldn't focus on anything, not even spending time with Chasity and Malajia, who'd been home on break. She needed to see her mother. "I just wanted to come see you," she answered.

"Okay," Grandmother Duvall smiled, giving Trisha's leg a pat. "Well, I'm glad you're here. I've missed you, you know." Trisha managed a smile. "Even though you only live a few blocks away, it'll be nice to see you *and* Chasity more often."

Trisha glanced down at her hands as she took hold of her mother's hand. "Yeah, I know," she agreed. She looked back up. "How's everything though, Mom?" she asked. "Did you go for your checkup? Is everything okay?"

"Yes sweetie, I'm good and healthy...*old*," she joked. "But healthy. I take my vitamins every day."

"Good." Trisha gave her mother's hand a soft pat. "And the house? Everything good with it?"

"Of course."

"You sure?" Trisha pressed. "Everything working okay? Is the gardener coming when he's supposed to? The pool cleaners? Do you need me to take you food shopping—"

Grandmother Duvall put her hand on Trisha's shoulder, calming her rambling. "Patrisha, everything with the house is fine. *I'm* fine," she insisted. She chuckled. "What's gotten into you? Why are you acting so worried?"

Trisha took a deep breath as she felt her emotions surfacing. "Mom, I just want to make sure you have everything you need. Everything you want," she sputtered. "I feel like I should be doing more for you...after everything that I put you through growing up—" a tear fell. "I should be doing more."

A seriousness fell over Grandmother Duvall's brown face. "Now you stop that," she ordered, voice stern. "Don't you go bringing up the past."

"I can't help it," Trisha sniffled. "I was a horrible daughter to you and Dad," she recalled. "I wish that I could just make up for everything—I just want to make everything right."

Grandmother Duvall placed her hand on Trisha's tear-stained cheek. She hadn't seen Trisha this distraught since she was seventeen years old. "You listen to me," she urged, voice comforting. "You weren't horrible, you were *troubled,*" she amended. "We *both* made mistakes back then." She shook her head as the memories of Trisha's adolescent years flooded back. "I admit that after your father died, I couldn't handle you anymore... I tried, but to be honest I wish I had tried harder...to this day I still feel guilty for kicking you out."

"Mom, you had *every right* to kick me out," Trisha recalled. She shifted in her seat when her mother shook her head in disagreement. "I disrespected you. I stole from you. I tried to *hit* you," she added, regretful. "Between that and me dropping out of school—I regret everything that I did. And I know that I've said this before, but I'm so sor—"

"It's forgiven *and* forgotten," Grandmother Duvall promised. "Sweetheart, have you looked at yourself lately?" she smiled proudly. "You have made a *complete* turnaround.

You went back to school, you graduated college, you even got your *master's* degree," she pointed out. "You own a business. You are a beautiful, smart, successful, kind-hearted woman...and I am so proud of you."

More tears fell from Trisha's eyes. "You really mean that?"

"Of *course* I do," Grandmother Duvall gushed, smoothing some of Trisha's bobbed hair from her face. "As much as I appreciate this house you bought for me, all I ever wanted was for you to be the best that you could be...and you're doing that, so I don't want for anything from you."

Trisha managed a smile, but despite her mother's reassuring words, Trisha still carried a guilt, a burden that she had yet to shed. "Mom—"

"I just wish that Brenda was the best that *she* could be," Grandmother Duvall said, cutting Trisha's words short. Trisha clammed up at the mention of her older sister's name. "I swear, I don't know what went wrong with her," she stated. "I haven't spoken to her. Have *you*?"

Trisha shook her head.

Grandmother Duvall sighed. "I wish I knew where things with you two fell apart," she sulked. "You two used to be so close when you were children."

"Yeah, I know," Trisha mumbled.

"I swear, ever since she ran off and married that boy...*Derrick* and followed him to Arizona, she's been different." Grandmother Duvall rubbed her arm. "I mean, the drinking, the way that she treated Chasity—I just don't get it. How could she treat a child with so much hatred?" She became angry. "And why didn't I see it sooner?"

Trisha found it hard to speak as her mother continued her rant about Brenda's questionable behavior.

"And you know what also has me so angry?" she fussed. "That Brenda kept the fact that she adopted Chasity a secret."

Trisha put her hand over her chest as she tried to steady her breathing.

"Why would she do that?" Grandmother Duvall asked as if Trisha had the answers. "Why would she hide it? From the family...from *me*, her mother?"

"Mom," Trisha pleaded.

"Was she ashamed? Was she embarrassed? Could she not have children of her own?" Grandmother Duvall fixed a pleading gaze on Trisha, who was practically falling apart in front of her. "Patrisha, you obviously knew about Chasity's adoption, which means at one point Brenda trusted you enough to tell you," she said. "You *have* to help me understand, because Brenda won't talk to me," she demanded.

"Brenda hates you because you still love *me*," Trisha sobbed.

Grandmother Duvall was both hurt and confused by that statement. "But why?" she asked. "Is it because I forgave you for your past? You didn't hurt *her*, so why is *she* so angry?"

"Mom," Trisha cried, holding onto her mother's hand, almost for dear life. Her mother stared at her in anticipation of what she was about to say.

"What is it baby?"

Trisha took a deep breath. "There's something that I have to tell you."

Chapter 26

Chasity picked up a colorful designer bag from its shelf and examined it. "You think this is too loud?" she asked Malajia, who was eyeing a wallet on a nearby shelf.

Malajia glanced at the bag then touched it. "For *you*, Miss Midnight? Yes, yes it is," she teased of Chasity's all black attire. She then grabbed the bag. "For *me*, no."

Chasity snatched it back. "Unless you have two hundred dollars in that dry ass bank account of yours, it isn't *you either*," she ground out, placing the bag back.

Malajia sucked her teeth. "Shit," she grimaced. "I guess I better stick to these twenty dollar wallets," she joked, picking one up.

The two girls, having spent the first few days of spring break holed up in a one-bedroom suite at the Wyngate hotel in Philadelphia, decided to take an excursion to the mall.

Malajia put the wallet down. "That shit's thirty bucks, I'm not buying that," she griped. "Where are the five dollar wallets?"

"Not in *this* store," Chasity muttered.

"Clearly," Malajia giggled. "Do you think we should order some more of those burgers from room service?" she asked. "That one we had last night was the best damn burger I've ever had."

Chasity shook her head. "Nah, I think I want to go home tonight," she replied.

Malajia shot her a glance. "Girl *why?*" she sneered. "Ms. Trisha already said that we can stay as long as we want. We got free reign to do whatever the hell we want...and *spend* all we want."

"See, you're always thinking about spending money," Chasity chided.

"I was joking about that part," Malajia amended. Her eyes shifted. "A little."

Chasity shook her head. "Look, as much as I enjoy all of the over the top amenities of that expensive ass hotel, I'd rather just be home." Chasity was confused and stunned when Trisha presented her and Malajia the option to stay at the hotel, instead of their shared home, for break. Had it not been for Malajia running her mouth every five minutes about it, she would have declined.

"I hear you," Malajia sympathized. "But you heard her. She wanted to make sure we have fun. She said she felt bad because she's been busy—"

"I *heard* what she said," Chasity abruptly cut in. "But that makes no sense. She can be busy all day and just leave us at the house. I'm not five, I can be at home alone."

"I don't think that's what she intended to say with the gesture," Malajia pointed out, voice calm.

Chasity rolled her eyes as she folded her arms. "I swear, she's been acting real weird lately," she fussed. "First it was getting all emotional for no reason over dinner a while ago. Then, when I got home it's like she could barely look at me...like she didn't want me there." Chasity recalled how standoffish Trisha was when she arrived home for break. She barely made eye contact with her, and every time Chasity wanted to talk to Trisha, she made up an excuse as to why she had to leave. Chasity and Malajia had been there only a day before she mentioned the hotel stay.

Malajia shook her head. "Come on Chaz, you know that's not true in the *least* bit," she said. "From what I've seen, you're like her favorite person."

"Yeah well, she's not *acting* like it," Chasity sulked.

Malajia rolled her eyes. "Girl stop bitchin'," she hurled, earning a frown from Chasity. "So, Trisha is acting funny. I'm sure she has a reason," she said. "I'm sure she'll tell you what it is later on. In the meantime, let's enjoy what the hell she paid for."

Chasity rolled her eyes again.

"And the bright side is that you get to spend some one on one time with *me*," Malajia beamed, a bright smile on her face.

Chasity stared at her. "I'd rather spend it with Jason," she hissed.

Malajia's smile fell, a narrow-eyed look replaced it. "Must you be a bitch *all* the time?" she sneered, earning a laugh from Chasity.

"Your feelings are so damn easy to hurt," Chasity joked.

"Yeah well, fuck you," Malajia huffed, folding her arms. "You're stuck with me, 'cause Jason is still at the shore with his family."

"He'll be back tonight," Chasity countered.

"And while he's visiting you in your room, I'll be in the *other* one listening 'cause I ain't leaving that damn hotel," Malajia spat. "You *and* him got me chopped."

Chasity frowned her face in disgust.

Malajia, picking up on Chasity's thoughts, nodded. "Yeah, I listen," she confirmed, unashamed.

Hearing a sound from her cell phone, Chasity retrieved it from her bag and looked at it. "Looks like you'll be going back to the hotel by your damn self," she announced.

"Why?"

"Trisha just texted me, she wants me to come home tonight," Chasity informed, placing the phone back into her bag. "Said she wants to talk to me about something."

"Well, have fun with that," Malajia shrugged. "I'll be enjoying that room service and those movies, alone."

Chasity pointed at her. "Don't you order those nasty ass movies, Malajia," she warned.

"You're not gonna be there to stop me," Malajia mocked, walking out of the store.

Chasity walked into a darkened house and sat her bag on the couch. Flicking on a nearby lamp, she looked around. It was quiet. It'd been a few hours since she received the text from Trisha, requesting her presence.

"Chasity is that you?" Trisha called from the den.

"Yeah," Chasity answered before heading for her. Trisha was sitting on the chaise lounge in the dimly lit room by the bay window, one of her and Chasity's favorite spots in the house. She took a seat on the chair in front of her. "What's up?" she asked.

Trisha, who was glancing out of the window, faced Chasity then gave her a hug. "Thanks for coming," she said.

Chasity pulled away. "Why *wouldn't* I have come?" she asked, confused. "What's going on with you?"

Trisha ran her hand over her hair as she sat up in her seat. "Chaz, I know I've been distant lately," she admitted, tone sullen. "It's just that I've had a lot on my mind."

When Trisha moved her face, Chasity noticed in the light, the redness in her aunt's eyes. "Were you crying?" she asked, concerned.

Trisha nodded as she tried to keep more tears from forming. "The things that I've been dealing with have just been..." she paused as she put her face in her hands and let out a long sigh. "It's been a lot for me to handle."

"Is that why you sent me to a hotel?" Chasity asked.

Trisha once again nodded. "I didn't want to subject you and your friend to my bad mood," she informed. "You've dealt with enough."

"Oh," Chasity replied. "I thought you just didn't want me around."

Trisha's head jerked up. "You *felt* like that?" she asked, feeling badly.

"A little," Chasity admitted. "I just—it's fine. I know that's not the case."

Trisha grabbed Chasity's hand and held it. "I'm sorry that I made you feel that way," she apologized, tone sincere. "I don't want you to ever think that."

"I'm fine. It's fine," Chasity assured. "Is this what you wanted to talk to me about?"

Trisha hesitated as she stared into Chasity's questioning eyes. *Am I really about to do this?* She asked herself. Trisha had been burdened with that question ever since her emotional visit to her mother's house just a day earlier. Upon leaving, she knew what she had to do, but wasn't sure if she wanted to. "No, it's not," she replied, squeezing Chasity's hand. "I'm about to share some things about my past with you and…I need you to just listen, okay?"

Chasity was skeptical. "Um…o-kay," she slowly put out.

Trisha took a deep breath. "Chasity, the woman that you see in front of you—" she paused to gather her words. "I wasn't always this way…When I was a teenager, I was bad, and when I say bad, I mean... I was a nightmare to your grandparents."

"*You?*" Chasity was in disbelief.

"Yeah," Trisha confirmed. "I mean, every bad thing that a fifteen-year-old could do, I did it. I snuck out, I skipped school, I argued with my parents, stole money, smoked, drank—*everything.*"

Chasity held a shocked look on her face, but remained quiet. She wasn't sure where the conversation was going, but she was intrigued.

"When I was sixteen, my father died, and the last strand of sanity I had, fled," Trisha continued, voice somber. "Your uncle John had been gone for like a year already, and Brenda, who'd just turned eighteen, ran off with Derrick and eloped."

"*That* young, huh?" Chasity sneered. Brenda nor Derrick had told Chasity about how they met, or when they got married. They'd been at odds with each other and *her* ever since she could remember.

"Yeah, they were high school sweethearts," Trisha revealed, managing a small smile. The smile only lasted a moment as more memories flooded. "Your grandmother and I were arguing like every day. I was so out of control, she couldn't handle me... One day, after she caught me sneaking back in from a party, she went to grab me and I tried to hit her."

Chasity's mouth fell open. "You hit Grandmom?"

"I *tried*," Trisha clarified. "She beat my ass and threw me out that night." She took another deep breath. "I had nowhere to go. My so-called friends turned their back on me, Mom had called every relative in Philly and told them what happened. Nobody would take me in... I had no choice, I called Brenda." Trisha adjusted the silk robe on her shoulder with her free hand. "By this time, Derrick had joined the military and they were living in Arizona... She didn't give it a second thought, she told me that I could come stay with her. Even sent me money for a plane ticket." Trisha paused as Chasity looked away momentarily. "You okay?" she wondered.

Chasity put her hand up. "Just give me a minute," she said. "It's a lot at once."

"I know," Trisha agreed. "But there's more...a *lot* more."

Chasity faced her again. "Why are you even telling me *any* of this?"

"Because...it's time that I *do*," Trisha vaguely replied. "I need you to know everything about me and to understand."

"I *do* understand you though," Chasity countered, still unsure of the reason for Trisha's revelation. "You're telling me about stuff that happened before I was born, before I ever *met* you. You can leave your past where it is."

Trisha shook her head. "No, I *can't*," she said. "Because

it always has a way of surfacing when you never thought it *would*."

Chasity decided not to argue any longer, and gestured for her aunt to continue with her story.

"Um…" Trisha tried to regather her thoughts. "I was living with Brenda and Derrick for about six months—I'd just turned seventeen actually. And…they started going through some issues."

"Such as?"

"They would argue a lot," Trisha answered. "Derrick was working two jobs while waiting to leave again for training, and she was upset because she knew that he would be gone for a year. She was stressing out about bills and—they were young and were starting to realize that they had bit off more than they could chew. Me, being the asshole that I was, sided with Derrick in all of their arguments. I accused Brenda of nagging him and just nit-picking everything that he did."

Chasity rolled her eyes. That sounded all too familiar. "Yeah, that sounds about right," she mumbled.

Trisha glanced at the ceiling. "To be honest, back then…I had a crush on Derrick," she admitted.

"You *what*?" Chasity scoffed.

Trisha nodded, shameful. "Yeah, I would flirt with him sometimes while we were still in school," she explained. "But he wanted my sister…I think that's what drove me to always take his side…I still liked him... we used to talk after they would argue. I would let him just vent." She felt a dark cloud fall over her as she prepared to say her next words. "Um…one night, I wanted to go out and didn't have any money… Brenda caught me stealing money from her purse, and we got into a fight. She tried to throw me out and Derrick stepped in… That pissed Brenda off, so, *they* fought. She threw a vase at him and left the house… That night, while she was gone, I went into their room to check on Derrick, because I knew that the vase had hit him really hard." She let out a sigh. "We were both upset; emotional… We started talking and trying to comfort one another and…one thing led to another and… We slept together."

Chasity snatched her hand away from Trisha and looked at her with disgust. "You slept with Brenda's husband?" she blurted out in disbelief.

Trisha felt tears fill her eyes. "Yes," she admitted.

Chasity put her hand over her mouth as she tried to process what she'd just heard. "You—you slept with your *sisters'* husband? After she took you in? You—Trisha that's terrible!"

"I know," Trisha sniffled.

"I mean, I don't know what the hell Brenda was like before she adopted *me*, but I'm sure she didn't deserve *that*."

"She *didn't*," Trisha agreed, regretful.

"And Dad—*Derrick* is just…" Chasity ran her hands through her hair. "That's disgusting."

"It was wrong," Trisha admitted. "*So* wrong…I told you I was horrible at that age. I didn't think about anybody but myself. Didn't *care* about anybody but myself… I just wanted what I wanted and while I was getting it…Brenda walked in on us."

Chasity shook her head. This story just got even sadder to her. She didn't recognize the woman sitting before her. She almost, for a moment, felt sorry for Brenda.

"Needless to say, she put us *both* out," Trisha said. "Derrick left for training a few days later and I…wandered. I had no money to fly back home, so I ended up staying in a shelter… A few weeks later, I found out I was pregnant."

"What?!" Chasity exclaimed.

Trisha wiped her eyes. "Yeah," she said. "I went back to Brenda and she told me to get an abortion… I couldn't do it. It didn't feel right." She put her hand over her face as more tears formed. "She told me that if I didn't get an abortion that I'd have to give the baby up," she recalled. "She said that there was no way in hell that the baby could ever be a part of her family…and she wasn't going to let me leave Arizona until the baby was born and she made sure it was gone."

"So, what happened to the baby?"

"I gave her up like Brenda wanted," Trisha said, wiping her eyes.

"You had a girl?"

Trisha smiled through her tears. "Yes, a beautiful little girl," she gushed. "I swear, putting my baby in someone else's arms was the hardest thing that I ever had to do…after that, I went back to Philly and crawled back to Mom…I was depressed for a long time…I just—I felt so guilty."

Chasity looked away momentarily. "Wow," was all that she could get out at that moment. "So, there's some product of you and Derricks' mistake walking around. With no idea of the bullshit that she came from."

Trisha sniffled again as she stared at Chasity. "She wasn't a mistake."

"She *was*," Chasity disagreed, feeling angry and relating with someone she'd never even met. "And because of your *mistake*, a child had to grow up with people who aren't her real damn family."

Trisha shook her head. "That's not—"

"Look, as much as I appreciate you revealing all your dirty laundry to me, if you don't mind, I'd like to have a minute to process all of this," Chasity hissed, standing up. "I'll call you tomorrow."

Trisha stood up as Chasity headed for the door. "Chasity, there's something else that I have to tell you," she said.

"I'm not interested in hearing it," Chasity threw over her shoulder.

"You might not *want* to, but you *need* to hear it," Trisha eerily put out, facing her departing figure.

Chasity spun around. "I'm not interested in hearing about your daughter," she spat out.

Tears stained Trisha's cheeks as she pulled every ounce of strength and courage she had. "Chasity—"

"What, are you gonna tell me that you want to find her now?" Chasity fumed. "You were against *me* finding my *mother*, and now you want me to be okay with you finding *your child*?"

"I already found her," Trisha revealed, much to Chasity's surprise.

"Oh *really*?" she sneered.

"Yes..." Trisha took a long pause. "She's standing right in front of me."

Chasity frowned in confusion, "What does *that* mean?"

Trisha put her hand over her mouth as she broke down. "Chasity, baby—"

"No, what the hell do you mean by that?" Chasity fumed.

Trisha took a step forward. "Honey... *you* are my daughter," she revealed.

Chasity felt like she'd been hit with a ton of bricks. Feeling the air being sucked from her lungs, she began breathing heavily. "Wait, what?" she panted. "I don't understand, I don't—"

"I gave you up to Brenda," Trisha sobbed, crossing the room as Chasity steadied herself against the wall. She reached for Chasity's arm, but Chasity jerked away from her.

"Don't touch me!" Chasity yelled. "You're a fuckin' liar!"

"I'm so sorry," Trisha cried.

"You sent me with her," Chasity raged, pointing. "You *know* how she treated me!"

"I swear to you, I had no idea that she would *ever* hurt you," Trisha explained, voice pleading. "I never thought that she would take her hatred for *me* out on *you*."

"How could you not think that?!" Chasity screamed. "I was the result of your affair with her fuckin' *husband*!" Chasity's eyes filled with tears as everything that she'd dealt with growing up flooded back to her. "You ruined my life," she cried.

Trisha sobbed. She was afraid of this. She knew that once Chasity found out the truth that she would hate her— that their relationship as she knew it would be over. That her world would come crashing down.

"I thought that I was doing the right thing for you," Trisha cried. "I didn't know—"

"Save it," Chasity hissed, pushing herself up from the wall. "I'm done. I fuckin' hate you."

Watching Chasity storm out of the room was like having the life ripped from her body. Trisha knew that there was nothing that she could say to change what she'd done, the lies that she told. Trisha had no way of knowing if Chasity would ever forgive her. Feeling her knees buckle under her, Trisha collapsed to the floor and dissolved into tears.

Chapter 27

Jason walked the hallway of the tenth floor of the Wyngate hotel, glancing at the room numbers in search for the one that he needed. Reaching the door, he knocked on it.

"Who is it?" Malajia called from the other side.

"It's Jason," he returned. The door snatched open and Malajia stood there, a panicked look on her face. "Thanks for coming," she said as Jason stepped inside.

"Of course, what's going on?" concern was written on Jason's face. He'd only been back from his family getaway at the shore for merely an hour before receiving a frantic call from Malajia.

Malajia ran her hands through her hair. "I don't know," she admitted. "She went to go talk to Ms. Trisha earlier, and she came back like an hour ago pissed off and crying. She won't tell me what's wrong and she locked herself in the room." Malajia pointed to the closed door in their one-bedroom suite. "I called Ms. Trisha and she didn't answer… I don't know what's wrong. Have you talked to her?"

Jason shook his head as he walked over to the bedroom door. "Not since this morning," he replied, knocking. "I was calling her after I hung up with you and she didn't answer."

After hearing no sound come from the room, Jason knocked again. "Chaz, baby it's Jason, I need you to open the door," he urged.

After a minute, he heard the lock turn. Glancing back at Malajia, who had sat back down on the couch, he gave her a nod, then opened the door and walked in. Jason stepped into the dimly lit room and crossed the carpeted floor. Chasity was sitting on the king-sized bed with a pillow clutched to her chest, face streaked with tears, and silent. He sat on the bed next to her.

"What's wrong?" he asked, tone caring, worried.

Chasity found it hard to speak at first; she just focused on breathing. "Trisha—she's—" She took a deep breath. "She's my mo—my mom," she stammered.

Jason didn't know if he'd heard her right. "You said she's *what?*"

Chasity looked at him. "Trisha is my mother," she confirmed.

Jason's mouth fell open. "Oh...wow...damn," he found it hard to form any comforting words, for he was just as shocked as Chasity was. "But how—"

"Jason, I don't want to get into all that right now," she hissed, feeling the urge to cry again. Jason put his arms out to hug her and she moved away. "Can you not touch me right now, please?" Chasity was already trying to fight her tears, and she knew that if she allowed Jason to comfort her the way that he wanted, the way that she needed, she would break down and she was tired of crying.

"I'm sorry," he said, putting his arms down. Instead, Jason took her hand and held it. He couldn't imagine the questions that she had, because he had them too. He couldn't imagine the confusion that she felt, the hurt. If he could've taken it all away, he would. "This may be a stupid question, but...how are you feeling?"

Chasity sighed. "I'm pissed the fuck off," she admitted, tone angry. "She's been lying to me my whole life... She left me with someone who hated me...she—" Chasity put her hand over her face. "I don't even want to look at her anymore."

"I can understand that," Jason sympathized. "Did she give you a reason why she did what she did?"

Chasity shot Jason a venomous look. "I don't care *what* her reason was," she barked. "You think what she did was okay? You think I'm just being dramatic?"

"I didn't say that," Jason replied, calm. "I'm not trying to upset you."

Chasity looked down at her hands; they were shaking. She felt bad for snapping at him. "I know," she assured him. "I'm sorry."

"It's okay," Jason promised her. "What do you need me to do?"

Chasity sighed. "I just want to be alone right now," she answered. Jason nodded before giving her a kiss on her cheek. "I'll be in the other room with Malajia," he said. "Just holler if you need me."

Chasity laid down without saying another word.

Jason closed the door behind him and ran his hand over his head, sighing in the process.

Malajia stared up at him. "Jase, what's going on?" she pressed. "What's wrong with her?"

Jason sat on the chair next to her and leaned back against the cushion. He'd only been in that room a short time, but he was already mentally drained. "Chaz just found out that Ms. Trisha is her mother," he revealed.

Malajia's eyes widened. "Huh?" she sputtered. "You mean mother as in *birth* mother?"

Jason nodded.

"As in Chasity was actually raised by her *aunt*?" Malajia added.

"Exactly," Jason confirmed.

Malajia stared at the closed door in front of her. "Damn," she said, sullen. "I can't even—wow… I wonder what happened. This is crazy."

"She doesn't want to talk about it," Jason stated. "I don't blame her."

"Yeah, me neither," Malajia agreed. "But…and I hate to pull an Alex here, maybe she *should*."

"I don't think that *we're* who she should be talking about this *with*," Jason said. "At least not until she sorts everything out with…her mother."

"God, that sounds weird to say," Malajia admitted, bringing her legs up on the couch. "So what do we do now?"

"Just hang back until she needs us," Jason replied.

Chasity pulled her car in front of her grandmother's house, turned it off, and jumped out. *God please let her be okay*, she thought, running for the door. Although laid up in her bed at the hotel the night before, Chasity had barely gotten any sleep. After everything that had happened, she didn't expect to get a frantic call from her grandmother that morning, telling Chasity that she needed to go to the hospital.

Chasity knocked on the door, then not wanting to wait, twisted the knob. "Why does she never lock this door?" she griped, running inside. "Grandmom, are you all right?" she panicked, hurrying into the living room. She paused and the worry on her face was replaced by a scowl. "You've got to be kidding me," she fumed, seeing her grandmother, perfectly fine, sitting on the couch. Trisha was sitting next to her.

"I'm glad that you're here," Grandmother Duvall said.

Chasity rolled her eyes. "I don't have time for this," she sneered, turning to walk out.

"Chasity darling, I need you to sit down," Grandmother Duvall ordered.

"No, I think I'll leave," Chasity refused.

"Chasity Taj-Marie." Grandmother Duvall's tone was stern. Chasity stopped in her tracks and faced both women.

Grandmother Duvall pointed to the chair in front of her.

"Come sit down…please."

Chasity was furious, but decided to comply. She'd never disrespected her grandmother before and wasn't about to start. She walked over and flopped down on the accent chair facing her grandmother and Trisha. She folded her arms and turned away from both sets of prying eyes.

Grandmother Duvall held her gaze to Chasity. "Now Chasity, I'm sorry that I deceived you like that."

"I thought that you were over here having a stroke or something," Chasity spat. She didn't appreciate being deceived, especially since it had put her in panic mode.

"I know, and I'm sorry," Grandmother Duvall apologized sincerely. "But I had no other way of getting you over here, and you and Patrisha need to talk."

"So, you knew about this whole thing *too*?" Chasity hissed.

"No, not until two days ago," Grandmother Duvall promised. "She came here and told me everything."

Chasity shook her head as her leg began bouncing up and down in a steady rhythm. She would give anything not to be in that room.

Trisha wiped her teary eyes with a tissue as she clutched something in her other hand. When she called her mother in tears that morning, Trisha expected a pep talk, some consoling words. She had no idea that her mother would orchestrate a sit down between her and Chasity. It was something that she was grateful for; she didn't have the courage to do it herself. "Chasity?" she called.

Chasity didn't respond; she just sat there, staring at the wall on the side of her. She had no intention of talking.

"Can you at least *look* at me, please?" Trisha pleaded. Chasity didn't budge.

Grandmother Duvall placed her hand on Trisha's knee and gave her a nod. "Listen Chasity," she began, looking at her angry granddaughter. "I know that you're upset, and you have every *right* to be. I was shocked and upset *too* when I found out… But this doesn't change the fact that Patrisha *is* your mother."

Chasity rolled her eyes.

"And because of that fact *alone*, you two need to talk this out," Grandmother Duvall urged. "Chasity, I know you have a million questions, and I know that Patrisha will have no problem answering every last one of them... Just know that neither of you can leave this room until you talk."

"First you lie, then you hold me hostage," Chasity muttered, tone sarcastic. "Great."

"Call it what you want, but you're *going* to talk." Grandmother Duvall reached over and patted Chasity on the arm. "Go ahead and ask whatever you want, sweetheart."

Chasity sat there seething, gritting her teeth. As much as she didn't want to talk to Trisha, she did in fact have questions. She faced Trisha, who stared back at her with wide, tear-filled eyes. "How the hell did I end up with Brenda?" she asked finally.

Trisha took a deep breath. "While I was gone for those weeks after she threw me out, Brenda found out she was pregnant too," she revealed.

"Dad got y'all pregnant at the same time, how gross," Chasity sneered.

Trisha sighed, she knew exactly how dysfunctional this story was and didn't blame Chasity for her snide remarks. "She said that Derrick was excited about her pregnancy and that they were going to try to work things out.... That despite what he did...what *we* did, she still loved him and wanted to build a family with him." Trisha pushed some hair behind her ear. "She told me that she was sending me back to Philly after I had the baby... She didn't want me anywhere near her *or* Derrick." She paused for a moment, then took another deep breath. "When we were both around our fifth month, Brenda had a miscarriage."

Grandmother Duvall lowered her head. Even though she'd heard this story prior, it was still saddening to her.

"It was horrible, she had to have surgery, and was told that she'd never be able to have more children," Trisha remembered. "She was devastated. Derrick was gone, and she didn't know how to tell him… He was so excited about becoming a father, and she thought that if he found out what had happened, that their marriage would be over." She sighed. "As much as Brenda didn't want to face it, she knew that I was carrying Derrick's baby…and she figured, since *she* couldn't have his child, that she would raise *mine* with him…and I agreed to it."

"So Derrick had no idea that I was *yours?*" Chasity snarled, disgusted.

Trisha shook her head. "Not until a few days ago…the day you came home for break," she revealed. "He came to see me because he couldn't get any answers from Brenda about your adoption… He'd gone away, and a year later came home to a baby girl, a baby girl that he thought was his and Brenda's. He had no reason to question that."

Chasity shook her head. It started to make sense. Trisha's behavior the day that she came home, Derrick's reaction to her telling him what Brenda said about her adoption. *Un-fuckin-believable.* Tears formed in Chasity's eyes. "So, you really thought that giving me to her was a good idea?" she asked. "I mean, I know you were screwed up in the head back then, but I didn't expect you to be plain stupid."

Grandmother Duvall put her hand up to halt Chasity's insults. "Chasity—"

"It's okay, Mom," Trisha assured her. "Chasity, in the beginning I had no reason to believe that she wasn't raising you right," she explained. "Brenda would send Mom pictures, and in every picture, you looked like you were happy… So yes, I *did* think that I was doing what was best for you."

Chasity stared at her for a moment as tears began to fall. "And when you found out it *wasn't?*" she spat, "Why didn't you come get me?"

Trisha fanned her face with her hands to try to keep from busting out crying, but to no avail. She couldn't hold it any longer, the guilt was crushing her. "You don't understand," she said between sniffles. "If I had gone and tried to take you from her...everything that happened would've come out and the whole family, *everybody* would have known, and it would've embarrassed her."

"So this was about *her*?" Chasity barked.

"It was about *you too*," Trisha clarified. "Do you have *any* idea the amount of ridicule you would have suffered from this family if they found out who your parents *really* were?"

"And the alternative was *better*?" Chasity asked, pain obvious in her voice. "You think that people talking about me behind my back would be worse than being treated like shit? Than being shown that being born was a damn mistake? Than being made to feel that you were the cause of every goddamn problem in your parents' life? Than being beat on and locked in my damn room for *days*, just because I did something that reminded Brenda of *you*?"

Trisha put her head in her hands and cried uncontrollably.

"She used to say 'every time I look at you, I see my triflin' ass sister'," Chasity remembered. "And I never understood why she kept saying that to me...but now it makes sense." Chasity shook her head. "You sacrificed *me* to protect her and your*self*... And you thought that throwing your damn money at me could make up for that...you *still* do."

"I just thought that I could give you some kind of happiness," Trisha cried. "I thought that giving you things, doing things for you would make you happy, I was trying to take care of you in my own way."

"*None* of that was about me," Chasity sneered. "You were trying to ease your *own* guilt."

"I don't know what I can do or say to show you how sorry I am," Trisha sobbed.

"Not a damn thing."

"Okay you two, enough," Grandmother Duvall cut in. She had let Chasity and Trisha talk and felt it was time for her to intervene. "Listen…I know that the way that this whole situation was handled, wasn't necessarily right," she said. "I know that Patrisha wishes that she'd handled it differently… *I* wish that she would've handled it differently. I wish that I would have known about your abuse Chasity. If I *had*, things would've been different… For not knowing, I apologize to you."

"It's not your fault," Chasity grumbled.

"I am their mother, so in a way it *is*," she insisted. "I was in a bad place with my daughters back then… I feel that if I had been different, then maybe Trisha wouldn't have had to go to Arizona and none of this would have happened…but then maybe *you* wouldn't be here."

Chasity looked at her grandmother as she spoke.

"Despite how you came to be, you're *here* and that makes me happy, because no matter how you were *made* to feel by your parents, you, my dear, are a blessing," Grandmother Duvall smiled to Chasity. "And that blessing…*you,* is what made my troubled daughter turn her life around."

"She's right," Trisha sniffled. "After I gave you up, I was so depressed. For *three years*, I didn't see you," she said. "Derrick finally convinced Brenda to fly here for the holidays and… I came face to face with my little girl…the *one* good thing that I did."

Chasity just sat in silence.

"When they took you back to Arizona, I couldn't stop thinking about you," Trisha said. "I had no idea when I'd see you again, but all I knew was that I wanted to be someone that you could be proud of…so I decided to make a change. I went back to school and got my life together…for *you. You* inspired me to be better."

"The bond that you two share is stronger than I've ever seen," Grandmother Duvall cut in. "It's one that only a mother and daughter could share. And I know that Trisha didn't raise you Chasity, but she did everything that she *could* to take care of you from afar. She would give her life for you."

"In a heartbeat," Trisha promised, placing her hand over her heart. "I'm sorry that I hurt you, and out of everything that I've done in my life, my biggest regret is not being strong enough to have raised you."

Chasity bit her bottom lip as she tried to keep from crying.

Grandmother Duvall took the item, which turned out to be an envelope, from Trisha's hand and handed it to Chasity. "I want you to open this," she urged when Chasity stared at her, skeptical. "I'll leave you two alone."

Trisha followed her mother's progress until she disappeared up the steps. She looked over at Chasity, who was staring at the pink envelope.

"What is this?" Chasity asked, voice drained.

Trisha looked at it. "There hasn't been a day that's gone by when you were away from me that I didn't think about you," she said. Chasity looked at her, confused. "I carried those things with me in my wallet everyday...I *still* do."

Chasity looked at the envelope and slowly opened it. Seeing two pieces of paper inside, she pulled them out and examined one of them.

"You were a day old in that picture," Trisha smiled, pointing to the small, worn baby picture.

Chasity gazed at the picture for moments before bringing her attention to a folded paper. Unfolding it, she stared at it, tears spilling. It'd been something that she wanted, had needed ever since she found out that she was adopted; her original birth certificate. Reading some of the words on the paper, her emotions took over and so did the tears. *Baby girl name: Chasity Taj-Marie Parker; Mother name: Patrisha Marie Duvall.*

Chasity broke down crying as she clutched the paper in her hand. Trisha rose from her seat and kneeled in front of Chasity. With tears in her eyes, she grabbed her daughter's hands and held them, before throwing caution to the wind and wrapping her arms around Chasity. After a moment, and much to her surprise, Chasity hugged her back.

Neither woman said another word.

Chapter 28

Sidra gave herself a once over in the floor-length mirror in her living room; smiling with approval. "Not bad, Princess, not bad," she mused to herself, smoothing down her royal blue short-sleeved dress. She stepped into her silver high heels and retrieved her matching clutch from the arm of a nearby chair. "I hope he likes my outfit." Glancing at her silver watch, she noticed the time. Ten after seven in the evening. It was only a matter of time before James would show up to take her on their anticipated date.

Mrs. Howard walked into the living room and looked at her daughter. "Honey, what time did he say that he was going to be here?"

Sidra turned around. "He said around seven thirty," she replied, giving her watch another look.

"You look beautiful," Mrs. Howard gushed, touching her daughter's hair. Sidra ditched her trademark ponytail in favor of wearing it down, softly curled. Her makeup was flawless.

Sidra smiled brightly, "Thank you Mama," she beamed. "I can't lie, I'm really nervous."

"Why sweetheart?" Mrs. Howard asked.

Sidra ran her finger through one of her curls. "Well, I mean this is our first official date," she declared. "Him living in DC working on his cases, and me being in Virginia at school...we don't get to do much but talk."

"Yeah, I know," Mrs. Howard said, sympathetic. "Didn't you tell me that he's older?"

Sidra rolled her eyes. "Mama."

"Princess, I'm not trying to nag," her mother promised.

"Yes, you *are*," Sidra contradicted, amusement in her voice. "I told you, he's twenty-seven."

Mrs. Howard reached out and adjusted the silver necklace around Sidra's neck. She did in fact remember Sidra disclosing James age and profession after their coffee date over winter break. Sidra was never one to keep information from her mother, but Mrs. Howard felt that as her mother, she had a duty to ask pertinent questions. "You don't think that's too old for you?"

Sidra shook her head. "I'm *twenty* Mama, I'm not a child," she replied, making sure to keep her tone in check. "And no, I *don't* think it's too old for me. I've always been mature for my age."

"I know that honey. You've always had a good head on your shoulders," Mrs. Howard agreed. "You know I trust your judgment, and I also know that if you like this man, then he must be a good one." She put her hands on Sidra's shoulders. "But it's my job as your mother to question things...and to worry."

"You don't *have* to worry," Sidra assured.

Mrs. Howard nodded. "Okay," she relented. "Now your father and brothers, *that's* a different story," she added, a hint of laughter in her voice.

Sidra winced. "Yeah I know," she muttered. "Mama, don't tell them how old he is, *please*."

"Um...I already told your father."

Sidra's eyes widened. "Mama!"

"I'm sorry honey, but you're his princess," Mrs. Howard chortled. "I *had* to tell him about the guy who was coming to pick you up."

Sidra sucked her teeth. "Well it's done now," she grumbled. "Thank God he's at work so he can't grill him."

"Well, look on the bright side. If all goes well, he'll get another chance to," Mrs. Howard teased.

She jumped when she heard the doorbell ring. "He's here," she panicked.

"Okay, calm down and just breathe," Mrs. Howard consoled. "I'll get the door."

As her mother headed for the door, Sidra watched, horrified, as her three older brothers trotted down the steps and sat on the couch. She'd almost forgotten that they had stopped by earlier that day for some of their mothers' home cooking. Sidra narrowed her eyes as they started cracking their knuckles.

"Seriously?" she spat out.

"What's the matter, baby sis?" Marcus asked.

"What the hell are you guys still doing here?" she fussed.

"Well, Dad called us and told us that you had a date. He told us to stay and interrogate him," the middle brother Martin answered.

"*I'm* not here for Dad," Marcus corrected. "I'm trying to find out for my*self* who the hell this old guy is, taking my little sister out."

Sidra shook her head. Being the youngest and only girl in her family, Sidra was used to being over-protected, but that didn't mean that she liked it. "Don't embarrass me," she warned through clenched teeth.

Her mother, who was speaking with James at the door, finally let him in. Sidra smiled at him as he made sure to shake her brothers' hands. He then approached her, holding a bouquet of white roses mixed with blue hydrangea. "Hi James," she gushed.

"Hi," James smiled back, handing her the flowers. "You look beautiful."

Sidra blushed. "Thank you."

Mrs. Howard held a single white rose in her hand. "He got *me* one *too*," she smiled, much to her sons' disgust.

"I'm telling Dad," Marcus bit out. Mrs. Howard waved her hand at him dismissively.

James leaned in to hug Sidra but stopped when he heard the guys loudly clear their throats.

"Hold that hug, buddy," Marcus demanded, standing up.

"Marcus, leave them alone," Mrs. Howard urged.

Marcus faced his mother and put his hand up. "Mama, I got this," he declared, earning a stern look from her. "Ma'am," he corrected.

Sidra put her hand on her face. "Oh my God," she mumbled, embarrassed. She looked at James, "I'm sorry about this."

James chuckled, "Sidra, it's okay," he assured her, holding her hand. "They're just looking out for you."

"So James, I hear that you're a lawyer," Marcus charged as James straightened his tie.

"Yes, that's correct."

"Are you any good?" Marcus asked.

Sidra sucked her teeth as James laughed, "I would say so," he confirmed.

"Oh word?" Martin cut in, rubbing his chin. "Yo, I might *need* a lawyer."

"For *what* boy?" Sidra hissed, over the interrogation.

Martin scratched his head. "Well, you know I got these parking tickets—"

"Martin, you're done. Go," Mrs. Howard ordered, pointing to the steps. "And take the quiet one with you," she stated of her youngest son Mike, who had done nothing but stare daggers at James.

"Fine," Martin mumbled, heading for the steps, with his brother in tow. "Nice to meet you man," he threw over his shoulder.

"Y'all aren't gonna get rid of *me* that easy," Marcus stood firm. "You seem to be a successful guy, from what I hear you're pretty smart, *older*. I see you own a suit and stuff," he sneered. "What does your thirty-year-old self, want with my twenty-year-old sister?"

"Mama, make him stop," Sidra pleaded.

"Marcus, don't make me get my belt," Mrs. Howard warned.

James put his hands up. "It's fine ladies, I'll answer," he assured, unfazed. Having a younger sister himself, he understood where Marcus's protectiveness came from. "Well Marcus, first of all, I'm twenty-seven," he corrected, staring the man in the eye. "And not only is your sister absolutely beautiful, but she is intelligent, funny, well-spoken and has a great head on her shoulders. I enjoy my conversations with her and look forward to talking to *and* seeing her a lot more."

Sidra couldn't help but blush at James words. Marcus, on the other hand, was confused.

"*She's* funny?" he joked.

Sidra sucked her teeth and directed a pleading gaze at her mother.

"Boy that's enough, you're holding them up," Mrs. Howard stepped in, grabbing her son's shirt collar. "Go eat dinner so you can go back to your girlfriend, or *whatever* she is this week."

Marcus let out a loud sigh. "Fine, I guess he's all right," he grumbled, heading for the kitchen. "You better not hurt her man."

"Wouldn't dream of it," James returned, confident. He then glanced at Sidra and smiled once again. "Shall we?" he proposed, extending his arm.

"Yes," she returned, looping her arm through his.

The restaurant that James chose was upscale and much to Sidra's liking. "This is a nice place," she mused, looking around at the space. The intimidate tables were covered with burgundy linens. The background music was soft and the crystal candle holders were filled with tall white candles, the flame adding to the intimate mood.

"I'm glad that you like it," James replied, reaching for his glass of wine. "I came here once before while I was here in Delaware on business, and I loved it."

Sidra nodded. "Nice," she replied as the server set her plate of pan seared salmon, steamed broccoli and rice pilaf in front of her. "So, how's work going?"

James unfolded his napkin as his plate of steak and lobster tail was set down. "Work is busy, which is a good thing," he answered. "I'm actually in the process of settling a case that I'm working on now."

Sidra sat there staring at James as he spoke. She took in his smooth deep voice, his handsome face, dark skin, his brown eyes and bright smile, his expensive suite. She glanced down momentarily. *You're staring too much, weirdo.* "Do you prefer to settle your cases over going to trial?"

"It depends honestly," he replied, cutting into his steak. "There are times when I look forward to fighting a case in court and there are others where I'm happy to settle… What do you think *you'd* look forward to when you become a lawyer?"

"I can say right now that being in court would be exciting for me," Sidra mused. "But I'm saying that because I've never actually *been* in a courtroom… That might change."

"No, I think you'll still have the same enthusiasm," James declared. "It's an exciting field." He took another sip of wine and pushed it to the side. "What part of law do you plan on studying? Criminal?"

"God no," Sidra protested, waving her hand. "I don't think I could handle it. I see myself more in corporate law."

"Ah, *my* field," James boasted.

Sidra cut a piece of her salmon. "Which is good, because I'll need your advice when I start practicing."

"I'd be happy to help," James smiled. "Unless we're on opposing cases of course."

Sidra giggled. "Of course," she agreed, before taking a bite of her food. She closed her eyes, relishing the flavors.

"So, are you ready to go back to school?" James asked, after some comfortable silence.

Sidra wiped the corners of her mouth with her cloth napkin. "Not really," she joked. "No, I am, I do miss campus, but just knowing the course load that I have to go back to has me a little antsy."

"Oh come on, I'm sure those classes are a breeze," James chortled.

Sidra shot him a quick frown. "Yeah okay," she sneered. "Between those classes and my neighbors getting on my last nerves, my stress level is about to hit the roof."

"Well, just wait until you go to law school," he forewarned.

Sidra shook her head. "Don't make me rethink my major," she jeered, earning a laugh from him.

"I'd love to come visit your school and see you in your element."

Sidra's heart jumped at the thought of seeing him again. "I'd like that too," she smiled. "But not around finals… It wouldn't be pretty."

James once again laughed. "I can't see you not keeping it together."

Sidra shrugged. "I told you, me and stress…not a good mix," she returned.

As the evening continued, Sidra felt like she hadn't stopped smiling. James's conversations were something that she had come to look forward to, his appearance something that she fantasized about. She knew that she liked him, but him sitting in front of her; Sidra became enamored with him.

The car ride home was just as relaxing, as they shared more stories and laughed together. Sidra didn't want the night to end, but sadly that reality set in when he pulled in front of her door.

"We're here," James announced, turning the car off.

"Great," she replied, even though inside she'd wished his car stalled at the restaurant to allow her more time with him.

Once he helped her out of the car, they both walked to her door. Sidra unlocked her door, then faced him, glowing.

"I had a really nice time tonight," James crooned.

"Me too," she smiled. "Thanks for asking me out."

"Thanks for saying *yes.*"

Sidra blushed, something that she'd been doing all night. *I wonder if he's gonna kiss me*, she thought as they stood there, admiring one another. Sidra got her answer when James stepped forward and placed his hand under her chin to lift it, allowing him easy access to her glossed lips as he kissed her. Sidra closed her eyes as she returned his kiss. Although short, the kiss was sensual and nothing that she'd ever experienced before.

Parting, James stroked her cheek and smiled one last time. "Good night."

"Night," Sidra returned, before walking into the house. As soon as she closed the door, Sidra leaned her back against the door and placed her hand to her chest. Smiling to herself and needing to tell someone about her night, she retrieved her cell phone from her purse and headed into the kitchen, dialing a number in the process.

Pouring herself a glass of cold water, Sidra placed the phone to her ear, holding the chilled glass to her chest with the other hand. "You girls there?" she asked into the line.

"Yeah Sid, we're here," Alex replied.

"Yeah," Chasity and Malajia answered in unison.

Sidra moved around the counter to the kitchen table and sat down. "Can someone conference in Emily?" she asked. "I tried, but this thing acts like it doesn't want to call anybody else."

"Chasity?" Alex prompted.

"You already know I'm not calling no damn Emily on my phone," Chasity hissed, stretching out on her bed. "I don't have time for her stalking ass mom tonight."

Sidra sighed as she took a sip of water. "I don't want to leave her out," she said. "I want to tell you all at the same time about my date."

"Well Mel, can *you* call her?" Alex pressed.

Malajia sucked her teeth. "Come on man," she whined.

"Why are y'all being like that?" Alex scolded. "We can't keep leaving her out of stuff."

"Nobody is suggesting that," Malajia countered at the same time that Chasity said, "why not?"

"Stop it," Malajia spat at Chasity. "Look, you know her mom is sitting by that damn phone. You *know* she has no life."

"Just call her," Alex barked.

"*You* call her," Malajia threw back.

Alex let out a quick loud huff. "Mel, you know I *can't*," she replied. "My house phone doesn't have that capability, and my cell phone won't three-way call for some reason."

Malajia sucked her teeth as she sat on Chasity's bed. "I hate that damn flip," she complained.

"Move," Chasity snapped, trying to push Malajia off the bed.

"Shut up. This bed is big as shit," Malajia shot back. "Stop acting like a stingy ass only child."

After Chasity and Trisha's emotional talk two days ago, Chasity, at Trisha's urging, came back to the house. Malajia, not ready to head back to Baltimore, was in tow and posted up in Chasity's bedroom.

"Why the fuck are you still *here*?" Chasity fussed.

"Because I love you and my purpose in life is to annoy you," Malajia jeered.

"Malajia, leave the girl alone," Alex urged, adjusting the towel on her damp hair. "I'm surprised she hasn't killed you yet."

"Hold on, if you two are in the same room, Chaz, why

don't you just put your phone on speaker so that Malajia doesn't have to use her line?" Sidra suggested.

"No," Chasity immediately returned.

Alex laughed, "Why *not*?"

"'Cause she's a bitch, *that's* why she won't do it," Malajia complained. "Hold on, let me try to call this girl," she griped. "I swear to God, if hover mother answers, I'm bangin' on her."

After a few agonizing rings, Emily finally picked up, whispering. Malajia quickly merged the call in. "Emily's on," she announced.

"Good, all my girls are on," Sidra beamed, adjusting herself in her chair. "So, my date was so freakin' amazing." The girls were silent as Sidra proceeded to give them a play by play of her date.

"I can't believe that he remembered that you like those ugly ass hydrangeas," Malajia teased.

Sidra made a face, even though Malajia couldn't see it. "*This* coming from the girl who likes weeds," she spat.

"Hey! Dandelions are not weeds," Malajia argued. "They're *wishes*."

"God, get out!" Chasity growled, smacking her hand against her forehead repeatedly.

Alex busted out laughing. "*Wishes,* Malajia?" she questioned. "What are you, ten?"

"Nah, I'm as old as that phone you got," Malajia threw back.

Sidra put her hand over her face and giggled. "We can never have a conversation without an argument happening," she said, laughter in her voice.

"Ignore her," Alex said of Malajia. "What did you end up wearing?"

"I sent a picture of my outfit earlier, you didn't get it?" Sidra frowned.

Alex pulled the cell from her ear and looked at it. "No, I guess I *didn't*," she concluded.

"Oh my God, it's that old ass flip!" Malajia snapped.

"Malajia, I'm gonna smack you the next time I see you," Alex warned, tone sharp. "I'm tired of you."

"Sidra, is he going to visit you at school?" Emily whispered, not wanting to run the risk of her mother hearing her conversation through the door.

"What?" Chasity bit out, annoyed. "The fuck are you whispering for?"

Malajia erupted with laughter.

Alex sucked her teeth. "Why the attitude, Chasity?" she huffed.

"'Cause I can't *hear* her ass," Chasity snarled. "Don't ask me stupid questions."

Sidra tried not to laugh, but was unsuccessful. "I can't with you guys," she chortled.

"What restaurant did you guys go to again?" Alex wondered, trying not to engage in an argument.

"Why you always gotta talk about food?" Malajia ground out. "Greedy ass."

Alex was silent for a moment. "Chasity," she called.

"Yeah?"

"Slap her for me please." Suddenly Alex heard a loud slapping sound, accompanied by Malajia's scream.

"Oh for real?" Malajia barked. "Don't make me tell your mom you're in here being an asshole."

"Wait, *whose* mom?" Sidra asked, picking up on what Malajia said.

"I'll call and tell you guys tomorrow," Chasity promised. She needed a break from talking about her recent discovery.

"Okay," Sidra relented. "Well, it's late. I'm gonna let your crazy selves go."

"See you Sunday," Alex returned. "Oh Chaz, just so you know, me and Malajia decided that we're riding back with you and Jason." Not hearing a response Alex laughed. "What happened?"

"She hung up," Malajia informed, amused.

Sidra shook her head. "Night, ladies." Ending the call, she remained at the table and let out a happy sigh.

Chapter 29

"Yeah James, I just walked up to my room," Sidra said into her phone as she opened her room door. "The drive back was fine. I probably should have left yesterday though." Her private conversation cut short when Alex walked into the room, with Malajia following close behind.

"Hey Sidra!" Malajia hollered, noticing the phone in her hand. "Who you on the phone with?!"

Sidra shot a glower Malajia's way. "Malajia, don't be an idiot," she hissed.

"Is that Rufus?" Malajia bellowed, much to Sidra's annoyance.

"Rufus?" Alex laughed. "You make me sick."

Sidra let out a sigh. "James, I'll call you back when I'm no longer in the presence of a moron," she spat into the line. "Okay, bye." Upon ending the call, Sidra picked up a pillow and tossed it at the laughing Malajia. "You play too much."

"Oh please, he already knew I was lying," Malajia joked. "Like you would ever talk to somebody named Rufus."

Sidra shook her head. "What time did you all get back yesterday?" she asked, changing the subject.

"Like around five or so," Alex answered. "Malajia was taking forever to pack and she almost got left."

"Please, y'all was *not* about to leave me," Malajia assured, waving her hand.

"Oh Chaz was *definitely* about to pull off without you," Alex chortled. "If Ms. Trisha hadn't come out to stall her, your procrastinating butt would've *still* been in West Chester."

"I can believe it," Sidra shrugged. "Where *is* Chaz anyway?" she asked after a pause.

"She went to the store to get a few things," Malajia replied, sitting on Alex's bed. "I would've gone with her, but she said I can't get back in her car for a week."

Alex giggled, opening a bag of chips. "She is so sick of you," she concluded.

Sidra sat in silence, looking down at her manicured hands. "Sooo, have either of you had a conversation with Chasity about the whole 'Ms. Trisha is her mom' thing?" she asked.

Alex shook her head, sitting next to Malajia. "Aside from the phone call that she made to us the day after your date to tell us, no."

"She hasn't said too much about it," Malajia added, reaching her hand in Alex's chip bag. "I think she's still processing."

"I think we should go talk to her when she gets back," Sidra suggested much to Alex's delight.

"I'm glad I'm not the only one who was thinking that," Alex beamed, clapping her hands.

Malajia rolled her eyes. "Y'all already know she's not gonna talk if she doesn't want to," she pointed out. "She's only gonna get pissed off, and then *I* gotta deal with her attitude when y'all leave."

"You'll be fine," Alex dismissed with a wave of her chip filled hand.

Malajia narrowed her eyes. "That's why your chips are stale," she griped.

"Why are you eating them then?" Alex threw back, placing a chip into her mouth.

"'Cause I'm *hungry*," Malajia returned, taking a bite of one.

Chasity walked into her room and dropped a grocery bag on the bed, along with some mail. After placing a slice of leftover pizza into the microwave, she heard the door open. Not bothering to turn around, she shook her head. "Y'all always seem to know exactly when I get back," she jeered.

"Yeah well, we were stalking the door," Sidra teased as Alex filtered in behind her and Malajia. "Get over it."

Opening her microwave door, Chasity grabbed her food and made her way to her bed. "What do y'all want?"

"We want to talk to you," Alex replied, sitting on Chasity's bed, next to her.

"They," Malajia clarified. "*They* want to talk."

"About?" Chasity asked, tone even.

"About you…and your mom," Sidra answered, sitting on Malajia's bed, next to her.

Chasity glanced up from her food, making eye contact.

"They, *they* want to talk about you and your mom," Malajia put out, pointing to both Sidra and Alex. "I told them you weren't gonna want to."

"Will you shut up?" Alex directed at Malajia, before turning her attention back to Chasity, who sat her plate next to her on the bed. "Look, if you don't want to talk, that's fine," she assured. "But we got the details, *not* how you felt."

"Yeah, we just want to make sure you're okay," Sidra placated.

Chasity sat quietly for a minute. She did in fact tell the girls the same story that Trisha revealed to her, but didn't get too much into how she was feeling because she was still dealing with it. But seeing how much the girls cared, made her want to give them some insight into what was going on in her head.

"Okay," she said after the pause. "What do you want to know?"

The girls were shocked. "Wait, you *actually* want to talk about it?" Malajia couldn't believe it. Especially after she tried to get Chasity to open up after she got back from her grandmother's house.

"Don't want to, but I'm willing to," Chasity clarified, adjusting her position on her bed. "Let's have it."

Sidra and Alex weren't expecting Chasity to be so accepting of their request, although they'd hoped. They gestured for one another to say something.

"Either ask me a question, or get out," Chasity urged, earning a loud snicker from Malajia.

"*I'll* go," Alex volunteered. "How do you feel about Ms. Trisha now? Like…are y'all okay?"

Chasity thought for a moment. "Um…I don't know right now," she answered honestly. "I mean, I'm angry at her, you know. But…I'm trying to get to a place where I can understand why she did what she did and forgive her for it."

"That's understandable Chaz, all things considering," Sidra consoled. "I can't even imagine finding something like that out."

"To be honest, I feel a little stupid," Chasity admitted.

"Why?" Malajia asked, confused.

"Because now that I think back, there were a lot of signs, and I didn't see them," Chasity said. "Like the fact that I *look* like her for one."

Malajia waved her hand dismissively. "Girl, that's 'cause y'all light skinned," she joked. "*All* of y'all look alike." Malajia's attempt at a joke was met with three pairs of agitated eyes. "I'm just playing."

"Pay this fool no mind," Alex urged, pointing to Malajia. "And you *shouldn't* feel stupid. You couldn't have known *any* of this, so why would you even look for signs?"

Chasity shrugged.

"Do you feel like you…*hate* her?" Sidra wondered.

Chasity slowly shook her head. "No," she answered. "I know that she loves me, always *has*… For that alone, I *can't*."

"I'm glad to hear that," Malajia commented. "Y'all are too close for that."

"Yeah," Chasity sighed, running a hand along the back of her neck. "Y'all got one more question."

"Ooh, ooh, its mine," Malajia charged, waving her hand wildly in the air.

Chasity rolled her eyes in anticipation of whatever silly question Malajia was about to ask. "What's your question, Mel?"

Malajia put her hand down. "Are you gonna start calling her 'Mom'?"

Chasity was taken back by that question. She hadn't stopped to think about it. "Well…shit I don't know," she admitted, honestly. "Am I *supposed* to?"

"*I* would," Malajia declared. "In a heartbeat."

"I spent my whole life calling someone *else* Mom," Chasity pointed out. "I don't think the name means the same thing that it would to *you*."

"Well, in my opinion, maybe it's time that word became something *good* for you," Sidra suggested. "After all, Ms. Trisha *is* your mom, and has loved you like one."

Chasity glanced down as she pondered Sidra's words.

"All right, y'all heard her, no more questions," Malajia cut in, standing from her bed. "Now get out."

"How are you gonna kick us out when *you* were just all up in *our* room?" Sidra griped, eyeing Malajia with attitude.

Malajia shrugged as she headed for the bathroom.

As the day went on, the sunny skies turned cloudy. Malajia laid on her bed, listening to the sound of the rain hit the window and let out a loud sigh. "I'm so damn bored," she complained to herself, kicking her legs wildly in the air.

She reached over, picked up her phone and dialed a number. "Hey Praz," she smiled when he picked up. "I'm good, listen any parties at the clusters tonight?... Nothing?...You start making those drinks again?... No? Not even *one*?" she rolled her eyes. "Damn it! Fine, let me call you back." Malajia hung up and immediately dialed another number. She tapped her nails on her nightstand as she waited. "Marla!" she shrieked, when the line picked up. "...No, no shut up for a second," she ordered when the girl began running off at the mouth. "Is there anything going on in the apartments tonight?... Nothing?... Damn, this campus dry as shit!" she sucked her teeth when the girl started rambling again. "No, no Marla....Marla, I don't care what you did over the break...Yes I'm serious—" She looked down at her phone and saw that Marla had hung up. "Funny lookin' bitch," she spat, then tossed the phone down.

Chasity emerged from the bathroom and grabbed something from her dresser drawer, putting it into her jacket pocket. "What are you out here whining about?" she quibbled, fixing her ponytail in the mirror.

"I'm bored as shit," Malajia complained.

"Sounds like a personal problem," Chasity returned, even toned.

Malajia sucked her teeth, then noticed Chasity grab her umbrella from her closet door. "Where the hell are *you* going?" she demanded, fixing an inquisitive gaze.

"Jason's," Chasity replied, heading for the door.

Malajia bolted up. "Really?" she ground out. "You gonna leave me here, alone and bored, while you go get *laid*?"

Chasity did a dance as she grabbed the doorknob. "Yep," she mocked. After a stressful week, she was looking forward to spending some one on one time with Jason and participating in some *adult* activities.

"Fine, carry your horny ass on," Malajia sneered, flinging her hand in Chasity's direction. "That's why I hope he ran out of condoms."

"Got one right here," Chasity boasted, pulling the square foil packet from her pocket.

"Freak," Malajia hissed as Chasity danced out of the room in a taunting manner.

Malajia sat for a moment and pouted, "Great, now I'm bored *and* horny," she grumbled to herself. "Might as well talk to Ty," she said to herself, reaching for her phone again.

Chapter 30

Chasity was laying on her bed days later, flat on her back, arm thrown over her face, trying to will her abdominal pain away. *I hate cramps!* Her mission to relax herself enough to fall asleep was in vain as Malajia barged through the door.

"Chaz!" she bellowed.

"God," Chasity groaned, removing her arm from her face. "What *is* it Malajia?"

Malajia walked over to her bed and sat down. "I need you to take me to the store," she informed, ignoring Chasity's tone.

"No. Leave me alone."

"What's wrong with *you*?" Malajia sneered, this time noticing the harsh tone in her roommate's voice.

"I don't feel good," Chasity hissed.

"*So*," Malajia hurled back. "That doesn't mean that you get to act all nasty to me."

"I have fuckin' cramps! Back the fuck off," Chasity snapped, sitting up.

"Ooohhh," Malajia sympathized. "Well, at least you know you're not pregnant," she joked.

"Yeah, thanks," Chasity grunted, trying to get comfortable.

Malajia scratched her head. "Cramps are even more reason for you to take me to the store."

"What?!" Chasity barked, confused and irritated.

"I'm on *my* period *too*, and I need stuff."

Chasity could've jumped across the room and choked Malajia. "*So*," she ground out. "Go ask Sidra to take you."

Malajia stomped her foot on the floor like a child. "Sidra's in the damn library and she'll be in there all day working on some dumb ass paper," she whined. "I need to go *now*."

"Not my fuckin' problem."

"Come *on!*" Malajia demanded, slapping her hand on her bed. "I'm down to my last damn tampon, and I need to change it soon!"

"ILL!"

"Oh what? You act like you have an infinite stock all the time," Malajia griped. "Can you stop bitchin' and just take me?"

"No, drive your*self.*" Chasity pointed to her car keys that were laying on her night stand. She normally wouldn't trust anyone to drive her car without her in it, but she was in too much pain to care.

Malajia eyed the keys. "My license expired," she hesitantly put out.

Realizing that trying to relax with Malajia in the room would never be possible, Chasity jumped up off the bed and grabbed her keys and pocketbook. "Just come the fuck on!"

Malajia hopped up and darted out of the room after Chasity, a smile on her face.

Once they reached the car, Malajia opened her mouth to say something and Chasity put her hand up to silence her. "I don't want to hear it."

Malajia laughed. "I was just gonna say thanks, crampy," she teased.

Chasity flipped her off in retaliation, as she prepared to step into the car. Hearing familiar voices, both girls turned around to see Mark, Josh and David approaching.

"What are y'all doing over here?" Malajia asked, placing her bag in the car.

"Looking for Sidra," Josh replied.

Of course you are, Malajia thought, amused. "She's at the library, working on her American History assignment," she informed. "She's gonna be a while."

"Damn it!" Mark hollered.

"What are *you* so hype for?" Malajia asked, annoyed.

"We were going to ask Sid to give us a ride to the store," David answered, voice laced with amusement. "We have to get some food and stuff."

"What's wrong with *your* car?" Malajia directed her question to Mark, who was avoiding her gaze.

"Go on Mark, tell 'em," Josh goaded.

"Man, fuck out my business dawg."

Josh flagged him with his hand. "His stupid self ran out of gas and now the car is stuck in the gym parking lot," he revealed.

Malajia looked at Mark with confusion. "What the hell is with you *always* running out of gas?"

"What is with *you* always minding my goddamn business?" he retorted.

"You're such a fuckin' loser," Malajia shot back.

Josh looked over at Chasity, who had her head leaned on the hood of the car. "Hey Chaz, can *you* give us a ride?"

"Fuck you and no," she refused, not lifting her head.

"Oh wow," David chuckled as Josh shook his head. Even after all this time, David was still shocked at what came out of Chasity's mouth at times.

"Come on Chaz, please?" Josh pleaded. "We really need to go, and there won't be another bus going that way for like thirty minutes."

Chasity raised her head and pointed at Mark, who had a big smile plastered to his face. "I'm not riding with *his* loud ass," she declared.

"Come on, friend," Mark teased. "There're no snacks in the room. Plus I need to buy a gas can so I can get gas for my car. Please?"

Chasity looked back and forth between, the guys, who were smiling, and Malajia who had just shrugged. Chasity didn't have the energy to argue anymore. She stepped into the car. "You know what? Just get in the damn car and don't *nobody* say a goddamn word to me," she ordered.

"Aye David, don't be eating all the snacks once we get them either," Mark said after minutes of riding through the streets of Paradise Valley.

"What are you talking about?" David asked, confused. "I barely touch them. *You* eat them all."

"Stop lying!" Mark shouted.

Chasity, after making sure no cars were behind her, slammed on the breaks, causing her passengers to jerk forward.

"Aww shit," Malajia laughed, knowing what was coming.

"Mark, get the fuck out!" Chasity hollered.

"What'd I do?" he asked, shocked.

"Get your loud ass out my car," she demanded. "I told you I didn't want to hear that shit."

"Mark, you play too damn much," David complained.

"I didn't even do nothing," Mark griped.

Chasity pointed to the floor by Malajia's feet. "Malajia, give me the damn club, I'm gonna crack his shit."

Malajia cracked up laughing as she moved the metal steering wheel lock out of Chasity's reach. "No, he'll bleed all over your seats," she joked.

"Chasity, we're sorry," Josh put in, leaning up in his seat. "He'll be quiet."

"Josh, one more outburst from him and *all* of y'all are getting the hell out," Chasity promised, then shot a glance Malajia's way. "That includes *you* Malajia."

Malajia returned a shocked look. "What? Why? What did *I* do?" she exclaimed, pointing to herself.

"It's *your* fault I'm out here in the *first* place," Chasity reminded. "I was supposed to be sleeping these damn cramps off."

"Is it *my* fault I ran out of tampons?" Malajia sneered.

"Can you ladies *please* not talk about period stuff?" Josh quietly put in.

"Shut the hell up Josh!" both girls snapped, glaring daggers at him. Josh put his hands up in surrender.

Chasity pulled into the Mega Mart parking lot and put the car in park. Malajia and the guys hopped out of the car, leaving Chasity to stay behind and take advantage of the quiet and her heated seats.

Malajia headed down the feminine aisle, while the guys made their way to the food aisles. "Yo, we need some bread," Mark suggested, picking up a loaf of white bread.

"No, don't get that kind," David said, reaching for a loaf of wheat bread.

"Man, don't nobody want that nasty ass wheat bread," Mark argued.

"Then don't *eat* it," David threw back. "*You're* not buying it anyway."

Josh sighed and rubbed his eyes. He'd grown tired of the bickering. "Mark, just buy your *own* bread," he griped.

"No, we agreed to buy stuff that we *both* like," Mark recalled, holding his loaf in a firm grip.

David held a confused look on his face. "Why would I agree to get something that we *both* like when *I'm* the one paying for it?" he asked, point blank. "You never pay for *anything*. Where's all the money that your parents send?"

"Man, you already know I gotta use my money to put gas in my car," Mark explained.

"That *still* doesn't explain where the *rest* of your money goes," David shot back, completely agitated. "I'm tired of paying for everything for our room, man. I can't wait until this semester is over so I can get a new roommate."

"Don't nobody *else* wanna room with your corny ass."

"Guys, come on. Don't start this mess in the store," Josh cut in.

"Nobody wants to room with *your* freeloading ass *either*," David snapped, ignoring Josh's request.

Mark glared at David. "Keep talking," he warned. "I'll punch those glasses three aisles down."

Josh tried to suppress his laugh at the offhand threat that Mark made. "Guys, chill," he urged.

"I wish you *would*," David challenged. "I hope that raggedy car gets towed from the gym lot."

Mark sucked his teeth. "Man!" he exclaimed, taking the loaf of bread that he was holding and slapping it across David's face, knocking his glasses off.

"Oh shit," Josh bellowed with laughter as he watched the glasses fall to the floor and slide down the aisle.

Mark immediately regretted the decision once he saw the anger in David's face as he lunged for him. "My bad Dave! My bad," he hollered as David grabbed for his shirt collar.

Malajia turned the corner just in time to see Josh grab David to prevent him from taking Mark's head off. "What's going on?" Malajia wondered.

"I'm sick of your shit Mark," David wailed, grabbing at Mark.

Mark, whose back was against the bread shelf, knocked David's arms down. "I said my bad, damn," he tried to reason. "I know you're in love with your glasses."

"Mel, can you help me please?" Josh begged, squeezing between the two guys in an effort to separate them. "Mark just smacked David's glasses off with a loaf of bread."

Malajia stared at the scene before spotting David's sliver glasses on the floor at the end of the aisle. "What the hell?" she laughed. "I can't, with y'all."

"You better pick them up and pray to *God* they aren't broken," David threatened, straightening out his blue and white shirt.

"All right, damn," Mark relented, straightening out the

collar on his black t-shirt. "You stretched my damn shirt."

Malajia walked over to Mark and grabbed a piece of lint off of his shirt. "You're so damn annoying," she ground out, nudging him in the direction of the glasses. She giggled as her phone rang. Her face lit up at the name on the caller ID. "Hey Ty."

"Hey, nothing. What are you doing?"

Tyrone's nasty tone shocked her. "Huh?" she replied, confused. "What are you talking about?"

"Where are you?" he spat out.

"I'm at the damn store with my friends," Malajia answered, voice laced with anger. "What's your problem?" When she didn't hear a response after a few seconds, she looked at the phone. "Did he just hang up on me?" she asked herself. "Asshole" she mumbled, tossing the phone back in her bag. Malajia went to say something to the guys but paused when she saw Tyrone walk in their aisle, a mask of anger frozen on his face.

Malajia was caught off guard and it showed on her face. "What the hell is wrong with you?" she sneered as he approached. "When did you get here?"

"Hey Tyrone man. Nice to see you again," Josh greeted with a wave.

Tyrone ignored him as he stood in Malajia's face. "What are you doing here with them?" he barked, much to Malajia's astonishment. "And why were you touching *that* one?" he added, pointing to Mark.

"Why *wouldn't* I be here with them? I've told you before, they're my *friends*," Malajia argued, folding her arms. She'd lost count of the times that she had to reassure Tyrone that the four guys that she spent most of her time with were nothing more than friends. She didn't understand why he kept questioning her. "And I wasn't *touching* Mark; I was taking something off his shirt." It took a few seconds before something registered in her head. "Are you spying on me?"

"No. I happened to already be in here when I saw you," he replied, voice angry.

"So why didn't you just come and say 'hi'? Why do you have to be so damn dramatic?" Malajia asked, voice steadily rising.

Mark was watching the interaction from the side. *Fuckin' jackass*, he thought. As soon as Malajia's voice rose, he went into protective mode and walked over. "Everything all right?" he asked Malajia, completely ignoring Tyrone.

"We're good dawg," Tyrone answered, facing down Mark.

Mark frowned at him, "I was asking *her*."

"Well *I'm* telling you… *We're good*," Tyrone reiterated.

Malajia looked back and forth between her boyfriend and her friend, both tempers on high. She did not want this to get ugly. "Mark, everything is fine, we're just talking," she assured, voice calm. "Go finish your shopping."

Mark's fiery gaze was still fixed on Tyrone as he addressed Malajia. "You sure?" he pressed. "Your dude seems to have a damn problem."

"Yeah, I'm sure. Go on," Malajia insisted. "I'll catch up to y'all in a minute."

Still skeptical, Mark did as Malajia ordered. Mark walked over to the other guys, who were watching from the side. "Let's finish up and get out of here," he ground out.

"Everything cool?" Josh asked.

"Yeah I guess…for now," Mark replied, walking off.

"You're being ridiculous," Malajia hurled at Tyrone once the guys were out of ear shot.

"I don't want you hanging around those guys anymore, *especially* that damn Mark," he demanded.

"Well I'm sorry, but that's *not* going to happen," Malajia let him know, point blank. "You can't stop me from hanging out with my friends. You're *not* my father."

"I *am* your *man* though. And I *don't* want you hanging out with other guys," Tyrone maintained, furious. "And I *especially* don't want you touching them."

Malajia put her hand on top of her head, she was so irritated with him and the way he was embarrassing her. "I wasn't touching—"

"Do you like him or something?" Tyrone rudely interrupted.

Malajia's eyes widened. "Are you crazy?!" she wailed. "*No*, I don't like Mark like that. He's just a friend. Like the brother I never wanted."

"Malajia, I'm not playing with you," he fumed. "Keep your ass away from him."

Malajia took a deep breath, trying to keep from flying completely off the handle. "Look, I don't know what you *think* you see, but you don't need to be jealous of any guy that I'm around," she assured, putting her hands on his chest in an effort to calm him. She frowned when Tyrone grabbed her hands off him and pushed them down.

"I *said* I'm not playing," he warned before walking away, leaving her astonished.

Chasity, sitting up and listening to the music blasting from her car radio, was relieved. The aspirin that she had taken earlier had finally kicked in, relieving some of her pain. She was lip synching along to one of her favorite songs when the guys walked over and got into the car. "Thanks for waiting Chaz," Josh said, fastening his seatbelt.

"Sure," she replied, turning the radio down. "Where's Malajia?"

"She's still in there with her dumbass boyfriend," Mark huffed, jerking his seatbelt on.

Chasity frowned. "Yeah?"

"Yeah," Mark confirmed. "He had a whole damn attitude. I swear, I can't stand that fool, yo."

"Yeah, you and me *both*," Chasity mumbled. She looked out of her window and watched as Tyrone stormed out of the store and over to a car full of his friends. Malajia followed out a few moments later, and Chasity could tell by the way she was walking that Malajia was upset. Normally her walk was more of a steady saunter; this time her pace was quick, arms were folded and face was masked with frustration.

Malajia got into the car without saying a word. Chasity, knowing that she herself hated to be spoken to when she was upset, decided against saying anything right away. However, after driving in silence for a few moments she changed her mind. "What happened?" Chasity asked.

"Nothing, I'm fine," Malajia replied, even toned as she gazed out of the window.

"She's lying," Mark chimed in from the back.

"Mind your business," Malajia snarled.

"Malajia, what did he do *now*?" Chasity pressed.

"He's being his usual asshole self," Malajia answered. "And I *don't* want to talk about it."

"Okay fine," Chasity relented, eyes focused on the road.

The awkward silence was too much for Josh to bear. It reminded him of his parents when he was young. Before they divorced, sometimes they would just sit in silence, trying to avoid arguing with each other. "Hey Chaz, Mark hit David in the face with a loaf of bread," he laughed.

"*Really* Josh?" David snapped.

"Come on man, we was cool and now you bring it up *again*?" Mark griped.

"What the hell?" Chasity said, not amused; Malajia managed a small laugh.

Josh sat back and smiled, proud of himself for breaking the silence.

Chapter 31

Emily sat with her head down, tears streaming down her face, blood roaring in her ears. "I—I failed every midterm?" she stammered, unsure if she heard the department head clearly.

Dr. Walker sat across from Emily, paper in hand, staring down at her through his glasses. "Yes Miss Harris," he confirmed. "*Every* midterm...all *five* of your classes."

Emily tugged the collar of her pink t-shirt as she felt a wave of heat fall over her. She had a feeling that she'd flunked her midterms, but to hear those words said to her was too much to handle. *Mommy's gonna kill me*, she thought. "I don't know what happened," she sputtered, still in disbelief.

Dr. Walker folded his arms. "Do you remember our conversation in the beginning of the semester?" he asked, tone stern.

"Yes sir," she meekly replied.

"So, you're aware that you are on your way to academic probation, right?"

Emily managed a nod. "Yes, sir."

"What happened?" he pressed, disappointed. "You finished your freshman year with so much promise. What is it, Miss Harris? Do you not like your major anymore? Do you need tutoring? Do we need to restructure your course load?" he asked, concerned. "Help me, help *you*."

Emily sat there, she felt more tears falling. "I—I don't know what happened," she repeated.

Dr. Walker removed his glasses and rubbed his eyes. "Miss Harris, I'll have you know that your mother called the office earlier, inquiring about your progress, and I had no choice but to tell her," he revealed.

Emily's eyes widened as she looked up at him, making the first bit of eye contact since she sat down nearly twenty minutes ago. "She—wha—you told her everything?" she panicked.

"Absolutely," he confirmed. "Now, I'm going to suggest that for the rest of this semester, you get yourself some tutoring in all of your classes."

Emily could no longer focus on the words that were coming out of Dr. Walker's mouth. All she thought about was the fact that her mother knew of how badly she was doing. She knew that her mom would eventually find out, but she still wasn't prepared for the consequences. Gathering her book bag from the floor, Emily stood up from her seat.

"I'm sorry Dr. Walker, I gotta go," she murmured, hurrying out of the office.

Emily practically jogged back to her room, and was greeted by a ringing phone. She dropped her book bag to the floor and slowly walked over. Judging by the six messages flashing across her brand new answering machine screen, her mother had been calling ever since she had spoken to Dr. Walker.

The phone stopped ringing and Emily sighed, then jumped when it rang again. Hesitantly, she answered. "Yes Mommy?" she said, already knowing who was on the other end.

There was a long pause on the line. "After everything I said, every talk that we had, you *still* screwed up," Ms. Harris spat out, finally.

Emily slowly sat down on her bed. There was nothing that she could say; she was busted. All she could do was sit there and take her verbal lashing.

"I gave you another chance to turn your grades around, and you blew it," Ms. Harris fumed. "You get no more chances. When this semester is over, you won't be returning to Paradise Valley University."

Emily couldn't speak as she felt a break down nearing.

"When you come home for summer break, we're going to look at schools here in Jersey," Ms. Harris added. "Enough is enough."

Emily continued to sit in silence, even after her mother ended the phone call. Her fears were becoming a reality. Finally able to stand, with tears stinging her eyes, she headed for the door and stormed out.

Sidra poured lotion into her hands and began massaging them as she visually surveyed the items on her dresser. She straightened out her perfume bottles and frowned when something caught her eye, or better yet, *didn't*. "Where's my apple body spray?" she mumbled to herself.

"You say something, Sid?" Alex asked, from her bed.

"Um yeah," Sidra replied, turning around. "You haven't seen my apple body spray, have you?"

Alex looked up from the book that she was reading. "Was that the one that you let me hold the other day?" she wondered.

Sidra shook her head. "No, that was the vanilla one."

Alex shrugged. "Then no sweetie, I haven't," she assured. "The vanilla one is on my dresser if you want that one back."

Sidra waved her hand slightly. "No, you can keep it," she said. She placed a finger to her chin as she pondered where she could've misplaced it. *I know for sure I didn't take it in the bathroom.* Her thoughts were interrupted by a knock on the door. "I'll get it," she announced, heading over. "Hey Emily," Sidra smiled once she opened the door.

Emily stared back at Sidra, eyes red and face wet with tears. "Hi," she sniffled.

The smile on Sidra's face faded as she grabbed Emily's arm. "What happened, are you okay?" she charged, pulling her into the room.

Upon seeing Emily enter, Alex sat up right on her bed. "Something wrong?"

"*Everything* is wrong," Emily broke down, plopping down on Alex's bed.

"Oh my God, what happened?" Alex panicked, putting her hand on Emily's shoulder. When Emily couldn't speak right away, Alex gave her shoulder a shake. "Em, you gotta say something."

"I failed all of my midterms," Emily revealed, wiping her eyes with the back of her hands.

"You *what*?" Sidra frowned, arms folded.

"I failed," Emily repeated. "And my mom knows… She's pulling me out of this school at the end of this semester."

Alex and Sidra glanced at each other in disbelief as Emily put her head in her hands. "God Em," Alex sympathized. "Look, it's terrible that you failed, but you can still turn everything around… Your mom should understand that you made a mistake…you shouldn't have to leave."

"Em, you *can't* leave," Sidra insisted, voice stern.

Emily shook her head; she had no hope. "She's gonna get her way," she resolved. "There's nothing I can say."

Sidra let out a sigh, while Alex tried to console a crying Emily. The door swung open and Sidra spun around, coming face to face with Malajia and Chasity.

Malajia put her hand up. "Ponytail, don't even start it. You already knew I wasn't gonna knock," she jeered, anticipating Sidra's rant.

Sidra, not saying a word, gestured her head towards Emily.

"What's up with *her*?" Malajia asked, pointing. "She's not drunk again, is she?"

"No Malajia, she's *not*," Alex snarled, handing Emily some tissue.

Emily lifted her head and wiped her eyes yet again. "I just found out that I failed all of my midterms," she revealed.

"What do you mean *all*?" Chasity scoffed. "Are you serious?"

"Damn. Even *I* didn't do *that* bad," Malajia teased when Emily slowly nodded.

"Not funny, Malajia," Alex scolded, handing Emily more tissue.

"Oh come on. She can still pull her grades up," Malajia argued, unaware the severity of the situation. "Even if she has to repeat a class, it's not the end of the world. Shit, I'm on repeat with Spanish 101, you don't see *me* crying."

"It may not be the end of the *world* for her, but it's the end of her time here at this *school*," Sidra put in.

Chasity frowned, "What does *that* mean?"

"Her mother found out about her grades and is gonna try to pull her out of the school," Alex sulked.

"What?!" Malajia exclaimed. "Emily, that's crazy. No, *she* is crazy. Your damn *mother* is crazy. She can't *do* that."

"Apparently, she *can*," Sidra contradicted. "And *will*."

Chasity shook her head as she fixed an angry gaze at Emily. "Emily, what are you gonna do about that?" she charged.

"She can't—"

"I was talking to *Emily*," Chasity barked, cutting Alex off. Chasity was done; she was tired of Emily's whining and crying.

Emily looked down at her hands, not bothering to respond.

"What are you going to *do* about that?" Chasity repeated, voice rising. "You're nineteen years old. Grow the fuck up!"

Malajia and Sidra stood in stunned silence as Chasity

continued to yell at Emily.

"You don't have to leave this school if you don't *want* to," Chasity ranted.

Emily cried once more as she continued to stare at her hands.

Chasity had grown more and more frustrated by Emily's weak disposition and silence. "So you're gonna pretend like you don't hear me talking to you?" she fumed. When Emily didn't reply once again, Chasity took a step in her direction.

"Chaz, stop it!" Alex hollered, jumping up from the bed.

Chasity pointed at Alex. "You want me to start respecting her, Alex?" she asked. "Well it starts *now*." Chasity turned her attention back to Emily. "Emily, get up."

Emily hesitated, then after a moment began to slowly rise from the bed.

Sidra took a step towards Chasity, "Chasity, maybe you should back off a little."

"Naw Sid, leave her be. I gotta see this," Malajia stepped in, pulling Sidra away.

Alex jumped in Chasity's face as she took another step towards a now standing Emily. "You better leave her alone," she snarled.

Chasity stared Alex square in her eye, eyes blazing, unwavering. "You wanna fight me, Alex?" she challenged.

Malajia began removing her earrings. "Alex, don't touch my girl, or I'm gonna jump in," she warned.

Sidra sucked her teeth. "Girl, you're not going to do anything but sit your ass down somewhere," Sidra cut in, guiding Malajia down in a nearby chair.

Alex faced Chasity down. "You *know* I don't," Alex threw back, ignoring Malajia. "But you need to leave the girl alone."

Chasity narrowed her eyes at Alex. "You gonna let her speak for you just like your mother does, Emily?" she directed to Emily.

Alex's mouth fell open. "That's *not* what I'm doing!" she wailed.

"Back...off," Chasity ordered through clenched teeth.

Alex opened her mouth to respond, then she noticed Malajia and Sidra quickly shaking their heads at her. "You condoning this?" she spat at them.

When they didn't respond, Alex had her answer. Resolved, Alex sighed and stepped away.

Chasity walked over and stood in Emily's face. "Look me in my face," she demanded.

When Emily didn't comply, Chasity gave her a little shove.

"Are you serious, Chasity?!" Alex screamed.

Sidra didn't know if she should step in or stay back; she was frozen with shock. Malajia, on the other hand, found it amusing.

Emily cried when Chasity shoved her again. "Stop it," Emily whimpered.

"What? I didn't hear you," Chasity taunted. "You wanna say that louder?" she shoved Emily again.

"Emily, you better stand up to her, or she's gonna keep doing it," Malajia urged. She, unlike Alex, knew what Chasity's intentions were.

"Maybe you should stop it," Sidra suggested, putting her hand up. "You're scaring her."

"Shut up," Chasity shot at Sidra before smacking Emily across the face. It was more of a soft tap, but it was more than enough to startle her.

"Oh shit, she just slapped her!" Malajia erupted, trying to hold her laughter in.

"It's not fucking funny, Malajia!" Alex boomed, pointing in her face.

Malajia looked at her, "How you mad at *me*?" she exclaimed, pointing to herself.

"Fight me back," Chasity challenged Emily.

"I can't," Emily sobbed, feeling another tap across her face.

"You fight me back, or I'm not gonna stop."

After the third tap to her face, Emily snapped. "Leave me alone!" She lunged at Chasity, grabbing her and knocking her to the floor. Chasity shielded her face as Emily began to repeatedly slap her.

"Oh my God!" Alex bellowed, darting over.

"Get her off my girl! Get her off my girl," Malajia hollered, jumping from her seat, only to be forced back down by Sidra who had sat on her lap.

Alex grabbed the crying Emily around her waist and pulled her off of Chasity. "Are you happy now, Chasity?" she seethed.

"Alex let go of me!" Emily yelled, shoving Alex's hands off of her. She then stormed out of the room, slamming the door behind her.

Sidra got up, allowing Malajia the opportunity to help Chasity off the floor. "Nobody wanted it to go that far, Alex," Malajia stated. "But the girl needed that."

Chasity smoothed her disheveled hair down and looked at Malajia. "Did she scratch my face?"

"Naw boo, you're good," Malajia assured, helping Chasity fix her hair.

Alex was fuming. She couldn't believe what had just taken place. She folded her arms and was pacing back and forth. "That was totally uncalled for, Chasity," she fussed.

"That's *your* opinion," Chasity replied, even toned as she examined her arms. The welts from the scratches were beginning to show. *Damn this shit hurts.*

"Wow, I've *never* seen Emily so angry," Sidra chimed in, still in shock. "You fell pretty hard Chaz, are you okay?"

"Yeah," Chasity replied, giving her lower back a rub.

"That's what the hell your ignorant ass gets," Alex sneered. "You got scratched the hell up."

Chasity frowned at her. "You *do* realize that if I wanted to, I could've snapped that girl in half, right?" she pointed out.

Alex rolled her eyes.

"And you can be mad at me all you want," Chasity threw out. "But the girl fought me back, so what I did worked."

"Yep, sure did Alex," Malajia agreed.

Alex shook her head at Malajia. "Look, I get it," she said to Chasity. "But you went too far. You *bullied* her just now."

Malajia sucked her teeth. Alex's complaining was getting on her last nerve. "Alex, you always gotta go to the extreme," she hurled.

"*Me?*" Alex questioned in disbelief.

"She didn't bully the poor *baby*," Malajia mocked. "She forced her ass to *finally* stand up for herself. Isn't that what we've been telling her to *do* all this time?"

"While I agree that slapping her was a bit much," Sidra added. "The outcome did work, Alex."

Alex let out a loud sigh as she looked away. "Whatever," she mumbled.

"Those slaps Emily gave you sounded like they hurt," Malajia teased, glancing at Chasity.

"They *did*," Chasity confirmed, amused. "Surprised the hell outta me."

"We could've used those slaps during that fight with Jackie," Malajia joked.

Emily tapped her highlighter on her desk while she tried to focus on her studies. Her efforts were in vain, she found it next to impossible to concentrate. Between the meeting with Dr. Walker, her mother's phone call and her confrontation with Chasity, she couldn't wait for the day to be over. Unfortunately for her, midnight was still three hours away. Hearing a knock on the door, she pushed herself back from her desk and went to open it.

Emily was startled. "Chasity," she stammered, seeing her standing there. *Please don't hit me again.*

"I'm not going to hit you," Chasity assured, noticing the scared look on her face.

"I'm—I'm sor—"

"Don't apologize," Chasity cut it, voice calm. "Come on, let's go for a walk."

Emily was taken back by her request. "Um, okay." She reluctantly grabbed her room keys from her desk and followed Chasity out of the room.

As they walked out of the apartment and started along the path leaving the complex, Chasity noticed that Emily kept looking around, as if she was searching for something or some*one*.

"It's *just* me," Chasity informed.

What is she physic? Emily thought. "Okay," she replied softly. "So what are you doing here exactly?" she wondered, pushing hair behind her ears.

Chasity took a deep breath. "Well...I came here to apologize," she revealed, completely shocking Emily; it showed in her face as Emily stopped walking and faced her.

"Really?"

"Yes," Chasity replied, halting her steps. "I shouldn't have put my hands on you."

Emily resisted the urge to glance at the ground. She held a gaze. "Thank you for that," she said, grateful. "Why *did* you though?"

"I just wanted you to stand up to me," Chasity explained. "You allow people to walk all over you and its eating away at you... I was trying to help, but I admit that I took it too far." Upon returning to her room after her confrontation, Chasity did a lot of thinking as she tended to her minor wounds. She realized that her methods might have been too much for Emily, for *anybody*.

"Why do you care, Chasity?" Emily asked, point blank. "I mean, you made it clear that you don't like me."

"I don't like how you *act*, that doesn't mean that I don't like you as a person," Chasity clarified. "If I didn't like you, you'd know, trust me."

"Oh," Emily breathed. That was a relief.

Chasity sighed. "Look Emily, I care because you're a good person...and I used to be *like* you in a way."

Emily's eyes widened. "You *what?*"

"*Shocking* isn't it?"

"Yes! I mean you aren't afraid of *anybody*," Emily pointed out. "People respect you, they're *scared* of you."

"That may be true Emily, but it wasn't *always* like that," Chasity replied. "I was once shy and quiet like *you*. I tried to people please my way through life. I thought that I needed people to accept and like me because I wasn't being accepted and liked at *home*," she continued, thinking of her past experience. "I was picked on a lot, and it wasn't until I started fighting back that I realized how much power I had." Chasity pushed hair behind her ears. "People respect me because I *make* them, people fear me because…well, I'm mean."

Emily managed a giggle before traces of amusement left her face. "I don't think I can ever change into the person that *you* are."

"I wouldn't *want* you to," Chasity admitted. "Being like me isn't necessarily a good thing all the time. I've hurt a lot of feelings and I've been in a lot of fights."

Emily sighed.

"It's okay to be yourself, Emily…just be a stronger version," Chasity advised. "You can still be *you* and tell people when they upset you, when they annoy you…or when they're *controlling* you."

Emily lowered her head. "I know you're referring to my mother," she said, somber.

"All I'm saying is that if you want to stay here at this school, and get some control over your life…you're gonna have to stand up to her."

"I know," Emily admitted after a moment. "I just don't know *how* to."

"You'll figure it out," Chasity assured, rubbing her own arm.

Emily's eyes zoned in on the band aids. "What happened to your arms?"

"You scratched me." Chasity eyed her as if she was

crazy. "You don't remember that part?"

Emily put her hand over her mouth. "No, I thought I just slapped you," she said. "I hardly even have any nails."

"Yeah, you got 'em," Chasity confirmed.

Emily giggled. "Well, I appreciate you not fighting back."

Chasity shook her head and chuckled. "You're welcome."

"So…you're probably gonna think this is weird," Emily began, shifting her weight from one foot to another,

"*What's* weird?" Chasity wondered.

"Can I have a hug?" Emily smiled, hopeful.

Chasity narrowed her eyes. "Do I *have* to?" she sneered. Emily held her smile as she opened her arms. Chasity rolled her eyes. "Fine," she scoffed, before allowing Emily to embrace her for a brief moment.

Emily let out a happy sigh as both girls continued walking. "Do you realize that this is the longest conversation that we've ever had?"

"I do," Chasity agreed.

"And it's without the other girls around," Emily pointed out.

"Your point?"

"Maybe we can start hanging out one on one," Emily hoped.

"Yeah, don't push it Emily," Chasity ground out.

Emily let another giggle come through. "It was worth a try."

Chapter 32

"I don't get why you're so damn mad!" Malajia hollered into the phone as she and Chasity were walking back from the fitness center. After a workout, Malajia's mood was in good spirits, but she was brought down once Tyrone called her to continue an earlier argument. "I told you that I couldn't talk to you right then." She rolled her eyes as his yelling continued. "I was in the middle of doing something. I alre—What? ...No I wasn't screwing anybody. Are you kidding me?!"

Walking beside her, Chasity tried to tune out the conversation by listening to the music through her headphones. But hearing the hurt and anger in her friend's voice while she talked to her boyfriend was making her angry. "Hang up," she suggested, pushing her ponytail over her shoulder.

Malajia flagged her with her hand, ignoring her suggestion. "Don't talk to me like that!"

Chasity glanced over at her.

"I swear I hate when you get like this… It's unnecessary… Yes it *is*!" Malajia's mouth fell open. "What did you just call me?"

Having heard enough, Chasity snatched the phone from Malajia's ear. "Oops," she said as she purposely hung up the call.

"What the hell did you do that for?" Malajia snapped, reaching for her phone.

"Don't take that bullshit from him," Chasity snarled, shoving the phone back into Malajia's hand.

"You don't even know what he *said*," Malajia argued, looking down at her phone.

"I *don't*," Chasity agreed. "But when I heard 'what did you call me?' it meant that he called you out your name."

Malajia rolled her eyes and put her hand up. "Whatever Chasity."

"So I'm *wrong*?" Chasity quizzed. Malajia's loud sigh confirmed what she already thought. "Exactly."

"It's like whenever I'm not with him, he thinks I'm messing around," Malajia confessed, pushing hair over her shoulder. "Talking about 'who are you screwing?'" she vented. "I haven't even screwed *him* yet. Why would I do it with anybody I'm *not* with?"

Chasity shook her head. "You don't see how possessive he is?"

Malajia sucked her teeth. She regretted venting to Chasity; now she was dealing with the ever popular boyfriend bashing lecture from her. "Don't," she hissed.

"Don't *what*?" Chasity returned. "You that blind?"

"Look, okay, so maybe he gets a little jealous," Malajia reasoned. "He's just protective of me…and so *what* he gets a little ignorant with his words when we fight, so do *I*."

"Yeah, okay," Chasity spat out.

"Not everyone handles their relationship the same way," Malajia barked. "You shouldn't judge… Yours ain't perfect *either*."

Chasity stared at Malajia for several moments. "I don't get you," she ground out.

"Well, now you know how *I* feel dealing with *you* all the time," Malajia teased, trying to make light of the situation.

"He's two seconds from hitting you," Chasity pointed out, ignoring Malajia's joke.

Malajia shot Chasity a lethal glare. "He would *never* do that!" she wailed. "Don't do that Chasity, don't you *dare* put that label on him."

"So you're snapping at *me* because *your* boyfriend is crazy?" Chasity bit back.

"No, I'm snapping at you because you always put him down," Malajia returned. "Yes, he may overreact at times, but he's *not* an abusive person."

"Whatever you say Malajia," Chasity relented. "You don't get it, and I'm tired of talking."

"Good, because I'm tired of *listening*."

Emily sat in the cushy seat outside of Ms. Smith's office, waiting. Glancing at the clock on the wall in front of her, she sighed. *What am I doing here?* Emily remembered waking up that morning, still reflecting on the events from a week ago. Her failing grades and the knowledge that she would be forced to leave her second home, had her reeling. That and her conversation with Chasity had her deep in self-reflecting thought.

Hearing her name called, she stood up and made her way into Ms. Smith's office.

"Have a seat Miss Harris," the woman smiled.

This room hasn't changed since I first walked in here, she mused of the familiar décor. Emily hadn't stepped foot into the counselor's office since the beginning of her freshman year. Emily nodded and took a seat in front of the desk.

"How have you been?"

Emily shrugged as she rubbed her arm. "Not good, apparently," she answered honestly.

Ms. Smith smoothed her hand down her green blazer. "Well, do you want to talk about that?"

Emily shrugged again. She knew why she'd contacted

Ms. Smith's office in the first place, but sitting in front of her now, she wondered if she made a mistake.

"I remember you Miss Harris," Ms. Smith stated, interrupting Emily's thoughts.

"You do?"

"Yes," Ms. Smith nodded. "You were one of the girls who wanted to run home after only being here a day," she mused.

Emily glanced down at her hands. *Great first impression,* she thought.

"You were so timid and afraid," Ms. Smith added. "It stood out to me."

"Yeah, not much has changed," Emily muttered.

Ms. Smith frowned in concern. "What are you afraid of exactly?" she asked, tone calm, professional.

Emily sighed. "To be honest..." she glanced out the window. "I'm afraid that by letting certain...*things* affect me, that I'm throwing away my opportunities," she carefully revealed.

"Can you elaborate on that?" Ms. Smith prodded, leaning forward.

Emily was trying to be careful with what she said. The last thing she wanted to do was badmouth the woman who raised her to a stranger. "I'm um... I'm failing my classes, because I'm stressed out," she said.

"What's stressing you?" Ms. Smith asked.

Emily looked down at her hands. "My mo—a relative," she eluded. "She's constantly on my back about everything and I can't focus... I feel like I can't breathe sometimes."

"Have you told this relative how you feel and what their actions are doing to you?"

"I've tried," Emily replied. "I guess not as hard as I *should*."

Ms. Smith paused as she jotted something down, something that always made the students who sat across from her nervous. "Miss Harris, you're *how* old?"

"Nineteen."

Ms. Smith nodded. "So you're an adult," she confirmed. "Which means that it's time for you to take responsibility and control over your own life. You can't let other people's actions affect how you deal with things…because at the end of the day, *you're* the one who has to deal with them."

Emily sat in silence as Ms. Smith continued.

"This relative *obviously* thinks that she has a right to control how you live your life," Ms. Smith continued. "Do you agree?"

"Do I agree that they have a right to control me?" Emily questioned. "No, I *don't*."

"Then what are you going to do to make them *stop*?"

Emily took a deep breath. Ms. Smith was saying the same thing that others have said to her, that the girls have said to her. Coming from an unbiased person, the words carried more weight.

"Do you have any idea how to do that?" Ms. Smith pressed when Emily didn't answer.

Emily nodded. "Yes," she assured, but secretly dreaded that conversation.

Malajia laid sprawled out on her bed, watching TV, hoping that the popular TV show would cheer her up. "Why do people still *watch* this shit?" she hissed to herself, turning the show off with the remote. The show episode was dry and so was Malajia's mood. Sitting up on her bed and leaning back against her headboard, she reached for a book on her nightstand. After flipping through a few pages, she tossed the book on the floor, letting out a groan in the process. With tensions between her and Tyrone at a high after yet another argument that morning, and her annoyance with Chasity over her accusing words two days prior, Malajia felt like she could punch something.

Hearing a light knock on the door, she let out a groan and jumped up from her bed. "I said I don't wanna go to that dry ass caf, Alex," she spat at the door. After declining

Alex's invitation to go to the cafeteria for lunch with her and Emily, she was sure Alex had come to try to change her mind.

Snatching the door open, the frown on her face remained once she saw who was *actually* there. "What are you doing here?" she sneered at Tyrone.

Tyrone held a dozen red roses in front of her face. "Can I come in?" he asked.

Malajia glanced down at the bouquet. Normally she would be excited to receive such beautiful flowers, but she was irritated with him; the gesture went unappreciated. "You can take those with you on your way out of the building," she hissed, closing the door.

"Hold on a sec," Tyrone insisted, sticking his foot in the door. "I came to apologize to you. Can I please come in?"

Malajia hesitated, but when he smiled at her, her lethal expression softened. *God, why can't I resist that damn smile?* She sucked her teeth. "Fine, come in." Stepping aside to let him in, she took the roses and sat them on her dresser. "These are pretty."

"I'm glad you like them," Tyrone returned, sitting on Malajia's bed. "Is your roommate here?" he asked, looking around.

"No, she's out with her boyfriend," Malajia quickly replied, bite in her voice. She folded her arms. "Don't you have something to say?"

Sighing, Tyrone reached out for her hand. "Malajia, I'm sorry for the way I've been acting."

Malajia took his hand and allowed him to pull her onto the bed next to him. She smoothed her mini skirt down and looked him in his eyes. "Why *have* you been acting like that?" she asked.

Tyrone ran his free hand over his freshly cut hair. "I just…I hate the fact that I can't be with you every day, you know," he explained, "I miss you when you're not with me, and when I can't talk to you, it drives me crazy."

"So you think calling me names like 'whore', and

accusing me of sleeping around is a justifiable action?" Malajia questioned, tone not hiding her disdain.

"No, it's *not*," Tyrone admitted. "But, I just can't deal with the fact that you're hanging out with other guys."

Malajia frowned. *Why do we keep coming back to this shit!* "Tyrone, I'm sick and tired of having this same conversation with you," she fumed, standing up. He stopped her by grabbing her arm, holding on to it with a firm grip.

"Sit down," he ordered, stern.

Malajia glared at him, then did as he said.

"You asked me a question and I answered," he pointed out. "You can't get mad because you don't agree with my reasoning."

Malajia jerked her arm away from him. "Look," she ground out. "Bottom line, I'm not hanging with some random dudes. Those guys that you're referring to are my *friends*. And contrary to what you *think*, I'm *still* a fuckin' virgin."

Tyrone glanced down Malajia's slender frame. Lust in his eyes. "I know," he crooned, gently taking her hand.

"You don't have to be jealous," she added, ignoring the way that he looked at her. "I'm not dealing with anybody else. I don't *want* to deal with anybody else. I need you to get that."

"I *do*," he promised, rubbing her hand.

Malajia let out a sigh as he kissed her hand. "I'm tired of arguing with you over stupid shit."

Tyrone was too busy focusing on how soft Malajia's skin was to pay attention to the tears forming in her eyes, to the desperation in her face.

"Are you listening to me?" she asked.

"Of course," Tyrone immediately responded, staring her in the eyes. He touched her face and she pressed her cheek into his hand. "Look, I didn't come here to argue," he promised. "*I* want things to be better *too*."

Malajia just stared at him. "So how can we make that happen?"

Without warning, Tyrone leaned in and kissed Malajia.

She was initially stunned; she didn't see the moment as a romantic one. Although she welcomed the feeling of his lips on hers, she wasn't finished with her conversation. She felt like nothing was resolved. She pulled away. "We still have to—"

Tyrone put his finger to her lips, silencing her. "You said you don't want to fight," he uttered, staring at her full lips. "Neither do *I*." Malajia stared at him confused. "So, let's not…let's make up?" he proposed.

Malajia didn't say another word as Tyrone kissed her once more. She tried to hold on to her frustration with him, but as his kiss deepened, she found it hard to keep that focus. She gasped when he moved his lips to her neck. Her body over heated as she enjoyed the feeling of his lips on her skin.

She freely allowed his hands to roam her body, but it wasn't until she felt his hand moving up her skirt to her underwear that she felt the urge to stop him. *You know what he's trying to do Malajia,* the voice rang in her head. *You're not ready for this*. Malajia tried to listen to the warning in her head, and even put her hand on his, to stop his fingers from slipping under the delicate fabric. Although Tyrone steadied his hand, he didn't move it. She gripped his hand as she fought the battle within herself. *Stop him, you're not ready*. Malajia ignored her inner voice. Tired of arguing and wanting her relationship with Tyrone to be stronger, closer, she removed her hand from his.

Taking the gesture as the answer that he sought for his nonverbal question, Tyrone removed a condom from the pocket of his jeans, then wrapped his arms around Malajia and laid her down on the bed, hovering over her in the process. Malajia laid in silence as Tyrone removed his clothes, then removed her skirt and underwear. He lifted her shirt up and Malajia stared up at the ceiling while he put the condom on. Or at least she hoped that he did, for she couldn't bring herself to even look at him, to make sure. She let out a breath as he laid his heavy weight on top of her.

Malajia moved her head, looking off to the side,

focusing her attention on the pictures on the wall in front of her as Tyrone positioned himself. With both hands, she gripped the covers behind her head as she prepared for what was coming. Something that she'd fantasized about, but was in no way ready for. Tears glassed over her eyes and she gritted her teeth, as she felt a sharp pain that she'd never felt before, followed by the revelation that something that she'd held onto for twenty years of her life was now gone. No sounds of pleasure flowed from her, although they flowed from him. Malajia just let out short bursts of breaths as she tried to adjust her body to the penetrating feeling.

Malajia sat on her bed, fully dressed, staring out ahead of her, not focusing on anything in particular. She'd almost drowned out the sound of the shower running in the bathroom. But a flashback of what happened merely fifteen minutes ago snapped her out of her haze. The reality had completely set in that she was no longer a virgin, and she couldn't come to terms with exactly how she felt about it.

The sound of the keys in the door startled Malajia. *Shit I wasn't expecting her back until later*, she panicked. She didn't have time to react, or even kick Tyrone's clothes under her bed, before the door opened.

"Hey," Chasity threw out, rushing over to her dresser in search of something.

"I didn't think you'd be back so early," Malajia put out, tone low.

"Yeah well, that movie was corny," Chasity replied. "And now your friends are whining about having to go to the damn store."

"Oh," Malajia replied, rubbing the back of her neck.

Chasity grabbed what she was looking for and went to head out of the room, when Malajia's down appearance stopped her. She knew that Malajia was sulking earlier because of an argument, and Chasity knew that she was annoyed with *her* as well, but the look on Malajia's face, the sadness in her eyes, seemed different.

"You okay?" Chasity asked, concerned.

Malajia opened her mouth to respond when a noise from the bathroom startled them both.

Frowning, Chasity pointed to the closed door. "Who's in there?"

Malajia hesitated. "Um…" Tyrone, walking out of the bathroom with a towel wrapped around his waist, stopped anything that was about to come out of her mouth.

Chasity spun around and came face to face with him, an angry look on her face.

"Tyrone, you remember my friend Chasity, right?" Malajia asked.

"Sure do," Tyrone answered, walking up to her. "How's it going?"

Chasity continued to stare at him with a venomous look. She had no intention of speaking to him. She was more concerned with why he was taking a shower in her bathroom. *If you don't step out my face.*

"Chaz, don't be rude," Malajia tiredly hissed, sensing the tension.

Chasity shot Malajia the same look that she had just given Tyrone, then focused her eyes on the man's clothes littering the floor by Malajia's bed. *You didn't*, she thought.

"Chasity, I get the feeling that you don't care for me," Tyrone observed, retrieving his t-shirt from the floor. "It's a shame, you should get to know me. You may change your mind."

Chasity shook her head at Malajia who just stared back, guilt on her face. "Yeah, I highly doubt that," Chasity fumed, before walking out the door.

Malajia jumped up, ignoring her soreness, and ran out after her. "Are you freakin' kidding me?" Malajia spat out, shutting the door behind her. "Do you *always* have to be so damn rude?"

"Yep," Chasity returned, continuing her saunter down the hallway.

"Chasity, you may not like him, but you better *respect* him," Malajia shot back.

Chasity stopped dead in her tracks and spun around. "Respect your*self*," she hissed.

"What the hell is *that* supposed to mean?" Malajia fumed, taken back.

Chasity once again shook her head. "I hope it was memorable for you," she said, tone dripping with disdain.

Malajia watched with contempt as Chasity walked away. Putting her hand over her head, Malajia let out a long sigh, before kicking the door in frustration.

Chapter 33

Leaving class a few days later, Alex was relieved to learn that the final for her English Composition class was going to be a paper, rather than a test. *That'll be a piece of cake,* she thought, smiling. Walking down the hall, she ran into Emily, who was just coming out of her class. She gave an enthused wave.

Clutching her books to her chest, Emily forced a smile. "Hey Alex."

Alex pushed some tendrils back up into her ponytail. "Have you started preparing for your finals yet?" she charged.

Emily sighed as both girls walked out of the building. "I know what they're *on,*" she said. "I have so much work." The light breeze felt good as the girls walked down the steps. It was the perfect weather for May. As other students ran and played on the lush green lawns around them, the two girls continued their walk along the narrow path.

"That you do, sis," Alex nodded in agreement. "Look, I know you think that staying off of academic probation is impossible…but you at least need to try."

"I know," Emily sulked, squinting her eyes in the bright sun. After a moment of ambling in silence, she glanced at

Alex. "I went to see Ms. Smith a few days ago," she announced.

"Really?" Alex asked, surprised. Emily nodded. "I thought you were gonna let me know, so I could go with you."

"It was something that I needed to do alone," Emily stated. "I just needed to sort things out."

"Well?" Alex pressed, curious. "What did you talk about?"

Emily shrugged. "Just about my stress and me failing," she informed. "I um…I didn't mention the drinking or the whole transfer thing. I figured some things she didn't need to know."

Alex stared at her intently. "Emily…" she began, unsure if she even wanted to ask the question that had formed in her head. "You haven't had any more drinks, have you?"

Emily shook her head and Alex breathed a sigh of relief. "I told you, I'm not an alcoholic," she chortled.

"I *know* you're not, but with finals coming up…" she took a deep breath. "I just don't want to see you fall back into that hole again, you know?"

"I get that," Emily assured. "But I think the reason why I was doing it was because I was holding everything in…to myself."

"I don't understand why you didn't come to us," Alex said.

"I think because I was, and still *am,* embarrassed," Emily admitted, reflective. "I'm fine though…for now at least… Until I have to leave."

Alex shot Emily a sympathetic look. "Don't say that," she pouted.

"Trust me, I don't *want* to," Emily insisted, somber.

"Well, if it means anything, we don't want to see you go," Alex stated. Alex loved Emily like she loved the other girls, like a sister, and knew she would be devastated if she left the school. Especially if it wasn't what Emily wanted.

"I know and I appreciate that. But…" she pushed some

of her hair behind her ear, "I don't know what to do. I mean I *know* what to do, I just don't think that I can *do* it."

Alex put her arm around her sad friend. "Well, the first thing we need to do is get you ready for these finals," she declared. "I'm gonna rally the others, and we're going to help you study. Maybe passing your finals will at least show your mom that you're turning things around."

"Yeah I guess," Emily murmured. *Nothing is going to change her mind.*

Sidra, having loaded up on coffee before her Economics class, sprinted back to her room once class let out to use the bathroom. *Stupid Professor Young, going on about economic principles, with his slow talking self,* she fussed mid-run.

Hurrying into her room, she tossed her books and purse to the floor and ran for the bathroom. Once finished, Sidra headed for her dresser, removing the pair of long, silver chandelier earrings from her ears. The new purchase was a bit too heavy for her ears; she figured she would give them to Malajia. Placing them neatly on the dresser as she searched for a small box to place them in, she had a thought. Sidra searched on the top shelf of her closet for an item. Having found it, she carried that and the earrings, and headed for the bathroom.

Malajia pushed the door open just as Sidra was walking back out of her bathroom, closing the door in the process. "Still not knocking, I see," she sneered.

"You finally caught on," Malajia returned, tone dry.

Sidra shook her head. "What do you want, child?"

"I need to borrow your iron," Malajia announced, holding the iron in her hand up for Sidra to see. "Mine broke."

"Sure go ahead; it's in the closet on the top shelf." Sitting on the bed, Sidra had a thought. "Why didn't you just borrow Chasity's?"

"Your ex-roommate is being a bitch," Malajia griped,

grabbing the iron. "She's not talking to me."

Sidra giggled, "You're always on her nerves."

"I'm not talking to *her* either," Malajia informed. "She's too much sometimes."

Sidra's interest piqued. It wasn't news that Chasity wasn't speaking to Malajia. Every other day, she was banning Malajia from the room, her car, or her life. However, it was rare that Malajia didn't want to talk to her best friend. "What happened?"

"I don't wanna get into it," Malajia ground out.

"Oh. Well, how long has it been since you two spoke?"

"A few days," Malajia replied, wrapping the cord around the iron. "Anyway, what are you doing now? You want to go watch this basketball game with me?" She was desperate to change the subject.

"Sure, let me change my blouse first," Sidra said, unbuttoning her dark blue blouse. "It's gotten warmer since this morning,"

"Change the skirt too, while you're at it." Malajia pointed to Sidra's grey wrap skirt, earning a glare from Sidra.

"Hush up." While passing Malajia to grab a new top from her closet, Sidra studied her. Something was different. "You look different," she pointed out.

Malajia frowned in confusion. "Um, I don't know *why*."

"Me neither. But it's *something*." Sidra tapped her finger on her chin. "I can't quite put my finger on it."

It could be that I'm not a virgin anymore, she thought. Malajia still had a hard time wrapping her head around the reality. So much so that she refused to tell anyone about it. "Put your finger on a damn shirt so we can go," she snapped. "I want to get a seat on the bottom of the bleachers."

"All right, fine. Don't get all testy," Sidra relented, pulling a new top off of a hanger.

Malajia was quiet as she walked alongside Sidra into the gym. Normally the drones of students, the loud music, the concession stands, and the fun energy would have excited Malajia. But not this day, she wasn't in the mood.

"Crap, I should've grabbed some fries or something from the stand," Sidra grumbled, rubbing her stomach as she sat down on the bleacher next to Malajia. "I'm starving."

"Here, you can have mine. I'm not hungry anyway," Malajia offered, handing Sidra her small cup of french fries.

Taking the cup, Sidra smiled. "Thanks." She waved to Mark and Josh when she saw them walk into the gym, then signaled for them. "Mel, scoot over so they can sit." Without saying a word, Malajia scooted down.

"What's up sis?" Mark greeted Sidra with a pat on her arm before turning his attention to Malajia. "What's up big head?"

"What's good Mark?" Malajia solemnly replied, prompting confused looks from both Mark and Sidra.

What? No smart comeback? No Insult? he thought. "What did you say?" He questioned.

"I said, what's good?" Malajia's eyes never left the court as she took a sip of her soda. "I'm trying to watch the game."

Mark looked at Josh, who just shrugged.

Leaning close to Malajia, Sidra said, "Okay, you're not acting like yourself." Malajia rolled her eyes. "You need to talk to your roommate and fix whatever issue you two have with each other," she urged.

"I have nothing to say to that bitch," Malajia scoffed.

Sidra frowned. "That *bitch* is your best friend, and you need to resolve it like *now*," she argued.

Malajia sighed. "I'll think about it," she said after a moment.

"No *thinking*, just hurry up and do it so you can get back to normal, because I don't like this 'calm' you." Sidra turned her attention to Mark; his face was as confused as Sidra felt. "And neither does *he*," Sidra pointed to him. "Look at him. He doesn't know what to do with himself since you didn't insult him," she added, voice full of amusement.

Malajia shook her head as she continued to focus on the game.

Malajia headed back to her room soon after the game was over. She and Sidra parted ways as Sidra went to dinner with Mark and Josh. Malajia had no appetite. That turned out to be a good thing; the solo walk back gave her a chance to think.

Walking in, she saw Chasity sitting on her bed, books spread around her, studying. Noticing that Chasity didn't even bother to acknowledge her, Malajia sucked her teeth and headed over to her own bed.

Twenty minutes passed, and Malajia, tired of working on her assignment and of the dead silence, slammed her notebook down on her bed. "This is ridiculous," she declared. Chasity still hadn't bothered to even look her way. It made Malajia's blood boil. "Chasity really? Are we *really* gonna do this?" she spat out.

"I don't know what you're talking about," Chasity muttered, eyes not moving from her book.

"Are we *really* gonna sit here and not acknowledge each other?" Malajia seethed, standing up. She placed her hands on her hips. "I'm *not* gonna live like that."

"Suit yourself," Chasity sneered.

Malajia walked over and sat on Chasity's bed. "We need to talk," she affirmed.

"Talk to your*self*." Chasity went to turn a page, and Malajia snatched the book away from her. Shooting her a venomous look, Chasity went to push Malajia off the bed, but was stopped when Malajia grabbed her arm. "Don't make me hurt you," Chasity warned.

"Don't be dramatic. We *need* to talk," Malajia barked.

"You've been talking *enough*," Chasity hissed. "Everybody and their damn mother thinks that I hurt poor little Malajia's feelings."

Malajia sighed. She did recall venting her frustrations with Chasity to a few of her acquaintances. She didn't give details, she just eluded to the fact that Chasity pissed her off. "Okay so *maybe* I vented to a few people about us having a falling out," she admitted. "You already know I run my mouth."

"Get out my face." Chasity enunciated her words slowly as she fixed a piercing gaze on Malajia.

"No, not until you acknowledge what happened," Malajia snapped.

"Don't take it back there, Malajia. You *will* get your feelings hurt," Chasity threatened.

"Whatever," Malajia fumed, letting go of Chasity's arm. "I don't appreciate you being rude to Tyrone, and I *especially* don't appreciate that snide ass comment that you made before you left."

Chasity folded her arms. "And what comment would *that* be?"

"That remark about me not respecting myself. And hoping it was memorable for me," Malajia reminded. "What the hell was *that* about?"

"You're really gonna act like you don't know?"

"Chasity, you *always* say smart shit, and there're times that I have no idea what the *fuck* you're talking about," Malajia shot back.

"Don't play stupid. You know *exactly* what I'm talking about."

"What do you *think* you know huh? Since you're always so damn perceptive," Malajia scoffed.

Chasity shot Malajia a skeptical look. "So you're going to sit here and tell me that when I walked in here that day, you hadn't just finished having sex with your bum ass boyfriend?" she questioned.

Malajia's eyes widened slightly, giving Chasity the answer that she was looking for.

"Yeah, that's what I thought." She stood up from her bed only to have Malajia do the same. "The clothes on the floor and the dumb look on your face was a dead giveaway."

Damn it, sick of her insightful ass, Malajia thought. "So *what* if I had sex with him? It's *my business*," Malajia fumed, stomping her foot on the floor.

"You're stupid as hell for that," Chasity argued.

Malajia rolled her eyes, "I'm *not* stupid," she seethed, feeling insulted. "I'm a grown ass woman and what *I* choose to do, with *my* body, in *my* relationship with *my* man, is *my* business."

"Who are you trying to convince? Me or yourself?" Chasity mocked.

Malajia felt her temper rising with each word that Chasity hurled back at her. "I'm trying to let your snide ass know," she began, trying to keep calm. "That despite what you *think* you know, I'm good with my decision to sleep with him."

"You know how I know that's a bunch of bullshit?" Chasity charged, folding her arms.

"How?" Malajia sneered.

"Because if you really *were* good with your decision, then your big ass mouth would've been running about it as soon as I stepped foot in the door," Chasity pointed out. "So you're a liar. Fucking that bastard wasn't what *you* wanted."

"You know what? I'm so sick and tired of you!" Malajia screamed. "You don't know what the fuck you're talking about!"

Chasity sucked her teeth. "You're right Malajia, I don't," she relented.

"You make me sick!" Malajia ranted. "You always have some smart shit to say. *Anything* I say, any *decision* I make, you gotta talk down about it. Your fake ass *acts* like you care about me, but you really *don't*!"

"You're right, I don't," Chasity reiterated. It was clear that she pulled out a feeling that Malajia wasn't yet ready to deal with. Chasity didn't regret it; the girl needed to be honest with herself. However, a screaming match was not on her to do list; her head was beginning to hurt.

Malajia didn't know what to make of Chasity's change in attitude. First she was overly vocal about how she felt, now she was backing off. "So what are you saying?" she asked, angry. "That I regret my decision?"

"I'm not saying *anything*."

"No, you seem like you want to say something, so come on and say it," Malajia challenged.

"I don't need to tell you what you already know," Chasity threw out, before heading for the door.

Malajia spun around to face Chasity's departing back. "You act like everyone's first time is all sunshine and freakin' rainbows," she barked.

Chasity stopped her progress and faced Malajia once again. "I *never* said that," she returned, pointing to her.

Malajia rolled her eyes. "Look, sometimes it is what it is," she said, tone sullen. "People lose their virginity all the time, sometimes they're not even sure if they *should. You* of all people should know that."

Chasity frowned slightly. *Did she just take it there?* "Don't bring *my* first time up because *you* didn't like *yours*," she spat out. "Contrary to what you *think* you know, I *enjoyed* losing mine, no matter *how* I felt afterwards. At least *I* didn't give it to an asshole, after he probably gave yet *another* excuse for why he treats you like shit."

Malajia's mouth fell open in shock. That comment cut her like a knife. "You are so fuckin' evil. That was totally uncalled for," she raged. "You're not acting like my friend right now."

"I *am* your friend."

"No you're *not!*" Malajia yelled. "Friends don't kick each other when they're down!"

Chasity put her hands up. "Oh, so you're *down*?" she threw back. "I'm sorry, I thought you were *good* with your decision," Chasity's words were laced with sarcasm.

Malajia shook her head as she felt herself tear up. "You know what, I am so fuckin' over you right now," she declared, voice trembling. "You are the most inconsiderate, ignorant, disrespectful person I've ever met," she hurled. "You walk around judging people, like your screwed-up ass is perfect."

"I never said I *was*," Chasity pointed out.

"You damn *right* you're not," Malajia returned. "*Far* from it. No *wonder* your fuckin' family and everybody else *around* you can't stand your ass. I'm not even *surprised* that your own damn father wants nothing to do with you, you fuckin' mistake."

Chasity stood there, hurt registered on her face. Malajia's words struck a nerve. Although they had argued plenty of times, Malajia had never been that nasty towards her. Chasity didn't know how to deal with that; this was a side of Malajia that was new to her. And to bring up her father, a sore spot for her... Chasity was livid. "So now you want to hurt *me* because you're mad at your*self?*" Chasity questioned, trying to refrain from lunging at Malajia.

"Fuck you, you hateful ass bitch," Malajia hissed before storming out of the room, punctuating her departure with a sharp slam of the door.

Chapter 34

"Yo, what's up with this campus cookout?" Mark asked, looking up from his notebook. "We all going together?" The end of the spring semester was fast approaching, and with that came finals. With cramming sessions needed, most of the group were huddled in the library studying.

"What campus cookout?" Emily questioned.

"Focus Emily," Jason scolded, pointing to her textbook. "You need to finish that math problem." After Alex informed him and the others of Emily's situation with her classes, Jason offered to tutor her for her Math final.

"Jason, this is so hard," Emily whined.

"Whining won't help you. He's gonna keep on you until you get it," Chasity put in, knowing her boyfriend's tutoring techniques all too well.

Sighing, Emily picked up her pencil. "Okay." She glanced up at Jason. "Can you at least give me the next step?"

"No," Jason answered bluntly, earning a snicker from Chasity. "We went over this five times before I gave you this problem to complete."

"She salty," Mark teased. As Emily solemnly went back to figuring out her math problem, Mark continued with his initial topic of discussion. "Anyway, President Bennett announced that after finals are over this week, she's gonna be throwing a huge cookout slash fair as a way to celebrate. Are we rolling together?"

"I don't see why *not*. We go everywhere *else* together," Sidra added, not removing her eyes from her book.

Josh looked over at her. "I must say that you're handling your finals stress a lot better than you have in the past," he observed. He knew all too well how crazy she could get during finals.

"Oh trust me, I'm trying my best," Sidra replied. "I *will* say that this Economics mess is on my last nerves though. If I have to read about inflations and public goods one more time, I'm going to flip a table."

"No, that won't be necessary," Josh chuckled.

Alex looked up from her book and stretched her neck. "Anybody seen Malajia?" she asked. "She's supposed to be studying for her Spanish final."

"She'll be here. She's on her way back from Tyrone's apartment," Sidra informed. Hearing Tyrone's name incited an eye roll and groan from Mark.

"Oh," Alex muttered. "She's been spending a lot of time over there, *hasn't* she Chaz?" she queried.

"I don't know and don't care," Chasity sneered, trying to remain focused on her notes.

Chasity's nasty tone made Alex frown. "What's the matter? You two fighting or something?"

"If you want to know, ask Malajia," Chasity bit out. She and Malajia had hardly seen each other or spoken since their argument nearly two weeks ago. Either Malajia was spending nights at Tyrone's, or Chasity was spending nights at Jason's. Malajia didn't feel the need to apologize, and Chasity no longer expected her to or even cared.

"No I'm asking *you*—"

"Alex, back off all right!" Chasity snapped. "Don't ask me about no damn Malajia. You want to know where she's been or what she's doing, ask *her*."

"Geez, no need to get mad," Alex shot back. "Are you at *least* going to help her study for her Spanish final?"

Fed up with Alex's prodding about Malajia, Chasity closed her notebook and began gathering her things.

"Alex come *on*," Jason griped, knowing how Chasity felt about the situation.

"Why are *you* snapping at me?" Alex exclaimed, staring at Jason wide-eyed.

"She already told you to back off about Malajia. You never listen," Jason barked. "Chill the hell out."

Alex let out a sigh in frustration.

Without saying another word, Chasity headed out the door as Malajia was walking in. Malajia glanced at Chasity, who in turn rolled her eyes and continued on her way. Shaking her head, Malajia walked over to her friends' table.

"Hey girl," Sidra greeted.

"What's up," Malajia sighed. "Can you help me with this Spanish, Sid?"

"Sure, just give me like ten more minutes to look over these Econ notes and we can start," Sidra promised.

"Cool." Malajia noticed as she began to unload her items from her book bag that Alex was looking at her. "Yes Alex?" she asked, voice laced with agitation.

"You're spending a lot of time off campus," Alex stated, folding her arms. "I hope you've at least been studying."

"I've been studying *and* minding my damn business, thank you," Malajia hissed.

"Yo, can you like *chill*?" Mark interjected. His words directed to Alex. "You always gotta nag. Leave people alone."

"Hey, you don't tell me what to do Mark," Alex shot back, pointing at him. "These girls are my sisters, and I can be concerned if I want."

"*Concerned* is one thing. Fuckin' nosey is another," Mark retorted, earning snickers from the table.

"Just shut up," Alex snapped.

"You mad 'cause I'm right," Mark teased. Alex flagged him with her hand as she sat back in her seat.

Emily looked up from her book. "Malajia, I *am* concerned about you and Chaz's friendship though," she put in. "You two don't even speak."

"Don't be Em, we'll be fine," Malajia assured. "We're just taking a friendship break."

Jason tapped Emily's book with his finger. "Hey, concern yourself with that math problem," he slid in. Emily groaned as she put her head in her book.

"Whatever you two are taking a friendship break over, I hope it gets resolved soon," Sidra added.

"I'm sure it will be, friends fight all the time." Malajia stated, staring at the highlighter in her hand. "We both said some things that were out of line, and we just need some time to get over them," Malajia happened to look at Jason, who let out a sigh as he tried to focus. "I'm sure *you* know what was said huh, Jason?"

"Most of it," Jason replied, eyes remaining on his book.

"Got any comments to make about it?" Malajia sneered.

"Nope." Jason knew exactly what was said; Chasity told him about the argument that same evening. He knew that Malajia had hurt Chasity's feelings, but wasn't going to admit that to Malajia or the rest of the group. Jason knew that this was something that she and Malajia would need to work out on their own.

"How about we take a break from the books and go grab some burgers," Josh slid in, hoping to diffuse the tension in the room.

"Not 'till Emily finishes this math problem," Jason proclaimed, earning laughs from the table. Emily couldn't help but laugh as she put her hand over her face.

Chasity had just finished dressing and styling her hair for her trip to the gym. After finishing three of her five finals that week, she was ready for a session with the heavy bag.

She was in the process of wrapping her hands, when she heard a light knock at the door.

She opened it to find a smiling Emily standing there. "Hey Chaz."

"What's up Emily?" Chasity questioned, tying her hand wrap.

"You on your way out?"

"Yeah, to the gym. What's up Emily?" Chasity quickly returned.

Emily glanced down at her sneakers. "Um... Okay I don't mean to interrupt you."

Chasity let out a sigh as Emily stood there, hesitating. "What's. Up. Emily?" Chasity repeated, this time slowly.

"Can you do me a favor?" Emily asked, voice full of hope. Chasity just stared at her. "My Spanish final is tomorrow, and I wanted to know if you could help me go over some words and sentences."

Chasity folded her arms. "You have Spanish 101 too?"

Emily nodded. "Yeah," she confirmed. "I've been studying all week long; I just need some extra help."

Chasity thought for a moment. She wanted to hit the gym as she was feeling wound up and needed some release, however she didn't want to turn Emily away, especially since she had the courage to come over and ask for help. "All right. Come on," she said, moving away from the door, allowing Emily to enter the room.

Twenty minutes into the tutoring session, Chasity was regretting her decision to help Emily. The girl kept trying to talk about things other than what was in her textbook.

"So how did you come to understand this language?" Emily asked, looking up from her book.

"I studied it," Chasity bluntly replied.

"Where? In high school?"

"Ask me that in Spanish," Chasity challenged, voice laced with frustration.

Emily gulped as she looked back down at her book. "Um....donde en el escuela secundaria?" she slowly asked after a few moments.

"Empecé a estudiar en la escuela primaria," Chasity answered, studying her nails.

Emily's face took on a confused expression. "Um...I don't know what that means," she admitted, ashamed.

Chasity rolled her eyes. "I said that I started studying in elementary school."

"Really? Wow." Emily was amazed. "That must've taken up a lot of your time growing up."

"Yeah well, when you grow up without friends, you have a lot of time on your hands. Emily, stop asking me questions and get back to those translations," Chasity ordered, looking at her watch.

"Okay," Emily relented, looking back down at her book. The session was interrupted by a knock on the door.

"Come in," Chasity called.

Sidra walked in. "Hey," she said. "What are you up to?"

"Chaz is helping me study for my Spanish final," Emily smiled.

"Oh? That's nice of you Chaz. How's it going?" Sidra beamed. Chasity shot her a look, basically telling her not to ask. Sidra giggled. "Anyway, did either of you talk to Malajia today?"

"Nope," Chasity spat out.

"No. Is something wrong?" Emily answered.

"Well, she needs a ride back to campus," Sidra informed.

"Don't know why you're telling *me* that," Chasity hissed.

Sidra adjusted the bracelet on her wrist. "Well, Tyrone's car broke down and she has to get back to campus in time for her Accounting final. Can you go pick her up, Chaz?"

"Sidra, *you* go get her. You have a damn car too," Chasity barked.

Sidra let out a quick sigh. "I *would,* but I have my Economics final in like ten minutes."

"She better call Mark then," Chasity suggested.

"Mark is failing *his* Accounting final as we speak," Sidra joked. "He *can't* go."

"Well, that sucks for *her*," Chasity sneered, unbothered. "She shouldn't have gone over there when she knew she had finals to take."

"Chaz, really? Are you going to be like that?" Sidra asked, hands on her hips.

"Yup."

Sidra sighed. "How is she supposed to get back in time?"

"She better hop on that autobús," Chasity shot back, inciting a chuckle from Sidra.

Smart ass, Sidra thought, amused.

Emily looked up from her book. "Does that mean 'bus'?" she asked innocently.

Chasity narrowed her eyes at her, "What do *you* think?"

Emily gave a nervous laugh. "Um, yeah I'm gonna just look that up," eyes returning to her book.

"Chasity, I know you two aren't on the best terms right now, but she is *still* your friend and she needs help," Sidra declared.

"I promise you, I'm not going to pick her up. She brought that on herself," Chasity refused.

God these two are so damn stubborn. "Fine," Sidra relented. "I'll just tell her to take a cab."

"And she *won't* have the money for that," Chasity assured, knowing Malajia's history with asking her to borrow money after spending what her parents sent her on frivolous things.

Sidra thought for a moment. "You're right," she agreed. "Can I borrow ten dollars to leave with Alex?" she asked.

Chasity rolled her eyes.

"I have money on my debit card, but I won't have time to go to the machine since I have to go to class," Sidra explained.

"Fine Sidra," Chasity replied, even toned, before taking the money out of her purse.

"Thanks, I'll give it back to you today."

"It's fine, don't worry about it." Chasity sat back down on her bed as Sidra left the room. She shook her head as she thought about Malajia's predicament. *She's so damn stupid.*

"That was nice of you to give her the money," Emily smiled.

"Don't say nothing else to me unless it's in Spanish," Chasity snapped.

Malajia's cab pulled into the dorm parking lot. She was relieved to see Alex standing there, waiting for her to pull up. She grabbed the ten dollar bill from Alex's hand and paid the driver, before hopping out. "Thanks girl," she breathed.

"No problem," Alex returned. "I have to run to turn in this paper, see you later," she threw over her shoulder as she hurried off.

Malajia, overnight bag and book bag in hand, hurried into the dorm and up the stairs. She was kicking herself for even going over to Tyrone's apartment the night before. She was already aware that his car was having mechanical issues when he came to pick her up, but because he, like always, begged her to come over, she like always, agreed.

Fumbling in her bag to find her keys, Malajia ending up dropping the entire bag. "Damn it!" she hollered, voice full of frustration.

She was relieved when the door opened; luckily Chasity was on her way out. Without saying a word, Chasity moved around Malajia to head out the door. Malajia noticing the snub, let out a loud sigh. "Well hello to *you too*," she sneered.

"Yeah whatever," Chasity shot back.

"Yeah whatever is *right*," Malajia scoffed, retrieving her fallen bag from the floor. "And thanks for coming to pick me up too. I appreciate it, friend," she added, voice laced with sarcasm.

Chasity turned around. "Oh now I'm your *friend?*" she threw back. "Screw you, bitch. I don't owe you shit."

Malajia glared at Chasity's back as she continued down the hall. Sucking her teeth, Malajia walked inside the room, shutting the door behind her.

Malajia's mind wandered as the professor sat the accounting final in front of her. "All right class, you have one hour to complete this final," she informed, taking a seat behind her desk. "If you finish before the hour is up, please place your test on the front desk and you can leave."

Well, here goes a big fat nothing, Malajia thought as she picked up her pencil.

Once she was finished taking her final, which ended up taking the entire hour, Malajia headed out of class and made her way for the exit. She stopped when she saw Jason and Mark walk out of one of the classrooms. "Another final down, huh?" she quipped.

"Yep. Aced it," Jason assured.

"*Failed* it," Mark jeered of his own efforts. "What's up fool, you finished failing *your* final?"

"I *hope* not," Malajia replied, adjusting her book bag on her shoulder. Mark tossed his hands up in frustration, accompanied by a loud groan. "What is your problem?" Malajia asked.

"Yo man like... Can you throw an insult or something?" Mark requested, making Jason shake his head and chuckle.

Malajia raised an arched eyebrow. "Soooo you *want* me to insult you?" she was confused.

"Yeah! I mean—" Trying to form a complete thought, Mark let out a quick sigh. "Look, I don't know what to do with this 'calm' Malajia. You need to get it together, big head," he sputtered, walking off.

Malajia shot Jason the same confused look that she had just given Mark. "He is so freakin' weird," she concluded.

"Yep, completely agree," Jason replied, before turning to walk off.

"Jase, wait a minute," Malajia called, halting is progress.

"What's up?"

"Can you ask Chaz to meet me in our room after her last class so we can talk?" Although Malajia wasn't planning on apologizing, she was beginning to miss her relationship with Chasity, and figured that sitting down for a talk would put them back on the path that they needed to be.

"Malajia, I'm not going to do that." Jason's response was blunt. "This is between *you two*. You want her to meet you? Then *you* need to ask her."

Malajia sucked her teeth. "Forget it."

"Suit yourself, Mel," Jason returned before walking off.

If she wants to act like that, then fine, Malajia thought as she too walked off.

Chapter 35

Saturday arrived, and the students of Paradise Valley University couldn't have been more relieved. Finals were over. President Bennett did as she promised and put together a campus wide cookout and fair. Held on the campus football field, the grounds were transformed to hold countless grills, picnic tables, chairs, benches, games and other activities.

"Oh my God, this is *awesome*," Alex mused, looking around. "This was so needed."

Taking her cotton candy from the stand operator, Emily smiled. "I know. The stress has been crazy."

"So, how do you think you did on your finals?" Alex quizzed, grabbing a bag full of popcorn.

"Well, I think I did okay," Emily replied, unsure. "The tutoring sessions that I had with you guys really helped me out." She placed a piece of candy into her mouth. "I mean, I know it's not enough to bring my grades up to where I *need* them to be, but it's a start."

"At least you made an effort," Alex pointed out. "Even *if* you are put on probation, it's not the end of the world. You can be off by the end of next semester if you work hard."

"Yeah, if I'm still *here*," Emily sadly remembered.

Alex put her arm around Emily, pulling her close. "You'll be okay," she predicted.

As the two girls started their walk through the event, they were joined by Sidra and Chasity who had arrived to the field moments ago. "Where are y'all coming from?" Alex asked.

"The dorm. I was deciding on what to wear," Sidra admitted.

"No, she was arguing with *me* because I told her she needed to put some damn sneakers on and not come out here, with all this grass and dirt, wearing heels," Chasity contradicted, pointing to Sidra's sneaker-covered feet.

"Say *what*? Sidra you have *sneakers* on? Outside of the *gym*?" Alex teased.

"Funny," Sidra sneered, flinging her ponytail over her shoulder.

"How did *that* happen?" Alex continued, amusement in her voice, "Because we *all* know you'll rock a heel on grass in a minute."

"Chasity's ignorant behind took all my heels out the room while I was in the shower and only left the sneakers," Sidra replied, earning a laugh from Chasity.

"You should've seen your face," Chasity laughed. Her attention turned to something as she walked. "Is that a bouncy house?"

"Yep. Isn't that cool?" Alex beamed, retrieving some popcorn from her bag.

"Oh I'm *so* in there," Chasity promised.

"I'm with you sis," Alex chortled.

"Are the guys coming?" Emily asked, pulling off another piece of her cotton candy.

"They're here already," Chasity informed.

Sidra pointed to the large rock-climbing wall off to the side. "Yeah, they're over at the rock-climbing wall, showing off," Sidra added, voice full of amusement.

Alex was about to respond, when Malajia interrupted her by playfully bumping into her. "Always have to be extra,"

Alex chuckled, nudging her back.

"I'm so glad this week is over," Malajia rejoiced. "I'm gonna have some fun today."

"Yes, me too girl," Sidra added.

Malajia glanced at Sidra, a surprised look on her face. "Princess Ponytail has sneakers on?!"

Sidra rolled her eyes. "Everybody has jokes today," she ground out.

Malajia looked over at Chasity, who hadn't even acknowledged her presence. "What's up Chaz?" When Chasity ignored her, Malajia sighed loudly. "Are we *still* doing this?"

"Don't talk to me," Chasity spat out.

Malajia frowned. "You need to grow up," she shot back.

"Don't make me embarrass you," Chasity sneered. She came to the field to have fun and relax, not to argue with Malajia. But if Malajia kept on pestering her, she was definitely going to do it.

"So damn childish," Malajia declared, shaking her head.

"Okay, stop this you two," Alex cut in. She was tired of the arguing between these two girls. "I can't believe this is *still* going on."

"Alex, let them work this out on their own," Sidra suggested. She knew that Alex's heart was always in the right place, but sometimes her prodding made things worse.

"No Sidra, come on," Alex protested, putting her hand up. "They're adults and they're both acting really juvenile," she fussed, looking back and forth between Chasity and Malajia.

"I thought it had cooled down. But I *guess* Miss holds-a-grudge-and-won't-talk-to-nobody hasn't decided it's over yet," Malajia mocked.

Chasity had had enough. "I'm leaving," she proclaimed, turning to storm off.

"No you're not," Sidra said, grabbing her arm. "You come with me."

As Sidra pulled Chasity off to walk with her, Alex

turned to Malajia, who was taking a sip of her soda.

"Enough is enough Malajia," Alex said, voice stern. "What's the deal with you two?"

"Get off it, Alex," Malajia warned.

"No, I *won't* get off it," Ales maintained. "This fighting is ridiculous. You two are putting, Sid, Em, and myself in an awkward situation," she added. "It's uncomfortable being around this damn tension."

Malajia sighed; Alex had a point. "I *know* that," she agreed. "My bad."

"That's not good enough," Alex harped. "What is the argument about?"

God, leave me alone! "I'm not trying to go into all that right now, girl! I'm tryna' relax," Malajia yelled. Malajia had no intention of providing Alex or any of the other girls with details on her rift with Chasity. As far as she was concerned, it was none of their business.

"I don't care *how* loud you get, I'm not gonna stop saying what needs to be said." Alex folded her arms to her chest. "No matter *what* the issue is, someone needs to apologize and you both need to move on. And by the way you two are interacting, I get the idea that *you* need to be the one to apologize."

"Not gonna happen," Malajia sneered. "I'm not the only one at fault. *She* said some shit too."

Alex rolled her eyes. The whole thing was frustrating.

"Is what was said worth your friendship?" Emily quietly put in. Both Alex and Malajia looked at her with shock.

"Look at Miss quiet adding her two cents," Malajia teased.

"And she's one hundred percent right in what she said," Alex added, turning her attention to Emily. "Nice work, Em."

Sidra and Chasity had ambled their way over to one of the many benches near the games. Chasity was quiet on their short walk over, but now seated, Sidra was determined to get her to talk. "Chasity, don't start this quiet mess that you do when you get mad," Sidra warned.

"I *just* got quiet," Chasity shot back, examining her manicure.

"Don't be smart," Sidra chastised. "Now, I'm not going to ask what the argument was about because if you wanted to tell me, you *would* have" she started. "But you two should resolve whatever your issues are."

"It'll be resolved once this semester is over and I no longer have to be her fuckin' roommate," Chasity sneered.

"You don't mean that."

"Sure *do*," Chasity maintained.

Sidra studied her. Chasity looked as if she was trying hard to hold her emotions in. "Do you *want* to tell me what happened?" she asked.

Chasity sighed. She didn't want to spread Malajia's business, but she felt that if someone else knew what Malajia was dealing with, then maybe they could talk some sense into her and the burden to do so wouldn't lie only with her. "Malajia…is just being stupid," she finally answered, deciding to keep it to herself.

"Yes, she has a tendency to be that way sometimes," Sidra jokingly admitted. "And loud and over the top… But she has a big heart and she's one of the most genuine people that I know."

Chasity shook her head. "I don't want to talk about it anymore."

Sidra sighed. "You know as a friend to you *both*, it's hard to watch this," she said. "I wish I could do something to make things better."

"You want to make things better for me right *now*?" Chasity asked.

Sidra's interest piqued. "Yes."

"Fine, come get in this bouncy house with me," Chasity challenged.

Sidra's eyes widened at the request. "What? No!" she shrieked. "Girl, I'm not going in there getting all dirty and wrinkled."

Standing up, Chasity grabbed Sidra's wrist. "Don't be corny. Come on."

Reluctantly allowing Chasity to pull her along, Sidra twisted her ponytail into a bun. "Fine, but if I get any dirt on my clothes, you're getting my cleaning bill."

"Yeah, yeah."

Sidra was hysterically laughing as she rolled out of the bouncy house. She was initially hesitant, however after ten minutes of being in there with Chasity and her other classmates, Sidra ended up enjoying it.

"Oh my God, that was awesome!" Sidra exclaimed.

"*Told* you," Chasity agreed, stepping out of the house. "But that high-pitched screaming, laugh thing you were doing, wasn't cute."

Sidra playfully backhanded Chasity on the arm. "Hush up. Let's go find the others."

After searching through the crowd for several minutes, they finally happened upon the rest of the group.

"Where did you two disappear to?" Alex chuckled.

"Don't ask, you'll never believe it," Sidra replied with a wave of her hand. "Where are the guys?"

"They were just here, but they left to get something to eat," Emily informed. "How about we go too? Anybody hungry?"

"Not for those nasty burgers and hotdogs," Malajia scoffed.

Sidra rolled her eyes at Malajia's complaining. "Yes Em, I'm hungry, but I have to run back to the room really quick."

"Why?" Malajia asked. "You're gonna be all long, and you *know* you expect us to wait for you to get back before we go eat."

"Because I have to go to the bathroom, smart ass," Sidra retorted. "And you know how I feel about strange toilet seats…all those nasty germs and nasty people leaving their 'sprinkles' all over the place."

Chasity shot her a strange look. "Sprinkles?" she scoffed. "You *know* you're too damn old to be saying that shit."

"Hush, you," Sidra hurled.

Emily giggled at the byplay. "I'll walk you Sidra," she offered.

Sidra smiled, grateful. "Thanks, I won't be long."

Chapter 36

Sidra hurried through the door and darted for the bathroom, leaving Emily to close her door behind her. "Stupid bouncy house has my bladder all crazy," she said from the bathroom.

Emily sat on Sidra's bed and ran her hands over the back of her neck. *It's so hot.* "Sidra, I need to pull my hair up, can I use your brush and a ponytail holder?" she asked through the closed door.

"Sure. Check on my dresser, on the left side," Sidra replied. "It should be next to my jewelry box."

Emily stood up and walked over, peering on the dresser. Admiring how Sidra had everything in a neat place, Emily was even more amazed that she could tell her exactly where something was located. Frowning, she looked where she was told. "Um Sid? I don't see a brush."

"What?"

"There is no brush on here," Emily stated.

The sounds of water running could be heard as Sidra opened the door. She frowned in confusion as she turned the sink off. "What did you say?" Walking over to her dresser, Sidra scanned the entire space with her eyes. Forgetting about the missing brush, Sidra's eyes fixed on her jewelry box. It was open, and appeared to be rifled through. "What the hell?" she fussed.

Emily watched as Sidra frantically searched through her box, then moved to both sides of the dresser, glancing at the floor.

"Where the hell is it?" Sidra grumbled, pulling her top drawer open and searching through it. Not finding what she was looking for, she looked at Emily. "My bracelet is gone," she panicked.

"Which one?" Emily asked. Sidra had so many, she wondered how she kept track of all of them.

"My cuff with the sparkles," Sidra informed. "It was a Christmas gift."

Emily stared blankly at Sidra "Um…maybe you misplaced it," she suggested.

Sidra shot her a cool glance. "*Me*? Misplace something? Not likely," she scoffed.

"Well, where do you think you had it last?"

Emily, don't start with the dumb questions, Sidra thought. "On my dresser, in my *jewelry box*," she hissed. Sidra put her hand over her head as she tried to think. *Alex would never touch anything without asking, and Malajia hasn't been over lately.*

Emily was searching for something comforting to say to Sidra when a horrified look appeared on Sidra's face. "What's wrong?"

Without a word, Sidra, realizing that her bathroom door was hardly ever locked from their side, stormed into the bathroom. She opened the small drawer on her side of the bathroom, and noticing something, or *not* noticing it, she slammed it shut. "I knew it," she hissed to herself. Fuming, she retrieved a small video camera from a corner on a shelf.

Sidra, not chalking her missing items up to lack of attention on her part, had discreetly placed a camera in the bathroom. Sidra hit rewind and stared at the screen as the images played back.

"Emily, come here a second," Sidra demanded,

prompting Emily to walk into the bathroom. "Look at this and tell me what you see," Sidra urged, holding the camera up.

Looking at the camera along with Sidra, they watched as Dee searched through the bathroom drawers until she found the earrings that Sidra hid. If that weren't shocking enough to the girls, the video then showed Dee knocking on their room door, and when it was apparent that no one answered, she walked in.

Sidra had seen enough; she was furious. Emily put her hands on her head in a panic as Sidra tossed the camera into her room and removed the earrings from her ears.

"Sidra, please calm down," Emily pleaded. "You have proof that she stole from you. We can take this to the resident advisor and even the dean." Emily knew that Sidra had suspicions about Dee; she vented to them after her conversation with Malajia about spotting Dee with what she thought to be her bracelet charms.

"No, *damn* the RA Emily!" Sidra yelled. "She does *not* get to steal from me and all she gets is a *talking to*. I'm gonna send her thieving ass in front of them with broken hands," she promised, then darted for the other door.

"Sidra, wait," Emily shrieked. When she didn't comply, Emily frantically ran back into the room, picked up the phone and dialed a number. "Alex, it's Emily," Emily sputtered into the phone as Sidra proceeded to bang on her neighbors' door. "Listen, you girls need to get back to your room now. Sidra found out that your neighbor has been stealing from her and she's going over there… There's no stopping her, please hurry."

I can't handle this, Emily thought, hurrying behind Sidra as she banged on the door for the third time. "Sidra," Emily called. The venomous look that Sidra shot her halted any further protests.

"Who the hell is banging like that?" a voice on the other side snapped. Snatching the door open, Dominique came face to face with Sidra's lethal stare. "What do *you* want? The bathroom ain't dirty, so you can't complain." she spat.

"Dominique, where is your roommate?" Sidra demanded, furious.

Dominique frowned. "What is your damn problem?"

Sidra's response was halted once Dee stepped forward. Without saying a word, Sidra shoved her way into the room, coming face to face with Dee, eyes blazing.

Emily followed Sidra in the room and cracked the door behind her.

"Deidre, where is all the stuff you stole from me?" she charged.

Dee brushed off Sidra's nasty tone. "I don't know what you're talking about."

"Don't. Play. With. Me!" Sidra exploded, accompanying each word with a loud clap.

"What the hell is going on?" Dominique put in, completely confused.

Ignoring the other voice in the room, Sidra put her hand up. "Dee, I'm gonna ask you *one* more time. Where is the stuff you stole from me?"

Dee's defiant silence caused Sidra to snap. Emily watched in complete shock as Sidra began tearing through Dee's side of the room looking for her belongings.

"What the hell are you doing?!" Dominique hollered.

"Bitch don't touch my stuff," Dee fumed, grabbing Sidra's arm.

Jerking around, Sidra grabbed Dee, pushing her into a desk. As the two girls began to tussle, Dominique hollered, "Hell no, she's not gonna be fighting my roommate!"

Seeing Dominique remove her earrings from her ears made Emily go from scared to angry. *Her roommate better not jump in it*, Emily thought. Although afraid of a fight, she wasn't going to stand around and let her friend get jumped. Lucky for her, before Dominique had a chance to do anything, the door to Dominique's room swung open.

Emily backed away from the door as Alex, Chasity, and Malajia stormed through the room. "Oh, we gonna brawl today?" Malajia bellowed, throwing her hands up.

Dominique went to charge at Sidra, but Chasity jumped in her way and stood in her face. "Try it, I dare you," she warned.

As Dominique swallowed hard at the lethal look that Chasity was shooting her, Malajia pointed at her. "Really Dom? You were gonna try to jump my girl?"

"She came in here trippin'!"

"*And*?!" Malajia shot back. Right or wrong, Malajia made sure to side with her friends against anybody.

Alex hurried over and grabbed Sidra off of Dee, just as she picked up a fallen clock and was about to hit Dee in the face with it. "No! Sidra that's enough."

"Get off me, Alex!" Sidra screamed, struggling.

"Naw Alex, let her go! Let Sidra snatch the rest of her hair off that head," Malajia instigated.

"Malajia, don't make it worse," Emily softly put in. She patted her chest in an effort to get her heart rate to slow down.

As Dee picked herself up off the floor, Sidra, being held by Alex, was still on a rampage. "You fuckin' thief! You better give back *everything* you stole from me."

"Nobody took *anything* from you, you prissy bitch!" Dee screamed back.

Emily took it upon herself to grab the evidence and bring it to the girls' attention. "What's this?" Malajia asked.

"Just watch," Emily urged.

The girls, including Dominique, huddled around the camera and saw what had set Sidra off. Dee gulped as all angry eyes fixed on her. "So not *only* do you steal stuff from the bathroom, you have the *audacity* to come into our *room*?" Alex seethed.

"Daaaaamn, klepto," Malajia mocked.

"Stupid bitch," Sidra fussed. "I knew it, I *knew* my shit

kept disappearing. And you had the nerve to wear it in my damn face!"

"Dee, you had me in here looking crazy defending you, and you were *stealing* from this girl?" Dominique added. "Were you stealing from *me* too?"

Before Dee could open her mouth to answer, Chasity, recalling earlier incidents, put her hand up. "Question. Dom who told you that Sidra was talking shit about you?"

"That has nothing—"

"I was asking *Dominique*," Chasity hissed, interrupting Dee's protest.

"*Dee* did," Dominique admitted. "Every other day she was coming in here telling me about how Sidra was talking all this mess about me. *That's* why I kept approaching you, Sidra."

"Daaaamn, liar," Malajia threw at Dee.

"What were you planning on accomplishing with that shit, dumbass?" Chasity barked at Dee.

"She just mad cuz Sidra look better than *her* gross ass," Malajia cut in.

"She was always coming over here complaining about that damn bathroom and shit," Dee hurled. "Looking down her damn nose at people, like she better or something."

"Just give me my shit!" Sidra hollered. She was not interested in what Dee had to say.

"Dee, give the girl her damn stuff," Dominique advised. "You already got tore up."

Fuming, Dee went to lunge for Sidra. "Bitch," Chasity barked, grabbing Dee's arm and twisting it before she had a chance to grab Sidra.

"Don't do it to yourself. Don't *do* it," Malajia goaded, moving close to Dee's face.

"Chaz, let her go. Malajia, stop instigating. Dee, give Sidra her things *now*," Alex commanded.

Chasity complied, and Dee headed over to her closet. The girls' eyes fixed on her as she pulled several items from the top shelf.

"A damn shame," Alex concluded as she took the items from Dee. She eyed Sidra's missing charm bracelet, cuff bracelet, apple body spray, crystal ring, cell phone case, and silver chandelier earrings. Alex shook her head in disgust. "Sidra, let's go. You have your stuff. No need to get kicked out the last week of the semester."

Although Sidra was still enraged, she allowed herself to be pulled out of the room by Alex, followed by Emily.

"Happy with yourself? With your stupid-looking ass," Malajia jeered at Dee, following Chasity out of the room.

Shutting the room door behind her, Malajia laughed. "Yo Sid, you straight turn *demonic* when you snap."

"Malajia," Alex warned.

"Don't 'Malajia' me. I can tease my friend if I want," Malajia shot back. "Shit, she just beat some ass, I'm proud of her."

Ignoring Malajia, Alex moved Sidra's long ponytail behind her shoulder. "Are you okay?" she asked, concerned.

"Sure, why not Alex?" Sidra grunted.

"Sorry, was just checking," Alex softly replied, not surprised by Sidra's surly reply.

"At least you got your stuff back," Emily added.

Sidra drew in a breath. She was trying to calm down, but for the life of her couldn't. She stood from her bed, walked over to her dresser, and in one sweep of her hand, knocked every neatly placed item off of it.

"Sidra, you need to calm down!" Alex exclaimed.

Sidra headed for her nightstand and began throwing the items on the floor.

"Oh shit," Malajia reacted as she watched Sidra's clock radio hit the dresser.

"That's enough, Sid," Alex urged, standing up.

"Alex, chill the fuck out," Chasity interjected.

Alex shot Chasity a glare. "Why do *I* have to chill?" she asked, confused. "Look at what she's doing."

"Let her get it out," Chasity threw back. "So *what* she's breaking shit? It's *hers*."

Alex sat on the bed and folded her arms to her chest as Sidra continued on her rampage. After several more minutes passed, the now physically spent Sidra flopped down on her chair.

The room was awkwardly silent, until Malajia decided to break it. "Soooo, anybody hungry?"

"Shut up," Alex snarled.

Chasity shook her head as she remembered all the times that she had gone on a rampage against her belongings when she couldn't calm herself down after an altercation. "Does this look familiar, Sidra?" she asked, recalling one incident in particular.

Looking around the room at the mess she made, Sidra chuckled slightly. "Yeah. Looks like *our* room after you had your first confrontation with Jason freshman year."

Alex thought for a second. "Oooh, you mean that night that you kicked him in the groin?" she recalled.

"Uh yeah, let's not relive that part," Chasity quickly dismissed. "But, now you get why I did that."

Sidra nodded, she sure did. "I'm still pissed though."

"Yes I know. Come on," Chasity said, signaling Sidra to come with her.

"Where are you two going?" Alex asked.

"We'll be back," Chasity answered flatly.

"Can *we* come?" Emily asked, voice filled with hope.

"No." Chasity's response was blunt, earning a snicker from Malajia.

Alex sighed and rubbed her hands on her jeans as the door closed. "Well, nothing else for us to do but head back to the cookout."

"Y'all salty. You wanted to go with them," Malajia teased, following up with a laugh.

"Thanks for taking a walk with me, Chaz. That helped," Sidra said, grateful.

"Yeah, you needed to get out of that room," Chasity replied. Half an hour had passed since Sidra's fight with Dee, and she was finally calm enough to return to the festivities with the rest of her friends.

As Sidra and Chasity approached the other girls, who were playing games; Emily smiled. "Hey you're back."

"Where *were* you two?" Alex questioned, putting her water gun down.

"We just walked around campus," Sidra answered.

"That's *it*? Y'all acted like you were going to some secret location or something," Malajia put in, shooting her water gun at a target. "Damn it! I keep missing it."

Sidra shook her head. "Yeah well, I *needed* it," she declared. "I hate not being able to control my anger. It's a terrible feeling."

"Tell me about it," Chasity mumbled.

"I'm sorry you had to go through that," Emily empathized, examining her water gun.

"Thanks Em. I'm okay now," Sidra replied. "We only have a few days until I no longer have to be the neighbor of a fuckin' kleptomaniac."

Malajia shot Sidra a side-glance, "I thought you were okay," she teased, picking up on Sidra's angered tone and the use of the F word.

"I *am*," Sidra hissed, rolling her eyes. She turned her attention to Alex. "Alex, sorry about the room. I'll clean it when we get back."

Before Alex could reply, they were joined by the guys. "Yo Sid, I heard you put the smack down on Dee," Mark laughed.

Alex shook her head. "Word travels fast on this campus," she said.

"I know Dominique. I just ran into her and she told me what happened," Mark informed.

"Yeah well, it's not one of my proudest moments, but it sure was necessary," Sidra boasted. "I'll bet you she won't touch my stuff again."

"All right, subject change," Alex interjected. "Let's go climb that wall," she suggested, pointing in the rock-climbing wall's direction.

"We climbed that like five times already," Jason stated. "I'm trying to do something else."

"Girls against guys," Alex persisted. "Losers pack up the winners' rooms when it's time to leave campus."

"They have to carry the stuff to the car too? *And* put stuff in storage?" David queried.

"Yep," Alex confirmed, smiling.

"I'm in," Jason declared. He pointed to Chasity "You ready to pack my stuff, baby?"

"Don't play yourself," Chasity bit back, inciting a laugh from him.

"No wait. How are you gonna make a bet like that without confirming with *us* first?" Malajia asked, face frowned.

Mark got close to Malajia's face. "What's the matter? You scared?" he taunted.

After a prolonged staring match between the two of them, Malajia squirted her little water gun into Mark's face, making him curse and jump back. "Stay out my face," she ordered. "And *no,* I'm not scared. I just don't want to make a bet like that when we have to rely on other people to win... People like *Emily.*"

Emily laughed. "Come on Malajia, I may actually surprise you."

"Doubt it," Malajia teased.

"Hold on!" Mark loudly objected.

"And he was *right* by my ear with that mess," Alex complained, rubbing her ear.

"It's five girls and four guys," Mark stated, ignoring Alex.

"No shit, Sherlock," Chasity sneered.

Narrowing his eyes at Chasity, Mark patted Jason on the shoulder. "Aye Jase, check your girl, man."

"Don't touch me," Jason calmly demanded.

Sidra giggled at the byplay. This, along with her walk earlier, was a welcome distraction. "All right, all right," she cut in. "What Mark is loudly implying, is that someone has to sit out so it can be fair," she clarified.

"All who vote Emily to sit out, raise your hand," Malajia joked, inciting all but Emily and Alex to raise their hand.

Mouth open, Emily pushed a stray hair behind her ear. "That's so mean," she pouted.

"*I'll* sit out," Sidra volunteered. "I'm not a fan of heights anyway."

Malajia sucked her teeth and groaned loudly. "We're gonna *lose*."

"Fine, it's settled," Alex stated, rubbing her hands together, ignoring Malajia's outburst in the process. "Let's do this."

Chapter 37

The campus was nearly desolate. Little by little, the student body departed for home to begin their summer break. "I'm gonna miss being your roommate, Sidra," Alex somberly declared.

"I'm going to miss you too," Sidra returned. "I've lucked up with two good roommates so far, hopefully I'll be lucky my junior year."

"Maybe we can all get into the clusters next year," Alex hoped. "That would be fun. All of us sharing a house."

"Oh my God, shut up," Mark barked, closing one of Sidra's many suitcases. "Y'all have been whining that 'I'll miss you crap' for like an hour."

Sidra and Alex shot him the same venomous glance. "Stay out of our conversation and finish packing our stuff, loser," Sidra commanded.

Alex laughed, "Yeah, you know the rules of the rock-climbing bet. Losing team packs the winners stuff."

Mark sucked his teeth. "I still don't know how we lost." He angrily tossed items from Sidra's dresser into a bag.

"Hey! You break *any* of my perfume bottles and you'll be replacing them," Sidra hissed.

"It's *your* fault we lost, Mark," Josh put in, folding the girls' blankets.

"Why is every failed thing *my* fault?" Mark fussed.

Josh shot him a glare. "Did you or did you *not* slide down the wall?"

Mark sucked his teeth. "Man, I told you I got a leg cramp."

"No, you lost your footing and slipped," Josh contradicted. "Stop lying all the time."

Mark flagged him with his hand. "Always bringing up old shit," he murmured. "That was days ago."

"Yeah and we're paying for it *now*," Josh shot back.

"Okay you guys. Arguing isn't gonna change the past," Alex cut in, voice filled with amusement. "You lost, just finish so you can load the stuff up."

"You better make it fast too Mark, because you still have to go over and pack Malajia's stuff," Sidra reminded.

Mark spun around. "Why *I* gotta go pack up her crap?"

"She beat you up the wall," Sidra said.

"So? David beat Emily and he's over there packing up *her* stuff," Mark disputed. "So who beat who has *nothing* to do with it. If so, we wouldn't be packing jack shit for *you* Sid."

"So *what* she didn't climb," Alex interjected. "She's part of the team, so cut it out and finish."

As Mark sulked, Sidra giggled. "You're going to have to pack up all those thongs she has," she teased. Mark just gritted his teeth.

"Chasity, how much more stuff do you *have*?" Jason tiredly asked, picking up her flat screen television off of the dresser.

"A lot," Chasity quipped. "Quit whining."

"I'm *not* whining. You just have too much stuff," he retorted. "You didn't even wear *half* those clothes this semester. You have a shopping problem."

"That sounds like whining," Chasity pointed out, looking at her phone.

He sat the television down by the door and wiped the sweat from his face with his shirt. "How is all of this going to fit in your car?" he asked. "You have four boxes and like five suitcases. Not to mention the TV, microwave, and refrigerator. Plus, you have to fit Alex's stuff in there since you're taking her home."

"Yeah, most of that is going in storage. So get ready to take it there," Chasity said, even toned.

Jason's mouth fell open. "Look here woman, this is crazy," he fussed. "I still have to finish packing *my* stuff."

"*What* stuff?" Chasity threw back, confused. "Your uncle came down here and picked up most of your shit the other day."

Jason rolled his eyes. "That's not the point."

Chasity, tired of his complaining, stopped looking at her phone and looked at him. "Jason, you should've gotten here earlier. That's on *you*," she bit out. "You're mad because you lost and now you want to complain. Get over it."

"I did *not* lose," Jason argued. Catching the glare that Chasity was giving him made him stammer. "Um, well…whatever. So what, I already told you that I climbed that thing like five times before we went back with y'all. I was tired."

"Yeah, yeah." Chasity went back to looking at her phone.

"Smart ass," he mumbled.

"Say what?" she snapped.

"Nothing," Jason lied, bending down to pick up a box. "Where are your car keys? I'm going to the storage place."

"On the nightstand."

Grabbing the keys, Jason pointed to her. "You're lucky I love you."

"Not trying to hear it, get to going," Chasity sneered. She dissolved into laughter once the door shut.

Malajia opened the door. "God Mark, stop girlin' and come on! My parents will be here in like an hour to pick me up," she shouted down the hall.

"Shut the hell up!" Mark yelled back.

Malajia shook her head as she shut the door. Seeing Chasity sitting over on her bed, head down looking at her phone, Malajia struggled with what to say to her. "Hey," was all that she could come up with.

"Hey," Chasity replied dryly, eyes not leaving her phone.

Sitting on her bed, Malajia pushed some hair behind her ear. "Is Jason finished packing your stuff?"

"Almost."

"Oh… Well, Mark still has to come over here and pack *mine*," Malajia laughed. "He's pretty pissed about it."

"Yeah, I heard." *Give it up Malajia*, Chasity thought. Although they winded up being civil to each other at the campus event, it still changed nothing.

"Look, contrary to how things are between us now, I'm going to miss being your roommate," Malajia admitted.

"Uh huh," Chasity responded.

Malajia sighed, *why is she making this so hard?* She tried to ease the tension with a laugh. "Maybe we'll all end up in one of the clusters next year," she hoped. "That should be fun."

Tired of the one-sided conversation, Chasity stood up. "Yeah, maybe."

Watching Chasity head for the door made Malajia feel like tearing up. The last thing she wanted was for them to end the semester on bad terms. She knew this would spill over into the summer, and that they would come back to start their junior year still holding resentment.

"Chasity, I'm sorry okay," Malajia blurted out, stopping Chasity in her tracks. Standing up from her bed, Malajia took a step towards her. "I can't do this with you anymore," she said. "I know we both said some things—" She let out a sigh. "Look, I didn't mean what I said about you. And the comment about your dad—" she took a pause and sighed again. "I didn't mean to hurt your feelings."

Chasity turned around and looked at Malajia. She was

making an effort; Chasity softened her hard expression. "It's fine Malajia."

"Obviously it's *not* fine if we're still on bad terms with each other," Malajia argued. "And your bland 'it's fine Malajia' acceptance just confirms it." She put her hands on the back of her neck. "You may not believe me, or even *want* to accept it, but I *am* sorry… You just made me so mad."

"Malajia, my intention wasn't to make you mad," Chasity replied, tone calm. "I just hate seeing you act so dumb over somebody who isn't worth it."

"But that's *my* business, Chasity," Malajia shot back. "And even though you're concerned, what you say and *how* you say things, is just nasty sometimes," she added, hurt registering on her face.

Chasity rolled her eyes and let out a sigh.

"Even if you may be right about—" Malajia looked down at her hands momentarily. "When it comes to my relationship… I just want you to stop treating me like I'm dumb…it's hurtful."

"If you thought that I was trying to hurt you by saying what I said, then *I'm* sorry," Chasity admitted.

Malajia stared at her.

"I have a right to feel how I feel. *Especially* when you tell me everything," Chasity pointed out. "But you're right, I shouldn't treat you like you're dumb." *Even though I think it.*

The words "I'm sorry" coming from Chasity threw Malajia for a loop. Especially since they were being said to *her.* "Did you *really* just apologize to me?"

"Don't be smart," Chasity scolded, inciting a giggle from Malajia.

The smile left Malajia's face. "Listen, let's just agree to disagree on the whole Tyrone subject," she suggested.

"Fine."

"And I think for the sake of our friendship, we shouldn't even discuss him anymore."

"*That's* fine too," Chasity agreed.

Malajia took a deep breath. "Good."

"And that means Malajia, that when he does something else to make you mad, don't come to me with it," Chasity stressed. "Because you say this *now*, but I'll bet money that you'll be at my door complaining about him."

Malajia sighed. "I thought we weren't gonna discuss him anymore," she reminded, tone sharp.

"I'm just making things clear for you. I *don't* want to hear about it anymore," Chasity reiterated.

Malajia put her hands up in surrender. "Fine," she agreed.

Both girls stood there, letting down their defenses for the first time in weeks. "Yo, I bet Jason is highly pissed about having to pack up all your stuff," Malajia joked.

"He sure is and I don't give a rat's ass," Chasity laughed.

Malajia, without warning, threw her arms around Chasity. "Aww, I missed my friend," she gushed.

Chasity briefly hugged her back. "Okay eww, get off me now," she jeered, shaking Malajia off.

"You make me sick," Malajia laughed.

Chapter 38

Malajia darted down the stairs to the kitchen to find her mother sitting at the table, reading a magazine. "Mom, what are you doing?" she asked, sitting down in the chair across from her.

Mrs. Simmons sighed at her daughter's silly question. "Malajia, what does it *look* like I'm doing?"

"It *looks* like you're sitting here bored," Malajia countered.

Rubbing her eyes, Mrs. Simmons closed her magazine. "I'm trying to have a few moments of quiet before Melissa wakes up," she ground out. "Is there something you need, child?"

Malajia smiled. "I wanted to see if you wanted to go to lunch or something?"

"Girl, I don't feel like packing up those kids—"

"No Mom, just me and you," Malajia amended. "Leave those brats with Dad."

"Since *when* do you want to hang out with me one on one?" Mrs. Simmons teased. She knew all too well that Malajia was the daughter that rarely wanted to be seen with her parents. She always had an attitude when anyone suggested that she spend any time with them or the rest of her family.

"Does it *matter*?" Malajia immediately regretted her flippant response once she caught her mother's glare.

"Don't start it. You're not too old to get slapped."

"All right Mom, chill," Malajia laughed. Truth was, even though she didn't want to say it, she wanted to spend the day with her mother in hopes of gaining the courage to ask for advice on how to deal with her turbulent relationship with Tyrone. The couple had argued several times since she and Chasity agreed not to discuss him anymore; she felt that she had no one else to talk to. Malajia had thought that finally having sex with him would calm him down, but it seemed that wasn't the case. He'd just gotten more possessive. "So do you want to go?"

"I'd love to honey," Mrs. Simmons declined. "But I have a ton of stuff to do today and your father has to go to work soon, so he won't be able to watch the girls."

Malajia rolled her eyes. "Isn't Geri here? Why can't *she* do it?"

"Geri has to work," Mrs. Simmons reminded. "You know her schedule; you've been home on break for *weeks* now."

Malajia ran her hands through her hair. *She's always brushing me off*, she thought. "Okay fine Mom. I'll go by myself."

Mrs. Simmons tilted her head slightly as she looked at Malajia, who didn't attempt to hide her disappointment. "We can go another time."

"Yeah, I know," Malajia muttered, standing from the table.

Malajia's mood hadn't lifted during her lunch at the quiet bistro that she found by the mall. She'd finished her turkey club sandwich and salad twenty minutes earlier, but she just didn't want to go back home and sit in her room. She

sighed, grabbed her cell phone from her small red clutch, and dialed a number.

After the fourth ring the line picked up. "Chaz?"

"Yeah Malajia, what's up?"

"Nothing much," Malajia sighed. "I just finished eating lunch…by myself…in public."

"Since when do *you* go eat by yourself?" Chasity laughed.

"Since, none of y'all heffa's live close by," Malajia shot back.

Chasity noticed the difference in Malajia's tone during the conversation. Her normally, loud, bubbly tone was a bit more somber. "What's wrong with you?"

Malajia played with the straw paper on the table. "Nothing I'm good. Why?"

"You sound weird."

Still perceptive I see, Malajia thought. "I'm just tired, I guess," she lied. "I was up early today. My body is still used to getting up early like I'm back on campus."

"You *never* got up early," Chasity contradicted.

"True," Malajia chuckled. "You know me well."

"Not sure if that is a good or bad thing yet," Chasity joked.

"Whatever bitch," Malajia laughed. "Anyway, how has your break been so far? I haven't talked to you in a while."

"Yeah I know. I've been traveling for the past weeks."

Malajia was intrigued. "Oh yeah?" she beamed. "With Ms. Trisha?"

"Yeah," Chasity confirmed.

"So…are things still weird between you two?" Malajia asked, hesitantly.

Chasity paused for a moment. "Um…not as much," she admitted. "The traveling has been forcing us to have fun, so there's not really much time to be weird."

"Well, she seems to be working overtime to put things back to the way they were," Malajia observed.

"Yeah, she's trying," Chasity agreed.

"Are *you*?" Malajia threw back.

"Funny," Chasity sneered.

Malajia shook her head as she reached for her glass of water. "Have you started calling her 'mom' yet?" she wondered. "I mean, it's been a few months."

"No, not yet."

Malajia frowned. "Don't tell me you're still calling her 'Trisha'."

"No," Chasity assured. "It's more like 'hey'," she joked. Malajia laughed. "I guess I'm working my way up to it."

"Well, look on the bright side," Malajia began. "At least calling her mom won't upset Brenda."

"Yeah, I don't give a shit about Brenda's feelings," Chasity hissed. "Change the subject."

"I should have gone home with *you* for the summer instead of coming here to Baltimore," Malajia laughed, honoring Chasity's request. "*I* could be living it up *too*." She leaned her elbow on the table. "I spoke to Sidra a few days ago, and she's in Florida with her family for vacation."

"Yeah I know, she called me earlier today."

Malajia sucked her teeth. "I wanna go some-damn-where. I'm so bored."

"Complaining isn't going to change that," Chasity stated bluntly. "Go visit Alex."

"Ain't nobody going to see no damn Alex," Malajia scoffed, inciting a loud laugh from Chasity. Malajia too laughed at her own reaction. "No, I'm kidding. I love Alex. But she's been working a lot so she doesn't have time to hang out. And we *both* know Emily can't have visitors....not that I would go anyway... I just hate her mom."

"Hell, I don't blame you." Chasity chortled.

"Look, I know you're busy so I'm gonna let you go," Malajia said. "Talk to you later."

"Okay."

Once she hung up the phone, Malajia took another sip of her water and let her mind wander. She felt much better. Leave it to her friend to lighten her mood. She paid her bill, gathered her belongings, and made a beeline for the mall to do some major retail therapy. With her father's credit card, of course.

Emily took a bite of her chicken salad sandwich as she tucked the phone between her ear and her shoulder. "Daddy, I'm really nervous about my final grades," she admitted. "I really tried to dig myself out of that hole."

"I know honey. Try not to stress yourself too much," Mr. Harris consoled. "Now, I'm not saying that I'm not disappointed in the fact that you let your grades slip in the *first* place, but I'm confident that you'll turn it around."

"Trust me Daddy, I'm disappointed in myself too," Emily sulked, pulling a piece of crust from the sandwich.

"Look sweetheart, you know what you have to do in order to get back on track," Mr. Harris said. "And you seem to be working towards getting there, and for *that alone*, I'm proud of you."

Emily smiled. Hearing her father say that to her, when she was so down on herself, was refreshing. Totally opposite from her mother. "Thanks. Truth is, I'd rather be back on campus studying than here in this house."

"Your mom?" He assumed.

"Yes," Emily confirmed. "I don't know how I'm going to survive the rest of break under her like this."

"Still bad, huh?"

"Daddy, she called the community college up the street from us to ask them about transferring my grades," Emily griped. "She's making me transfer."

Mr. Harris let out a sigh. "Emily, I really think it's time for you to come live with me," he sternly suggested. "You're an adult. She can't keep controlling you like this."

Emily rubbed the bridge of her nose with two fingers. *Tell me something I don't know.* "I don't know...I don't know if I *can* Daddy. It would crush her."

"I've told you before, she is a grown woman. She'll survive," he argued.

Emily sighed. "I know."

Sensing the torture in his daughter's voice, he softened his tone. "Listen sweetie, I'm not trying to bad talk your mother to you," he declared. "She's a good woman, but she has become too dependent on you. She has made *you* her entire life, and she needs to let go and get one of her own... I'm just being honest."

Emily knew that her father was right in everything that he was saying, but she just didn't have it in her to turn her back on her mother, even if it would make her life easier. "I hear you," she assured. "Um, I have to go though, I'm supposed to be going to the grocery store with her, so I'll talk to you later, okay?"

"Seriously, think about what I said," he urged.

"Okay, I will," Emily promised. "Love you."

"Love you too."

A long sigh left Emily as she put the phone back in the receiver. *What am I going to do?*

"Mama, do you need anything while I'm out?" Sidra asked, sticking her head back in the door.

"No sweetie, enjoy your time out."

Sidra shut the front door and headed for her parked car. Hearing a text message notification sound from her cell phone, she looked down at it. After reading the short message, she rolled her eyes. "So dramatic," she said to herself as she dialed a number.

"Girl, what's up with your text?" Sidra asked Chasity once she answered.

"What? Me saying that your idea is stupid?"

Sidra chuckled as she sat in the driver's seat. "Yes *that* one."

"Well what do you want me to say? It *is*," Chasity spat out.

"Look Chasity, if this is going to work, you need to tell Malajia that we're going away to celebrate Alex's birthday," Sidra insisted, fastening her seat belt "And *I'll* tell Alex that we're going away for *Malajia's* birthday."

"I don't get it. Why tell them *anything*?" Chasity asked, exasperated. "We can just say we're gonna spend the night in New York just for the hell of it."

"But it will be more *impactful* this way," Sidra insisted. "They'll *both* think that we forgot about their birthdays, and that'll make the surprise that much better."

Coming up with a plan to surprise Alex and Malajia for both of their twenty first birthdays wasn't an easy task. Since Alex's birthday was in July and Malajia's was in August, Chasity and Sidra figured that they would do something jointly, and Sidra felt that her plan was perfect.

Chasity let out a frustrated sigh. "This is so extra," she complained. "Besides, if I tell Malajia that we're doing something for Alex's birthday and not *hers,* she'll bitch and moan about it up until she finds out the truth," she griped. "She'll blow my phone up every day."

Sidra laughed. "You're so dramatic," she teased. "Just ignore her phone calls."

"I already *do* that. But she'll show up at my house, Sidra," Chasity replied, inciting a louder laugh from Sidra. "She's done it before."

"Are you serious?"

"Hell yes," Chasity exclaimed. "Last week she said she wanted to come over my house and spend the week, I told her to fuck off, and stopped answering her phone calls... Two days later she showed up at my fuckin' house with a suitcase."

"Oh my God," Sidra laughed. "How long did she end up staying?"

"She just left *yesterday*," Chasity hissed. "I'm telling you, I'm not dealing with that drama for another two weeks."

"Yeah well, Alex won't be a treat *either*," Sidra bit out.

"Her birthday was two days ago and she already called me telling me off about forgetting."

"Yeah, I got that call too," Chasity said.

"Right, so when I tell her that we're going to celebrate Malajia's birthday, *I'll* be hearing about it until then, *too*," Sidra assured. "She doesn't ask for much, but she feels that her birthday is important. I mean we *all* feel that way about our birthdays."

"Not *me*," Chasity argued.

Sidra sucked her teeth. "Maybe not before, but *now* you do," she amended.

"Fine. I don't want to talk to you anymore," Chasity joked.

"I don't know *why* I continue to call your evil self," Sidra countered after a sigh. "That's fine, I'm on my way to go get my hair done anyway, so I'm finished talking to you too."

"Getting your hair done for *what*? You only wear ponytails," Chasity jeered.

"Goodbye Chasity," Sidra barked, before hanging up on the laughing Chasity.

Alex hurried into the diner where she worked and closed her umbrella. "Damn rain," she scoffed to herself as she examined her wet shoes. She'd overslept and had to practically run to work for fear of being late.

"Hey Alex, is it raining bad out there?" her manager asked her.

"Bad is an *understatement*," Alex complained, sitting her umbrella in a basket behind the counter. "That wind blew my poor umbrella inside out."

"Sorry to hear that. Hopefully it will clear up by the time you get off."

"Yeah maybe," Alex replied solemnly as she pulled her wet hair into a ponytail.

"With the rain, it might not be much of a rush today, so I

may let you go early," the manager said, adjusting menus at the counter.

"If you don't mind I'd like to stay the entire day. I can always do something else like wash dishes if I don't have enough tables to wait," Alex replied. "I can use extra money."

"Are you sure?"

"Absolutely." Alex grabbed her notepad as she watched a customer walk in. *Time to get to work.*

Her manager was right; it was slow because of the storm outside. Alex didn't mind, she was able to still make a day's pay and not have to work too hard. Truth was, she wasn't in too much of a good mood to be dealing with a bunch of people anyway. She hurried into her home, dropping all items but a paper bag to the floor by the door.

"Alexandra, is that you?" Mr. Chisolm asked from the kitchen.

"Yeah Dad," she replied, walking to meet him. "I brought some burgers from work for everyone. Ma doesn't have to cook tonight."

"Aww that's sweet," he mused, taking the bag. "How was your day?"

Alex sighed as she sat at the kitchen table. "It was fine, considering the rain."

Mr. Chisolm studied his daughter; she wasn't acting quite like herself. "Are you okay?"

Alex delayed responding as she took her wet hair down from its ponytail. "Truth is Dad, I'm feeling a little let down right now."

"Why is that?"

"Well…you know my birthday was last week… And as much as I appreciated spending the day with family…" Alex paused as she wiped her wet hand on her shirt. "I'm disappointed that none of my friends bothered to do anything with me," she admitted.

"Oh…I'm sorry to hear that," Mr. Chisolm sympathized. "Did they say *why* they didn't do anything with you?"

"No. I mean they said happy birthday." Alex thought for a moment. "Well Malajia and Emily actually called me *on* my birthday. Sidra and Chasity only said it *after* I called *them*." She let out a long sigh. "But I at least thought we would hang out... I don't know, maybe I'm just being dramatic."

Alex tried talking herself out of her hurt feelings for the first few days after her birthday, but she just couldn't get past it. She made an effort to try to make each of her friends feel special on their birthdays, and she hoped that they would do that for her in return. Especially since this was a big birthday for her, with her turning twenty-one and all.

"Sweetheart, I'm sure they have a good reason. I wouldn't write them off just yet."

Her father's big smile and hopeful voice caused Alex to give a slight smile. "You're right Dad, thanks." Her father was trying to make her feel better, and instead of leading him to believe otherwise, she feigned content. "I'm gonna grab a shower. So you can go ahead and start eating without me."

"Okay, if you insist," Mr. Chisolm stated, removing a burger from the bag.

Alex retreated to her room and prepared herself to take long, hot shower. Before Alex could make it to the bathroom, the phone rang. Holding her towel secure with her hand, she ran for the phone. "Hello?"

"Hey Alex, what are you doing?" Sidra asked, voice bubbly.

"Um, just got home from work, about to hop in the shower. What's going on?" Alex hoped that Sidra didn't pick up on the slight disdain in her voice.

"Oh okay…" Sidra hesitated momentarily. "Hey, are you going to be working next Friday?"

"Um, I have to double check the schedule, but I believe I may be off. Why?" Alex's voice was hopeful. *Maybe they're going to do something after all.*

"Well, you know that Malajia's birthday is the Monday after next," Sidra reminded. "So I figured we would do something for her the Friday before," Sidra informed. She shut her eyes tight as she waited for Alex to respond.

"Oh," Alex began after a few moments of seething silence. *Really? You call me about Malajia's birthday and don't say anything about mine?* "So…." She rubbed her forehead in an effort to remain calm. "Okay."

Sidra knew that Alex was trying to gather her thoughts. She looked over at Chasity, who was sitting right next to her listening on Sidra's speaker and mouthed the words, "She's pissed."

Chasity nodded in agreement. Chasity had driven to Delaware earlier that morning so that she and Sidra could plan together in person.

"And what do you plan on doing for *Malajia* exactly?" Alex made no attempts to hide the scorn in her voice this time.

"Well, me and Chaz thought it would be fun to take her to New York for the night," Sidra replied. "We could party and the next day, we can take her to eat and do some sightseeing maybe."

"Oh Chasity is in on this *too*, huh? How sweet," Alex's voice dripped with sarcasm.

"Yes," Sidra confirmed, giving Chasity, who'd just rolled her eyes, a soft nudge. "And it's a surprise, so please don't say anything to her about it."

Alex sighed, "Sure Sidra. Look, I have to go. Talk to you later."

Sidra didn't get to respond because Alex had abruptly ended the call. "Sheesh," Sidra quipped. "Did you hear her voice? She wanted to cuss me out."

"Yeah I heard," Chasity said.

"All right girl, *your* turn. Call Malajia," Sidra commanded.

Chasity sighed. "Ugh, fuck my life," she complained.

Sidra nudged her. "Hey, watch your mouth," she scolded. "My parents are here." Chasity plucked her in retaliation. "Ow!" Sidra shrieked.

"Look here, damn it, I can go back *home*," Chasity hissed, pointing. "I can cuss at *my* house."

"Oh hush and call her."

Chasity began dialing Malajia's number. "I don't know why the hell I had to come down here *anyway*," she griped. "You could've come to *my* house."

"I didn't want to take the highway," Sidra explained.

Chasity frowned in confusion. "You still on that? Delaware is nothing *but* highway," she pointed out.

"Shhh, it's ringing," Sidra said dismissively as Chasity activated her speaker.

"Hey BFF," Malajia gurgled, inciting an eye roll from Chasity.

"Hey Buttons," Chasity bit out.

Sidra put her hand over her mouth to conceal a giggle at Chasity calling Malajia by her hated childhood nickname.

"Listen, are you going to be busy next Friday?" Chasity asked.

"Girl no. You know I have no life anymore outside of campus," Malajia chuckled. "Why, what's up?"

"Sidra and I were thinking about surprising Alex by taking her to New York overnight to celebrate her birthday," Chasity explained. She then put her hand over her face; she already knew that Malajia's response wasn't going to be as calm as Alex's.

"What the hell do you mean for *Alex's* birthday?" Malajia erupted. Sidra chuckled as Malajia ranted on. "Her damn birthday was over a *week* ago! She don't get no late birthday celebrations. Those aren't the rules."

"Malajia, what fuckin' rules are you *talking* about?" Chasity snapped.

"It doesn't *matter*," Malajia shot back. "What about *my* damn birthday? *I'm* turning twenty-one *too*. I want a celebration. What about *my* damn surprise?"

"Bitch are you coming or *not*?" Chasity barked.

"Yeah, I'm coming you ignorant, light skin bastard," Malajia shot back, causing Chasity to snicker. "And Sidra is in on that *too*?" Malajia fumed. "That stuck up, ponytail wearing bitch got some nerve. She wanna be planning shit for *Alex*? *I* knew her *first*."

Chasity quickly pushed the mute button as Sidra's silent laughter came to an abrupt stop, followed by a look of complete shock. "That was so rude," Sidra sneered.

"Hello? Hello?!" Malajia hollered.

Chasity unmuted the phone. "Shut the fuck up, and have your ass at my house next Friday by one," she demanded.

"You mean you're not coming to get me?!" Malajia bellowed after a few seconds of silence.

Chasity felt herself about to snap. "You must be out your dumb ass mind, if you think I'm driving to Baltimore to pick you up just to go back up north to New York," she argued. "You better get on that goddamn train."

"Don't talk to me like that, you—" Malajia's words were cut off as Chasity hung up on her.

Sidra giggled. "She is so damn extra… And *rude*. I shouldn't do *shit* for her."

"Are you really surprised?" Chasity wondered, shooting Sidra a glance. "I told you she was gonna react like that."

"Yeah I know, but *damn*." Scratching her head, Sidra laughed. "She's going to call you back and cuss you out, Chaz."

"She's not gonna cuss me no-damn-where because I just blocked her ass," Chasity informed. Sidra shook her head as her laughter continued.

Chapter 39

The next week flew by for Sidra and Chasity as they were busy trying to finalize all the details of their dual surprise. Not so much for Alex, who was still quietly seething over the idea of her friends celebrating Malajia's birthday without having any regards for *hers*. Malajia felt the same about Alex's surprise, but wasn't quiet about it... Not at all.

"Malajia I swear to God, you've got *one* more time to call me a bitch or a bastard and you are *walking* from that damn train station," Chasity threatened. She then hung up the phone as Malajia yelled another obscenity in her ear.

"Is Malajia still complaining about this trip?" Trisha asked, voice full of laughter. She and Chasity were on their way to pick Malajia up as her train was just about to pull into the station.

"You *know* she is," Chasity snarled. "She's been bugging the hell out of me all damn week. I *told* Sidra I didn't want to put up with this mess."

Trisha giggled. "Despite how annoyed you are with your friends, this is a really nice thing that you and Sidra are doing for them," she mused, giving her daughter a side-glance.

Chasity was silent for a moment. "Yeah well, I regretted my decision a long time ago," she jeered.

Trisha smiled to herself as she shook her head. Trisha, knowing that Chasity was planning on making Malajia take a cab from the station, and wanting to get as much time in as possible, offered to drive Chasity to go pick Malajia up.

Chasity sucking her teeth broke through the silence in the car. They'd just pulled up to the station to find Malajia waiting with her suitcase by her feet, a frown on her face, and her hands on her hips.

"Oh what? You not gonna help me with this bag?" Malajia scoffed when the trunk popped open.

Chasity clenched her jaw as she tried to refrain from firing of a list of obscenities at Malajia in Trisha's presence.

"Hi Ms. Trisha," Malajia said, sliding into the back seat.

"Hey. You all ready for tonight?" Trisha returned. "You girls are going to have a great time in New York. Chaz and Sidra picked a really nice hotel."

"Yeah, I can't wait to see how they went all out for *Alex*." Malajia's nasty tone caused Trisha to glance at Chasity, who was beginning to turn red. She was always amused by the girls' banter. "I hope *Alex* enjoys her twenty-first birthday experience. She has some great friends... It's a shame that *I* can't say the *same*," Malajia vented.

Chasity was over Malajia's smart comments. She looked over at Trisha. "I apologize in advance," she ground out.

Trisha, knowing what that meant, put her hand up in submission as Chasity snapped her head towards Malajia.

"If you don't shut the *fuck* up!" Chasity erupted. "I'm sick of hearing your bullshit,"

"Hey! You can't cuss in front of Ms. Trisha like that," Malajia shot back as she pointed at her.

"I will snap that ugly ass finger off your hand, if you don't get it out of my damn face," Chasity warned. "You are the most annoying person on the face of this goddamn earth," she ranted. "Don't say another thing to me this whole trip, or I swear to God Malajia, I'll ship your whining ass to Emily."

Malajia sat back in her seat and folded her arms. "I'm not going to no damn Emily's," she mumbled.

"What?" Chasity snapped.

"I didn't say nothing," Malajia lied as she looked at her freshly painted fingernails.

Trisha shook her head as Chasity adjusted her seatbelt. "You feel better now?"

"No," Chasity spat out.

A party-ready Malajia walked into Chasity's room a few hours later, just as she was putting the last of her items into her small suitcase. "Can I just say one more thing?" Malajia requested.

Chasity threw her head back in annoyance and let out a loud sigh. "Go ahead, Malajia."

"I still don't think it's right how you and Sidra are treating me," Malajia complained.

"I *know*, Malajia," Chasity's tone was condescending.

"Just so y'all know, when you two heffa's turn twenty-one next year. I'm not gonna do *shit* for y'all."

"That's *fine*, Malajia," Chasity responded, tone not changing.

Malajia rolled her eyes and folded her arms. "Whatever."

Chasity flipped her curled hair over her shoulder and smoothed down her short, black halter cocktail dress. "Can *I* say something now?" Chasity requested, voice full of attitude.

Malajia waved her hand in Chasity's direction. "If you *must*."

"Any more whining that you *feel* you need to do, get it out before Alex gets here," Chasity urged. "You *better* not ruin this surprise, or you *will* get slapped tonight."

"Are you gonna apologize after, like you did for Emily?" Malajia jeered.

"Fuck no," Chasity returned, much to Malajia's annoyance.

As Malajia searched for a snappy comeback, the doorbell rang. Chasity darted down the steps to let Sidra and Alex in.

"Ready to have some fun?" Sidra did a little dance as she walked through the door.

"Don't y'all look cute," Chasity mused of her friend's party attire.

Sidra, dressed in a short, one strap silver party dress, had her long hair down, curled and pinned to one side. Alex, dressed in a pleated tan, sleeveless skater dress, gave a slight, unenthused wave as she stepped into the house and headed for the couch. Chasity glared at Alex's back before turning her attention to Sidra.

"She's been like that the *entire* ride up here," Sidra whispered of Alex's attitude. "I can't wait until this surprise is over."

"*You*?" Chasity sneered. "I'm two seconds from punching Malajia in her freakin' mouth."

"Where *is* Miss Sunshine anyway?" Sidra chortled.

"Upstairs," Chasity replied, adjusting her diamond chandelier earrings in her ears. "You talk to Emily?"

"Sure did," Sidra sighed.

"And?"

"Poor thing can't come," Sidra revealed, tone somber. "Her mom has her held up in South Carolina at her grandmother's house."

Chasity sucked her teeth. "I bet her miserable ass mom did that shit on purpose," she scoffed. "Fuckin' hover craft."

"Yeah, I wouldn't put it past her," Sidra agreed, adjusting her dress strap. "Emily said she thought that her mom overheard her talking to me about New York... It's a shame."

"Sure is. We need to go," Chasity urged.

"Yeah, let's get this show on the road," Sidra agreed.

The two and a half hour ride to New York felt longer than it actually was. Chasity and Sidra could have cut the tension between Malajia and Alex with a knife. Between Alex's constant loud sighing and Malajia sucking her teeth and flopping around in her seat every five minutes, Sidra and Chasity couldn't get out of the car fast enough once they reached the hotel parking lot.

Sidra and Chasity stood in the back of the elevator, exchanging amused glances as Alex and Malajia solemnly stood in front of them during the ride to the designated floor. Chasity sent a text as she and Sidra silently laughed and poked fun at the two mopey girls.

"What's so damn funny?" Malajia barked as they approached the door.

"Girl, shut the hell up, and open the damn door," Chasity demanded.

Letting out a loud groan, Malajia twisted the knob and pushed the door open. Sidra gave her and Alex a little nudge into the room.

Upon seeing the room full of people yell, "Surprise!" both girls' faces took on the same stunned expression.

As applause and cheers rang throughout the suite, Alex and Malajia turned to Sidra and Chasity. With tear-filled eyes, Alex hugged Sidra, then hugged Chasity. "Oh my God," she gushed, emotional. "This is amazing."

Malajia let out a scream of delight as she went to hug Chasity. "Awww Pebbles, I love you."

"No bitch, don't touch me," Chasity joked, smacking Malajia's arms away several times before actually returning her hug.

After hugging Sidra, Malajia, along with Alex, went around the room, happily greeting their guests. The one-bedroom suite, equipped with a pull-out couch, table, chairs, a kitchenette and two bathrooms, was beautifully decorated with balloons and streamers, accompanied by an abundance of food, drinks, and party favors.

Malajia screamed as she ran over and hugged her three older sisters and mother. "Y'all were in on this?"

"Girl yes," Geri confirmed, flinging her long braids over her shoulder. "We knew about this *weeks* ago."

"I couldn't wait to see the look on your face," Mrs. Simmons put in, fixing one of Malajia's curls with her fingers. Malajia smiled brightly as she hugged her mother a second time.

"I can't believe you actually kept something from me, Ma," Alex teased, placing her arm around her mother.

"I know. It was hard, especially knowing how bad you felt when you thought that your friends had forgotten your birthday," Mrs. Chisolm mused. "But it was worth it. I'm glad you're happy, baby."

Sidra rushed to her mother's side in the kitchen and began removing the lids from the food containers. "Sidra, I made the potato salad. I know that's Malajia's favorite," Mrs. Howard stated, placing plastic spoons in the containers.

"Thanks Mama. And yeah, she's always going on and on about how good your salad is." Sidra dipped a fork in the salad and tasted it. "So maybe now, she'll shut up about it."

Mrs. Howard chuckled. "I'm so proud of you and Chasity for pulling this off." She put her arm around her daughters' shoulder. "I love how close you girls are. I know you always wanted sisters, now you have them."

Sidra smiled. "Yeah, they're all right sometimes," she joked.

"What time is that party bus supposed to be here?" Chasity asked Trisha, as Jason gave her a kiss on the cheek.

"In about an hour and a half, so everybody has time to eat and relax a bit before it gets here," Trisha replied, glancing at her watch.

"How bad did they get on your nerves?" Jason asked Chasity.

"I don't even wanna talk about it," Chasity replied with a

wave of her hand.

"Yoooo, what's up with that food?" Mark asked. "When can we eat?"

"In like two minutes Mark," Mrs. Howard replied from the kitchen.

Malajia sucked her teeth as she walked over to him. "You *would* ask about the food," she spat.

"Shit, that's the only reason why I came," Mark retorted. Inciting a glare from Malajia. He then smiled as he playfully poked her. "Happy birthday weekend, big head."

Malajia returned his smile with one of her own. She tapped him on the arm. "Thanks," she said, giving him a hug.

Alex was too excited to eat anything. She continued to make her way around the room, greeting and thanking everyone. She squealed with excitement when she saw a few of her cousins. "I can't believe y'all left Philly for me," she joked, giving them big hugs.

"Only for *you* cousin," one of the pretty, dark-skinned, full-figured women cooed. She touched Alex's, full, shiny wavy hair. "Girl, you gotta teach me how to deal with my hair. You are rockin' that natural."

"Trust me, its work, but I love it," Alex laughed, giving another hug.

Malajia made a beeline right for the kitchen and loaded up her plate with Mrs. Howard's potato salad. "Oh my Gooooooddd, this potato salad is hittin'," she complimented, mouth full.

Mark slid up beside her. "For real? Let me get some." Before Malajia could react, Mark had scooped up more than half of her serving with his fork and walked away.

"You play too much!" Malajia yelled after him, throwing her napkin in his direction.

Josh shook his head at Mark. "You're always messing with her," he quipped, before turning his attention to Sidra, who was pouring herself some soda. "You look really pretty," he crooned.

"Thank you sweetie," Sidra gushed, picking up her cup. "I admit this dress is a little shorter than I *normally* wear, but hey, what's one night huh?"

"No, no it's…really nice. You look *really* good," he reiterated. Josh found himself staring at Sidra as she began to drink her beverage.

Catching the way that he was looking at her, Sidra raised an eyebrow. "You okay?"

That question snapped him out of his trance. "Oh, yeah, yeah. Sorry." *Nice going.* "Um… I'm gonna go see what David's doing."

Sidra just shrugged as he walked away.

"Chaz, how do you work this radio you bought?" Mark yelled over the chatter.

"Boy I don't know, figure it out," Chasity sniped.

"Aye David, use some of that nerd power, and hook up this radio," Mark ordered, pointing to David, who was eating his food on the couch.

Chasity shook her head at Mark, then walked over to Trisha, who was fixing herself some food. Chasity tapped her on the arm, grabbing her attention. "Can I talk to you outside for a minute?"

"Sure." Trisha sat her half-fixed plate on the counter, then wiped her hand on a napkin before following Chasity out into the hall. Trisha faced Chasity as she closed the door behind her. "What's up sweetie?"

Chasity glanced back at the door before looking back at Trisha. "I just wanted to take a minute and say thank you for helping me and Sidra put all this together," she began.

Trisha smiled. "You don't have to thank me," she assured with a wave of her delicate hand.

"Yes, I *do*," Chasity insisted. When Sidra and Chasity began their planning process, they had no idea where to begin. Trisha, having contacts and experience in planning events, was happy to step in to offer assistance and funds to make the surprise party happen.

Trisha stood there as Chasity continued to express her gratitude.

"You didn't have to do *any* of this, and you did," Chasity continued, she fiddled with her hands as she took a deep breath. "You do a lot for me and for the people I care about and...I appreciate that."

Trisha was beaming on the inside. Although she and Chasity had been speaking since her revelation, she still felt the strain; she felt that Chasity had walls up. To see Chasity finally let her walls down made Trisha want to cry happy tears. "I'm happy to do it."

Chasity stared at her. "I just don't want you to think that you have to go above like this just to get back on my good side."

Chasity's statement took Trisha by surprise. "Listen, I'm not trying to *buy* you, Chasity," she assured her. "I just...I want you to be happy, that's all."

Chasity nodded. "Look, I know I've been giving you a hard time lately—" she glanced down. "I'm just angry...*was* angry, and hurt and confused and..." she took another deep breath as Trisha stood there, listening intently. "I may not like what you did, I may never understand *why* you did what you did but... I realize that I can't change what happened."

"*I* wish I *could*," Trisha admitted, sorrowfully. "If I could do things over again Chasity, I would've kept you."

"And then maybe you or I wouldn't be where we are or *who* we are today," Chasity realized. Trisha sighed as she ran her hand over her hair. "Bottom line is, I wanted to know who my mother was...and now I *do*, so thank you for telling me."

Trisha nodded, trying to fight the urge to reach out and hug her daughter. "You're welcome."

"If it's worth anything...despite how I reacted....I'm glad to know it's *you*," Chasity said. "And at least I know you didn't give me up because you didn't want me."

Trisha felt tears fill her eyes. She'd been waiting for the day that Chasity would come to terms and forgive her for her past decisions. "I love you," was all that she could get out for fear of blubbering like a baby.

"I know," Chasity replied. "I love you too..." she hesitated, trying to decide if she should even say the next thing on her mind. "Mom," she muttered.

Trisha looked perplexed as a tear fell from her eye. "Did...did you just call me *mom*?" she asked, hopeful as she put her hand on her chest.

"*Did* I?" Chasity immediately replied. Trisha just held her gaze. "Is that okay?" Chasity wondered when Trisha didn't immediately respond. "Or would you prefer Mommy?... Ma?... Mama?... Madre?"

Trisha managed a laugh through her happy tears, she always appreciated Chasity's dry sense of humor in serious situations. "Whatever *you're* comfortable with, baby," she sniffled.

Chasity smiled. "Mom it is," she said, before Trisha moved in and wrapped her arms around her. Chasity, feeling like a weight had been lifted, smiled as she retuned her mother's hug.

An hour and a half later, Malajia was full and beginning to feel the effects of the wine coolers that she had been drinking; she was ready to hit the town. Turning the music down, she grabbed another bottle and pointed at her mother. "Mom, I just want to say that I'm *so* happy that you came and helped with everything. I love you and when are you leaving?" she said.

Mrs. Simmons's mouth fell open as she tried to hold in a laugh. "Well damn it, child."

"Malajia, that's so rude," Sidra scolded.

"Oh no it's not. When are y'all old people leaving?" Chasity agreed, turning her attention to Trisha. "That includes *you* too."

Trisha looked back at Chasity with shock. "Old?" she scoffed. "I'm only seventeen years older than *you*," she reminded.

"*Only?*" Chasity jeered, earning a light pinch on the arm from Trisha.

"Smart ass," Trisha chortled as Chasity rubbed her arm. "And why do we have to leave?" she questioned, hands on her hips.

"Are you saying that y'all don't want to party with your mothers?" Mrs. Simmons questioned.

"Hell no!" Malajia exclaimed, she tried to back pedal when she saw the stern look on her mother's face. "Um…I mean…well… Okay I can't think of anything nice. Mom, y'all gots to go."

Alex laughed. "*I* don't feel that way Ma," she said to her mother.

"She's lying to you Mrs. Chisolm," Chasity joked.

"Oh, I know she is," Mrs. Chisolm laughed back.

"You know what, y'all act like we're not fun," Trisha put in, striking a pose.

"I know right?" Mrs. Simmons agreed. "*We* can party too," she added as she and the other mothers huddled in a group and began dancing.

The girls watched in horror at the dances that were taking place in front of them. Between that and the, "Hooooo. Go girl, go girl," that kept flying out of their mouths, it was too much to bear.

"There isn't even any music on," Chasity observed, embarrassed as Sidra put her hand over her face and shook her head.

"Go Mom, go Mom," Maria, Tanya, and Geri chanted in unison as their mother broke it down to the floor.

"No! Don't 'go Mom' her," Malajia scoffed, signaling for her mom to get up. "Don't encourage that mess. Don't nobody wanna see them actin' all freaky."

"Oh shut up girl," Mrs. Simmons laughed.

"Yeah, how do you think *y'all* got here?" Mrs. Howard

added.

"EEW!" the girls loudly complained in unison.

"Mama really?" Sidra exclaimed.

"I can't. Ya'll have to go," Chasity commanded, pointing to the door. Trisha laughed as she grabbed her purse. "I already know how *I* got here. I don't need to hear that story again. Goodbye."

"That just gave me a really bad image," Malajia complained, before smacking herself on the head. "Eeeewww get out of my head."

"Okay fine. We don't want to hang out with you kids anyway," Trisha stated. "Come on ladies, the limo is waiting for us. Time to go have some *grown up* fun."

"All right, have fun, Ma," Alex giggled, waving.

"Stay out those strip clubs Evelyn," Malajia warned.

"I'm not making any promises," Mrs. Simmons joked, slinging her purse over her shoulder.

"Eww! Just go please." Malajia put her hands on her hips as the door closed. "They are so damn embarrassing."

"The party bus is here, come on girls," Sidra announced, grabbing her purse.

"Whatchu mean 'girls'? What about *us*?" Mark asked.

"Sorry bro, we have to take a cab," Jason informed. "The bus is for the girls."

Mark sucked his teeth. "Come on man, they always making us take a bus or cab," he complained. "Besides...*I* wanna sit next to Geri."

Malajia rolled her eyes as Geri began smiling brightly. "Boy, my sister don't want your raggedy ass," Malajia scoffed.

"Hey, I can speak for *myself* you know," Geri argued as Malajia grabbed her arm and pulled her out the door.

"You *heard* what I said damn it," Malajia hissed, teeth clenched.

The party bus full of girls pulled up to the designated

club around eleven thirty that evening.

Malajia, who was thoroughly enjoying the ride in the large, black, twenty-passenger bus, equipped with loud music, snacks and drinks, requested that they just ride around the city for a half hour before going to the club.

After standing in line for a good fifteen minutes, the group got their hands stamped and headed inside the packed club.

"Hooooo, I'm twenty-one! Give me a shot," Malajia yelled over the music and loud chatter, as she headed over to the bar with her sisters. "Buy me a birthday shot, buy me a birthday shot."

Geri laughed as Malajia tapped her hands on the bar counter, repeating her chant.

Maria signaled for Malajia to move away from the bar. "Girl, calm down, you didn't *officially* turn twenty-one yet. You have a few more days to go." she scolded.

"*I* know when my birthday is," Malajia barked as Maria grabbed her arm.

"Shut on up and come away from the bar with all that noise, so we can sneak these drinks to you," Maria urged.

Malajia smiled from ear to ear. "Whatever you say," she beamed, moving off to the side with Maria.

Geri walked over, holding two shots. "Here girl, it's cherry vodka," she informed. "Happy birthday weekend, little sis."

"Yeeeesssss, my sistah. Getting it started," Malajia bellowed, wrapping her arms around Geri.

Malajia was about to down the shot, but before she could put it to her lips, Mark slid up beside her and snatched it. "Yoink," he said before dancing away.

"Seriously?" Malajia shouted after him as Geri busted out laughing. "It's not funny Geri, he's a butthole," she hissed at her sister.

"Oh shut up. Here, take the other one," Maria offered, signaling for Geri to hand Malajia the other shot.

As Malajia put the small glass to her lips, Mark's hand reached over her shoulder and snatched it from her. "Yoink," he repeated.

"For the love of God!" Malajia hollered at his retreating back.

Cocktail in hand, Alex was dancing by David. "Thanks for buying this for me, David."

"Anything for a birthday girl," David smiled.

Chasity and Sidra danced up to Alex and grabbed the drink from her hand. "What are you two doing?" she asked with amusement.

"Shut up," Chasity jeered, taking a sip.

Sidra laughed. "We can't buy any alcohol, we're not *legal* yet," she said, before taking a sip and making a face. "Eww what *is* this?"

"Something not meant for a minor," Alex teased, taking her drink back.

Malajia danced over to them with three shots in her hands, handing one to Alex, "Here Alex, take a birthday shot with me."

"What's this?" Alex asked.

"Cherry vodka, and there is more where *this* came from," Malajia declared. "My sisters are being real generous tonight, might as well take advantage."

Chasity held the third glass as her two friends toasted each other. Alex downed her shot and was about to be joined by Malajia, but once again Mark managed to slide up and take it from her. "Yoink."

Malajia stomped her foot on the floor. "I fuckin' hate him," she seethed.

"Here, take this one," Chasity said, handing her the third shot. Malajia quickly downed her drink, relieved that Mark didn't snatch that one. She steadied herself as the strong liquid poured down her throat. "That's my song!" she yelled as she began dancing with her friends and the rest of the crowd.

After a long, fun night of partying, the girls were finally able to relax in the hotel suite. The mothers had gone home and the guys slept in their own hotel suite after clubbing all night with the girls. "That was the best night of my life so far," Alex mused, taking a bite of one of her birthday cupcakes.

Sidra was stretched out on the pull-out couch. "I'm surprised you actually drank tonight," she put in, running her hands through her fallen curls.

"Me *too*. But it was a special occasion," Alex replied, sighing happily. "I probably shouldn't have drank those shots though. I'm gonna feel that in the morning."

"You drank *what* shots?" Chasity slurred, trying to lift her head up from the chair she was sitting in. "You snuck them to *me*."

Alex laughed. "Oh yeah that's right. *That*'s why I'm not drunk."

"Mark is an idiot," Sidra chuckled. "He kept stealing Malajia's shots."

"And yet she *still* managed to get pissy drunk," Alex pointed out, gesturing to Malajia who was sprawled out on the floor, still in her party clothes.

"I heard you, you...you…fuckin' mop," Malajia slurred, voice muffled from laying face down on the floor.

"That's fine. At least this mop won't be hung over in the morning," Alex shot back.

"Whatever," Malajia grunted, slowly rolling over. "Chasity you bitch, you stole my margarita and swapped it with that virgin shit."

Chasity laughed. "I sure the hell did." She stopped laughing and put her hand over her mouth, then ran for the bathroom.

"Ewww vomity," Malajia teased, before a wave of

nausea hit *her*. She grabbed the nearest waste basket and threw up into it.

"Oh God. *Always* with these two," Sidra laughed. She herself was feeling tipsy off of the drinks that she had through the evening, but was nowhere near as drunk as Malajia and Chasity.

Alex grabbed another cupcake. "Yep, best night of my life," she gurgled.

Chapter 40

"Alex stop asking me about those damn eggs! Don't nobody *want* those," Malajia snapped, rubbing her temples with her fingers.

Alex was confused. "What are you talking about? This was the first time I mentioned them," she argued. "I *just* opened the menu."

The girls were sitting at a booth in a small diner a few blocks from their hotel. Although the weather was beautiful, with the bright hot sun and slight breeze, Chasity and Malajia couldn't have cared less; they were hung over from the previous evening's festivities.

"Ughhhh, I'm never drinking again," Chasity groaned, leaning her head against the window. She had woken up with a killer headache and bad nausea. Sitting in a diner where the entire place smelled of food was not helping the situation.

"You said that the *last* time you got drunk," Sidra pointed out with a laugh as she thumbed through the menu.

"No, I really *mean* it this time," Chasity whined.

"Serves your ass right for stealing my drinks," Malajia hissed before frantically rubbing her eyes. "God, why is it so bright in here?" Her headache and upset stomach were no better.

"Well *I* feel great," Alex mused, smiling brightly. "No hangover at *all*."

Chasity and Malajia shot her the same glare. "Shut the fuck up," Chasity sneered.

"I outta throw up right in your orange juice," Malajia threatened, inciting a laugh from both Alex and Sidra.

"Learn how to hold your liquor," Alex teased.

"Anyway, when did my sisters leave last night?" Malajia asked, taking a sip of her water.

"They left right after we got back to the hotel," Sidra informed. "They left with your mom."

"Oh," Malajia replied, sitting her cup back down. "I was so done. I didn't even remember that they were there," she admitted, giggling.

Twenty minutes had passed before the girls received and began eating their breakfast. "Chaz, you're not eating your french toast," Alex observed, pointing to it with her fork.

"'Cause I don't want this shit," Chasity grunted. "*You* ordered this."

"Look, you went to the bathroom and I figured I would be nice and order you something," Alex replied, cutting her blueberry pancakes. "You need to eat."

Chasity was about to reply when the guys walked up to their table. "Morning ladies," David greeted, pulling a chair up to their booth.

"Hey, I thought y'all were heading back home this morning," Sidra said, sprinkling sugar on her bowl of fresh fruit.

"We're heading out after breakfast," Jason put in, grabbing a piece of french toast off of Chasity's plate as he slid in the booth next to her.

Mark sat next to Malajia, who was resting her head on the table. He then grabbed one of her sausage links off of her plate. "Yoink," he said.

Malajia popped up and smacked him on the arm. "Don't start that shit today," she snapped.

Josh laughed. "Yo, that was hilarious last night," he recalled. "Mark stole like five shots from Mel."

"How the hell did I get drunk when he kept stealing my drinks? This don't make no sense," Malajia wondered, folding her arms and sitting back in her seat.

"Hey, is that any way to treat me after I stuck up for you last night?" Mark questioned, pouring syrup on Malajia's food.

Malajia shot him a confused glance. "Boy, what are you talking about?"

"Your dude called last night acting all stupid on the phone with you, so I took the phone and checked his bitch ass," Mark revealed.

Malajia's eyes widened. "What?!" she exclaimed, then began rummaging through her purse in search of her phone.

"Wait a minute, is *that* who you were arguing with on the phone at the club Mel?" Sidra asked. "I thought that you were just drunk talking to yourself."

"I don't remember *any* of that." Malajia turned her phone on. She saw that Tyrone did in fact call her the night before. She also saw that he had called her five more times that night and texted her four times that morning. "Shit. I'll be right back."

Chasity shook her head as she watched Malajia jump up from the table with her phone in hand and run out the door.

"What's going on with her?" Alex asked. She had never seen Malajia nervous over a phone call before; it was odd.

"Her dude is a jackass," Mark commented.

Chasity kept her mouth shut as her friends made their comments about Tyrone. She had no intention on offering her two cents on the situation. As far as Chasity was concerned, it wasn't her business.

"What do you ladies have planned for today?" Josh asked, smoothly changing the subject.

"Umm, we were planning on doing some sightseeing, and maybe some shopping," Sidra answered.

"*Window* shopping," Alex amended with a chuckle.

Mark nudged David to bring his attention to Josh who was staring at Sidra with longing in his eyes. Mark smiled slyly. "Sid, look at Josh right quick."

Before Sidra could turn, Josh had snapped out of his trance and picked up a cup of water that was sitting in front of him. "Mark, what are you talking about?" Sidra asked.

"Never mind," Mark shrugged. He looked over at Chasity's cup of tea sitting in front of her and reached for it. "Yoink!"

"I will punch you in your fuckin' neck," Chasity threatened as Jason quickly grabbed the cup and moved it out of Mark's reach.

"Chill your dumb ass out," Jason scolded him, handing the tea to her.

Mark continued to eat Malajia's food as Malajia walked back to the table. She was quiet as her friends were conversing around her. Malajia glanced over at Chasity, eyes red from crying; she looked as if she wanted to talk to her closest friend. Chasity caught her glance and slowly shook her head no. Malajia looked down at the table as she pushed some of her hair behind her ears. Chasity sighed as she glanced out of the window. She figured that Malajia just had an argument with Tyrone and knew that she would want to talk about it. But due to the pact that they made before leaving campus, talking about him was no longer an option.

"Malajia, are you okay?" Sidra asked, noticing the sadness in her face.

"Yeah I'm fine," Malajia solemnly replied. She figured lying would be better than having everyone asking her a bunch of questions. She only wanted to talk to one person, and it was clear that the person was not having it.

"Well, obviously y'all hangovers are going to prevent us from doing anything else today," Alex concluded, placing her balled up napkin on her plate. "Let's go check out and head back home."

Emily was sitting at the kitchen table, silent as her mother rambled on with her sister on the phone. Emily's face held a scowl; she was so mad that she could spit fire. *I missed another event with my friends because of her,* she fumed.

Emily had been back in New Jersey for two days before she called Alex to see how the New York trip was. She feigned enthusiasm as Alex went on and on about the fun that she had. Emily had been avoiding her mother in hopes that her anger would subside. But it hadn't, it'd only gotten worse.

Emily looked up from the table as her mother hung up the phone. "So Emily, did you take a look at those forms that I bought home from Plains Community College?"

"You mean that school five minutes away from here? *No, I haven't,*" Emily replied, voice dripping with disdain.

Ms. Harris raised her eyebrow. "You want to check that tone of yours, little girl?"

"Mommy, why did you lie to me about Grandmom?" Emily spat out, ignoring her mother's scolding.

"I don't know what you are talking about."

Emily shut her eyes tight. She was trying not to raise her voice. "You *told* me that we had to rush down there to see her because she was really sick," she recalled, remembering the frantic conversation that she had with her mother the day before the New York trip. "When in *reality* all she had was a cold."

"How was *I* supposed to know that? She sounded sick on the phone," Ms. Harris argued.

Emily shook her head. *She is such a liar!* "Mom, I'm sorry but I don't believe you," Emily seethed. "I know you overheard me talking to Sidra," she accused. "You *knew* that my friends' party was in New York and you made me leave with you. You just wanted to get me away so that I couldn't go. You used Grandmom's health to keep me away from my friends. Does that sound *right* to you?"

Hands on her hips, Ms. Harris searched for something to say. Emily had never been this vocal before. "Emily, that's not true. And besides, even *if* we hadn't gone to Grandmom's house, you *still* wouldn't have been going to New York," she countered. "Did you *really* think that I was going to allow you to go?"

"I'm nineteen years old Mom," Emily sniped. "Technically, I could have gone *without* your permission."

"Who the hell do you think you're talking to like that?!" Ms. Harris hollered. "Are you crazy? You *never* used to talk to me like that. You think you're grown and can do what you want? Huh?"

"Mom—"

"You think you can take care of yourself?" Ms. Harris continued to rant. "You're failing in school, you're talking back to me, you've lied, and you're hanging out with people that are no good for you. I should have *never* let you leave the state to go to school."

Every word that her mother yelled made Emily angrier and angrier. She felt herself losing control of her emotions. "Mom, please," she begged.

"I don't give a damn *what* you say, you are *not* going back to that school in a few weeks," Ms. Harris promised. "You will *not* turn out like those girls. I refuse to let that happen!"

"STOP IT!" Emily erupted, no longer able to hold everything in. "Just stop it. I can't do this anymore."

Ms. Harris struggled to gain her composure. "Little girl—"

"I'm *not* a little girl anymore," Emily countered, pounding her fist on the table. "Why can't you see that?"

"You've proven over and over again that you cannot be on your own," Ms. Harris seethed. "You have screwed up so much in these past two years."

"That's because of *you* Mom!" Emily wailed. "You have

me stressed out all the time! I can't focus. I'm depressed. I'm missing out on so much worrying about what *you'll* think. That's no way for anybody to live."

"You will *not* sit here in my house and accuse me of causing you to flunk."

Emily ran her hand over her hair. "Forget it Mom, you're missing the point."

"Oh no, I think I *get* the point." Ms. Harris's tone was ominous. "Instead of taking responsibility for your *own* messed up choices, you're pointing the finger at *me*." She folded her arms. "I tell you *what* though, this little attitude that you've developed *will* stop. I'll see to that. Just wait until you transfer schools."

"I'm *not* transferring," Emily's tone was firm.

Ms. Harris stared at Emily in disbelief. "What did you say?"

Emily shook her head. "I'm sorry Mom. I love you and I don't mean to be disrespectful, but I refuse to change my school." Emily stood from her seat. "So you can keep those brochures," she added, pushing the papers across the table.

"How *dare* you defy me like that? As long as you live in *my* house, you'll do as I say." Ms. Harris made a beeline for the stairs. "You are filling out those papers."

Emily took a deep breath. "I'm moving in with Daddy," she blurted out. Emily watched as her mother came to a complete stop and put her hand to her chest. Seeing her mother look so devastated made Emily tear up.

"You—you're doing *what*?"

"I'm moving to North Carolina with Daddy," Emily reiterated. "I talked to him last night. I'm leaving today."

Ms. Harris held her hand on her chest, unable to speak.

"I'm sorry," Emily said. "I can't let you control me anymore… I'm done."

Ms. Harris steadied herself on the nearby magazine stand as Emily darted past her and up the stairs.

Closing the door to her bedroom, Emily rested her back against it, glancing at the wall in front of her. She smiled slightly amid her tears. For the first time in a long time, she was proud of herself. *I did it. I finally did it*. Although it killed her to hurt the one person who meant the world to her, Emily knew for her own sanity it had to be done.

She wiped her face with her shirt and headed to the closet to grab her suitcase.

College life 301;

Junior Seminar

Book five

The College life series

Coming Soon!

9 780996 981767